D0208499

The Final Quest

Richard Monaco

BERKLEY BOOKS, NEW YORK

This Berkley book contains the complete
text of the original hardcover edition.
It has been completely reset in a typeface
designed for easy reading, and was printed
from new film.

THE FINAL QUEST

A Berkley Book / published by arrangement with
the author

PRINTING HISTORY
G. P. Putnam's Sons edition / January 1981
Berkley edition / April 1983
Second printing / August 1983

ISBN: 0-425-06994-X

A BERKLEY BOOK ® TM 757,375
Berkley Books are published by The Berkley Publishing Group,
200 Madison Avenue, New York, New York 10016.
The name "BERKLEY" and the stylized "B" with design
are trademarks belonging to Berkley Publishing Corporation.
PRINTED IN THE UNITED STATES OF AMERICA

For old and new friends and family

Special thanks to:
The Lampack Crew
The Leone Company
Victoria Schochet
and
Shelter Restaurant

PROLOGUE

Parsival stood on the hilltop at dawn. The gray was brightening into a fuzz of pink in the east. The burnt-out forests below still smouldered right to the line where the flooding rains had finally checked the blaze.

He squatted and pondered the tracks in the muddy trail, but they told him nothing useful. Glanced again at the twisted body of the young man. Two sets of footprints passed over and around him. The mud had dried on his face. Like a mask.

He stood up and decided to follow the tracks. Passed the dead man (wondering how he came to be there, imagining it might make a tale in itself), then stepped over the black armored body: one of Clinschor's killer knights, washed clean of last night's blood, one arm dangling over the cliff edge. Paused, turned the man over and freed the great, fanged, faceplate. He'd never taken the trouble to look at one unmasked before.

A thrust had slipped through the eyeslit and ripped into the brain. The dark, dried blossom of blood took color as the sun lifted into a cloudless, shining morning. The cool air seemed to wash the world clean.

He stood up. Shook his head slightly.

Just an ordinary dead man, he thought. *Only the mask was inhuman*. Stretched. Cracked his joints. *I'm nearly forty. I must have seen everything by now*. Smiled. *Well, I'm going back to the beginning again...I never seem to give up...Which way did my strange son go, I wonder?...I owe him so many years and that's a debt can never be repaid, in truth...Which way?...not there, surely no one would go back to that...*

He was looking over the blackened heap of countryside that filled the horizon: charred and crumbled trees, choked rivers, vanished towns, castles that were burnt-out shells...Turned and looked north: the trail ran across the hilltop, then curved down the slope, steeply, an ancient mortarless stone wall running beside it...vanished into the dense pine woods and rugged rock cliffs below and then, beyond, in the dawn haze, led into open, rolling country. Well, he couldn't see where the trail came out, but he'd find a way through. He always did, he reflected. He'd never gone there before which made it a good choice. This was as far as he'd ever come. He'd been to these forests as a boy when he found the Grail Castle (which lay out of sight down the reverse slope) the first time. Then again, a day ago, fighting Clinschor's men in the terrible storm...sliding down the long, muddy, steep hillside battling hand-to-hand with the ruined warlord...He hadn't even bothered to go inside the castle this time because he knew the Grail was gone and believed he was free of it at last...well, perhaps he was...except he couldn't really believe this hope or dream or truth that always had drawn him on was finished...he hated it too because his whole life seemed somehow to have been dimmed in a light that might not even have been real and he partly believed he'd lost his son because that image distracted and depressed and haunted all his days. Now he wanted his son back...he refused to think about anything else...

I'll go where I've never gone, he thought. *There's as fair a chance he went that way as any other*.

The pathway was so steep in places that he had to hold one hand up to the stone wall as his feet skidded in the slick mud. He felt relaxed. Didn't miss his sword. Didn't think now because there was nothing to trouble himself with...rested his sight on the cool, stunningly bright forest below. The air was washed pure...

He was almost to the bottom of the jagged, cliff-seamed woods where the trails twisted and crisscrossed steeply. He stopped by a gleaming curve of metal. Stooped and picked up a helmet, ripped, battered, crusted with mud and dried blood. Turned it in a spray of sunbeams that penetrated the massed trees, saw the letter L elaborately worked in gold on the faceplate.

If that's for Lohengrin, he thought, *then once more I'm wandering as if I traced a perfect map. In any case, miracles have become almost ordinary...*

Tossed it aside into the dry brush and began picking his way down a rough cliff face beside a hissing, ringing thread of waterfall that twisted, spattered, and vanished into shadows, sparkled in spaced fragments where the leaves cleared and rocks pulled away and then finally lost itself somewhere in the softly rolling, grassy fields where the almost perfectly round hill ended. Flowed down like himself, he thought, only quicker...And smiled...and kept climbing down...and down...Gray hairs and blond catching the light...

I

Hot, noon summer sun. Baron Howtlande squatted beside the road, blinking sweat from his eyes, uncomfortable in his rusty chain mail shirt, wiping his bared behind with one stubby hand. Then, wiping the fingers on the resilient earth, he hitched up his leather pants, staring across the rolling fields of brush and scattered trees where the yellow dust road twisted and dipped. The light was a rich shimmer.

He moved a few steps along the grassy shoulder and squatted down again where shreds and bones of pig still crackled on the dying coals. He reached and pressed a seared rib to his sucking, surprisingly thin lips, tongue reveling in the sweet, hot fats.

He wiped his mouth into his reddish, grease-knotted beard. Squinted hard: he swore something had just moved again in the soft, honeylight-stained greenness. It was too soon, he reflected, for the raiding party to be coming back, and, anyway, it was the wrong direction... his men wouldn't have gone south, to the barren country... so these might well be refugees from starvation and plague... yes... His stumpy limbs creaked him to his feet.

"Where's Finlot?" he asked, chiseling a scrap of chewed gristle from his back teeth with a thick fingernail.

A skinny, short man with tight, incredibly detailed muscles and a blond beard had just come out of the underbrush.

"He went for water," he said.

"I think we have travelers." Gestured. The other squinted and shielded his eyes.

"There's ten, at least, Howtlande."

"Ah?" The bulky man was uneasy.

"Several are women and children," the wiry man said. "You need not fear."

"Ah..." Howtlande sucked his lower lip, thoughtfully. "Well, Skalwere, your Viking eyes are keen."

"Why do men like you always say more than is needful?"

"Eh?"

"It's clear my eyes are sharp. Why talk about it?"

Howtlande grinned, sucking the end of the stripped bone again.

"Because," he explained, "we're civilized, unlike you northern dogs, and enjoy the pleasures of words. You've never been to a noble court, that's plain."

Skalwere spat.

"I prefer the pleasures of deeds, fat one," he muttered.

"In that case, find Finlot and let's hide ourselves. Mayhap these pilgrims yonder bear all their worldly treasure on their backs."

For, he thought, *without wealth, I cannot bind enough men to me as will satisfy my purpose. In the end, I must have coin or fail.*

"If their women be young that's wealth enough," Skalwere said, moving off through the green wall of bushes as Howtlande kicked dirt over the coals, never taking his eyes from the distant figures that wavered in the heat reflections as if they were images from lost worlds straining to take substance in the still, hot, golden afternoon.

Howtlande moved behind the screen of leaves and squatted in the cool shadows. Belched and relaxed...half-heard birds quarreling in the dense branches overhead...mulled over his plans. At first, survival had been enough. He preferred not to think about the past, but the final days of the war for the Grail haunted him and leaked into his dreams still. Survival had been a rare luxury for a time. Everything had gone wrong: the fire they'd set to raze what they didn't want to hold had trapped and destroyed their own army as well as the crumbling Briton opposition, and in a matter of hours he'd become a general commanding only his own hide, crawling down the muddy mountainside through a raging storm and struggling on through the charred countryside where tens of thousands of soldiers lay heaped in fragile ash shapes, sealed together in melted armor. Moving on past what in the moonlight he took for unending rows of them blurred by the flooding and darkness. He had gone mad for a time (though he blanked that out): he'd felt them all following him, rolling over the earth in a tide of shadows, and he'd fled, pale, frantic, choking on the bitter ashes, flinging away most of his armor and finally, towards dawn, blacking out . . . waking in the pallid sun just outside the vast line of desolation, his body smeared, mouth and nostrils half-plugged with soot and muck . . . wandering in staggers over the still wet, green ground, then dropping into a tepid, muddy stream and cleaning himself as best he could, rinsing his mouth with foul water that had flowed from the heart of the ruined country.

He peered through a break in the leaves and watched them coming. One was riding either a pony or a mule. The heat shimmers still shook and bent the forms severely.

Men and gold, he thought, *gold and men* . . . There were more survivors than he'd expected. They kept turning up.

A slight stir in the undergrowth told him that Skalwere and probably Finlot were getting into position.

I left Germany a lord and I'll not return a beggar, he reflected once again. It was one of his favorite thoughts. The bitterness of it was a consolation. *Lord master was a fool. I'm not a fool. There's all the logic I'll ever need . . . My dreams stay in my sleep where they're harmless. What I see I see . . . even if you suffer from seeing devils, if you know they're made of nothing then you draw the teeth of madness* . . . Nodded self-agreement. *That was his error: the stinking Grail dream . . . It caught all of them and ruined all of them* . . .

Shook his head, thinking of the armies and immense wealth that had been spilt and lost.

"Fanatics," he muttered. Stood up behind the screen of glistening leaves floating in the bright, hot, droning afternoon as the party, in traveling capes and peasant clothes, came around the near curve of road. The scraggle-faced man mounted on the dusty mule looked, Howtlande thought, vaguely like a priest, though he wore no cross or beads.

He counted thirteen of them. Then stepped out to bar their way, noting that only two had weapons visible: the rider had a short sword, and a gray-haired, massive fellow in weathered hides rested a spear over his shoulder. A hooded woman and two children stood close to the armed peasant. The dust blended everyone together.

Howtlande noticed how the middle-aged man stopped alertly and looked (instead of at him) left and right. *This,* he thought, *was the one to watch*.

"Who blocks our course?" the rider demanded in a thin, violent voice.

"Say rather, 'my lord baron,' you ass on an ass," Howtlande suggested.

"You're a nobleman?"

"You say true, ass."

"Few are met with in these days," the man said. He seemed to be spokesman for the group that watched and waited, uneasy, silent.

"Well," Howtlande answered, "you've met with one. And he waits for you to pay the toll."

The rider was scornful.

"Pay what?" he said.

"The road toll."

"Hah. You do better to join us. There's nothing at your back but trees, I think."

"The rate goes up apace," Howtlande said.

"I serve a great leader," the man said, "who is gathering the country together again. We always can favor a fresh sword."

"A great leader." Howtlande was smiling, quite relaxed now. Kept watching the big man with the spear, who was a little apart from the others as if he'd been following along without commitment. "These are troops, then?" He indicated the ragtag peasants.

"Follow us and bear your own witness." The man's face was very red around the eyes.

"Who's this great leader? Lord who?"

"The golden eagle, he's called."

Howtlande guffawed. Spat and wiped his greasy lips with the back of his hand.

"Ah," he said, grinned, as Skalwere and Finlot (a bleak-looking, wintery-eyed, long man) stepped out of the cover on either side of the road. He noted the massive man seemed unsurprised. Had expected that. "More like the golden asshole." Drew and pointed with his sword. "Leave the women and your purses." Smiled. "Even that fat one. Skalwere likes to harpoon blubber like a true Norseman."

Only Finlot seemed remotely amused.

"That's good," he said.

"That's the toll," Howtlande continued. "You may as well pay and ride on."

"You fools!" exploded the violent, flat voice. "Mere brigands. I offer you—"

Howtlande hit him alongside the head with the flat of his blade, moving with remarkable celerity. Watched him flop into the ditch.

"And the mule too," he said.

The rest were already moving, most bolting, the fat woman (he noticed peripherally) hesitating, looking from Finlot to Skalwere as if to see which were the Norseman, he thought, amused, as he sliced the leg from under a fleeing teenager and left him screaming and twisting in the dust, as the other two ripped into the rest, hacking, stabbing and tripping and herding the women together at the same time. A young peasant pushed Skalwere away from a girl and Finlot jabbed his spear between his ribs and dropped him to his knees in the dust, thick, dark blood flooding from his mouth. Howtlande gripped the mule's reins now, watching the massive man with the long spear backing into the underbrush with the hooded woman and two children. One girl and a couple of peasants had broken away and were scrambling into the trees. He'd never expected to take them all but they'd done quite well for three men, he decided. Soothed the mule, absently, watching Finlot trip a woman who tried to get up, using the butt of his spear as Skalwere smashed another in the temple, knocking her flat in the ditch, and then turned and plunged after the spearman and family, leaves rasping, branches snapping, as he vanished into the brush. Howtlande, still soothing the mule, stood over the rest with Finlot.

Skalwere was surprised not to find them instantly and trotted and struggled deeper into the greenrich, sunshook tangles, tripping on roots, ripping a path with his sword, slapping stiff, barbed branches from his eyes . . . stopped and listened . . . wasn't sure if he heard movement or not . . . voices floated vague and muffled from the road behind him.

"They move like Picts," he muttered to himself.

And then he turned, surprised, as the big man appeared behind him and his body ducked and twisted to miss the vicious thrust. Then he squatted down, grinning.

"Ah," he said, "you be no common Briton." Waited for the man to take advantage and charge, ready to roll under the spear, close and kill. Except the massive, iron-gray bearded fellow (whose eyes, he noticed, were bright blue chips in a nest of squinting) moved forward one easy, patient step after another, spear cocked just enough, held just high enough. Skalwere appreciated this and began hunkering backwards into the screening berry bushes, shaking the faint threads of sunlight. He decided there was no point in empty risks what with solid booty waiting. There would always be another day. There always was, he reflected. Paths, he thought, always crossed in those narrow times. After a few yards he stood up and began working his way back to the road. Everything was quiet there now except for a shrill weeping that he assumed was a woman or a hurt lad. All around the birds took up their chirping again.

As Broaditch moved quietly the few steps to the thick tree where Alienor and the children crouched, he gestured with the spear and all silently and quickly went on through the tangles, finally coming out, farther back, into a rolling field of dried grasses and tuftlike clumps of brush and spread-out lines of coppery cypress that seemed to flicker up into powdery sky, like flames.

"Well," he said, at length, leading them on in a wide circle that he reckoned would bring them back to the valley road a mile or so beyond the raiders. "We've become wild creatures enough. All of us."

Alienor had pulled back her hood. Red-gray hair glistened in the steady, heavy sun.

"Water flows, husband," she said, "the nearest way it can."

"Well, it don't please me, woman," he answered, "put it any way you like."

"How far is it, father?" the girl, Tikla, wanted to know. She was keeping pace with her slightly older brother, who was whipping a willow switch at tall, stooped sunflowers as he walked.

"I would restore to them," Broaditch said, peering alertly around, "their lost childhood...Aye...and my own lost everything else too, had I the power."

"Father?" she repeated.

"Not far, child." Frowned and murmured. "No more than eternity away."

"Your father," Alienor put in, "has come to riddling like a mystic hermit since we found him."

"It was this hermit, woman, did the finding."

"Oh?"

"Aye. Right enough. And were not easy as finding shit in a cowbarn."

"A sweet comparison."

"Well, just, anyway."

"Oh? And were we not where we were when you come upon us you'd not have found us."

He frowned and smiled and shook his head as if struck.

"Woman," he said, "there's no denying that, I think."

"So, were it not for where we chose to be you'd have missed us." He couldn't tell how amused she actually was. She always could sound a little fierce.

"No question," he murmured, peering around.

"So," she said, with a twinkle of triumph, "without our help you'd not have done the thing at all." She smiled then.

"I found nothing quite the same," he said, and she glanced at him, faintly unsure of his full meaning.

"Do you mean to forever hold that little business up to me?" She was almost coy.

"Little business." He brushed the grayed hair back from his sweaty forehead. "A springtime bud in winter, more like."

"What? Winter? You say I'm come to that? Hah. Oaf." She cracked her knuckle into the side of his head. "Oaf. So you make a hag of me already?"

"Well, well, *autumn* then, woman." He was grinning now, faintly. "In any case, finally you admit it in full." He wasn't sure himself how much it actually mattered to him. But not knowing bothered him; suspecting bothered him.

"Ah, do I indeed, Broaditch?"

"I'm hungry," said Torky.

"We'll eat soon," she assured him.

"That long-faced chap, that Lampic," Broaditch was saying, "he showed his thoughts in his eyes." Spat and pursed his lips. "His squinty eyes," he amended.

"And what do thoughts come to?"

"The turnip comes from the seed."

She chuckled, reaching down into the foodsack now, tilting it over her shoulder.

"Broaditch. At our time of life? You act like a young swain jealous of his first love's every look."

"Well, well..."

"I might profit from this mood had we time and place at hand."

He stopped again. The weedy grasses here reached nearly to Torky's face. His sister was over her head.

"Sit down, everybody," Broaditch said. "We wait and see what we see."

"What's in your mind?" Alienor asked. He shrugged. She frowned. "There's nothing to be done about those folk. No sense to think on it."

He nervously thumped the spearhaft into the soft earth.

"I hate these things," he said.

"I know," she said.

"Mama," Tikla asked, sitting crosslegged, braiding a few long, yellow-green strands of grass, "can I have water? I'm *hot*."

"Stay in the shade," her mother responded.

"I'm sick of having to see these things," Broaditch was saying. "I hate it."

She touched his shoulder with her weathered cheek. Squeezed his thick arm.

"I know," she repeated, shutting her eyes against the bright pressure of sun. "But there's nothing to be done. Ah, my gruff love, we've had many years, you know... many years..."

"Can I have some cheese?" Torky asked, plucking at the sack as she set it down.

"Ali," her husband was saying, "I have been led around and around... each time I followed fate... each time I came full circle..."

"And found me again." She released him and sat down among the warm softness and little violet flowerpoints. She unwrapped the wheel of dry cheese. The children knelt close to her now.

"Yes," he murmured, twisting the spear into the ground. The children were both at the cheese. "Yes..."

"You're sad, father," Torky said, chewing, eyes clear, grayish.

"A little, my son," his father answered. "Because I let the

world mark me." He almost smiled for a moment. "If you can wake each morn and forget yesterday, you'll grieve but lightly in your life." He looked tenderly at them both, Tikla involved with a bite too big for her mouth. "Do you understand?"

Torky was serious. Stopped chewing. Blinked. Watched his father's face almost gravely.

"I think so," he said.

"Let each day pass like the dreams of the night," Broaditch went on, leaning his weight into the spear. "They too seem real enough until you wake." Alienor was looking at him now.

"That's fine advice," she remarked.

"Don't mock me, woman. Well I know my weakness..." He broke off and held his hand out, cautioning them to stillness. He poised, listening to an oncoming swishing of grasses. He peered over the foliage and saw the flapping robe, pale, flat face streaked with blood, the sucking mouth as the man rushed across the dense, sunsoaked field. Broaditch readied his spear, thinking:

If the others are at his heels I'll trip them to hell!

Then the priestlike man staggered through a wall of bushes, stumbled to one knee and stayed there, puffing, staring at Broaditch with disgust, fury, and fear until he recognized him.

"You were...with us on...the road..." he gasped and Broaditch nodded.

"Your life seems a miracle, clerk," Broaditch said, thoughtfully, aware now there was no pursuit.

"They were busy with their booty." The man seemed relatively unshaken by events. He seemed to take no account of his slashed, swollen head or anything else but getting on: his dark eyes seemed to be looking past whoever or whatever happened to be before them and his body made little, impatient movements while still.

"They were your friends, back there?" Broaditch wondered as Alienor came closer and the children ate and watched.

"My brothers and sisters," the man answered, getting up, eyes, Broaditch thought, almost like holes, staring past and slightly over their heads.

"That was your family there?" Alienor wondered, skeptical.

"My brothers and sisters in the holy cause."

"Ah," said Broaditch, comprehensively. He shut one eye.

I'm ready for any measure of madness, he thought. *My whole life has prepared me for it.*

"Nothing was said about it on the road," Alienor put in.

"It's not a subject for chatter, woman," was the reply. A faint tic rippled across his cheek as he spoke. "God's true people led by a great man. He's gathering his flock."

"Ah," Broaditch repeated, not quite rolling his eyes.

"I thought all the great men," Alienor said, "had, praise Mary, passed from us. They must grow back like wild weeds in a garden."

The dark eyes with their invisible pupils flicked at her accompanied by a fluttering twitch. She noticed there were no smile wrinkles at his lips.

"Our leader is no weed, woman. Say, rather, a rare and precious flower."

Both of Broaditch's eyebrows went up at this intelligence.

"A precious flower?" he murmured.

"A man inspired." The black, bottomless eyes were on him now, for the first time. "Follow me and you'll see for yourselves."

"Then, for a time," Broaditch responded, "we tread the same way. There's no harm in a direction, all else lying equal."

"Which it never does," Alienor interjected. "Children! Don't wander!" Torky was drifting into a berry bush, whipping his willow wand at the blossoms. They reached the road and waded into the rich, golden dust. Broaditch glanced back and there was nothing behind, just the lush shimmer of the day.

"Come on, my doves," he said, still amused. Grinned and spat to the side. The man went on straight, a little ahead, as if he heard nothing, the dust billowing like smoke around him.

II

The pale man was virtually naked as he crossed the fields. His big bare feet were calloused and filthy, rent with scabs and sores. The faded, tattered shreds of a robe fluttered around the bony limbs. His pale, washed-out, grayish eyes were perpetually widened and resembled pools of still water on a dull day. His left hand clutched a warped stick. His hair was greasy and knotted like a mad bird's nest, the boy thought, watching him come out of the tree shadows, step on and then over a low wall that ran partway along the cart-rutted roadway that twisted like a dusty scar through the green rolls and dips of countryside. The man rushed on, that is, the angles of his body and clothes seemed to rush, and he leaned as if into the violent wind of his passage, everything moving rapidly, tireless, in frantic suspension, although (the boy noted) his forward progress was actually slow. The energy that shook and danced the skinny body seemed to scatter his motion in all directions. He moved as if yanked by an invisible leash. In fact, as if to bear out the simile, his head and neck seemed to be wrenched forward at the onset of each somehow unwilling step.

Behind the boy (who was perhaps nine) a tanned, bright blond young woman in her late teens rose from where she'd been washing her face, dipping the water from a foamy thread of stream. She stared after the ragged, bony figure, whose gait was such a stiffness and struggle, sloshing through the fine dust, shadow a black, jagged shock across the glowing greenness.

"He walks like a blind man," she remarked, "with the saint's twitching."

"Mayhap he is a holy man," the boy suggested, wiping dull-brown locks from his eyes.

"Or a village loon." She plucked his rough peasant's shirt. "We ought to go on. I dread to rest too long in any place until we are farther from the ruined lands."

"Is the death come this far, lady, do you think?" he asked as they went on roughly north towards the rock-boned, green foothills beyond the peaceful, hot, motionless valley.

"It's not just the sickness," she told him, "that we need fear, boy."

"What then?"

Her expression was like a shadow and a shield for a moment. Her eyes went away, inwardly . . .

"Never mind, boy," she told him. "Come along. It's enough when troubles are here, I think, without calling them on by name."

She took his hand as they walked alongside a dense wall of trees until they found a break and pushed through the dazzle of shaking leaves and sunlight and pieces of shadow . . .

"Do you know where we're bound?" the boy asked her, following the loose shimmer of her pale blue gown that was dusty, stained and torn at the hem.

"Never mind that either," she said. "You're all questions, boy."

The pale, ragged man was violently going around a long, empty curve of road, eyes wide, shocked-looking. The stick cut and twitched at the air when his hand would spring suddenly to life as if to punctuate some obscure inner process otherwise unreflected. He jerked on and on, the dust gradually gathering in his hair, blurring his face and body . . . and all he saw was the brightness before him passing steadily in dips and leaps, saw the banked, white and yellow flowers on the slopes; loosely sketched poplar trees; bright, vacant sky . . . shifting shadows . . . until finally the sun was at his back and his own angled, jerking shape gradually grew out before him as if his substance flowed into darkness and he thought nothing, merely watching out of calm yet hungry emptiness as he was seemingly dragged along by a force oblivious to bone and blood's frailty, until his shadow and the night were one and he reeled a little, the stored, burning sunlight beating in his head, the stick jerking, gesticulating . . . then the rising moon spread new shadows and he staggered straight ahead as the road looped away. Then suddenly stepped over an edge and fell silently into a slash of darkness that might have been bottomless, and he still seemed to be walking as he dropped, the stick fanning vacancy . . .

III

The knight was young, fairly tall, wearing chipped, weathered red and black armor, lacking a helmet. His black, dusty, tightly curled hair resembled a Moor's, the rawboned woman thought, watching him through the underbrush that clustered on the slope before the little wooden bridge. She gripped the pitchfork tightly. Beside her crouched a short, goatish man in his fifties holding a spear with a cracked tip. There were other women, a few older men and teenage boys and girls hiding in the brush and willows that overhung the stream and path. It was an ideal spot and when the stranger was well out on the narrow, railless span a dozen or so of the motley ambushers fired and heaved and lobbed a volley of stones and makeshift javelins that twisted in flight and went end over end. One old man, as he let fly, fell forward down the slope. The missiles were rattling and splashing down everywhere, one, then another ringing lightly off his armor. The wrong end of a pointed stick struck him in the throat, puffing out his cheeks as the people scrambled, cheering (for some reason), and by the time they were jammed shoulder-to-shoulder on the narrow span he'd recovered enough to draw his sword and fan a single cut that sheared away two out-thrust spears and sent the leaders piling back, screaming, skirts flapping, white beards flopping. A little girl tossed a rock and scurried off, and at the end of the bridge (as the others tripped and skidded, slipped and rolled for the undergrowth) the big woman with the pitchfork and a bent old crone with a carving knife stood their ground together, the old one snarling:

"Curse all thieving bastards! You put no fear in a good woman!"

The knight seemed puzzled. Let his point fall and rubbed his throat where he'd been hit. Swallowed experimentally.

"What means this?" he wondered. "What folk are you, to use me thus?"

Some of the bolder hesitated now on the slope and under the willows that dryly shook the burning sunlight.

"And who be you, then, sir?" the big woman asked. "If not a brigand or worse."

"Ah, well put," said the crone in a voice like coughing, brandishing her knife, a little wasp of a woman with steel-colored eyes, threatening him almost symbolically. The rest were waiting partly in peace, fear and menace... "Who be you?"

"I?" the armored man frowned. Knit his eyebrows. One hand unconsciously fingered a raw, uneven scar alongside his right eye. "Why I am..." Broke off. His bare fingers flicked sweat from his eyes. "Never mind that," he said, staring, then starting forward and all but the two rippled back as if a wind blew them, even the old one giving a step or two, painfully stooping and, as he passed, flailing the blade in his wake. The long woman just stood there, watchfully.

"Cowards!" raged the crone. "You're all cowards! God curse you all for cowards!"

The knight marched on, surrounded at an impotent distance by the ragged peasants; some raged, some pleaded... some children were already playing.

"Go away! Go away!" a little girl screamed.

"Mercy, lord," importuned an ancient man.

"Good folk," the knight said, "I'm hungry and thirsty and have come far."

"More will follow," the crone coughed after them. "You'll see. Feed one dog and the wolves follow!"

He stopped at the well, surrounded at a safe distance. Drew water for himself and leaned his sword on the stones. The people were quieter now. The crone was still coming across the grassless stretch of field, hobbling, knife flashing the fierce, steady summer light.

"I don't understand all this," he was saying. "I've come a long way and much...much is clouded in my brain." Drank deeply. "I'm alone, as you see. None follow me."

"What do you want?" a voice asked from the crowd.

He was staring at the road that veered under the trees beyond the village and vanished. His hand touched his hurt skull again. The barn was behind him and one of the boys was standing on the big stone to get a better view.

"To eat," the knight was saying. "Rest..."

Rest from time, he thought, dark eyes troubled. He kept finding strange things in his mind: pictures...words...things inexpressible as longings, too...He sighed and stared at the road, the dark bluish tree shadows barring it...

IV

"You needn't bind this one," Howtlande said, pointing to the short, soft-faced woman who was staring, numbly, straight ahead, not even trying to cover her breasts where the cloth was ripped away. The sacklike garment hung to the ankles, streaked blood showing on her thighs through the rents. Skalwere was knotting the ropes on a sullen, chunky girl's wrists and looping them to the next in line, a weeping, thin red-haired woman. "Get them moving," he went on, staring meditatively at one of the peasant men who was face down in the ditch, legs uptilted as if he were diving into the earth, up to his eyes in his own caking bloodmuck.

Howtlande was sitting on the mule. The bulk of his men started straggling ahead in drifting and approximate line. No one even bothered to joke about the women now among the twenty-five or so bandits. Most, he reflected, were masterless men-at-arms, with a few gallows birds and that one, odd, actual knight. The only other knight besides himself in the band. A dark-haired, longjawed, dour middle-aged bastard who told you nothing in any conversation and was unmatched in battle viciousness. Howtlande felt certain he would know the name if he ever were to learn it. He'd only asked once and the eyes had looked at him like dark stones as the fellow said:

"You have the sword." Voice hard and smooth. "Why trouble further? Call your own horse your own way."

Howtlande had readily agreed, though he hadn't tried calling that horse anything just yet. But he couldn't help speculating about the possible past... he was well-trained, that showed at once, a perfect captain. He must have served kings; perhaps even his own former master, the ball-less wizard.

Hah, he thought, *who finally ran short of spells, too ... the cringing son-of-a-bitch, I don't see how he ever took me in to begin with ... well, he took enough others. There's no such thing as a lonely disgrace, it's always shared with someone ...*

He spat into the fine dust that was rising and hanging behind them like yellowish smoke. A butterfly rose, erratic, sudden, falling, tipping, tilting through the air with exquisite awkwardness. He barely registered it stuttering across the road and vanishing as if blown dissolving into the glitter of underbrush and long grasses.

"How far do we march?" Skalwere wanted to know.

"Tired already?" Howtlande joked.

"No, fat man," was the unsmiling reply. "But it be well to know your destination."

"Not far. Half a day on foot. I know the place, Viking."

"Spare me," Skalwere cut in, "more answer than question." And moved toward the head of the scraggly column, past the roped women, the part-armored men in varying states of personal scarring: one-eyed, -eared, -armed; bloated, lean, short, long; bent and straight; speaking and silent, all hot ...

Vicious, runty bastard, Howtlande thought, and half-muttered. The knight was striding, silent, at the flanks of the mule.

"How do you fare today, sir?" Howtlande asked. The man didn't look at him. "There may be horseflesh in this village. There's few enough steeds left in the country for our finding. Else I'd not be mounted thus, eh?" Smiled. The man glanced at him and said nothing.

A fit companion for Skalwere. The pair of them could match their wits and elegance together ...

He went on, still trying to stir a wriggle of conversation from the fellow:

"Once we have good mounts beneath us and raise more men then things will be different."

"Once we're dead, things will be different too," the knight reflected, not-quite-smiling.

"Don't give in to the pessimism of these times," Howtlande insisted. "That's a great mistake. In my view, sir, there's a whole new world of opportunities opening before us. Look you, men rise up in any condition of life. There's a leader in prisons . . . among serfs . . . beasts . . . you take my meaning?"

"I don't take it very far," the knight returned, composed and aloof.

"Oh? Hear me, first we take this town, then the next, and so on. Then we keep heading north. I have a route in mind that will allow us to gather strength like . . . like a ball of snow rolled down a winter's slope."

"And so," the knight replied, "we only grow by speeding to the bottom."

"What? Hear me, sir, we're both cut from the same sheet." His voice was confidential. "Don't yield to this pessimism. I say there's no limit to what may be ours, in the end."

"The length of a grave may be ours, in the end."

"You're worse than a monk." Howtlande was exasperated. "You have to use your imagination."

The other smiled.

"I do, baron," he said. "I've had to or else I'd face the truth."

"You served great men, in your time, I think."

"None but. All dead. And the greatest of them once told me his whole life was hollow at heart. And I didn't understand him then." He scratched the back of his neck where it showed reddened and thick above the bright links of mail. "Later I came to understand him."

Howtlande opened his round mouth, then closed it again. Watched the man sink back into himself, into a granite silence . . .

V

Suddenly the sickening falling ended with a shock that was pressure before it became chill suffocation and he kicked and struggled up from the muddy bottom, sucking air and remembering everything instantly, bursting into a mounting wail that became (at the end) a howl as teeth flashed and chewed water and air in the bony edge of a face, the cry echoing from the riverbanks, a bitter eruption so violent it seemed the scarecrow frame would burst to pieces ... and then he was swimming, lashing, pounding at the dark water, clawing, scrambling, kicking at the shore as if to wound the earth itself, spitting fury, racing over the land now without even taking the trouble to straighten up, hands still flicking at the ground, hissing, over and over:

"So ... so ... so ... they think me set aside, do they? ... so ... so ... so ..."

Jerking along now, following the stream, too caught up in a frenzy of remembering to grasp or even care that he was plunging blindly into the silver-haunted shadows, bulging eyes fixed on bright, vivid shapes, the flowing past lost and then becoming (as he gradually slowed and stood upright) the future ... pleasant images, so that he was down to a reflective walk a few yards later as he gradually gained control of himself. The shock of remembering was fading... that that he'd lost; the sickening frustration of seeing it all slip away... now he was watching each enemy, each betrayer dragged to justice, and the details absorbed him: he watched Lord General Howtlande being bound to the wheel, his fat, sweaty flesh quivering, mouth shrieking and pleading, rolling his eyes as the executioner stepped closer.

His smiling mouth murmured into the peaceful, silvery glowing night, just louder than the throbbing of frogs and general screech of nightbugs.

"No mercy, general," he said.

Then he mouthed the other's desperate reply:

"Please, my lord, I beg you, please! Pity me! I'm sorry I failed you... I'm sorry..."

"Too late, general," he told the image in the darkness, "far, far too late."

"Please... please..." Sobbing, bubbling, chewing his foamy lips, then screaming as the burning red steel drew a ring under one eye and the socket suddenly filled with bubbling, charring jelly.

"Far, far too late, traitor." His voice was smoothly, contemplatively calm. "Now the other eye."

"Please... O mother of God... please... no more... I beg you, lord... I'm sorry... I'm sorry..." Only one eye still could weep. "Don't hurt me more... this is enough... I've learned my lesson... I'm sorry... I'll do anything... please..."

"Burn it out!" he hissed, clenching both fists. "Burn it out! Out!"

And then he tripped and went to his knees. Groaned, rubbing his foot. One toe throbbed terribly under the splintered nail. A log lay across the path in the faint gleaming. He stood up and limped on a few more steps, then nearly walked into a wall. Wooden. He pressed his palm to the timber; groped along it thinking this was a great defense built by his enemies to keep him outside, blocked off from the source of his power. He smiled with grim determination. Could feel the power pulsing deep in the dark country ahead like a sunken sun within the depths of the earth fitfully guiding him. He clenched his teeth, drawing himself back a little. He would smite this wall with his concentrated will. Did they think his force waned so far that this pitiful barrier would check him? He paced a few steps and began muttering a spell, chanting, singsong, reaching one big soft hand out, pouring the energy into his fingers, visualizing the wood bending, splitting under the psychic impact, his body and then the earth beginning to vibrate as his immensely bass and resonant voice filled the night and hushed the droning sounds . . . then, suddenly, violently, thrust himself forward and sagged, surprised, into unresisting darkness, toppling over what he didn't know was a window ledge (the invisible sill hitting him just above the knees), getting up inside and straining his sight into the corners, chuckling under his breath.

"A new enchantment," he muttered.

He was quite satisfied. The merest touch of his strength had been enough.

He crouched and groped around the thick-smelling interior: earth, smoked wood, old sweat . . . heard a fly buzz somewhere, invisible . . . touched something soft, crumbly; smelled it on his hand: cheese. Very good . . . He murmured a spell to take off any poison or curse and ate some, feeling a little gloat of smugness. Crammed it in, swallowing and spilling moist crumbs.

"Rest now," he half-said.

Began creeping around the floor looking for something to wash it down. His wet clothes sloshed. Found nothing. There was no telling how vast the place might be. He saw it running off into an endless, treacherous labyrinth . . . He had to sit and rest his eyes a moment. Leaned against the cool, mudchinked wall; started to repicture Howtlande on the wheel, one eye seared out . . . lost it . . . saw armies under a blazing greenish sky hurling themselves against a vast, black stone fortress . . . slid down the wall onto something soft; dimly felt cloth on his cheek . . . the massed troops glittered like black ants; then darkness lapped over him totally in a massive, soft surf . . .

Then brightness, harsh, digging into his eyes and head. For an instant he felt the attack of magical forces and struggled to collect his power; then blinked and shook fully awake. Stared around the hut, which was a small shock to him: a sagging little kennel with the sun coming straight in the window and cutting through slight spaces in the wall and roof.

He saw the hunk of cheese on the low table, gourds hanging above a hearth overflowing with ashes and then the peasant man, face blackened and bloated, lying on his back, tongue thrust out as if in violent mockery and defiance of the flies that

spiraled and hummed around him, arms starfished out, great,
lumpy swellings under the armpits, belly bulged up; then the
woman on the low pallet in her shapeless garments. He turned
his head on the softness and saw the third face, much too close,
just as the woman exhaled a terrible rasping that he didn't know
were words. The young girl's face was inches from his own,
blue, empty, frozen eyes staring out from purple-black flesh;
soft, golden glints of hair caught in a stir of air and the edge
of a stray sunbeam; inches away; the tongue that at first he
took for a chunk of dark sausage; and he knew they'd won,
his enemies had tricked him here, to certain, horrid death.
Heard the woman's words now, a gurgle and hiss across the
room:

"...waaaar...teeerrr...waar...terrr. Wa...rter..."

And he jerked his head from the soft, cold breast he'd lain
on all night, staring, hearing too (as if amplified) the burring
buzzing of the gathering flies, their bright flash and greenish
flicker at the window where the sun spilled in.

He scrambled to his feet and saw the open door and was
already stumbling, fleeing into the gold-lanced green outside,
moaning under his breath, straining, angular, jerky, over the
crest of hill; across the road in a spume of dust; along the clean,
smooth hillside through the scraggly wheat...across the village proper, the huts moving past; a blur of faces he didn't
even glance at, fleeing by an old woman working the well-
rope; a group of playing children rushing past, shouting at him;
one running along for a few of his panting yards as he went
up the reverse slope shouting, dry, vacant, violent:

"Death is come! Death is come!"

He did not see the knight in black and red robes just coming
out of the barn, yawning and stretching in a flood of clean, hot
sunlight, then staring curiously after the gangly figure in the
rent rags who struggled up the hill as if pushing his outsized,
twisted shadow ahead of him and, still running, jerking up and
down, disappeared over the far crest.

The knight turned quizzically to the matronly woman beside
him.

"I wit," he said, "that fellow grew tired of this village."

"Nay, lord knight without-a-name, I know him not. He had
the look of a holy man."

"Mayhap he flees the Devil," the knight returned.

"Or his fasting cracked his brains," she offered.

I know about the Devil, he thought, *that's curious. But what do I know about the Devil? Curious*... He frowned, puzzled.

Her face wasn't quite fierce but set against all times and weathers. There was iron in her, he thought. He was amazed again at all he knew, the words and images at his command. Except so much was missing... his name... when he tried to remember too much he saw brief, vivid, inexplicable flashes of what he assumed was the past; flashes out of a general dimness. He frowned, trying again:

What's my name?... Nothing. *A name is the sound or a mark they make to*... *to separate a thing from other things*... Frowned. *Why do that?*... *the things are the same anyway*... *Where did I come from?*... Shook his head slightly. *Why does it matter?*...

He saw the same scene: an unbelievable storm, wind and rain sheeting almost horizontally into a hillside that leaped and shook in the incredible continuous lightning... flashes of sword and armor in chaotic fragments... slashed bodies... a robed man, mouth yawning, screaming into the thunder and rage, long moustaches fluttering, pale eyes burning as if invoking the fury through himself... he felt sick and nervous, remembering this, and then shook himself out of it. Blinked at the sunny brightness, the brilliant points of dew, scattered bright flowers.

"They don't name each one of those, do they?"

"Well," he said, "where are those wicked men you fear, woman?" He felt warm and strong, He realized he had little fear in him. Whatever he had been, he decided, he must have been fairly successful at it. Smiled, faintly. Or comfortable with it...

"Never mind, good sir," the woman said, holding out an onion and piece of cheese to him, her eyes seeking and finding a boy and girl playing together at the edge of the cultivated fields, a mother's automatic checking. "Troubles always find their way home. This is a thing I've come to trust for truth."

VI

The air was sparkling and fragrant. Parsival stood in the walled garden inhaling the day, the flowers and spice, the cool gray stones rich with sweeps of ivy, the heavy hanging trees creased and nicked with yellow light and blue shimmer. The moment seemed charged with something from long ago and he felt a strange, sweet sense of time last and of no time passing at all . . . smiled and stretched his limbs till they shuddered a little. Sat down on the grass with the sunlight pushing against his bare face and arms.

"What delight," he whispered. This was a day from the purest depth of childhood and if he forgot to tell himself how many years had come between, there suddenly were no years at all, just this moment . . .

He smiled and shut his eyes and the brightness still glowed into them.

He shook his head. Was startled because the shadow of the wall had shifted noticeably though he was certain his eyes had been closed but a moment. And now one of the monks was standing there, young, round-faced, nervous-looking, partly smiling.

"I feared to disturb you, sir," he said.

"I must have dozed."

"Do you really think so, sir?"

Parsival concentrated on the man.

"I ought to know," he declared, at length.

The monk nodded nervously and brushed a hand through his unevenly tonsured hair. Parsival noted that for all his uncertain looks his voice seemed quite assured.

"So you ought," the holy man said, ambiguously. "There's food and drink waiting, if you are ready."

He'd been there perhaps two hours. Since mid-morning. He was hungry. He'd passed an empty, crumbling, white stone church and followed a cart trail across a dense, flowery glade under full trees (that rushed and creaked) to where the thin double ruts ended at a white, overgrown wall whose stones were spilled among the high grasses. He'd thought it odd for tracks to end where there was no gate. Noticed the rusted fragments of an ancient suit of armor and a broken sword lying as if the rocks had been dropped to shatter them there. Clambered over the wall and saw the monastery with the brothers working in the fields around the large, low, rambling structure, the same bright white building rock. No one had spoken or seemed to notice him until this one monk led him through cloistered passages that wound within and without the inner buildings past vistas of sudden bright green richness at the end of long, dim halls. Strips of crystal sky vibrated through slitted windows. Finally the fellow had left him in this silent interior garden.

"Yes," he murmured softly, thoughtfully, "I'm hungry enough."

"Are you awake now, sir?" the monk asked with the same ambiguous overtones, still partly smiling.

"If you mean to say something, brother, why don't you say it straight out?"

The monk brushed irrelevantly at his hair again.

"Some things," he replied, "can't be said plainly or they vanish like a moonbeam in a candle flame."

Parsival nodded.

"Very well," he said.

"We're still waiting for you to wake up and come and eat and drink." Rubbed his head vigorously. "The table is laid, the wine poured."

Parsival stood up. For an instant afraid he lacked the strength to do it all in one motion, as if he'd been stuck to that lawn under him.

"I want nothing to do with that anymore," he said.

"With nourishment?"

"You know what I mean. It's all trick roads that lead in circles. Sweets that turn bitter, drink that sours." He shook his head and stubbornly set his lips. "If you tell me the Grail is here I'll run away." He paced back and forth under the trees, body breaking thin threaded sunbeams that spattered the grass like golden coins. "I want none of it and no *powers* either. Look, fellow, I'm an ordinary man. That's the remarkable thing about me."

He stopped and planted his hands on his hips. A fragile trickle of light creased his face almost in half. "Was I led here? Is that it?"

"You're led everywhere," the monk said, "whether you know it or not." Played with a smile.

"I know all this talk," he said. "I've heard it for years." He moved and the thread snapped. "Talk to me after the grave. I'll listen then."

"Too many 'nays,' sir, if you ask me. You're free to do all you choose. God has granted us that much."

"I want none of it," Parsival said, remote, shaking his head. "I paid my debts on that mountaintop. I did all I needed to. I was once a fool and famous for it. I lost my family and my peace of mind." He was heading past the monk now, aiming for the arched passageway. "I've been your damned hero and damned magician too and that's all done with." He stepped out of the sunlight and seemed to vanish into the hall, still talking, voice echoing back directionless, suddenly distant and hollowed. "So lead me to your food, and I'll starve at your table or chew my own flesh before I'll touch *your* meat!"

The monk had moved to the archway standing just outside as if speaking to the shadowed void before him.

"You opened a door, sir," he said, pleasantly, "that can never be shut. You're needed. When the wolf comes to the fold what shepherd turns his back on the sheep?"

Parsival's answer was lost in its own rattling reverberations far down the hall but the monk seemed to understand well enough. He looked faintly wry.

VII

The red and black knight was standing with the least old of the men, the lithest women and the strongest boys. He lined them up with homemade spears, poles, clubs and a few rude axes. The afternoon was hot and cloudless. The heat pulsed on the dry ground.

Whoever I am, he was thinking, *I seem to know about fighting. I clearly had a bitter trade.* He could remember fragments of battles, armored warriors clashing with blind fury, himself ripping into them, a flash of burning cold power and satisfaction as his blade hit home again and again, sheared metal, sprayed bright blood... *I suppose the woman's telling me the truth.*

He'd confided somewhat in her this morning, explaining that his memory was in pieces, that he didn't know who he was or what he stood or didn't stand for, and asked her opinion of his possible history. She'd sat in the dust beside him, worn, hard, work-twisted fingers steadily enmeshed in complexes of yarn, pulling, knotting, stringing the shapeless tangle (as if by a kind of magic) into what gradually was becoming a child's garment.

"It's clear you been a knight," she'd told him. "None would dispute that, me lord."

"Well then," he'd replied, fingers drumming on his sword hilt, "but what do I do now? Where do I go? Or do I?"

"If you stay here, me lord knight," she'd said, carefully, not looking at anything, the threads flowing through her unceasing hands, "you'll be soon set upon, as we all will be, for the few grains of food we have. We'll all be put to the sword, sooner or later."

"How know you this?"

"A week since, old Halpp was found in the back hills, chopped fine by an ax."

"Did he tell you aught?"

"His wounds did. And the single pair of feet marks in the ploughed earth. We was seen and where there was one they'll come more."

"But what must I do?" He'd gone back to that. "Wander and hope to recover my yesterdays? For all I can tell, those who knew me are dead and gone ..." He'd shaken his head.

"Aye?"

He'd shrugged. Poked his fingers in the dust.

"It's difficult to say these things ... but what should I do? Where do I look?"

She'd never ceased twisting the material into form, fraction by inescapable fraction.

"Why not plough the earth God gives you?" She'd knit her eyebrows, watching him now.

"What?"

"You're bound by a code." Not looking now.

"Code?"

"Aye. Chivalry, me lord. You need go nowhere to do your duty."

"How do you know this?"

"Knights are all bound thus."

"To what end, woman?" He'd let the yellow dust run through his fingers. The sun was beating almost straight down.

"Ah," she'd said, "to help them as has great need a help and deep distress."

She'd explained it well enough, he was thinking now.

Out of this chivalry may come something I need to know ...

"The first thing," he was telling them now, "is to get them to fight where *we* wish." He smiled. Obvious. Necessary.

The long-boned woman, his advisor, was watching, sitting just in the shade of the barn on a backless stool. Her hands still worked on a garment. He couldn't tell if it was the same one.

"If there aren't too many," he told them next, "I'll keep them away from here." Squinted at the woman, whose head was tilted forward as if absorbed totally in her working. He touched his raw scar again. "I need a headpiece," he said. "Have you one here?"

An old man looked uneasy.

"We're but villagers, great lord," he said, "how could we—"

"Go on, Palit," the woman said from the shadow, not looking up, "bring him all the gear."

"But . . . Maryls . . . we—"

"Be still, old fool. Get him the gear."

The man nervously labored away, signaling one of the boys to follow. She explained:

"There was a battle in the valley. We gathered what we could. Who could blame us?"

He shrugged.

"I'll do what I can," he said, "but you all must fight and not flee as you did from me on the bridge." Went over to one boy. "Hold the spear like this . . ." He began instructing them and continued as the sun tilted down into the burning west and the landscape began receding into dim spaces and shadow.

The sky was like dark blood, the sun under the smooth-topped hills that were purplish black, depthless as the twilight seeped among the trees and huts in a glimmering, grayish tide.

He sat in front of the barn, the woman behind him. He heard nothing beyond the steady droning murmur of the July night. He knew she would still be working, that her hands were moving unceasingly. He'd watched her peel potatoes for his supper, clean greens, fill the pot, cut, slice, shred so neatly as to seem almost magical to him, and he'd recalled a woman seeming dreamlike in flowing golden silks, a bright-blue tent behind her, a long, fine-boned, smooth face tilting down, long hair piled high and bright and she moved as if balancing it, holding something he knew was a sweet out to him, smiling in her violet, shadowed eyes . . . and then lost it and thought:

Was that something holy? Or something I remember?

And then he was standing up, intent, alert, before he even

caught up with his body's responses, as if lifted to his feet by unseen hands, and he realized he'd felt rather than seen the blot of movement on the far hillside that rolled down to the river, and he was already running, the mail links shaking and ringing softly, holding the sheathed sword still at his hip; pushing the boy who'd fallen asleep by the low brick wall that partly encircled the village with a wobbling and crumbling arc.

"Are you so full-fed and safe, boy?" he demanded. "Go softly and tell everyone to prepare." Watched as the fourteen-year-old scurried away, became a blur lost in the deepening dusk. The huts and trees were now indistinguishable dark blotches. The stream was a faint, silvery trace creasing the twilight-blended shapes.

He felt a strange, cold anticipation as he trotted easily, then moved into a quiet walk down the slope to the bridge. They wouldn't see any reason to get wet. They'd send a scout or two at best to cross over the hard way. Well, the peasants would have to deal with that.

Chivalry, he thought, recalling his conversation with the woman. He stopped under a willow, screened by the dense, sweeping wands that whispered and shifted in the veerings of air. The sunset was a lost violet hint above the single darkness of hills, woods, fields . . . the water splashed faintly past . . . the bridge seemed to arch into nothingness . . . *Chivalry . . . ah, would but these pieces in my head unite themselves! I might then give a name and reason to my life! Well, these folks here are afraid for their potatoes and so I'll do this chivalry . . . my God, but this is passing strange . . . I know names and the world and yet my own is absent, my traces faint . . . I must wait and watch and learn what I may . . . wait and watch . . . ah . . .*

Heard a clinkering of metal . . . then a loud whispering voice. They were just across the water now.

If I try to parley they'll think me weak and attack anyway . . . He knew these things without particular memories to tie them to: the way you swing a sword without having to recall any or every particular time in the past.

I'm a somewhat cynical fellow, as I begin to see. But that comes from watching life . . . no . . . watching people. Life is indifferent to anything . . . He smiled. He was learning. He expected everything would come back to him in time.

He saw them across the short, narrow arc of bridge that darkly spanned the faintly luminescent water, saw a vague metal gleaming and then shadows separating from the deeper background, the wood reverberating slightly as they crossed, an unintelligible voice half-whispering over the cricket's summer hysteria in the warm, seamless night full of immense ripeness and perfume.

He stared into the deep blanknesses, seeing only the blurred edge of their movements. He felt his throat tense, mouth dry, heart quicken, and suddenly this all seemed absurd. What was he actually doing here? He didn't know these men or their purposes . . . why not just live and eat and sleep and enjoy all the richness of this world? Absurd . . . this had nothing to do with him, his inner blanks left him free and innocent, and he struggled as if to break invisible bonds as feet drummed softly on the wood and a voice, hushed, fragmentary, said:

" . . . some . . . if God wills or . . . Devil . . . sleep for a fortnight, I . . ."

I have naught to do with any of this. Whatever I once had to do with is lost in bottomless shadow and let me leave it there . . .

He watched the vague sheen of a river and felt a deep urge to follow it up and around the shadowed, mysterious bends . . . on and on . . . remember nothing . . . start all time from now . . .

And then he found himself already walking, the draped willows whispering over his armor, turning his back on the raiders, almost strolling along the soft riverbank, faceplate open to the tender breezes.

"I'm free," he murmured, partly aloud. *I don't want to know anything more.* "I'm free."

Except something in him knew, expected and so was unsurprised when a crouching, lithe figure, dripping water, cursed and swept a two-handed ax stroke at him. The hushed, flowing moment receded and was lost and he was caught again by his own motions, smoothly stepping aside, hearing the blade hiss past his ear as he drew and cut in one fluid motion and the man (hit glancingly in the upper torso) was shocked shrill and fled yelping, hoarse, crashing through brush; could be heard falling and getting up.

He turned now into the inevitability of the men charging from the bridge, all surprise lost for everybody, and he wondered why he had no fear. Then, as the blots and gleams and voices rushed up out of the fallen night to meet him, he leaped ahead (waiting for the fear and then forgetting even that) as if in a fast current, curious and ferocious, amazed (from some inner distance) at what he was doing, at his ducking, blocking and near-miraculous slashing that seemed to blow the vague, raging forms away from himself with hardly a felt shock, seeming to float in almost peaceful suspension above the actual cries and crashes and shadowy tumult. Then he heard the yells of the peasants farther up the slope and wondered how many there were coming on . . . but it was all so easy, moving in the dark, in and out of the screen of willow, great hissing rents cut in the branches. He felt supple, twisting and moving like a dancer; thrilling in little shocks each time a blade or ax brushed past his face or skidded from his chain armor, each shock whirling him deeper and more intricately into the ferocious dance, sparks flying, the shadows falling and fleeing, and he felt towering and coldly sweet and beating with a strange joy . . .

This is what you are without even a name, a voice that was probably his own kept repeating, *this is what you are . . .*

VIII

Dawn was mixed gray and little chips of wet-looking greenish blue. Broaditch was peering down a long, gradual hill into the valley, where a stream and a footpath wound more or less together, the path straightening the steeper curves. He was sipping a bitter root tea from a wooden mug. The children were partway down the slope, Tikla watching her brother digging in the earth with a short stick. Alienor was setting the light copper kettle upside down on the grass. The man (whose name, it turned out, was Pleeka) was squatted near the fading fire, chewing a dried fragment of something Broaditch had noticed him extricate from the robed recesses of his person. He hadn't troubled to wash his face and the ragged, lumped wound was black and ugly. Even crouched like that he seemed impatient, eyes withdrawn, pitlike.

"It could rain before the day's done," Broaditch commented.

"Mayhap it will break the heat," Alienor said, picking up the pot.

"Mayhap I will break the wind," he said, looking dourly into his cup, "if I have to drink more of this brew."

"Don't complain," she told him.

"There's not a bean in it yet it billows up my innards like a bellows."

"It's healthful," she said. "You're a gross man."

"Not me, I swear, woman. It's my bowels betray me." Burped. She made a face.

"Your life will be altogether different," Pleeka was suddenly saying, as if these weren't his first words since waking. There was the same cold contempt on his face, contempt that was not particularized so that, Broaditch saw, a man could resent him without having to bother about it.

"I have found that to be my plague, fellow," Broaditch said back, draining the tea and flicking away the dregs and belching again. "My life has ever been different without becoming particularly satisfactory."

"Once you admit the living light into yourself," Pleeka informed him, not looking at him, "all things are born anew."

"So have I heard." Broaditch stood up, wiping his hands on his hams. Downslope Torky had unearthed a fairly large rock which he was struggling to lift and lever free, but the stick kept breaking. Broaditch could hear his daughter's voice, high and giggly.

"That's cracked, Torky," she was saying. "What will you do with it?"

He didn't respond. He was on his knees, straining, feet slipping in the weedy dirt.

"There's lots of other rocks," she said. "Look . . ." Pointed, but he paid no attention.

"Be still," he said, straining. He puffed breath a little.

"I will not," she said.

"I like this one." Braced his arms and took a new angle.

"Hear me," Pleeka was saying, eye depths aimed at Broaditch, "the man I serve will move mountains in the name of God." He stood up as though he would leap into the air, though he did not.

"So you're his prophet?" Broaditch asked, straight-faced.

Alienor took in the conversation sidelong, swinging the foodsack over her back as her husband took up the other pack and set the ropes over his shoulders before hefting his spear.

"It's just cracked, Torky," Tikla insisted, as the stick broke off short again and he fell over on his side.

"Devil curse it!" he said.

"Mind your words, smart lad," his mother called down to him. "Get yourselves ready to travel. If you've any business to do, take it to the bushes before we start. Trifle not with Satan's name."

"Life can be simple and good," Pleeka was saying, "when each day's course is known and fitting."

"I had that as slave and serf," Broaditch answered. "Well, Pleeka, were you a priest once?"

They were heading downslope now. The day was grayly brightening. Tikla was going out ahead while her brother still struggled with the half-buried stone.

"No," Pleeka said, "I were worse even than that. A scholar." Broaditch grinned, liking the reply, for once.

"Then you were a hard fellow," he suggested.

They were passing Torky and his father raised an eyebrow.

"What are you doing, boy? Do you want me to free that for you?" He smiled. "Do you mean to bear it away? I'll give you a burden if you feel such a need."

"No," his son said, "I'll do it." Was digging savagely all around the sides with the stub of stick, flinging earth everywhere in frantic, raging, inefficient industry.

"Why," Broaditch asked over his shoulder, part pausing, "do you want it? I misdoubt it has much value, son."

"I care not," was the answer. He was kicking at it and rocking the heart-shaped chunk.

His father nodded and went on.

"Finish quickly then," he said, "and follow after." To Alienor and Pleeka (if he pleased to listen) he said: "With all my years and snowy hairs I think I have done no better than that boy." Rested the spear over his shoulder and aimed a word at the angular man: "Well, more-than-a-priest, what—" Broke off, squinting into the valley. Gestured for them all to wait. It was far enough away to blur in the early mists but he could just make out vague figures and wet gleamings of steel and (to clinch it) a bulky mounted man. "So they've come out ahead of us," he muttered, leaning on the spearbutt. "Well, let them go on in peace."

They seem to have swelled in numbers, he thought. *And the countryside seems to be shrinking . . .*

He glanced back at Torky, who was putting his back into it now, squatting, hands clawed around the chunk of rock.

"He touched me," Pleeka was saying, looking across the valley, expressionless, or rather with one expression that could have meant anything or nothing.

"What?" wondered Broaditch.

"This is what I must share. His touching."

Broaditch glanced at Pleeka, then back at Torky, unconsciously tensing, straining with him as he heaved, staggered half-upright, cradling the stone against his legs, holding it free for an instant, braced, awkward and fierce as if against the hillslope, the massing clouds' vast shifting overhead, the vast tilt of the earth itself . . . then buckling, dropping and flinging it back into the hole. Stood there wiping his hands against his baggy leather shorts.

His father smiled.

"There was light," Pleeka said, harsh with that abstract contempt, "do you understand?" The tic shook his cheek and he half turned towards Alienor, who said not a word. "Do you understand?" he repeated. "There was suddenly light . . ."

IX

Howtlande was sitting on the mule in the darkness at the far end of the narrow bridge when the fighting started. He instantly understood and was shouting:

"Skalwere! Mind the flanks, Skalwere! I'll see to the rear!"

From the sparking, clash and fury across the water, he believed half-a-dozen at least opposed them. The rest of his men (save for one guarding the women) went racing past him, boards rattling and booming underfoot...

The nameless knight had forced a way to the path and was holding the last roll of high ground before the village, but he realized men had already slipped around him through the bush and willow even before he heard the screams and shouts among the huts.

The moon was just lifting through the hill treetops and he saw vague figures all around him. None seemed too anxious to close altogether but he was panting now, sweat flooding over his face, and his limbs felt swollen and heavy. The spearmen kept darting up, thrusting and leaping back from his vicious counterstrokes. Each effort drained him perceptibly. He moved towards the huts, blocking and shifting. A squat shape hunched too close and, an instant slow in getting back, was clipped by just the swordtip in the face; gestured; lurched; bawled and fell and vanished as though into the earth's deeper darkness. The men around him were just hints and glints, stirring, shifting as he half ran up the slight slope towards what (through the sweat-blurring of his sight) seemed warring beings of flame and darkness.

Is this magic here before me?

And the word was a shock: something he knew and didn't know.

There are holes in the world, his mind said, *and magic is a hole in the world . . .*

He slashed . . . then whacked a furious spear aside. Closer, saw the huts were aflame and a mad tangle of shadows flew around the men holding the torches: women, children fleeing, falling in the wild light and then he was (panting and wobbling) near the barn and saw the big woman, two teenage boys and others, old people (in the ruddy, flaring torchlight) crouching around the mound of potatoes, makeshift weapons poised in despair, fury and something like embarrassment too: an old man with a scimitar (brought from God-knew-where), a boy with an oversize mace . . . The raiders gathered at the door to charge inside. One of them was down, sitting, holding his wounded midsection. A woman sprawled half out the door, face lost in blood and shadow.

He turned as a fully armored knight strode with drawn sword out of a blazing hut in a rush of sparks and fire-flashing, seeming to draw the flames behind him a moment as he headed straight over, businesslike, holding a smallish, round shield casually.

"Here's the knight!" a spearman was shouting, pointing him out to the newcomer, who tugged his red-reflecting vizor closed and came on quickly now. The rest waited as the two armored men closed, circling briefly, and the nameless one thought:

This is a new manner of fellow . . . And then struck, and his terrific, bone-wrenching cut was deflected by the shield and the air was ripped by the percussive counter. Over his opponent's shoulder he glimpsed fragments of the scene in the barn, the flurry and screaming, raging, a woman falling into the potatoes, dress and limbs flopping like a dropped doll, blood spattering over the food, the raider keeping his spear in her chest, still rushing, crashing into the mound himself, spilling the bloody lumps like a sack of stones everywhere underfoot, combatants, victims, everyone skidding, going up and over . . .

He ducked away from the knight's next cut, legs wobbling a little, lungs raw with each sucked breath. Sensed, heard someone moving behind him, tried to twist around but knew it was too late and without even surprise felt a titanic weight bang over his head and a white light flared everywhere and his sight and mind went supernaturally clear in the shock of it and he recorded every face and every detail of the scene: the people flailing, tumbling and bleeding and screaming, rolling on the potatoes, clinging and clutching like dancers at a mad feast, reeling singly and in locked groups and pairs around and around as panic and hate kept them spinning, reaching for passing walls, partners and enemies, gripping forever-failing support as flames burst out all over and in blind escape now dragged one another back in a welter of fire, blood and shadow . . . Then something sharp ground in his skull and brain and he screamed wildly, clutching at his head as all light winked out and he knew his true name and was trying to shout it out within the silent blackness that was himself.

X

Parsival was still fuming, walking rapidly around a curve in the passageway, unconsciously turning right at the next crossing, thinking:

I've been fate's fool for forty years and I won't be tricked into anything again...never...no witchcraft or empty praying...I've seen all the visions I need to see and I have heard if you deny it, it all goes away like a dreaming...which way here?

He faced a forking. High above a line of slit windows streamed whitish daylight that was swallowed by the general dimness. Dark pennants hung unstirring, obscure.

He looked left, then right. Both passages gaped blank and dark.

"You bastards!" he abruptly raged aloud, gritting his teeth. "May you lick the Devil's hind in hell!"

Thinking in fury:

More tricks! To trick me into what this time? Sarcastic: *"Why take the road that always rises, boy."* Oh, yes. I heard that nonsense before, you mystical bastards! *No more empty journeys warring with ghosts and unwitting men...*

"I fought your fucked wars for you, you sons-of-bitches!"

he shouted. The muffled echoes rattled dully back.

Raging again he stormed at the right, checked himself, and plunged into the leftward way.

The Devil's way is left, I hope, he snarled to himself. *I've had enough of what they say God's was ...*

The passage dipped ... rose ... then he was in a huge, round hall, windowless, lit by man-tall candles set around the wall. He hesitated, looking up, squinting. There was a gigantic mural composed like a wheel around the entire ceiling in equal parts lit and dim. There was what seemed a flowering garden outside a little castle, a bar of dark blotting part of the scene where a woman stood among flowers. She had long hair and large, shining eyes that reminded him of someone. In the next lit panel a deer was fleeing, a spear angled into the chest ... darkness ... then death, as a skeleton, jousting with a knight. He looked back at the woman: yes, he thought, it somehow resembled her ... his mother ... the eyes at least.

Dear God, he said to himself, *I haven't thought of her in so long ...*

He looked elsewhere on the incredibly detailed picture: A great battle, tantalizingly at the edge of a shadowy area where a knight in what seemed tattered gear was moving through dense forest, holding something in his hands that appeared to shine like a jewel ...

I could think this all meant just for me ... perhaps all men could ...

He pulled away and crossed the hall to the narrow door at the far end. Pushed it open, expecting anything (except "anything" would have to be thinner than his shoulders' width to get through there) and was dazzled by a hot burst of sunlight. Blinking, he twisted sidewise through the doorway.

He found himself in another walled garden, this one very large, outside the monastery proper, with walks and tall trees. It seemed deserted. There was such a flood of sweetness he felt dizzy. Banks, no, waves of flowers swayed in an unbroken glow everywhere up to the shadows of the ancient, massive oaks that all but covered the high outer walls.

He waded knee-deep through the incredible sea of color and scent, rich with bees and butterflies. He paused at a delicate stream that flowed blue over pure white stones, glittering like cut crystal. He stooped and drank from his hands. The water was cool and tasted of sunshine and slow green earth. The breeze was a vague whisper and fingered his long, blond-gray hair. He took a full, lush breath and sat down . . . then reclined, looking at eye level across the shimmering field.

I'll climb the wall, he thought idly. *It'll be simple.* He didn't move. *In a little while . . . First a little rest . . .*

He lay back and shaded his eyes with his arm. The sun was always so much hotter when you were prone. He let the drowsy warmth sink into his flesh . . . drifted with the coils of laden breeze . . .

No, his mind said, *this is a trick too . . . this . . . is . . . is butterfly bread and God's forgetting . . .* and then with a whooshing of leaves and shaking light the trees were explaining things to him, laying the whole problem out with the help of thin pencils of sunlight, sketching on the sweet grass . . . he understood he'd fallen through the inner hole in himself guarded by dreams and the sun kept him awake within his sleep, and then she was there in a radiance soft but intense as daylight, and he was absorbed in watching each shifting, gleaming part of her, each slight breath of movement that stained the iridescent atmosphere; her body clothed and bathed in unending, unrepeating color, her face a sweetness beyond expression, and he feared to move his mind at all and perhaps disrupt the ineffable unfolding of that silent womanlight . . .

And thought said:

No . . . No . . . You cannot merely watch like this . . . you'll be lost . . .

He was amazed at how conscious he actually still was. He felt that if he opened his eyes the vision and field would both be there.

No, no, not just watch!

Because he sensed he would be absorbed forever in watching, that he'd sink and drift passively away into eternities of silent, soft beauties. He had to do something with this or be lost, drained away . . . What? . . . What? . . . He tried to somehow get closer to her, feel her . . . wordlessly speak . . . wavered there, rising and falling over the blank depths of sleep . . .

Is this my mother too? Is this my own heart's image? Is this holy? He felt a golden rush of joy suddenly. *Is this flowering from me?* He asked the tree voices. Felt the ecstasy as the sun wrote answers on the field. He couldn't read it. Strained but couldn't read . . . Was trying to wake up now and the tender, feathery being of purest flame was gone and he was thinking as he struggled back:

Do things do things...

He sat up sweaty, shocked in the sea of blossoms. Stood up, rubbing his face and eyes. Swayed a little. Then he was wading across the field through the cool, fragrant shade towards the high, white garden wall.

I'm not fighting everybody's battles, I'm going to put my life together...I don't need visions...I'm going to find my child and try to show him something...

He touched the wall with one hand, absently, as if surprised to find it solid and sun-heated.

I need a woman too again...I never really loved anyone enough...

He locked his fingers and toes and began climbing, and on top he looked back at the odd monastery, which seemed deserted from here: empty fields, no smoke from any chimney. It looked totally abandoned.

He shrugged. More of their tricks, perhaps. Or it meant nothing. He really didn't care.

He swung over and dropped a body length into the weedy outer field.

Let it be, he told himself. Because he was going to live his own way, let them fill the world with visions, portents and all mysterious, vast significances...

He strode away and didn't look back again.

I'm going to put my life together...

XI

The pain in the amnesiac knight's head was so intense (as if beyond mere feeling) he found he could stare right through it. He blinked at the morning light. The pain leaped a little each time the world shook and then he looked around, saw the trees passing slowly and unevenly through the hazy heat... saw soldiers... women... boys and girls... blinked at the long, rabbitlike mule ears for a moment before realizing he was bouncing behind them atop a cart loaded with raw and scorched potatoes. A pair of cows were snubbed close to the rear and lowed from time to time. He smelled their rich, sourish warm breath.

He tried to sit up and the pain was white iron claws in his skull.

"Aiii," he sighed and held his head with one hand.

"Good morrow," a bluff, smooth voice was saying.

He turned his eyes that way. The speaker was mounted, keeping pace with the toiling cart, the rising sun behind him so that he was a bulky, blinding silhouette.

"Good morrow," the voice repeated, "knight in the cart."

A chuckle. "Better such disgrace, I think, than be left behind, don't you agree?"

"Ahhh," the hurt knight sighed.

"I thought you were dead."

"Why . . . Why . . ." He was still trying to see the man clearly, but the sun was almost directly behind him and the beams stabbed into his sight. He twisted his face away.

"The next village is in view," the voice (he couldn't know) of Finlot called back to Howtlande who, mounted on his mule, looked away from the knight on the potatoes. Howtlande rattled a crudely sketched map of the territory.

"Excellent," was his response. "Unless they have famous lords like this one among them I expect little trouble." He smiled with oily satisfaction, sucking on a scrap of cold pork fat, tongue lashing at the greased edge of his moustache. He leaned out of the sun over the sides of the halting wagon and fixed the injured fellow with his dark, active eyes that coldly belied the netted, perpetual humor wrinkles surrounding them. "Well, are you with us, lord general?"

Holding his head with both hands, the knight struggled up to a semi-sitting position on the food heap that shifted under him. His neck was stiff, back out of joint. The unrelenting pain clawed at his head. He sighed and leaned against the wicker side that sagged a little and creaked with each slow jounce of the wheels . . .

"Ahhhh," he murmured.

"He ought to been dead," was Finlot's opinion. "I lain a five-pound hammer over his noggin. His helmet's all flat." He sort of sniggered. "He ain't bled a lot, considering."

"Well, well," Howtlande declared, "you were not treating with an ordinary knight. This is a great and legendary fellow."

"Oh?" Finlot wasn't too sure. "All them what I hits on the noggin is fair ordinary."

"Which great one, do you say?" a new voice behind the pain and sunbrightness pushed in: the dour warrior with a red silk surcoat.

Howtlande leaned back up into the brightness, holding his mule's neck. Sucked thoughtfully at the ball of fat in his stubby hand. He looked suddenly sly.

"The lord general," he said.

"Which lord general?" the dour, nameless knight persisted. "And of what?"

"Do you know him not, sir which-and-who?" Howtlande narrowed his already squinty eyes. When the dour knight said no more he went on: "Well, if you will not say who you are yourself expect no floods of information." Grinned, the fat shining on his lips which he ineffectively wiped with the leather sleeve end that hung raggedly below his steel wristlets.

The knight in the cart was staring, holding his hand up against the sunglare.

"You," he said at the bulky figure featureless with the hot sky behind.

"Yes, general?" Howtlande was feeling expansive.

"You know who I am?"

"Would that not take much knowing, sir?" was the reply. "Had you a wife it might tax even she to know you altogether. Or your mother, say, I—"

"By Odin's dangling fuck-maker," a new voice interjected with disgust, and the knight didn't bother to turn his eyes because there was pain enough in looking straight ahead. "He's like a great wind that blows and rages to shake a straw!"

"Well put, Skalwere," Finlot called out. "If we could fight as fierce as he speaks long and to no point, why none could hold us for a heartbeat." Guffaws here and there.

Howtlande sneered.

"And if all your brains were gathered in a pile," he told them, "an ant would step over it unseeing."

"Do you know who I am?" the wincing knight demanded. Adjusted himself on the potatoes. He realized there was no hope of (or point in) getting to his feet. The pain even seemed to be ebbing slightly. "What is my name?"

"Know you it not yourself?" the fat man wondered, scratching his hawk nosetip. He was finished sucking the lard. Cocked his round head. The nose was the second warning (after the eyes) that nature had placed on that jolly mask.

"Would he then ask?" Skalwere called over. "Though *you* might, in his place."

"What be he lord general of?" Finlot wondered. "That village of mud and cowflops?" Guffaws here and there in the marching line.

"Say, if you can," the knight insisted, holding his lumpy, bloodcaked skull, gingerly.

"Why scatter your advantages?" Howtlande asked no one,

licking the last sweet traces from his shiny lips. "The blow took your memory, it would appear, sir. So your name now would be little use. Surely it's a blessing to have a light mind. I'll not be the one to weigh it heavier." He spurred the mule, whose sharp hooves plip-plopped more rapidly than the actual forward motion justified.

The mysterious subject of conversation finally shut his eyes. Sighed under his breath with each rut and stone the warped wheels battered into and over. He decided to wait until the pain eased, then he'd follow up. Here was a key to his past . . . but right now he'd rest . . . yes . . . that was it . . . rest . . . *Ah* . . . it hurt . . . *Ah* . . .

The pain and dreams jarred in and out as the day flashed on and off. He saw the dark-eyed, beautiful woman again and this time with a man . . . flash of burning sun prying at his eyelids, into his raw skull . . . The man and woman under cool trees by a glittering stream. He was tall, blond, in red, silky robes and the woman crooked a basket of thickly-gleaming red berries under her long arm. The green spring light was cool and sweet. This couple was so tall, godlike, somehow . . . his head was ripped into again as if by sawblades that ground over the bared bones . . . Then the peace and coolness, the purling swish of water, the birds, breezes high up in the pine-tops . . . voices . . . her voice, saying words he didn't really follow . . . divine, mysterious utterances . . .

"So," she was saying, "I spent a lifetime getting away from there and now you want to go back."

"What harm in a visit?" he wondered.

"They love you little enough, great husband."

"Your father's ill."

"Not enough by half." She didn't look at him. "I don't want to go back there."

. . . he knew these were memories . . . then the light stabbed and pounded at him but he sank under it again into the cool, easy lushness of that shady afternoon somewhere in his lost past. The tall, blond man was drinking from a wineskin. Stained lips and chin with what seemed a dribble of blood which he didn't wipe away. A little girl, ash-blond, about three, naked, was kneeling at the stream's rocky edge, piling smooth, dark, round stones in a heap, careful and grave. Threads of reflected sunlight flicked over her intent face as the awkward, stubby childfingers sorted and plucked and added to the stack.

"You hate your own father so?" he asked.

"You know all this," she said. The sun glowed in the basket of berries but missed the woman's face. She seemed to be watching the waterflow. "You were different for a time," she told him.

"For God's name, Layla," he said, setting the wineskin aside.

"In God's name," she corrected.

"I am different," he insisted. "I'm changed."

"Mayhap so . . . but still you are weary of me, my husband."

"Nay."

"Yes."

"I am not." He was so tall he seemed (in the viewer's angle) to be leaning back into the green-gold blur of forest light. His robe was fascinating: the shimmers of silk flashed when he moved, like water. The voice was deep and strange. There was a strange taste . . . he wanted the deep voice to stop . . . just stop sounds . . .

"I didn't want the other child," she said next. The voice was a calm softness. "You truly want to go away. Why not admit it?" She was staring at him finally, eyes wide and bright dark. "God . . . God . . ." She was crying and he tasted a tense dryness . . . was it him she didn't want? . . . who? . . . what? . . . "You tried, Parsival. You tried. I grant you that . . . you tried to be a man and decent to us. I grant you that."

"So I failed you?"

". . . *don't say things anymore,* his mind pushed in. *It tastes* . . ."

"You tried." She turned now, walking away, hands gripped together. "I grant all that . . ." Sobbing, tearing at him with sobbing and the fear and the taste . . .

. . . *wait,* he thought, *don't* . . .

And he was running, the shadow and golden light flickering past, passing the tall, red blur of blond giant and the little girl who never looked up from piling the wet stones, rapt, squatting . . . tree boles, branches, leaves flashing past, hearing his voice raw and filling everything, mind beating over and over, running, beating, tasting it:

. . . *wait for me . . . for me . . . wait for me* . . .

Hearing the resonant male bass high behind him:

"Sweet Jesus...Layla! Sweet God, make your peace with me! I beg you! I beg you!"

And then the light that was pain slashed his flayed consciousness and the cart leaped and banged, lumpy potatoes shifting and spilling around him...

XII

The legs and arms flopped stiffly through the spaces in the wagon sides as two sturdy, dusty men heaved it across a network of hard clay ruts to the edge of the ditchful of bodies. Behind them was an empty village of huts. Smoke from a single fire rose into the mild, windless morning.

The bulkier of the pair was looking down the hard scar of road to where a few sagging logs crossed what was once a stream, but now was stones and caked mud.

"Where'd this one come from then?" he asked his companion, who was wearing his hood up. They both were already sweating. The first was bareheaded, balding and missing the tip of his nose.

"Arr, what's this?" the other responded, letting the traces drop, clattering, to the harsh earth.

"Another customer." The first pointed to where a ragged, bony man lay flat on his face by the bridge, legs and arms starfished from the swellings.

"What fine work we got, eh, Flatface?"

The bald man shrugged.

"Well, we gets the pickings, at least that," he reflected, harsh, squinting, lumbering over as puffy, rainless clouds inched across the sky. The edge of one caught the sun and briefly dimmed the fierce light. He bent above the pale, ravaged man, flipping through his rags expertly and finding nothing, rolled him over and stared with disgust into the long, bony face with filthy, outsized moustaches plastered to the hollow cheeks by dust and grease. "Some bloody pickings," he said, "this one be." Pondered the black blotchings on the abdomen. Gripped the emaciated wreck by one knifelike ankle and dragged him to the burial pit. The head bounced over the rough ground.

"What spreads the death, Flatface?" the hooded one asked, conversationally. "Some say flies . . . others the wind itself."

Flatface grunted. Rolled the body into the heap. Then they backed the cart around and dumped the rest.

"Not so many no more, eh, Flatface?"

"Who be left but us to get it now?"

When the corpses hit, clouds of flies rose grating and seething.

"I know not why we still live," the hooded one said.

"Some it won't touch." Shrugged. "Ask God or the Devil. I wit not which be in charge of plague."

They were pulling the empty cart back. It rattled lightly over the stony earth.

"It's a strange thing, Flatface, a strange thing. Me old woman, she went right off . . ." Snapped a finger. "Like that . . . The old Gaf too . . . That was back when we used to bury'm."

"I think they poisons the fucked earth, Vordit, that's what I think."

"It's been unnatural dry." Vordit peered around and crossed himself. "No doubt a that."

"I think the dead poisons the earth." Flatface reiterated his declaration. Jerked his head in a nod.

His associate was squinting down the pale thread of main road that ran across the low-rolling valley fields and vanished in the haze.

"So," he said. "Ah."

"Eh?"

"Is that wind work? I think not. Oh, I think not."

Flatface turned and stared himself at an almost motionless streak of dust that floated in the horizon haze.

"Must be more of'm coming north," he said. "The road lies there."

"Let'm come, and go too."

The light briefly dimmed again as they jounced the cart past the first houses, sagging, tilted, forlorn with gaped, empty doorways and overgrown, sunbleached yards.

"Well," Vordit said, "there's room enough for all in the pit." He glanced distractedly at the slowly passing, empty shells that seemed to still hold (somehow suspended in their mist and shadow) the harsh intensities of all the lives there, all hopeless rages and tender moments . . . A crow arced overhead, a dark, rough fluttering, and folded itself down on a tattered thatch eave. The bird eye was a sudden, dim bead.

Flatface was looking behind again. The dust was closer. Whoever they were, they were not dawdling. Now he could see there was a second cloud somewhat behind the first.

"So," Vordit was saying, "what troubles me still is why they worked so hard? If it all comes to the same. Eh?" There was a kind of furious amazement in his tone. "Folk was clearing them worthless fields when the plague took them. What use was it all? They should've run off . . . what use?" Shook his head and sniffed violently, part blew his nose, then sniffed again.

"Go ask them, why don't you?" suggested Flatface, walking now, looking backwards as he pushed at the traces.

It was nearing sunset before the first bandits actually reached the wasted collection of broken huts and houses. Howtlande gestured with drawn sword at Flatface and Vordit, who were sitting on the cart, munching hard bread. There was no one else in sight or hearing.

"Fan out and search around," Howtlande told Skalwere and Finlot. "See what's to be seen."

"Why would I do that?" Skalwere questioned, sarcastic. "I'd walk around with shut eyes save that you just opened them with your fat wisdom." He was already slipping up into the shadows, short, wiry, dangerous, quick and quiet. He was wishing he could go home again. More than ever . . . If only he'd slain Tungrim, the son, too, and not just the others . . . He'd imagined himself raising a force of disgruntled Britons and Welshmen and renegade Norse and going back home on better terms than he'd left . . . except these men were not much of a match for half their weight of Vikings.

Howtlande smiled his best smile and advanced the pale mule a little closer to the two peasants, whose flesh glowed through the grime as if they were made of embers as the last sunbeams leveled into them.

"Hail, goodfellows," he said, "we're travelers on a long route with more coming behind. Be there room in your fine town here?"

"If it be not empty," Skalwere called down from the hut shadows, "your talking will soon clear it out."

Flatface just watched as his partner said:

"There be room to spare here, traveler."

"Another tragically wasted place," Howtlande sighed. He wondered if anything useful would be left. How could he expect to build his forces in this land of the dead and missing? "How many are left, goodfellows?"

Vordit shrugged and bit into his bread as if he had eternity to swallow and digest.

"Can you count?" he finally asked back.

"Just you both?"

"No," Vordit allowed.

"Well, how many then, fellow?"

The other raiders were poking around the deserted huts behind Skalwere and Finlot. The sour knight stood silently near the mule.

"Should I name those already in the grave?" Vordit wondered.

"Were we to wait on that tally," the dour knight said, "we needs must stay past our own deaths."

"So this town is empty?" Howtlande said, exasperated. "You low-born sons-of-bitches weary me. Is it empty or nay, thick brains?"

"Not so long as we be in it," Vordit pointed out.

"Enough of this nonsense." Howtlande was losing his temper as Finlot and Skalwere returned.

"No one about," Finlot declared, a trace breathless. "No food . . . no folk . . . empty huts, fires cold on the hearth . . ."

The second group of raiders (with the women and the cart) could be heard now in the darkening stillness. The wood creaked and strained, shockingly loud. Everything seemed to be sinking, receding as the last red glow was sucked away into the faintly luminescent hollowness of night.

"All fled on," Flatface said. "We stayed."

"Why?" asked the knight. "You prefer the peace and quiet?"

"No," said Vordit.

Howtlande was frustrated and impatient.

"Answer questions as put, you dogs," he suggested.

"You sound like a nobleman," Flatface thought aloud.

"All of us are most noble," the knight said. His armor was a vagueness like a lost gleam on dark water.

"We stayed," said Vordit, "to care for the dead ones."

Finlot was squatting, leaning on his braced spearbutt. Skalwere had his back to the conversation, apparently staring into the last deepening smear of blood-colored light.

Contempt ate silently at him. Except for that knight who rarely spoke the rest were cowards and carrion who in his homeland would live best by begging or mending nets. Men needed an iron code. The code was becoming clearer and its importance paramount. These people had nothing to bind them but the whims of their feelings. He'd kept the code and would keep it, they'd remember his example, because by now his single slip was blurred over by reasonings and circumstance and time. He never really looked at it anymore, one small blurring in a long, clear lifetime . . .

"Why bury them?" Finlot wondered.

"Someone had to," Flatface felt.

"But that's daft, you foolish bastard."

"Well," Howtlande offered, grinning faintly, humped up, a massive blot against the sunset, "there's that which sticks to the fingers, eh?"

"Don't put nothing on me mother," Flatface said. "I were no bastid, you bastid!"

"Well," Finlot allowed, "still it be daft."

"Then why?" asked the knight. "Duty?"

"What?" wondered Flatface. "Daft? We just stayed. Why not?"

Skalwere kept turned away.

Duty, he thought. *Duty . . . What do these ragged swine know about that?*

Howtlande was watching the oncoming cart and pale mule rise out of the vast, tidally advancing night. The brighter stars were softly wet-looking. No moon yet.

"Say what you fucked and bloody please," Vordit suggested. "If I was you I'd press on me way. The death ain't gone from noplace till there's none left to die." The last red tint had just faded from their faces.

"I'd not have stayed," Finlot said, reflectively, "as wise as you make out to be."

Skalwere finally turned around.

"Why don't you talk for another hour or two?" he said. "The moon has yet to rise."

"Get these gravediggers into line with the rest," Howtlande suddenly seemed to break out of a reverie. "We'll have plenty of work for them ere long." Then to the mule, kicking it lightly: "Stir your bones, you baggy-assed son-of-a-bitch!"

Finlot ushered the two along with cocked spear. A slight breeze came up and swished the still trees.

"Somebody had to stay," Vordit muttered. "Otherwise what's the sense?"

"What sense?" Finlot wanted to hear.

"We lived here," the other replied, sullen, downlooking.

"Oh, aye," commented Finlot, "that makes all clear, like a map to a blind man."

"We lived here," the other repeated.

"Why do you take us off?" Flatface asked, watching the gleaming spear point.

"Why, we're forming a great host, and we'll need good buryers."

Back in the ditch the flies quarreled and grated. The bodies shifted here and there as their internal halations dictated. Some bizarrely erupted into long-latent flatulence; a stiffening arm cocked itself at the dark sky as if with purpose, with only the other dead to witness the unseen salute...

The ragged man on top of the heap suddenly breathed hard and heavy, chest creaking and popping...gurgled... clenched and unclenched his long, wide, soft hands, volitionlessly plucking at, clutching the twisted, flopped corpses...

He discovered he was staring at a perfectly round blur of whiteness that floated in a vast dark, and he thought he might be underwater, held enchanted by a spell at the bottom of the sea. Stared at the magical light he knew was holding him in thrall...began gathering the scattered shreds of his will power to fight the imprisoning whiteness...gathering...

Ye cannot hold me...Ye cannot hold me...I will it! I...

His body was a soft smear of flesh strung over frozen bones. There was a memory of pain beyond imagination. He vaguely believed the fevers had melted him to this, that the only life in him pulsed like a heatless ember behind his sight, had retreated back and back from the flashes of wild pain...

Stared and fought the great whiteness, eyes tracking it across what he didn't know was the sky, never shifting, never releasing the pressure that held the speck of life back from what was lulling away his unfelt body. He felt no peace and sensed no restful darkness or sweet fields, only the struggle, the unending pressure to live, to master the round glow, and knew he'd won when it was chewed to nothing, bottom to top, fraction by fraction by what he didn't know was the western horizon... then it was gone and he was freed... freed...

Victory, his mind exulted. *Victory...*

Tried to move now...speak...strained...croaked a sound... was blotted out...

XIII

"Another cursed and empty place," Alienor said, holding Tikla close to her skirts. Sourceless, subtle first dawnlight shadowlessly lifted the broken huts from the void night. Tikla was leaning into her, yawning. Torky was poking around the abandoned place with his bulky father. Long-faced Pleeka was pacing nervously, looking, apparently, at nothing.

No dead here, Broaditch mused.

"Father," said the boy, "did the sickness slay them?"

"Then the dead buried themselves," he pointed out. "As scripture says."

The hills rose before them, a featureless wall.

"Did God say that?" Torky asked.

Broaditch shrugged, flexing his powerful hands.

"Jesus Christ," he said. "Which we're told is all the same."

"God and Jesus are the same?"

"Well, son, as water in the sea and water in a bucket are the same." Shrugged. "But I think, unless I grow a pair of Christ eyes myself, I'll never see if such be sooth or costless words. Meanwhile, we'll have to trust the priests. That has its defects, however, if you've known many priests." He nudged something with his toe. An empty, cracked pot. "It *may* be true. It may all be true..." He started walking past the last shadowy hut. He stared into the imperceptibly dissolving night. Thought something had moved across the field by the road.

"So they're the same?" Torky persisted, matching his strides to his father's.

"That's no problem for words, son." Was sure of it now: a gangling figure swayed towards them as if drawing vaguely glimmering form from the substanceless air itself. "Well, someone lives here, mayhap."

He glanced back to be certain Alienor was all right. She was still outlined (as the stars faded above the old hills) grayish in a shapeless sack dress. Pleeka was behind her. He turned back to the strange, jerky-stepping man who reeled to a halt just ahead. Broaditch saw the dead-white flesh streaked with dark, eyes that seemed to palely drain the light into themselves; overlarge, pale hands on broomstick wrists, gesturing before him, and then the voice, hoarse but tremendous, ringing, the force of it overwhelming its own raw, painful rasp, saying, singsong:

"Devils fall back from thy master!"

Torky, startled, went back a few steps behind his father's solid, shielding shape.

"What?" Broaditch wanted to know.

Alienor was watching. She'd heard the voice, muffled, flattened by dull earth and musty air and it had startled her: familiar... something from the deep, disturbing past... She moved a little closer, Tikla swaying reluctantly against her, rocking her head back and forth over her mother's hip. Pleeka paced and muttered inaudibly behind her, lost in his reveries.

"Ideals," he whispered. "Ideals..."

"Devils be bound to my will alone," the bizarre stranger insisted.

"What a greeting," Broaditch allowed. Watched the ragged man totter, still twitching his outsized hands and long, thick fingers at them in what he finally realized must be magical passes. "Fellow, you seem to have but few steps left in you. You'd do well to husband your strength for walking along."

The wide, empty, bright eyes glared as the body (as if to confirm Broaditch's prophecy) suddenly sagged and was gone, leaving the big man surprised there'd been no rattle and clatter when all those bones hit the ground.

Broaditch bent over him. Torky watched. Alienor sat her daughter on a stone and came over.

"What new trouble have we now?" she wondered. "I've grown tired of my easy life."

"A very thin man," her husband said. Stooped and lifted one of the arms and let it limply flop back. Wrinkled his nose. "From the smell he's been dead a week and moving on from spite only."

"What said he?"

"Nothing with sense in it, woman." Broaditch straightened up. "We'll attempt food and drink on him."

"What little we have, you mean. The water jug's low and where's the next well, I wonder? All the streams been dry so far."

"Well, since four days' hike anyway." Wiped his hands together. "It's always the poor has got to make loans."

She didn't react. Glanced back over her shoulder.

"How far do we follow the *crusader?*" she asked.

Broaditch shrugged, rummaging in the foodsack as the sweet, dampish air filled imperceptibly with light and the trees and huts and the hills shaped themselves from the draining night.

"It doesn't matter yet," he answered, bent over the sprawl of bones in question.

"Give him not enough to kill him or it's a double waste." She sniffed and looked around again at the emerging village. "He had a loon's voice."

Broaditch held the waterskin to the raw slash of blackened mouth. Heard the breath catching and wheezing. The dribble of water sparkled and vanished into the shadowy gaping that chewed the air now and sputtered slightly.

"Well," Broaditch murmured, "here's a face that shows some wear."

"We have to decide," Alienor was saying, watching Pleeka pace. Tikla had slumped on the grass with her back on the rock. Torky remained standing close to his father, watching, intent, absorbed, as if about to utter some grave profundity. She asked herself why they had to remember. If there were just some potion that would blot away all ill and leave only the sweet. She smiled.

There would be, in that case, she thought, *more hollow in life than hill . . .*

"Who is he, papa?" Torky wanted to know.

"He neglected to say."

"A hermit?" The boy drew back a little again. "He stinks bad."

"That may well be holiness, son," Broaditch said as the man's eyes popped open without a flutter and he resumed his coldly flaming, vacant stare. His lips shook and then smiled for an instant.

I have them in thrall, he was thinking. *Fortune is turning my way...*

His look went sly. There was light enough for shadows now. A warm, dry breeze stirred the trees and the sunseared, yellow-brownish field grasses. The east was a pale, flame-colored melting wash.

"Good morrow, fellow," Broaditch said, watching the sly eyes that reminded him of pond water on a rainy day.

Alienor didn't speak. Went back to stand near her slumbering daughter. Pleeka was still now and stared over at the newcomer. Broaditch gave him another drink. Watched the dry, chapped lips work and smack. Up close the eyes were sunk in, bloodshot, and Broaditch thought if he wept he'd weep blood like those pictures of Christ in churches...

"Are you a holy man?" Torky wanted to learn.

I have them... I have them... am I not back from the dark lands?... have I not learned much there?...I begin again here, on this morn... He tried to really smile. Great chunks of memory slammed home in his burning brain along with flows of strangeness and pictures he didn't bother about yet. *All is not lost...*

"Look," he whispered, then said rich and loud as Broaditch and Torky moved closer as if called. "Look at the marks on me... the marks!"

The morning showed them plainly: the fingerprints of the plague on face and chest, pocked, black...

"I passed through darkness," he told them, eyes tracking nothing. "You pitiful devils..." Tried to laugh this time. Pleeka came nearer, staring at the long, mad, concentrated, bony face as (with an effort, but suddenly, as if a well of energy flooded the sagged body) he sat up in triumph, not actually looking at anything; standing as if he rose to oversee the brightening fields and ruined huts, calm and remote, big, pale hands folded over his loins. The scraggly, filthy face seemed contemplative, the dark mouth parted.

"I'm hungry," it said, ringing, filling through its hoarseness like a flood of stones down a hillside, crashing, clashing, clacking. "I'm hungry."

Broaditch, on one knee, paused reaching into the foodsack, as if he'd mistakenly looked for the wrong food, as if they actually had something else to offer this unsettling stranger.

XIV

Parsival was halfway across the ceramic blue, wide, shallow river, striding and hopping from stone to stone, watching the foamy swirls twist and bubble away around the willow-over-hung bend—a few hundred yards, in fact, from the wooden bridge where the villagers had abortively battled the amnesiac knight...

He felt as though a spell had lifted, that darkness had passed from his mind...

All of that's gone, he was thinking. *Sword, shield and stupid life chasing Christ-knows-what-and-never-tells...*

Because it was not abstract for him now. He intended to find his son so he could finally just say it: *I'm sorry, forgive me*...and after that what they did wouldn't matter...perhaps he'd go home again, see crops planted...open all the doors...find a wife?...let age come in its time with grace and ease...

He noticed how low the water level was. Dried, pebbly banks cracking and crumbling...

And then there were too many reflections: shadows that laid the water open to the bottom (where weeds unwound and infinitesimal minnows glinted like steel chips), superimposing heads and shoulders like a thick palisade, and he was already stopped in midstep, taking in the row of them, the high sun's shadows blotting out all the eyes above wild beards that (he saw without noticing) puffed and stirred as they breathed, and he didn't have to count to know there were over a dozen before even bothering about the long staves and bent clubs and dull, ragged-looking blades.

Ah, he was thinking, *a forest of hermits . . .*

Except he felt the gazes he couldn't see through the shadow hollows and hairshag, felt the malice that went even beyond religion . . .

He was halted on a round, slick stone that rocked a little at each slight shift of his weight. Raised both eyebrows. Hoped none of them carried bow and arrows.

"Good day, sirs," he said, glancing covertly behind himself by lowering his head.

"An unbeliever," one of the beards stated, clipped, flat harsh. He couldn't tell which had actually spoken.

"In what, pray?" Parsival was curious. So it was religion after all. These men were amazingly gaunt. Part of his sight was aware of the undulant weeds, abstractly thinking: *They show the movement . . . until something shows the movement you can't tell anything's passing . . .* Watching the men, who hadn't stirred yet. *Too many to argue swordless . . .* Still he didn't regret throwing his blade away because now he was even with everyone and equally threatened. That was important. A weapon always set him somehow smug, detached, isolated, masked his ordinary heart behind extraordinary skill.

He found himself strangely distracted by the waterflow, the fish flickers, the light bouncing, scattered by the long willow shimmers overhead. He became absorbed in the richness of the moment, aware too that he feared dying because something was stirring within him, something like speech trying for a voice that the water and light and fragrant earth and fear too could shape, and he wondered if he were brave enough yet to simply flee. Frowned as the shortest, gauntest one was talking, stepping down the steep, dried-up bank to the sand-laced shoreline. The green and gold light winked over him. Their dark, greasy-looking robes had been folded around their waists, bare chests tanned and burned unevenly. Some were barefoot, this one missing random long toes, eyes like polished pebbles.

"Unbeliever," the leader was saying. "You look fat-fed." His light beard seemed stained with blood about where his mouth should be.

"So?" Parsival returned unregretfully. *What absurdity!* "You are all on a holy fast, then?"

The man looked back at his fellow's beards.

"A fast?" he mocked. "To be sure, unbeliever."

"Are you children of Mahomet?" Parsival tried.

The man was amused now. The others were inching down the bank and spreading out silently. He squatted down and played with the stones near his mutilated feet.

"Mahomet," he laughed, holding his pale, gritty-looking stare perfectly still. "Hear me, fellow, we are the Truemen. The children of the father."

"Truemen? So you never lie?" Parsival relaxed his legs to back up to the flatter rock he remembered was one long step behind him.

"We are the inheritors," the wiry, crouched man replied. "We are the father's flail."

Why is it, Parsival asked himself, *when men mean to do truly ghastly acts religion is their first armor?*

"Inheritors," he remarked, "you were all named in some will?" He part-leaped back and came down firmly on one foot. He was pleased he hadn't missed and looked a fool, up to his knees in sand and water.

"Where are you going back to?" the chief inheritor asked, standing up like a steel coil, walking, then wading, step by step. "Like you not our company?"

The others were pretty well spread out along the opposite shore now and were entering the water too. He saw their point: the ones at the extreme ends would move fastest and close him in the center, bag him, he thought.

Well, they've done this business before.

"Inheritor," he said, "or whatever you decide you are, pass me in peace. I've had a hundred times my fill of stupid battling."

"Nay," the man said, "not quite, eh, lads?" He smiled as he looked at his men. The end ones were already across and running into the trees, starting to close a wide, loose circle with Parsival in the middle. "But you'll have it soon."

"As you see, I'm unarmed."

"Well, there's a pity." The man and the two or three nearest him were closing quickly. He was cut off.

I'm always wandering, it's my curse, I have to get someplace and stay . . .

"You have to force me into it, don't you?" he said. "Someone always has to do me that service."

"Take him!" the violent, wiry man cried. The line had closed

Richard Monaco

behind him. They came on splashing into the stream.

Parsival stooped and clawed free two handfuls of smooth, cool stones from the stream-bottom and without a break in motion charged the two nearest (the leader and a fatnecked bull of a man), whipped the missiles away *left* (hit a bald skull and rebounded twenty-five feet in the air), *right* (hit a runty, one-eyed man between the legs who hopped straight up and howled). Then the massive-necked one (the blur of his moving registered, metallic reek of body and breath, wirelike hairs on the smooth, sweaty chest, deep grunts) was chopping his ax down as Parsival (already ducking without having to pay attention) spun so fast he already stood behind the man, who tilted off-balance, trying to check his committed swing and needed only a light kick to send him over on his bushy face. This became a dance with Parsival loose, free, floating... Next, he spun close to the leader (broken teeth, snarling mouth, furious glare), inside the vicious jabbed blade, picked him up under the arms and tossed him into the next coming, a pointy-faced redbeard leaping from stone to stone with poised mace. Without glancing back Parsival ran, feet rebounding from the shore, then bank, slashed through the brush and willows (that flickered his shape a moment before shimmering back into loose dangling), howls and curses fading behind... the strident cry of the leader:

"A hunting! A hunting! Call the brothers! Call the sons of the holy father!"

Some other:

"Then the feast! The feast! Arrrr!"

Almost lost now as the landscape shook slightly, zipping past:

"First the praying, brother! The praying..."

He followed a vague scribble of trail, effortless and swift... up and lightly over a fallen tree, swinging and dancing through the crisscross of sidewise branches... racing on... sun flick-flashing... racing partly in sheer exuberance, barely panting after half a fast mile but beginning to feel his legs thicken with pumped blood and his stride splay and wobble a bit.

The Truemen, he was thinking, *the brothers... what dunglumps... I flee to where I can when I can as far as I may... this is the art of living in this world...*

XV

Howtlande was eating a chicken wing, chewing the crispy skin, fraction by fraction, the grease slick on chin and cheeks. His eyes were narrowed and jovially wrinkled. He spoke as he chewed. The young amnesiac knight with the fiercely beaked profile was crosslegged across the low fire, the flames rushing in the uneven breeze, flaring the soft brightness into the heavy, starless, warm dark. Howtlande's round face glistened.

Ah, he was thinking, *and why not me? Most men have no more energy than a serf whose crops are ripe and the sun presses him to sleep the long afternoons . . . men sleep, though they walk about, notwithstanding . . . It's time to wake up curly-hair here . . . we'll trade him his memory for something useful . . . I was curdwit Clinschor's sword-polisher years enough . . .*

He glanced around to make sure no one was near. At the next bonfire a large group was still eating. The women were in a rope pen strung between trees, most of them: two were at the cooking fire and another was snoring at the edge of the rosy, restless light in the arms of a long man. The dour knight who wouldn't name himself sat apart, hands on knees, staring straight ahead . . .

"Hear me well, fellow," Howtlande said to the young man.

"I'm not deaf," came the reply, "that I can tell."

"Never mind, never mind." He shifted the slick, bony fragments in his mouth, watching the younger man's dark eyes that seemed as inscrutable as the wall of darkness beyond the feeble straining of fireflicker. "There's time enough for wit when the world's won."

"When which?"

"Heed me, raw fellow. I will guide you to your memory if you help me in turn."

"Can you do this?" And Howtlande nodded, sucking his fingers, face (but for the eyes) beaming. "How can you do this?"

"I knew you," the fat lord whispered, spitting bone and gristle into the fire, which hissed.

His hearer took it in.

"Ah," he murmured, suddenly wanting to get up, walk away, hear nothing more. "Well," he said.

"Want to know your name, eh?" Tossed aside the fragile, unstrung remains and finally wiped his face with his greasy sleeve.

The other waited. Then spoke:

"I think you want something now," he finally said.

Howtlande shrugged, heaving up his round shoulders.

"Who does not?" he philosophized. "You were a great fellow, you see. Oh, yes, by heaven. And I want you to serve me. Be my true vassal. I intend . . ." He shifted his rump and emitted a long, low, liquid fart. Sighed, eyes misted with brief satisfaction. "I intend, I say, to restore order to this land."

"What has that to do with my name? Where did you know me?"

The tentlike shirt went lumpy as the huge man twisted around to make sure none had crept close to him.

"In the army of Lord Master Clinschor," he informed him, "and you're lucky such as *I* found you, young sir knight. For I never hated you. Ah, but countless do. You were a cruel lord, Lohengrin."

"Lohengrin? So that's it."

"Aye, right." Howtlande sighed and leaned back on a sack of garments, locking his hands behind his neck. The upper round half of his face was obscured, the lower glowed reddish, grease slick.

The name triggered nothing. He was disappointed. A name couldn't be that important, he reflected. Frowned and tried to concentrate, bring something back . . . nothing came . . . Was this fat man lying? . . . Why would he?

"Now you know your name."

"I need to know more, I think, if it's to do anything."

"Oh? Most folk would be pleased enough to forget all their old ills. Yet you seek them out."

He probably was smiling, Lohengrin decided, but he couldn't tell. He stared across the fire where the shifting heat suddenly raised up a long blackened twig, running sparks, snapping, bending with forked end almost like a crippled arm beseeching the night that pressed and blotted at the dwindling flames.

"My name isn't enough," he repeated.

"Whose is, young knight?"

"You say I was cruel?" He wondered what sort of man this murdering pillager would judge so. A disturbing idea.

"So many claimed," Howtlande answered.

"Was I more cruel than you?"

The bulky leader wasn't amused.

"Well asked," he said. "You surely were more dangerous." Pause. "In those days." Let his massive legs flop down, belly mounded up behind the fire, bare where the leather shirt had ridden up. "What I now need," he remarked, irrelevantly, "is a fair woman or a sweet boy." Chuckled.

"Who was this Clinschor?" the younger knight asked. Howtlande grunted and again broke wind and Lohengrin said: "I'm glad the flames are between us."

"So you've forgotten *him?* Small wonder, for he's well worth forgetting. Him and his great plans . . ." Yawned immensely. ". . . and mysterious powers . . . bah . . . His helm was cracked . . . How he'd babble on about what he was going to do, until your ears buzzed and eyes lost focus . . ." Yawned and stretched out his limbs with a creak-cracking . . . let himself sink towards sleep. "Clinschor the great . . . ha ha . . . the ball-short wizard . . ."

"What?"

"Medusa with words . . ."

"What?"

"Turned men to stone with talking at them . . ." Howtlande heaved onto his side with a vast shifting of flesh and shadow.

"What things did I do?" Lohengrin asked, then waited ... was rewarded by a long, shuddering snore ...

So he sat there watching the coals glow and soften. All the twigs had sunk deep down into the general, dimming mound. It pulsed in the drafting air like, he didn't quite think, a failing heartbeat ...

There was nothing, just the vague spill of violet embers now, that seemed a trick of the sight ... the sticky, lightless night ... snores close and far ... insects screeching in the trees ... and he woke to find he was still sitting there, slumped forward, face near the vague coals and soaked-in heat. As though forming there he saw what he knew must be Clinschor's long, bony, pale face and big cat's eyes; silly, uptwisted moustache. He was standing on a hilltop in mists or smoke, grayish robes fluttering as he declaimed (silent in vision or memory) and gesticulated with one violent, abrupt arm ... and then sound and words, the booming voice close behind him, Clinschor's voice, saying: *All my secrets are yours, Lohengrin* ...

He knew he had to be asleep now, saw the beautiful woman again (*mother,* he thought) in a long, pale gown, bare feet flicking up the hem, holding a single candle whose flame tossed wild shadows along the stone wall (he knew he was a child, just awakened, on his way back to bed, a urine droplet hitting his leg as he stopped and nervously held himself there; he'd just been to the bucket), turning into a chamber he knew wasn't theirs (because he'd turned left as always coming out of his room in the stone stillness, through the long, rattling snores of his nurse, padding along the dim, moonstreaked corridor past the empty doors that he never would look into at night and open places where the stairs rose and sank into obscurity, moving quietly in his flannel sleeprobe, thinking the kitchen is only one more bend away, already tasting the soft cheese that always hung from the second arch, bravely ignoring the darkness at his back). He hesitated, rubbing his eyes, then went over. The door was shut and he stood there a few moments (or minutes even, he'd never be sure), then pushed it lightly and it swung inwards with one sharp creak, except he thought it was repeating again and again so he nearly fled and then, chilled, sinking within himself, stared through the blurring of moonbeams at the window arch and saw her face tilted back on the pillow, the bed creaking and the strange, bearded face seeming to float above hers until he registered the arched bodies, gleaming skin, creaking, rocking shadows . . . He stood in silence, stared, felt something stirring down there, shocking, surprising him, and his hand went to the heat and shock, something new opening as if the cold stones he stood on were sinking away into fathomless night depths . . . he wasn't even thinking about it yet and then her voice, an endless sobbing moan that he somehow knew wasn't pain, and by then he was already running back, bends flying past, air rushing at his ears with the pound pound pound of stricken blood . . .

"Mother," he murmured, half into and out of his sleep, remembering his father too: smooth-shaven, light-haired, greenish-blue eyes brooding, inward (he always thought), stubborn, stonehard . . .

Father.

No.

But father . . .

No.

Will you teach me to . . .

When I get back.

Gone. And then to her:

You don't love him, mother.

Be still, son.

You don't there's no love he's always gone . . . I saw you . . . I saw . . .

Woke full up. Sat there staring as the images fled. Let himself sink back onto his side, the warm hush of night filling his ears . . .

XVI

Broaditch leaned into it as the slope steepened, gripping the bar exactly like a Chinese coolie (though the simile would have been lost on him), tugging the flatbed wagon into the depthless gray morning, sky a dull wall above the hills. He went on steadily, wincing once as an uneven wheel jounced over a stone.

Alienor and the children followed a little behind; lean Pleeka strode ahead while the ragged, plaguestruck man lay on his back in the wagon and flopped with the bumps. He hadn't stirred since speaking his last the previous morning. After he'd toppled on his face Broaditch had located the vehicle, refitted both wheels, telling Alienor (who'd been dangerously silent on the whole subject):

"We can always use it later for something."

And she:

"Aye. We can load all the wandering madmen we pass on it. Save then *I* must pull it."

"Why so, woman?" He enjoyed these exchanges.

"Because you'll have to lie there too, being one of them."

He'd grinned and felt warm, for some reason...

Well, he was now thinking, *I couldn't leave him to die. He weighs no more than a man of straw and how such a body made all that voice...*

"How about you lend your back here?" Broaditch called ahead to Pleeka, who didn't turn.

"I don't want him," he said.

"Not even to swell the ranks of your faithful crusaders? He looks a fair choice man. Sound of wind and brain." Chuckled.

"You're the one finds him so precious," Pleeka returned. "Truemen want the living, not the dying..." Then murmured inaudibly. "The best of us, at least... the best..."

"What's that? But what do the *falsemen* want?" Felt a twinge in his lower back and carefully adjusted his leaning stride.

Be this the first pinch of old age? he asked himself.

Was just topping the little rise leaving the deserted village and valley behind them. The day was going to be hot. The flick of pain didn't repeat.

"That's your business, fellow," Pleeka said, not turning.

"How far is it?" Torky asked. He had just come up beside the clunking wagon, half-trotting, half-skipping, walking backwards now, arms extended at his sides.

"To where, son?" his father inquired, glancing behind at his burden: the man still lay perfectly flat, filthy, feet wobbling beyond the rags, a few, he thought, happy flies circling and settling in.

"Which is what he wants to know," Alienor put in.

"Woman," he told her, tapping his forehead with a blunt thumb, "there's a picture *here* and I'll know it when I see it again."

Because he intended to find that tiny kingdom again where he'd been a serf under Parsival's mother... if it still existed...

After how many years?... Yet as fair a place as any to make for...

They were never happy, my brother always said so, Leena was thinking, remembering, crossing the field beside a wall of pines: dense to the ground their bluish, hushed energy dulled by the sunless, tin-gray, hot, sticky day. Her feet and calves were sore but she kept the pace, goading the boy through his complaints, because she knew they weren't far enough yet and she wasn't going to risk either plague or capture.

They always were fighting...why am I thinking about this? Lost days...Lohengrin was older so I think it hurt him more...

She didn't want to stop because then she'd have to think about what they were going to do next...

Hills and woods and hills and more hills...my poor brother...poor Lohengrin...

"No," she'd said to him, "don't go for then I'll be alone here."

And he, hookfaced, furious, eyes hard and remote like dark stones under shallow, still water, she'd thought, sitting his thicklegged black horse, sun spilling blood-red over the western hills behind him, saying:

"Then get out of here, Leena."

"How can I?"

They were alone beyond the outer wall. The stones, she'd thought, seemed smeared with sun's blood.

There was always blood everywhere, she thought now, tilting herself up the hill, the boy laboring in front, drifting from side to side, ready (she knew) to complain any second, and she prepared to say: *No, keep on...* she wanted to halt, drop in her aching tracks but the blood was behind like a creeping, tidal wall. Always blood and the shadows and loneliness...and those men...those men...she refused to think about that, or about where they were actually going, because the first thing was distance and time, which were the same thing only so long as you kept moving, she thought, since time was no friend when you were still, waiting, chained to blackness or cold stone...back...back to where her father had lived, find it somehow...perhaps...perhaps...distance and time...

"Leena, can we—" the boy started to pant, rocking his head from side to side.

"No! Go on." He said nothing more but she repeated: "No."

"Please don't go, my brother," she'd said at the horse and man shape, a motionless, dark sculpture in the burning, dying light, the road winding down and away stained by the ruby glowing that fired his black armor (*the blood touches each of us it's a marking I know it's in my eyes too,* she'd thought) and she knew he didn't really see her.

"I want to find him," he'd said, cold, furious, the light bleeding and old.

"Father? Is that—"

"No," he'd said. "No."

"I don't under—"

"All of them, then." His hand was on the hilt of his sword where the light dripped. "Those sons-of-bitches...all of them...I'll teach them something."

So melancholy, she thought now, *and then he was gone too like father...mother was always wet-eyed...no one was happy...always going...going...*

Hollow-eyed mother, Layla, flesh purpled beneath where the creases showed in the candlelight, brushing her hand at her loose hair, smoothing it, swaying a little across the table.

Mother, she remembered, *you didn't cry that time and you were always crying...*

"But he didn't tell me," she'd said.

"It matters not," Layla'd said.

"I said please stay."

"Yes," her mother'd replied, staring, swaying, and from the bedchamber the deep voice she didn't really like to have to hear called something she wouldn't register or recall and her mother said: "Yes..." again. The deep, male voice.

"I asked him if he went to find father."

Layla laughed dryly, without smiling. The flames moved and ran like blood on the red silken robe as she swayed and caught the winestains at her mouth. The male voice.

"Wait," Layla said, "I'm just coming."

"Mother..."

"Look for him," she said and didn't even laugh this time, bloodlight rippling...

And then time went past and she didn't recall much and then coming out of the sewing room holding a candle and the shock, the shadows moving in the hall, crashing and cries, a servant staggering past, mouth open, full of blood, his silver hairs parted with a neat, dark gash, the whiteness chipped and he fell, vanished into the shadows that moved and there were big men and stairs fleeing beneath her and terrible sounds, shadows, swords, and her mother shouting from above somewhere and the man, the bearded man, falling out of a sheet (*he must have wiped his blood with it,* she watching as he lurched and twisted, feet still tangled, body spouting like a fountain (*so many holes*), like, she'd thought, the saint on the church altar sprouting arrows (she used to stare at it during mass), neat red arcs spilling gracefully from his curved and

tranquil form ... the nakedness of the falling body a shock too
("Call me uncle, child," he'd liked to tell her in that deep voice
she pictured somehow as changed by the beard), rolling past
her on the stairs. She'd held her head in a rush, a soundless
vacuum of knowing that she was screaming as if she screamed
silence, blood splashing and sprinkling over her pale face,
arms, loose robe, hot and raw from all the holes and the shadows moved and the men and the long silence rushing away ...

"We don't stop now," she told the boy, breath short, legs
shaky as they topped the hill and looked down the smooth
grayness and dulled green to where the thin road slashed
through the empty country and she thought: *It must have circled
around us* ... and then noticed the people and the wagon and
hesitated, reached for him, thinking *No,* hands just missing
because he was already running, wobbling downslope, calling
out, and the coppery-haired woman had stopped, looking up,
and then Leena saw the two children and relaxed a little as her
legs suddenly sat her down on the stony earth among bleached
tufts of weedy grass. She watched him go on, wide-legged and
weary.

They all were waiting, the young boy down there pointing,
she could see his mouth moving. She let herself not think
now ... not anything ... for a while ... she absently brushed a
smoothing hand across her hair ...

XVII

Stupid curse why do I remember him now? It cannot be the drink for I am ever drunk and he taught the vice to me the pretty bastard...

"Don't snore so," she said, jabbing her elbow into the sleeping man beside her. "You're all sons-of-bitches anyway."

The man mumbled something between a gurgle and a gasp. Stirred.

"Well I know it," she muttered on. "Why?...Why must the Devil poison my brain?..."

The man didn't quite speak. Sputtered and sighed.

To make me see his face again...Dear husband, I don't forgive you...She saw him: tall, restless, eyes sparkling like sky in the stray sunbeam that slanted in the high chapel window, the priest's voice a drone, all the guests a blur, just the whitish-blond hair that flamed in the light, she thinking: *I have you now I have you forever my sweet dearest*...not even aware of her brother John, the mad priest, in his vestments, watching, leaning on the stone wall in back watching from his pale, nervous face, eyes steady (*like a snake's,* she often thought). *I'll never forgive you, Parsival, you shitstain!...You left me...with two children...stupid curse*...

"Peace, damn you!" she snarled, sitting up in the bed, the dried straw rattling and creaking. Hit him as hard as she could in the massive blur of chest and hurt her fist. He belched and said no words. "Son-of-a-bitch barbarian bastard!" she said. The narrow, low-roofed hut was spinning very slowly and steadily at an angle.

Sweet Mary, she thought, *that brew . . . no lady drinks such-like swill . . . I'm no low-born bag of shit . . . like this barbarian bastard . . .*

There was a blurring of moonlight at the window that traced some of the wall and the rough beams above.

"Sweet Mary," she muttered, holding her torso with long, still graceful hands. Her body had stayed slim and the prints of years didn't show in such subtle light. The moon caught fine traces of silver in her long, dark hair as she stood up and the floor spun faster . . . dropped to her knees . . . sucked in deep, desperate breaths . . .

Sweet Mary . . .

Crouched there, naked, shivering in the hot, sticky night. The man was snoring again.

"I want . . . to go home . . ." Nodded. "Yes . . . for I am a lady . . ." The snores penetrated the spinning blur around her. "Be still, scub . . . scubscum . . ." Crawled through the shifting darkness, desperate now, fingers scraping and clawing the planks, desperate for the cooler air spilling around the sagged door, fumbling, scrambling along the wall, hitting her head, then knotting, twisting, spilling, spewing on and on and on . . . finally she pulled back and sat on her hams, gasping and coughing, mouth and nose bile-fouled. She knew she'd be able to sleep now. Didn't move, rested on her heels facing the wall, eyes shut and his face still there: the unstained eyes, the shadowy crease down his cheek like a faintly ruled line . . . so long . . . so long ago . . .

Her hands stayed in her lap as slow tears squeezed out one after another . . .

"Oh, you bastard," she whispered. "You bastard . . ."

I'll leave here tomorrow . . . no more of this for me . . . no more . . . I've been weak . . . go back south it can't be bad as they say . . . something must be left . . . the castle's still mine . . . I should find my children . . . what kind of mother are you? . . . Nodded. Then laughed, short, sharp like steel on stone.

"Wonderful children," she muttered. Opened her eyes, which changed nothing. Listened to him getting up now, the mattress crackling like fire. His grunts. A racking set of coughs and hawkings. Then big feet slishing over the planks.

"What's that stench?" he wanted to know in a thick, blurry voice.

"Wonderful son..." She swayed a little on her knees.

"Did you befoul yourself again? You needs learn to drink like a Norse woman." She heard him bump into a stool. It scraped ahead. "Where are you?"

He opened the door with strain and banging. Pale light spilled in. The setting moon was over the hills, framed as if in a painting, and then his shadow went through and she heard the spat spat spatting trickle hitting the packed dust outside in the hot, still night. A dog was yapping somewhere in the distance. There weren't many animals left in the country. Wherever they'd been people were hungry and it was getting worse...

"Sweetsilk daughter..." Muttered, then, loud: "She's dead, you bastard!"

"Be still," he commanded from outside. She listened to him spitting again.

"You bastard," she hissed.

His blurred shape dimmed the doorway, feet skissing on the gritty floorplanks.

"Have I been hard on you, woman?" he asked her through a creaking yawn. "Clean yourself, why don't you? Ah, or come not to bed again this night."

"My son... my son was sad... always sad... In his eyes, you could see it in his eyes..."

"Your son." The door swung shut and the feet scraped away and then the bed burst into cracklings again. "Clean yourself and sleep..." Grunting... cracklings... yawns... "Wine is your curse, I fear..."

"What wine, Tungrim?" she wanted to know, struggling upright, suddenly frantic, holding onto the rough wall of this hut they'd found deserted yesternight. "Cheap swill brew!" Laughed in derisive triumph. "Cheap swill brew, you bastard! Whore's son!... I'm noble... and drink noble drinks... whore's son..."

"Be still," he muttered, from just the near side of sleep. "I do... you... well indeed..."

"You scum!" She reeled along the wall, splinters rasping her forearms. "Clot of asshole spillings..." She took breath and leaned there, pale, naked, frail-bodied, as the door swung open, sucked by the freshening wind. His face was still there, looking at her, tender, remote...

I'm going away right now...

The tragic blue eyes, the fine girl's blond hair, Parsival as he looked twenty years ago...

"Leave me alone!...Leave me alone!...Scum..."

She moved and the wall was suddenly gone and the moon, hills, stars went tilting overhead and the warm, packed dirt hit her softly on the back and her body knew there was no point in trying to move while her mind was taking her away...she saw the castle, long table set...servants, knights, ladies...she was talking, smoothing her gown in rich candlelight...the young, smoothskinned knight in red silks leaned in close and it was *his* face again and she shook her head in violent spasms and (from where she lay) the moon was bitten into by the wall of trees, the last beams like a mist over the dooryard and the other huts...the distant dog yiped shrill and petulant and a bass voice wordlessly cursed and there was suddenly a violent silence...the nightmare returned, the ropes on her arms, the stinking oil torches filling the halls with greasy smoke...then outside, barefoot in her shift, the voices she didn't listen to...they dragged her to the waiting horses as fighting still flurried in the castle yard. Voices raged and suffered, torches and shadows rushed everywhere in tumult and then she was staring at the girl on the dark ground in slashed silks, drowned in blood and shadows (*Leena*, she'd thought once only, then stopped her shocked, overloaded mind), face chopped to shreds, arms and legs outflung as if she were actually leaping away...then the warm horsereek, massive muscles under her, her own voice screaming (she didn't hear it or realize until the raw pain in her throat finally closed it off) and the night rolling and bouncing past, wrists gripped by steel hands, yieldless armorplate against her flesh, hopeless sinking within beyond even fear and her voice only whispercrying over and over into the rush of air, sounds lost utterly:

"You weren't here for this...you weren't here...you weren't here..."

XVIII

He kept running, steady, easy, watching the forest fly past, feeling very good after miles, his legs still fairly firm at each impact. His breathing was even. Tomorrow everything would hurt, but that was tomorrow...

The trees were old here, massive, bent and turned as if the woods were sagging down under a vast weight of sky, everything grayish-green under strips of tin-bright cloud. The scribble of trail he followed had become a faint thread. He wondered who might use it, as he'd passed nothing but unworked landscape and no travelers. Trails, Parsival reflected, should link something to something else.

He sensed something suddenly... felt odd... slowed into a walk, listening hard behind himself... nothing, just leaves stirring sluggishly overhead. Sweat clung to him in the humid air now that he moved slowly. Something, he believed, was somehow familiar here. Something...

They're not too hard on my heels, he thought. *If they followed. Even that lean devil would have his work cut out to hold my pace.*

His flushed legs carried him through floaty, pleasant steps. He was hungry.

I've been here before ... wherever this lies, between God's navel and the Devil's asshole ...

Another fifty steps and he broke through into a screen of dead saplings, moving carefully, the slightest touch of elbow or foot snapping one or more—they'd fall dryly and lean on the rest. The path had vanished in a scrawl of moss and pebbles. He could only see an arm's length in any direction, sight blending away into impenetrable grayness.

There must be a swamp close at hand ...

He went on, twisting through the brittle interstices, ground damp, black and slick. The important thing now was not to turn aside because he'd have to come to low ground and water soon and if this belt of rotting trees was at all thick he could wander pointlessly and be forced to retrace his steps. Meanwhile the grayness was subtly dimming as he used up the afternoon ...

Except it wasn't really a swamp, just a sluggish twist of stream banked by reeds and soggy-looking, cabbagelike plants.

One direction or another there's bound to be a river or lake near ... Smiled, sarcastic. Lost again, mighty finder of the nonexistent Grail, among other nonexistent things ... Finder in the main of women who dream into his stupid, lost eyes! Stopped smiling.

And he was almost past it before he noticed the campfire ashes and the straw and timber huts that sat like mushrooms along the bilious shore, vacant, gaping but not quite deteriorated enough to be altogether deserted ... It wouldn't surprise him if those "Truemen" lived here because, he thought, they'd suit a place with scummed and slimy water at the doorstep.

He paused at the campfire, kicked at the wet, old coals. There was a chunk of what looked like meat on a stick. He idly picked up the charred wood and frowned in surprise; decided his imagination had him in thrall but it looked (the bone and burnt shreds) like a smallish hand ... human ... thumb and forefinger at least ... possibly ...

No, he thought, *nonsense ...*

There wasn't enough left to be certain.

He tossed it back to stick in the ash, incompletely gesturing, fingerlike bones tilted as if to pluck at the darkening air.

He went on, following the stream now, against the current, hoping to find the main source ... he was passing the last, squat, tilted hut when the blur-faced, naked, dead-white man half-crawled out of the doorhole and half-stood on bandy legs, frizzy, wild beard bushing around his head into his filthy, knotted mane. His voice, Parsival decided, was about what you'd expect.

"Where are the brothers?" it crackled and strained to say. "Has not the father taught that none should walk alone save himself only?"

It was as if the greenish-gray muck, water, and soggy, crumbling forest were melting into the air, and dusk itself into seamless dankness.

"Whose father was that?" Parsival said, watchfully.

Did only creatures like these monkeys survive?

As the head was cocked to the side there was a fugitive gleam that, he thought, might have been eyes.

"Not one of the brothers, are you?" the screechy voice demanded.

"Whose?" Parsival watched the man trying to decide how deeply sunk in madness he was.

"You are not," he concluded, shambling forward, walking on two feet and one hand (more or less). "Well, abide awhile."

"To supper?" Parsival wondered, thinking about the strange, clawed fragment that might have been a hand.

"Ah," said the man, "if you wait a bit the pot will be full."

"What place is this?"

The beard nodded. There were signs of possible amusement.

"A place of brothers," was the answer.

"Forgive me, fellow, but I'm in haste." He turned to go on and the hunched man with surprising speed scuttled over the slick slime and stood in his path.

"Wait a bit, sir," he suggested. "The pot will soon be full. Wait for the brothers."

Parsival moved on, not fast. Watched the beard still resting one long arm on the dark ground, a blotted distortion in the failing light. Dusk ate deep blanknesses into the woods and the stream seemed to fall away into a void, a grayish gleam...

The man gave before him, keeping pace on the narrow space between the foul water and the netted dead saplings massed alongside in a blurry wall.

"Who are you?" Parsival asked.

"Ah. I?"

"No. I but spoke to the frogs as is my custom," the tall knight said scornfully.

Which were booming here and there. He brushed his hand at a cloud of gnats that were suddenly, faint and frantic, flicking at his head.

"I am called Mogwut," Parsival was informed.

"And what do these *brothers* do, brother?" he further queried the humped blot that still retreated, keeping pace, long arm down like a monkey's. They were past the last hut. The water-reek was heavy with mud and decay, almost sweet.

"The brethren be the Truemen," Mogwut explained. "We follows the father."

Parsival was listening above the growing swamp din of insect and frog, chittering, ringing...

"Lord Jesus Christ, you mean?" he wondered.

"The living father. John. John of God." He'd halted now, the dimness like a cloud around him, and Parsival slowed, squinting to see where he was... everything was one blurring... He knew (without actually seeing it) Mogwut had moved again but he didn't realize how close he was until the shapelessness had scuttled into him, low, hard, all harsh, slippery angles and hot spoiled breath, ripping fingernails, and Parsival felt surprise first, that he'd been so easily closed with, then anger as he tried for a grip on the obscene, panting, tearing, terribly strong, crouching thing (a touch of fear now) that kept grunting and spouting about God as it gnashed at him and Parsival was skidding sidewise, back foot going down the invisible bank, on his knees now, defending his face quick and desperate, blocking and ducking his head as his opponent spoke like a barking:

"Unbeliever...Unbeliever...stay for the feast... unbeliever..."

Felt the snaggly teeth rip a strip from his forearm and he was swinging now, snapping terrific punches, catching edges, bone, hair, the creature incredibly rapid and active, teeth snapping, chewing at his midsection, too close... too close... heaved him back, driving to his feet and flailing his elbows, and heard it grunt and curse in the near darkness and a fraction later (*too fast*, he thought, *by Christ!*) the ripping, snapping, stinking whirlwind was back, drawn as though yanked by an elastic rope.

"Jesus!" Parsival swore, embraced it now, teetering on the skiddy embankment, short-stepping, puffing, reeling backwards again, going over locked tight, nails, mouth, barking,

steaming breath all close to his face and then the sickening
moment, the tepid, foul watershock as the faintly luminescent
darkness arced and staggered, then under and up (it was shallow) and the thing he battled was a churning of muck, hung
with slimy weeds. Bottom ooze sucked at their steps. The
malicious creature was fearfully strong. Parsival worked his
elbows again, desperate with fury, and inexplicably found himself with a grip on the pumping, bony arms that felt like leather
and steel, and roaring in frustration he lifted the surprisingly
light form free of the sloshing, scummy flow, that poisoned
each breath and clung in gobs, and spun him, still gnashing
his spitting mouth and flapping his hard clawing hands (Parsival
felt his own blood running warm over his face) and jammed
him, reversed, into the thick bottom and plunged and dragged
himself to the shore, hearing the others coming now, the popping rattle as they cut through the dead trees. He ran, blood
and breath bursting within him, sight torn by light flashes that
illuminated nothing.

If there's but a single other like that one I am lost . . .

Running, keeping the dim gleam of stream on his left, skidding but holding the pace, the barking screech (it was out of
the mud already) raging, calling out to the others:

"Follow," it screamed, "follow Mogwut!"

Running, running through his scrapes, bruises, rips, thinking he was just starting to discover how ordinary a man he'd
really become . . . or always was, perhaps . . .

XIX

"The holy citadel lies below," Pleeka told them as Broaditch was just heaving the wagon to the crest of a suddenly acute slope that fell away into a stony valley where the twilight died in slow mists and campfire smoke among dim blots of what, he thought, must be huts and hovels and what seemed a broken-backed fortress or at least an uneven, high wall that (so far as he could tell) blocked off nothing from nothing ...

The girl, Leena, was beside him, Alienor next to her. Then Tikla. The teenage boy and Torky paced along behind the cart.

Broaditch was sweating. The boy and Torky leaned into it with him at difficult twists and rises. The inert madman or hermit, tortured victim, he thought, or whatever he was, lay flat and still but for his almost random, sighing breaths. Pleeka hurried ahead like a man who finally sees home, long-striding down the twisting, slashed scrawl of trail, his form dimming, Broaditch fancied, as he descended like a sinking swimmer.

"From here," he suddenly, shrilly said, "the brothers go out to all parts of the country to pray and bring peace to the suffering. This is the heart of the great crusade of truth." As the dusk thickened his voice seemed suspended, bodiless. "To heal this wounded land where war, sickness and desolation hold sway ..."

Broaditch was blinking to keep awake and his mind rambled abstractly . . . thought about roads and trails . . . about how the earth was so perfectly made that everything had its space and being, and only a hopelessly diseased mind could miss the tender wisdom of arrangement, of breath and air, light, growing, and all intricacies of leaf and blossom, food, water; earth beating like a vast heart, nourishing itself and its creatures endlessly . . . and then men tracking over it, their needs and fears and hopes pouring them down paths that feet made roads. Where men clustered huts sprouted (because the land ordered this too, its fecund nodes drawing life like water to a pool) and then the lord's castle, the village . . . city . . .

Leena was staring above the hill at the last stripe of sunset and was thinking:

It's there too not the burning it's not the burning it's the blood . . .

Her fingers worked nervously with the stained linen blouselike garment, rolling, smoothing, bunching it over and over. Because there had been smoke everywhere too, pouring through the halls, filling the chambers, stinging . . . scorched flesh . . . and in the yard (where the gate was down) flamelight mounting, roaring, flinging the shadows all around the inner walls, cords chewing into her arms, iron fingers gripping too. The shadow bodies, arrows stuck in (her mind said) like sticks in mud . . . she wouldn't focus so they were just curds and spillings of the flailed darkness and as they dragged her to the gate she couldn't blot away the firecolor and then she knew flame bled too, the restless, running, spilling of it and she shut her eyes tight.

"Leena," Alienor broke into her reverie, "that was the name you gave?"

"Yes." She didn't break her stare, holding the blood away carefully.

"Where came you from, child?"

She blinked slowly. The last rubyglowing trace was dimming into purple. She held it carefully, watching the night lap over it . . .

Broaditch was trying to see Pleeka on the descent. The trail twisted and vanished into the evening. He shrugged, leaning on the tracebar.

"Save for going backwards," he announced, "there's no choice of directions here."

"You never cared to do that even when sensible," his wife

pointed out, still studying the teenage girl whose wide, still eyes held the last stains of the sunken sun almost without a blink. "Child," Alienor asked gently. The girl had really said nothing beyond her name and "Yes, I'm thirsty . . ."

"You're not stopping, are you?" Leena inquired, staring.

"Not for long, methinks," Alienor answered, glancing at Broaditch.

"I want to sleep, Da," Tikla said, rubbing her eyes.

"Not till we sound bottom here," her father told her. Turned to the two boys. "Stay behind and when I tell you, pull back and dig in your heels, eh, lads?"

"Aye," Torky affirmed. The other nodded in the virtual night.

The last red was gone and when Alienor looked the girl was already heading down the zigzag slope.

"What's his name," Broaditch asked.

"It's Bink," Torky supplied.

"Ah, Bink."

"Yes, sir," the quiet boy responded.

"Hold on well when I say so."

"Yes, sir."

"A polite lad," Broaditch said to Alienor.

A rose in the winter, she thought.

"No doubt," he muttered, slipping slightly, catching himself. "Curse it . . . no doubt I only do this . . ." Bit his lip as he twisted the stiff bars and flat cart around a violent bend in the spare footing of the trail down. ". . . this wonderfully senseless enterprise . . . Grip fast!" he suddenly called back to the boys. Alienor was ahead with his daughter, walking just behind Leena. "The Devil's piss," he muttered. "No doubt . . ."

I only do this because I started it . . . no, I amend that, only because it's senseless . . .

He could see what had to be campfires in the valley. He could almost smell the roasting and broiling. A few steps on, cooking flesh scented the rising wind and just that hint triggered his hunger.

Potatoes are silver these days, he reflected, *and meat gold . . . watch it!*

"Grip, boys!" he said, louder than he intended. Felt the slight tug as they held on and he dug his heels in the stony surface. A step side went down into vague glimmerings and deeper blots . . .

I'm mad...it took me fifty-odd years to be certain of it...easy...easy...

They were rolling smoothly again but just enough faster so that his legs had to dance a little and he knew it was too late to halt now. Gaining on Alienor and the girl he called ahead:

"Ali! Clear the path when you can." Over his shoulder: "You lads hold well on unless I call *release,* you mind me?"

"Aye, father," said Torky, voice quavering from the bounces.

The cart was terrifically loud now, booming, crackle-creaking at his back, leaping high (when he looked), a dark, tormented crashing out of all proportion to what he knew the actual bulk was, looming in fixed pursuit, the fragile tracebars seeming but straws holding off a vast, dark weight, rushing him faster and faster...legs snapping up and down, jarring his skull, stones digging through his sandals, ahead the blur of Alienor (Tikla invisible in her arms) and Leena's blond hair a faint gleam, and him shouting now, voice feeble in his throat as the creaking, smashing exaggeration of sound and mass were swallowing up everything...faster...faster...Torky and the boy yelling too and himself, craning around:

"Let go! Both of you! Let go!"

The wagon seemed to lift over him, feet churning mainly air as the lank figure suddenly sat up and clung to the rattling sides against the madly shifting tilt and his tremendous voice flattened all other sound for a moment (Broaditch couldn't tell if they were actually words) and Alienor flashed past, ghostly, pressed flat against a bulge of rockface, then the girl not even turning aside, barely glancing up...

Christ! he thought. *Christ!*

...and then, somehow, they were past as if shadow and substance had melted together (he never understood how) because the path was too narrow...then the terrific voice ceased and his own was shouting into the rattling din and rushing wind:

"Jump out! I cannot hold!"

And where was Pleeka, could he be far ahead?...Then he was suddenly sitting on air, then the racing earth pounded his buttocks with warm, dull pain and the banging dinning passed like a dark wing flutter over him and he waited for the impact and then it was past and lost and he just sat there, panting, numbed (the pain underneath just beginning to come through), halted in shock and silence, one leg over a sheer cliff edge, thinking:

What a thing to have died doing . . . Carting a madman . . .

Listening to it going on, clacking, banging, suddenly frail again like (he imagined) a child's toy . . . gone . . . and then Torky and the boy were breathlessly beside him while he just sat there looking out over the wide night, staring into the indecipherable emptiness below where faint spots of flame reminded him of smeared fireflies . . .

He felt the rush of air and opened his eyes, knowing instantly that the demons had shattered his defenses while he lay weakened and were dragging him through the earth to the pits of hell. Felt himself flung back and forth and sat up already fighting for control, beginning his chant for power, hands gripping what he didn't know were the sides of the wagon, booming out his magic as he sped faster and faster down into the gaped darkness towards fangs of fire; he saw his magic drive the female demons back (heard their pitiful shouts of dismay), knew his power and fell silent and smug, holding on as the wild ride accelerated and he gathered his strength, calmly waiting for the bottom where he would subdue the king of devils because all this was ordained by destiny. He would descend and gather the forces he needed to fulfill his final quest . . .

He was smiling as he reached the long, smooth, grassy hill where the cliff path twisted suddenly straight. He watched the fires grow, his rags fluttering in the wind . . . grinned . . .

Broaditch finally thought he heard a crash sufficient to mark the end of the cart, but much later and far, far, below, so he couldn't be sure . . .

Alienor was there now, close enough to see the hint of his big face. She said nothing.

"Mama," Tikla said, "I'm *so* tired . . ."

Broaditch, aware of her, said nothing either. Finally, one leg still dangling down, he raised his heavy shoulders and shrugged.

He saw the fiend forms dark against the long, hot blaze, rushing up at him. Readied to will himself motionless, sorting over his spells for the purpose, then starting one so that the shadowy figures were turning, standing, reacting as he came bellowing vehemently, the wagon leaping high and wild, still gaining speed until suddenly (soundless to him) it was gone from underneath (he had no perception of the wall-like ridge that ripped it away) and he was flying (much to his satisfaction), sailing over the flames in a flash of bright and terrific heat that lit loose ends of his rags so that he trailed fluttering sparks as he sat comfortably on the wind, passing over the upturned faces (none of which had seen the cart anymore than he'd seen the rock), and then he was caught by a great, clawed hand that plucked him from the air and shook, bounced him violently as his breath struggled and arms gestured magically, fighting this lord of devils, spinning and rocking up and down in the sure grip of what he didn't know was a gnarled treelimb, voice finally bursting forth again so that the astonished audience, peering into the night, heard the flying figure's thunderings pounding rhythmically from midair as rows of them fell on their knees. Finally he felt, with satisfaction, the fierce grip impotently relent and drop him to soft earth where he incredibly stood on bony, vibrating legs and declaimed at them with titanic authority:

"I have come," he roared, shaking their very bones and the trees and ground too, "I have come among you!! I have come to take hold of all that is mine!!"

XX

Howtlande looked with smug pleasure at his raiders as they marched (in semi-order, he had to admit, but at least with a look of purpose and force) across the misty morning meadows beside a gently twisting trickle of stream under the hot, sweet sky. He chewed a strip of pork rind as his mule tap-stepped almost delicately along.

When I came down that mountain after defeat, he was musing, *I was one man alone and now I'm over a hundred strong and tomorrow, who can tell?*

He squinted above the dry-looking treetops at a high battlement. Just as Finlot had reported, there was a castle in this rich riverbottom valley—he hadn't completely registered the significance of the dwindling streams and browning, heat-shocked countryside. He was concerned with food, weapons, horseflesh . . . Finlot had seen few armed men. All these strongholds, he knew, were depleted by war and disease.

Glanced at bushy-haired Lohengrin who was walking ahead beside the dour knight. Decided he'd buy the young princeling with bits of his own history an inch at a time.

Lohengrin was frowning at the ground—sharp, dark face downtilted. He was leafing through memories, testing connections . . . feelings . . . repeating his name to see what that might bring to the surface. His wound had healed and the scarred tissue was less red. But it always ached.

He felt trapped, somehow, and tense. There was nowhere else for him, he believed, so here he was . . . But once there was a real clue, a clear road, he vowed, he'd follow it . . .

He glanced at the grim knight beside him, in grayish, pitted armor.

"Sir," he said and the fellow cocked a long, hooked eyebrow in his direction, "what would you make of the name *Lohengrin?*"

The knight took it in, showed nothing.

"Why ask you?" he finally responded. The sun pressed steadily on the dry earth. Tree shadows flickered over them.

"I wish to learn things concerning him."

"Do you mean to meet him in single combat?"

"Is he a strong fighter?"

"He's known to be. And a vicious bastard, so they say."

They had just passed through a row of close-spaced poplar trees and the big, rambling castle lay just ahead. A few ragged peasants were already fleeing the half-parched fields, a plough still falling, the pale, shirtlike garments flapping around bare, skinny limbs.

The raiders spread out quickly with curses and yells. Howtlande was bellowing orders that were only partly effective.

"Come on, youngblood," the longfaced knight at his side told him, "let's pass the time. One way's like another."

They moved out at a half-trot in a jingle and clatter of arms, crossing bare, furrowed earth, fine dust billowing like smoke around their legs.

"Do you know this Lohengrin," he called over to the other man. The line was fully extended now. They entered the ragged, chest-high, dried-out wheat that swooshed and crumbled around them. He thought how strange it looked: head and shoulders seemed to float as the wind blew long, slow brittle waves into them. They appeared to rush blindly at the looming walls as if borne by an irresistible tide. "Do you?" he repeated and the knight glanced over, eyebrow hooked.

"Never saw him," he said. "I knew his father."

"What?" For some reason this idea stunned him. His father. That hadn't occurred to him — as if he'd had none . . . or mother either . . . mother . . . "Who?" he asked. "Who is his father?"

One of the fleeing farmers (who'd been scraping around the hopeless crop) was slow and fat and some of the fleeter raiders were all around him before they actually broke out of the wheat field. The serf's round head bounced along, the rest of him covered and then his lump of hat flew off and he made (Lohengrin thought) a strange bleating oinking sound and vanished under the browned grain that shook the hot, slanting sunlight where he flopped and struggled.

They must have struck him low for I saw no blow, Lohengrin thought.

"Who is his father?" he shouted now, because the men were cheering and hooting and clashing their weapons. There was a flash in his mind: the golden hair and the sweetfaced, dark lady and in a mixed rush of anger and outrage he knew them both ...

The serfs ahead, shouting and gesturing, scurried through the moatless gate and Howtlande, behind everyone on the pale mule, was yelling something hoarse and moist. Then the gate banged shut in their faces and they pulled up, panting and cursing.

"That was well-crafted," Skalwere piped up from under the outward tilted wall. "What cunning!" He spat into the dust and watched Howtlande, whose cheeks puffed in and out around his scowl.

"Rip down the gate!" he shouted. "It's wooden. Hack it to shreds! There's no army here."

"Hack it yourself, you bloated toad!" Skalwere suggested.

Some of the men fell to work with ax and sword, chipping and banging away at the thick boards.

Lohengrin was suddenly swaying, legs rigid, locked, palms pressed to his head, an incredible white, flaring pain searing the side of his skull, so violent that the massive wall before him shook and shimmered as though a wind blew empty fabric and the solid earth went cloudy and he felt a raw brightness, beating, beating in his head, pouring out through his eyes so that the sunlight mixed into one blinding perception that seemed to suspend all movement and penetrate earth, stone, all open space ... himself too ... felt himself, the flowing forward of his life, saw (as if all time were a flat terrain) a road and a place that was solid in all the wild, roiling mists of life, smoke-like castles, towns, people, deeds ... a thin road running to a solid ground (not earth), a place closed without sides, shelter without roof or walls, water without flow or wetness...his imagination briefly flailed at these images that were not pictures of anything...people without form too but solid...so firm and safe and solid...

He realized he was falling, but since no falling was possible, knowing bubbled up like warm, sunny, melting laughter and he understood that Lohengrin had melted and yet was so solid, so strong, so irreducible...the names melted and the limbs, torso, head but what was left was solid...

He landed forward, hands gripping his skull as if struck down by a blow and fell about a foot or so into the rough-set stones under the battlements, locked legs holding him almost upright, back arched, face resting on the wall as if he meant, somehow, to push himself through it, body still as the mossy granite itself. Howtlande and the others stared...

XXI

Parsival followed the rank, vaguely hinted stream under the heavy hanging trees that strained the risen moon to faint threads. The water was a cloudy gleaming he kept losing and finding again. It seemed to shift and melt away each time he tried to focus, the slippery mud splatting as he went on quickly, always backlistening, trying to feel pursuit with his tensed nerves.

He went on and on as if suspended in a flow of soundlessness, the swamp noises dying as he passed and filling in behind...the air was thick breathing in the mudreek and rot...He wondered how far they'd follow...without the thin wet luminescence he'd be lost in minutes under these massed leaves.

Suddenly he was out as if leaving a cavern: suddenly stars and deep spaces all around, the moon fading as the east (towards which he fled) brightened steadily and he glanced at the blotted wall of darkness he'd just left behind.

The slow stream was a trickle here and gleamed like polished metal. His feet dragged through the dry grasses as he crossed gentle country into clear, soothing, warm air.

He was starting to feel the clawmarks and bites that monkeylike devil had left in his flesh...and the general soreness too...

By late morning he was wincing at the sunglare, looking

across the bare fields for at least a significant clump of trees where he might lie down with even minimal security. There was a spur of woods at least a mile ahead. Nothing nearer. The thread of water led there so he followed on, eyes burning with brightness, sleeplessness and the already pounding heat pressure . . .

It was nearly noon now. Parsival's legs wobbled a little. He kept shutting his eyes for a few steps at a time. He went into the long line of trees and the first shade was a soothing impact.

Suppose I never find my son? he suddenly asked himself. *What then?* Looked behind. *I doubt they're still at my back . . . I need to rest . . .* The sun flashed in pieces through the dense, stiff netting of drying leaves. *What do I do next, in any case? . . . Save follow or be followed which I always am doing . . . my whole lifetime . . . Because I won't go where they want . . . whoever they are . . . that's it, isn't it? . . .* He almost looked around for some supernatural sign. Almost expected one. *Because I once did or didn't do something or other with the stupid Unholy Grail . . .* Kept closing his lids. Sleep pressed at him with hunger's aid. *Because of that or something they won't leave me in peace . . . they follow or lure me . . . I need a good plan . . .*

He stood still and was about to stretch out when he heard the shouting and stared through the rest of the bunched line of trees until his vision ceased in an odd grayness . . . squinted, thinking it might be mist . . . no . . . seemed solid . . . He glanced back the other way across the dun-green sweep of openness . . . nothing there.

He went forward, staring at the dull fragments of blankness. He couldn't tell how far it was . . . was it mixed among the leaves? . . . Finally he put out his hand and was shocked by cool, rough hardness . . . stone . . . heard the shouting again and clash of arms.

Moved out of the trees inches from a massive, high wall and for an instant he imagined (he expected anything from *them*) he'd been spelldrawn back to the monastery; no, that was white stone. Came to a corner, peered up at the castle and down the sides and around . . . saw no troops . . . nothing . . . The sounds were coming from around the front face of the fortress and he decided to climb up and seek shelter and food.

The grooves were wide and deep and he topped the battlements in a few minutes, weary as he was. If the place were more strongly held than it appeared he could sue for protection as was custom. He looked through a narrow embrasure into the castle yard, all yellow scorched grass and hot dust. A single bony horse stood in the narrow strip of shade beside the main building where a scraggly row of trees shook spare, brittle leaves.

He went quickly along the deserted battlements, then leaned over in front and saw armed men standing in the fields and near ground while a big man on muleback gestured with a sword and yelled. Pointed up suddenly and a handful of bowmen tried their luck as Parsival saw two armored knights, one helping carry the other back from the gate, his hands pressed to his head. His son, though he didn't know it.

An arrow chipped stone near his face and he watched the next few come in, ignored them as they zipped overhead or snapped against the wall. He was turning to look for the defenders (someone in the yard was banging a metal alarm), and then crouched, spun low to confront a tall knight in light green steel, many times mended, long mace over his shoulder. Cocked his helmeted head and spoke through the grillholes.

Voices in armor, Parsival thought, *never sound human. Unless you're inside of it . . .*

"Well, by Christ," the voice said.

"A meet moment for prayer," Parsival commented.

"Whenever we meet it is."

An arrow hummed high over them and lost itself in the courtyard where peasants and a few armed men were stirring up the dust, frantic, jerky.

Parsival straightened, starting to look amazed.

"This may pass belief," he murmured.

"Yes."

"Fate seems bound to fate as though by cords." He shook his head. *They* were at it again, no doubt. Looked wry. "Because you don't even have to open that faceplate, do you?" Shook his head. An arrow hit the walltop and spun end over end. *They'd strike us best,* he thought, *by aiming elsewhere.* "Gawain," he said. "Again."

Saw the scene of their last meeting, vivid as a painting: the mounting smoke, the wild flames everywhere walling them in, thousands on all sides trapped and screaming, roasting, tossing away their hopeless weapons, the conqueror's vast army dissolving in fire as the blaze crowned, leaped over them, sparks raining, swirling madly, the terrible charring stink, the bubbling fleshfats. Lancelot and Gawain flailing at each other through the smoke and heat, horses roll-eyed, swords ripping air and sparking iron, charging and prancing over the fallen, squirming, lost heaps of men as the vast press, fleeing, lifted Parsival up and ahead, mount and all, and bore him uphill, and looking back he had one last glimpse of the two of them, battling, sealed behind towering fireblasts, sinking into bitter haze as though hell had opened and (he thought then) welled up from the agonized heart of the world . . .

"Not dead," he said. "Not dead."

"That would have been too easy." Gawain was leaning over the wall. "They'll bang and hack until the fat one thinks of climbing, as you did." Glanced over at him. "Are you part of that . . . amateur exhibition?"

"Not likely. How many knights have we in here?"

"We?" Gawain seemed amused and sardonically pleased. "If it's we then two's the number. And thirty-odd peasants and suchlike. Six men-at-arms. This place is greatly depleted since it saw you last, old friend." Flicked a well-shot shaft aside with his gauntlet. "Actually, Parse, I came here to wait for you, and haven't I had rare luck?"

"Wait?" *What is this place, then?*

"I were weary and half-seared and half-mad and half-blind with smoke and many other halfs besides, to follow the theme straight to my face itself, half as you know . . ." Where he'd been sliced from forehead to chin, years ago: cut so his teeth showed through his cheek. A pair of armed men were coming up the carved stairs from within. Gawain gestured with his good arm. "Stand a lad at each corner," he ordered. "Use crossbow and stones when they try to mount up here."

The men nodded. One was young and very pale. Parsival knew how he felt. The other was a chesty veteran who was already shouting commands into the courtyard.

"You haven't asked yet," Gawain said. "I commend your patience."

"Asked what?" he frowned. "You mean, how you lived to tell the tale?"

"No. But that's a fair question too."

"Well?"

"That bastard has limbs of stone, I swear, by Mary's grace. I hit him two dozen good strokes. His armor folded, yet I saw no blood and he battered me..." Shook his head. "He snapped my blade, and had not the flames come between us, I were a split hare and the skillet only lacking!"

"Who?..." Remembered. "Ah, Lancelot."

"Pass him by, Parse, at every chance."

"Ah."

"When I came free of the flames my horse's tail blazed like a comet and my single eye was sightless. I was a shorn Samson, I think. Well, come on." He started down the stairs. "We'll have to clear the gate for a bit. That's sweaty work." Down into the dusty yard, passing the nervous men-at-arms ascending. The peasants stood by the main castle door in the biting, flat sunlight, their shadows clear and hard. "Why do you not ask me?" Gawain wondered, plucking a sword from among several leaning on the wall and tossing it to Parsival. He held the mace braced under the forearm with the missing hand.

"Ask what now? Need we play riddle games?" And then he had it: looked down the yard and saw the barn, sagging, dried-out looking, a sketchy pair of chickens roosting on the violently down-angled roof. Remembered...she was stunningly soft and fluid in the staining moonlight that seeped through the split and separated boards, shining on the gathered hay as on silver...the spot of her navel, the soft-stroked, misty wash of darkness shaping thighs to groin...even the memory drew away his breath...

Unlea...ah...so I've been led back to this...

"Is she here?" he asked.

"I would have thought," his friend replied as they took station by the barred gate where the two fighting men waited, "you'd have asked otherwise still."

"How, damned riddler?" Smiled briefly, hefting the broadsword.

I threw all these away, he thought. *Yet someone's always handing me another...*

He debated dropping it. Went on to the rest of his problem, the old problem of leaving her in the torn silk gown by the river (now a trickle, unrecognizable), watching her return home across a misty morning and then wandering himself, depressed, weary, baffled, and her husband, Bonjio, cathing him later as he drifted vague and lost and didn't look up as they boxed him in and then he slashed back at them out of depressed mistiness, cut with body only in the deadly reflex of all his bitter years and then the shock and outraged *No!* in his mind as the knight's hand intersected the bright arc and flew off in a mist of blood as he thought: *No, no, I've cursed myself I can never I can never*... "Very well," he was now saying to Gawain, "that's why I got rid of my sword for the second time."

"Fling open this gate," Gawain was saying, "on my word." To Parsival. "Ready, old slicer?" Tilted his covered head. "Or do you want a helm and better armor?" Parsival shook his head. "He's not here," Gawain finally said.

They were within the cool shadow of the wall and Parsival was staring back across the white-bright yard at the woman who'd come out into the high arced doorway, gown a watery blue blurring within the interior dimness. He didn't have to see more than that.

"Not here?" he vaguely responded, remembering, almost violently... tasting it...

God sweet God has nothing changed?... nothing?...

"Nor there either, Parse." Drew his very long sword and stood solid and easy as a man about to hammer nails or cook a meal. "Nowhere at all. You came back here in good time."

"I never meant to," was the unintentionally ambiguous reply.

"Open it!" Gawain ordered.

Parsival hesitated and then light glared in and half-a-dozen surprised raiders stood off-balance in the gateway behind suddenly impactless ax and blade, leaning forward as if against the air, and as Gawain rushed into them like a whirl of wind Parsival thrust his sword deep into the dry, hard-packed ground and followed.

Better to take one of theirs, he told himself, *if it must come...*

The first ax stroke flicked the hot light and Parsival danced beside it and drove his fist above the leather, vestlike chestpiece and hit bare throat, twisting himself into the tangle of shadows and desperate limbs, flashing steel, all angles and turnings and he kicked, then rammed a bony knee into a massive torso at the moment of balance, tipped him away, turning through the outcries, grunts, raw breaths, rages... heard Gawain's butcher's blade humming and chopping... saw others coming at a run, the mule rider charging, too, flanked by one of the knights, shrill voice above everything, coming as if riding the dust like a storm . . . next two spearmen blocked him, backed him to the outer wall and he thought:

Now it's for life entire . . .

Let them thrust, took the first spear, yanked, snapped it away from the shocked man who instantly tried to run as the other point scraped along Parsival's chest, burning, and he swung the broken shaft like a club and cracked the puffy face along the cheek and Gawain shouted what became words a pause later:

"Back! Back inside!"

As he jabbed the other, turning, desperately thrusting the man in the side and then there were too many and he ducked arrows, a tossed ax, and moving, spinning with an electric, thoughtfree speed he was inside and the ax-chewed gate thumped and rattled shut and his heart and breath went thick and wild again.

She was crossing the yard, sun flashing in her hair . . .

So he's dead, he was thinking, *that's what Gawain was trying to get me to ask about . . .*

"Plague took him," Gawain panted, as if hearing his thoughts. "He were left unburied in his chamber."

"Are we doomed, Gawain?" was the first thing she said, standing just outside the imperceptibly shifting shadowline. She was actually looking at Parsival. "Well," she then said to him, "*you* seem well enough."

He pressed his lips together. Watched her face, taking the moment in, effectively blank about what to do about anything . . .

"Yes," he finally murmured.

Hammering and chopping shook the portal again. Dust puffed out from the interstices of board and iron. He knew they'd have at least one of those knights posted there now. Another sortie wouldn't be so easy . . .

"We cannot hold after dark," Gawain told her.

What do I want? Do I still want this woman? Is .hat what brought me back though I knew not I were coming until I came . . .

He saw she was afraid and holding it in. Her hands showed it. He remembered she was skittish and very emotional.

Gawain stepped out into the fierce light and craned around at the walls.

"What can be done?" she was asking him.

"Fly," he said, reasonably.

"He's right," Parsival added, unnecessarily. She didn't look at him. Was she being cold or just preoccupied? For a moment he thought she'd been having an affair with Gawain. The idea was disturbing as well as absurd. Gawain, with half a face...

"Cut our way out?" the tall man-at-arms by the door wanted to know.

"Eight against a hundred?" Gawain pointed out. "So only Parse here or myself might live to boast?" Chuckled within his steel outer head. "Mind, you cannot kill this bastard or me. We're like fellows in a minstrel's tale. We wade through everybody's blood and never reach the far shore." Chuckled, hollow, ringing.

"What can be done?" she repeated. "How can we—"

"We let them in," Parsival said and Gawain paused, then nodded.

"Just so," he agreed. "While the husband's at the gate the lover's out the window." He paused, suddenly self-conscious.

A nice choice of words, Parsival said to himself. Held his face expressionless. Didn't quite look at her. Gawain went on.

"Parse and I will wait to greet the—"

"Just one of us," Parsival said, cutting off the next remark.

"Yes," Gawain altered his statement. "One only."

She looked at both. Said nothing. Parsival studied her eyes again, almost hesitant to meet her there... *Like deep forest colors,* he'd once mused, *where the sunlight is strained to a few precious drops...*

Yes, he found himself strangely considering, that was life. To see like that was life. The rich wonder... stared, almost tranced... aware that the sweet colors were simply there as the sunlight itself was, impersonal yet intimate... How to express such things?

And then the light flashed within him too and the colors were trees, slanted sunbeams, hushed shadows, and he saw the madly ragged man again standing on a jagged rent of rock. He knew the face, the long nose, wide bony brows plastered with hair and filth... couldn't quite place it... the mouth was wide, moved steadily in the silence of the vision. There were others there, shapes that seemed melded into the dark treespaces that wavered like seafronds now... the same man superimposed over the sunbeaten yard, fading like an afterglow, strange, shifting, blotted forms around him, the mouth that gulped and spewed its air, starved, hollow, infantlike... what appeared to be a peasant, bulky, stoopshouldered, leaning on a spear in the background against an edgeless solidseeming screen of dark leaves...he namelessly knew him too...these things were somehow joined somewhere to his life like obscure trickles that find a flowing stream...

Unlea was intent on him now.

"We'll keep them off the walls," Gawain was saying, "for the rest of the afternoon. It's too hot for much more of this nonsense. They'll soon be under the trees."

The hammering at the gate was slackening. Muffled voices called to one another. Gawain stepped farther into the yard, looking up, tilting his head to give his single eye coverage. A pair of middle-aged serfs were laboring up the steps with baskets of stones.

"Let it rain on their parched heads," Gawain suggested, shouting to the men on the walls. Then, to Parsival and Unlea: "Rocks and heat are great discouragers of men."

"Why don't we ask who they are?" she tried, hands moving slightly, nervously, "And what they want? Perhaps we might—"

"Lady," Gawain informed her (Parsival thought he seemed more the way he was when they first met twenty-odd years before, as if, perhaps, his mutilation had finally been absorbed too), "what use to parley with the wolf at your throat?" Gestured. "I've been wolf enough in my time."

"All courses would fail, in any case," Parsival added, almost self-consciously. "They'd likely lie and seek advantages." To Gawain: "I would say they want food above all else."

"I would agree, Parse. Soon it will be water too. There's little enough of either in here to boot."

"Why can't we tell them so?" she still wondered.

"And would they heed?" Gawain asked in turn. "Even in normal times?" His voice was tinny in the helm. "Much less now that the world's dying."

Her smooth hands went to her face. She was, Parsival noted, trying to be brave. This was her home, after all, bare and lost as it was.

"Could we give them some of our store?" she asked.

"You might return here," Parsival said, softly, "at a later time."

"To what, sir?" she asked him. He saw she wasn't far from tears.

He said nothing. Felt vague and uncomfortable. Gawain headed up the stairs to supervise. Unlea was waiting. He didn't want to see her weep.

"We'll see," he said, taking her hand. It was hot and dry. He felt the slight tremor that wasn't always visible. "Let me try to help."

"As before?" she murmured without even rancor, too shaken to really concentrate.

"I tried," he said. She took her hand away.

"Did you?" she barely said.

"Yes, Unlea," he said, watching her, "I did."

All my magic seems to have drained away, he was thinking, as the dusk spread like a pool in the courtyard. *Not mine only either* . . . Looked up: the men on the walls still seemed to be waiting, except he knew they were dummies, scarecrows (*or scaremen*, he quipped) . . . Unlea, Gawain and the rest were all at the other end of the castle moving through the old moat drain tunnel that now opened into the dried ditch itself. He'd make certain they met with little or no resistance. The sky was a whitish fuzziness above the hollowing courtyard.

He went to the gate where they'd been prying and thumping rather than hacking for the past half an hour. One of the planks was already wrenched free, leaving a strip of slightly brighter blurriness.

He kept his vow technically intact by wielding a long, slightly knobbed horseback mace. Didn't bother to test swing it as he approached the gateway. A nail burst free with a punnggg. He wondered, distantly, if this time he'd find himself overmatched. The idea didn't frighten him. He always assumed the time would come . . .

Always the same epitaph, he said to himself, *I tried* . . . *Parsival, son of Hertzelroyd and Gahmuret, always tried* . . . *succeeding was another matter* . . .

He could be dead, blotted away in a moment, and that wasn't even exciting anymore. His blood didn't beat in his ears. He repeatedly resisted the urge to simply stand there and contemplate the moment, the subtle feelings in him that bent with and mirrored, somehow, the shifts of still warm air, melting tones of light, the stored day's sunheat in the earth . . . smell and taste . . .

I owe this to her even if I hadn't crippled her husband . . . *I hópe I slay no one tonight unless it be ordained beyond my power . . . if power I have left, or has that all faded with the lost magic and left me in the shadows of a dying world, as Gawain put it . . . there's been no rain and not long before there was too much water . . . how mercies shift and turn to torments . . .*

Several more nails shrieked and popped. Another board gone. Vague forms beyond laboring, grunting.

Dying . . .

He threw back the lockbar and jerked the gate inwards, spilling two men in the warm, dark dust. The rest seemed empty shapes in dissolving twilight. Dark gleams of armor . . .

He ran forward, silent, tranquilly determined, heard the fat commander's voice yelling a blurred command, someone snarling back at him and then the first impact shivered up his fluid, violent arms and the man was gone . . . his body ducked (he was in the flow now and didn't even have to not think) and he heard the missed swing . . . struck again a little amazed himself at the almost casual force he freed through himself . . . another fell, bellowed horribly . . .

"Come on, lads," he cried to his nonexistent troops, "charge these womanly bastards!" He hoped he sounded convincing . . .

Lohengrin was waiting as they attacked the gate, watching the sunset discolor and die beyond the towers. He was watching himself too, monitoring his head, waiting to see if it would betray him again . . . there was just a dull, pulsing near-pain now . . .

The other knight stood next to him.

"Note how those bastards on the battlements keep so still," he said, mockingly.

"Hmm?" Lohengrin was bemused. He was actually wondering if it wouldn't be better to slip away from all this confusion and violent nonsense. Why overthrow this place? He felt pointlessly pulled along by that fat man's odd hints and blurred part-promises. He sighed. Did he really *want* to remember anyway?

"They aren't living men," the knight told him, amused, "or my name's not . . ."

"Not what?" *Mine might be Lohengrin . . .*

"You wouldn't know me, boy. But it was Galahad."

"Was?"

"I let him die."

"Why not tell the others no one's up there? We could scale—"

"Is there anyone inside you particularly care to kill?"

"Nay. What reason would I—"

"Just so. Let them flee. I've slain enough to keep me."

"Then why are you here?"

"One place is like another. I pass time." He grunted. "All were shallow when I recall them. This jelly-gutted scum is no worse than great Arthur."

"Say you so?"

The first nail sprang loose. Punngg!

"I saw much in my time," the knight went on.

"What do you know of Lohengrin, then?"

"What? Still on that? They say he is cruel, unlike his sire. That he came to be Duke-whatever by fouler means than were common. And served the brute beast Clinschor."

"Clinschor?"

"Can that name be unknown to you?"

The other nails ripped free and they heard the plank clatter loose. Howtlande was ordering someone to do something just behind them.

"I have forgotten almost everything, sir," Lohengrin said.

"Then God has blessed you, sir," said the other. "I remember everything. Which is why I don't talk much."

And then the flurry at the suddenly open entrance, cries, a crunching blow . . . another . . . They went forward and Lohengrin dimly saw a figure stooping, dodging, striking out, then shouting for his men and Lohengrin braced for the coming shock and the other knight called out over Howtlande's irrelevant din and Skalwere's vicious riposte:

"He's alone!"

And then the suddenly flickergleaming, dancing shadow passed close and Lohengrin's sword was barely up in time to save his skull (the power of that blow, he semi-thought, was like a lightning bolt) and he fell to one knee—cut hopelessly at the phantom. The other knight, cursing in a mutter, charged past and he heard the mule, shrill, startled, and the fat man's nasal raging: the dark was all swirling men, grunts, outcries, crashing, as the terrible opponent weaved among them, Skalwere's voice, diminishing:

"Follow me! Follow me! To the rear!"

Lohengrin stood there, head throbbing. He held it, waiting . . . waiting . . . afraid it was coming back, the strangeness that whirled self and the solid world away . . .

I don't want to be cruel, he told himself. *I don't want to be Lohengrin . . .*

The crashing had moved farther off along the river road. Shouting drifted back:

". . . bastard! . . . no . . . here . . . You cut me you dung-sucking fool! . . . aiii! . . . help me . . . here . . . here . . ."

Then more screams, a different quality now. He knew they had seventy-odd fighters and no single anybody could conceivably . . .

Men were fleeing past him suddenly, routed, blurring up out of the night, Howtlande's voice shriller, hysterical:

". . . Castle! Inside! . . . Inside! . . ."

Others:

"Save me . . . Devils . . . aiiiiiii! . . ."

The night reeled with shapes and cries and blind clashing and he fell back with the rest, thinking:

Counterattack . . . all this for what? . . .

Parsival saw the thin gleam of the stream as he paused a fraction to crack a blundering pursuer across the knees and then saw them coming, shaped by the faint waterglow and knew:

They followed me from the swamp, good God . . .

And there were many more this time. They loped and sprang snarling into the whirling confusion with the certainty of predators from hell. He decided this was diversion enough, and an act of heaven, from his point of view. Pounded himself a free path and took off at full sprint . . .

Lohengrin suddenly found himself moving as the elusive and terrible fighter passed like a ghost blown by a phantom wind. He followed as if an invisible tether joined them and the air rushed into his open helmet, light armor links ringing faintly. Passing close along the wall, the combat and agony fading behind, he felt (rather than actually saw or heard) the man ahead as they cut around the rear of the castle and someone shouted:

"Who's that?"

Another:

"Gris?"

"Aye. Right enough."

Then they were past and the earth was gone and his mind said *relax* and he hit and rolled in softness and mudreek.

There was a half-moat here, he thought.

Crouched to his feet. Heard a whisper of metal and headed along the head-high ditch that ended, crumbling to no more than shin deep, and he was back in the open night straining by starlight at half-forms, following a ghostly hint, cold with sudden anger, determined to do something about something for once, memory or no memory.

"Where are you?" he muttered. Set his teeth. Followed another slight noise, passed through a hush of pine trees, tripped, rebounded ... went on, compacted into the furiousness he knew would sustain him, preserve him until he came to solid grips with something ... anything ... Whipped out his sword as if that could help and charged on, believing his rage would keep him from hitting a tree full tilt, feeling like tensed steel. "Show yourself," he crooned under his breath.

XXII

Broaditch had backed himself, his family and the two newcomers against a squarish shelf of rock, spear ready, watching the dim crowd gather in the wildly wavering shadows around the firelight. The air stank of sweetish charred meat.

Broaditch had noted the shattered wagon when they entered the camp. He'd assumed the man was dead and, looking for Pleeka, came out of the fallen night and met him almost at once, standing under the trees at the outer rim of reddish brightness. He seemed uneasy, watchful, not pleased. There were clumps of people nearby. The men all seemed bearded and the women wore hoods. Murmurous movement all around, fragmentary phrases surfacing here and there.

"...in truth...aye...a miracle...proves justly what father...Father is with him now...aye..."

"What ails you, fellow?" Broaditch wanted to find out, face close to the other's flattish, brooding features. "You look stricken."

"Things have...changed," he partly replied.

"Ah," Broaditch was impassive, "but they were ever ill, I'd take oath."

One of the people passed nearby and Pleeka took him by the shoulder with his long hand.

"Brother," he said.

"Aye?" The smallish, pointed-faced woman, hair fiercely pulled back from her narrow forehead, responded.

"Sister," he corrected, "what means all this?"

"The flame spirit has come among us," she said, voice dry, inflectionless.

"Sister," he shook her shoulder, "what doctrine is this?"

"The father's," she replied, twisting her head back to stare greedily towards the spurting fire. There was a jagged wedge of rock behind it.

"Where are the hymns and the vesper brothers in white?" Pleeka demanded.

"What?" she responded, struggled vaguely to free herself to stare. "Are you Trueman?"

"I've been traveling. Converting."

"The service has been changed by the father," she informed him, inflectionless. "And the vesper brothers..." She craned her neck.

"Yes?" he insisted. "What about them?"

"They proved false to God."

"What's this rot?"

"Father John discovered their heresies and denounced them a fortnight since. He then proclaimed a miracle to come, and lo, it has come." She was exultant.

"What miracle was that?" Broaditch put in.

"The flame spirit appeared among us! The sign we awaited!" She peered briefly into the shadows at the newcomers.

"Are these with you?" she asked Pleeka. "Where's your beards? All must wear beards. It's the law."

"Law? Law? What..." Pleeka broke off. "What was done with the vesper brothers?" Broaditch guessed he must have been one himself.

"The brothers and sisters took them as God instructed."

A stir swept through the crowd and she struggled away to get closer. Broaditch leaned back to his wife.

"Ali," he whispered, "I like this less and less."

"The children need resting but my feet plague me to go," she replied.

"We best wait for dawn."

"And mayhap never see it, husband."

"They don't seem . . . well, murderous."

"Don't they?" she muttered.

Someone had mounted the rock, no, two figures, one a long sticklike shape that Broaditch, with shock, realized was the madman from the cart. He planted his long bony feet on the rock like birdclaws. The other moved with sudden jerks, gesturing in what must have been meant, Broaditch thought, as a benediction, then, reedy-voiced, spoke over the instantly hushed crowd.

"You have all eaten?" he rhetorically demanded.

The crowd howled back assent. Broaditch was startled by the flat, harsh grating sound.

There must be a thousand out here, he thought. *That's a few mouths to feed in these times!*

"Has the miracle come?" he demanded.

Another howl sprang back from the firewrung night.

"Have I given my promise?!" he virtually shrieked.

This time Broaditch made out:

"Yeesssss!!"

"All the world has been put to God's sword," he yelled, and Broaditch found the thin, fierce, whip-cracking voice familiar. "All the world is dark, brothers and sisters . . ." There was a low tremulous moan. Broaditch noticed a dwarflike fellow clambering up the back of a near giant, with a pointed knob of a head, to improve his view. The woman was on tiptoes in front of Pleeka.

"Who is this?" Broaditch asked him.

"John. The golden eagle."

"John?" Broaditch was incredulous and not-quite-outraged yet. "Did you say John?"

There was more shouting and agreement in the crowd and then John was kneeling before the skinny figure who suddenly stepped forward into the wavering, dramatic forelighting. John's voice, screaming:

"The spirit of fire beloved of the Almighty! Did ye not behold him descend?!"

"Yyyeessss!" Ecstasy and pain. "Yyessssss!"

Broaditch felt Alienor's hand dig into his upper arm. Tikla was collapsed, sleeping at her feet. Leena and the boy were pressed to the treebole; Torky was drifting a little closer. The dwarf was perched on the giant's shoulders as if a single creature with a doubled, ominous body towered there or, Broaditch fancied, a demonic father playing with his distorted child.

He shuddered as the new voice crashed into the night like a great stone. The madman spoke.

And the other is him...John...my God, what a fit pair if this be so! Except he still didn't want it to be.

Alienor remembered more: recalled that voice from behind two decades (as she'd first heard it standing in the castle yard, a prisoner, when he rode up with his black-armored mute knights and hurled a savage speech into them that set the barbarians dancing in frenzy; when he was fuller fleshed, with those absurd upcurled moustaches flipping up and down as he spoke that now were pressed flat to his filthy face, and she instantly wanted to flee from all the impossible madness of all impossible meetings...

We bore him here, she thought, *we bore this thing...*

"Broaditch," she was saying, crying out, "Broaditch, we did this..." Voice lost under the mounting, hoarse shocks exploding from that spare, shadow-hollowed, gesticulate frame. He bent closer to her.

"What?" he yelled. "What?"

"Clinschor!" she raged in his ear. "Clinschor!"

Clinschor stared at the balding, intense man in the priestlike dark robes a short time after dropping from the pine branch, which he now believed was the giant hand of providence, and watched him tremble with a mixture, he well understood, of cunning, excitement and awe too. He was satisfied. Victory was certain.

"Are you *He* that I raised?" Father John had asked.

"I am the power and the flame," Clinschor found himself saying. Then he muttered a spell of control. Heard the people gathering, calling to one another, pressing as close as they dared. The circle of space they left around him, he clearly understood, was due to the pressure of his inner potency. He took the man's right hand in both of his own. Felt cold, irresistible strength flowing into himself as if drawn from all of them. The man John was shaken even through his cunning.

"Speak to them," he asked, eyes rolling a little, staring into the other's unfathomable, grayish hollows. "Come, my lord of flame."

Yes, Clinschor thought, *that's correct, my lord is the correct form...*

Standing at the edge of the rock, the fire and shadowforms at his feet, he saw what had to be done. The enemies were already doomed. This time nothing would save them. Root and branch... He'd been purged to utter cold and would never relent again! Stood and let his vision penetrate the night and saw his enemies in the air, on the earth and under it, the walls and spell-barriers that he would shatter to black dust!... yes... Looked over his gathering forces without the slightest hesitation. Felt the feeling, the growing as if he were tall now as the stone he stood on, his head among the treetops. He let all the vast, dark, wheeling space fill him, felt his vast voice and the earth tremble and his eyes fill with tears...

"I am the fire and the sword," he told them. "I have come back from death and the bottom of heaven. I shall lead you to the glorious presence. I am come to make all things new!" Barely aware, as he soared, of the howling response as his words took fuller hold... "All things new!"

XXIII

She stared at the mule's backside that, she idly thought, seemed to somehow grow flies of itself, since she never actually noticed any arriving from anywhere else. They stirred, bunched and spread whenever the brushtail flicked and coiled. The sun was steady, harsh on the dry fields where grain and long grasses were bleached and crumbling. She was trying to remember how many days had passed since the rain and found she couldn't remember; then found she really didn't care, because her mind was on the wineflask hanging at the mule's flank.

She barely noticed Tungrim, chunky, barelegged, straddling the animal, just the leather sack swaying and spinning . . . Swallowed, telling herself:

Noon . . . it's barely noon . . . I can wait . . .

Telling herself it was merely thirst except she had no real urge for water. On all sides the Norsemen marched quietly in leather-trimmed armor and conical half-helmets, canvas-strapped carts squeaking along, her own mount rocking under her, heat beating at her hood . . . She kept dryly swallowing, fighting the faint nausea, the pain only a hint around her eyes now, a casual claw touch.

She thought about asking him for the drink, trying out different ways of circumventing his refusals. Shifted in the saddle and tried to distract herself by looking around at the band of them marching in from the coastline where their famous dragon ships lay moored.

Tried to interest herself in where they might be going. Failed. Thought about discussing it with him... discussing something, anything with him.

Hear him grunt or regale me with tales of the virtues of the freezing northlands... God, what a dullard!

She already knew the answers to her own satisfaction: they'd loot the next starving village. Then the next... What a life, she mused. For senseless waste, it compared favorably with the last years of her marriage. Well, Tungrim had saved her, she had to admit, and her fucked, breakwind husband had "saved" her from her family. At least she owed him that.

Good Mary and her sweet son what a life! He helped me, the dreary, honest bastard with his platitudes like stale bread... O the wisdom of the Vikings, who can match it? Surely not donkeys or mere stones?... Mayhap a lump of steaming dung might narrow the gap... She glanced again at the sloshing winesack. Then pulled her eyes away. *No... no good troubling my mind... but God, wine is a medicine for time! The only one...*

The world was a hot ache, a soreness, and she kept thinking of the soothing taste and gentle touch of the drink, a soft embrace, an intimacy with herself alone, a fullness with herself alone, the thoughts, the wit of herself and the slow, sweet passing of shapes bright and dark, the rolling sun and moon no trouble to her... passing into quiet sleep...

Can he deny me just a single sip?

She knew he would. Well, he'd helped her.

None of them else cared a shitstain... none...

And there was still the nightmare, the dank passageways under the cold earth of the recent and crudely dug den where the terrible people who'd stolen her from her home hid under the green hills and waited for something she never discovered. The terrible people: squat, yellowish and pale, jabbering endlessly in a raucous tongue (she never learned to decipher a fragment), knights in jet black armor who never spoke or were seen with their helms off or even open... stink, stagnant air... human waste dropped everywhere in the muddy, timbered tunnels for flies and long, shuddering worms... guttering

torches, muddy sleeping straw... her rusty chains... waiting
in sunless fetidness... waiting so she'd no longer wondered
if she were mad but simply how long she would remain
so... stringy hair caked with foul mud, lice nipping, skin
scratched to bloody streaks... she became so dulled she'd no
longer even asked the mute knights or the babblers anything,
no longer begging: "Please, why am I kept here? Please! Why
did you slay them?"... finally numbed out of time and caring,
there was commotion, clashing, cries, and the squat people
fled past going deeper into the inner tangles, followed by black
gouts of smoke thickening until she gagged and in blind reflex
struggled for a life she no longer distinguished from the choking
dreams that came and went as hopeless as the grim muck and
stones that pressed endlessly in... then flame roar, furnace
heat blasting into her as she twisted and roasted, smelling her
hair burning, preserved so far only by the layered filth and oil
that coated her gaunt flesh and then the rusty chainring snapped
from the wall and she was rolling and crawling away through
crackling timbers and raining sparks... somehow powerful
hands were gripping her, lifting her into a rush of sweet, cool
air, a new incomprehensible language all around her... shock
of brilliant daylight, hot sun impacted in the sea and shimmering
on the lush hills, the blur of battle all around, furred and horn-
helmeted warriors striking down the black knights and their
dwarfed companions... saw on the horizon immense masses
of black smoke and ripping stormcloud. She couldn't know
that this was where the war for the Grail was ending in defeat
for everyone and the nearly total destruction of the heart of
Britain... now a reddish-bearded face with eyes like steel chips
peered, smiling, into hers and she heard a screaming she didn't
know came from herself until (as the shock of everything hit
and the madness vanished) she was already falling into soft,
soothing darkness...

His mule was beside hers now and her hand already reached
out before she was really aware of moving and then he had her
wrist, steelchip eyes on her and she heard herself curse him,
mechanically, furious, hopeless...

XXIV

Lohengrin sped out of the nearly invisible trees, holding his sword ahead as if it somehow lit his way. He was certain he'd missed his man, lost him back at the moat, but was sure, too, there was no reason to go back... and so he nearly ran into the horse, a plunging dark mass that suddenly was motion against an infinitesimally lighter background of field and sky, and then it snorted and there was another ahead and whispery voices. He froze, straining to check his burning breath.

"He'll find us," a male voice was assuring someone, "never fear, Unlea."

"I'm not certain I do fear it," she replied.

"Well and whatever," the other rejoined, then to his mount: "Come up, you silly fartwit."

Lohengrin saw him now, a vague metal gleaming. Heard the muffled hooves.

They must have bagged the feet, he thought, *to dull the sound...*

"Do we go straight on?" a coarser voice asked.

"Till we pass what used to be the river," the knight Lohengrin didn't know was Gawain said. "Are you not pleased he's come back?"

"Am I not?" she ambiguously returned.

Lohengrin only partly listened. He stood, indecisive, sword unmoving. Should he speak up? Perhaps this knight knew something about *Lohengrin*...The sounds, movement faded quickly into the muffling night...The breezes shook the trees into an invisible hissing high up, out in the fields...

As he started to follow someone spoke close behind him and he turned, nearly in panic, scanning to pull a sure shape out of the hollow blottings of the night.

"Will you spare me slaying you?" the man asked.

"What?"

"Walk back the way you came. Follow not this path."

There were still shouts, ringings, shifted and swallowed by the wind.

"Are you certain to best me?" Lohengrin asked.

"Save my breath and yours," was the answer.

The young knight felt his scalp prickle and he inched back a few paces, testing the vacant air with the tip of his blade. He recognized death in the voice that touched a memory somewhere in the lost, empty recesses of himself.

"I mean no harm," he told the darkness that he felt completely exposed in. His running sweat was chilled. Who was this terrible man who'd stood against a hundred?

"Leave then." The voice was behind him again. Lohengrin twisted around, backed and circled. He felt his cold rage flowing into him. Fear made him furious.

"Very well," he said. "Are you a wizard, sir?"

"In the dark," came the amused answer, "there's magic everywhere."

Lohengrin barely listened. He was inching up to where he thought the fellow was. He was sure he'd caught a dim steel gleaming a bare sword length to his right. The rage poured into him like iced blood. He told himself it was time to act, to conquer, lead. That was all that appeared to bear reason in this absurd world he found himself wandering through, with rent past and no purpose...Unfair!...Stupid...He'd give them back the only coin anybody seemed to count, he'd have this much purpose: slay whomever dared stand before him! Command the rest. Ring himself with power...other things stirred now and he remembered, peripherally but intensely, one of the captured village girls, long graceful hands, long back...He was awakening, so there was going to be that too, pictured her sweet mouth with his angled hardness thrust into it . . . he was awakening, at last! Gritted his teeth.

"Sir," he said, "I am not one of those men back there. I am a lost knight whose memory has been stricken from him like pages torn from a book. I need good counsel above all else. Why I know not even my *name,* for certain."

"Is this truly spoken?" the unseen warrior wondered. Except he just could make him out now: a tall shape, the vaguest glimmer of chain mail and light hair.

You son-of-a-bitch! Lohengrin thought. *I have you now.*

"I swear it, sir," he said.

"What name have you?"

"Someone said Lohengrin . . ."

And then, body whipping like a steel spring, he uncoiled a terrific stroke, sidewise and level, that stunned even himself with its frenzied malice and power, anticipating the impact, crunch, split and shatter, his own voice beating in his ears and head, exploding a warcry!

Howtlande felt the mule shudder just before it spilled him, going down spraddle-legged, the shadowy attacker still hacking the long, flopeared creature with relentless and senseless savagery that terrified the pop-eyed leader because the killer was so totally unconcerned with him and the sword he snicked the air with, reaching for the small, rapid shape plying its long-handled ax, chopping the beast's skull to unnecessary splinters. Howtlande rolled backwards with surprising agility. He somehow was convinced his enemy could see in the dark, imagined reddish feral eyes . . . He scrambled away still hearing the frenzied ax, splat, splat, hack, crunch, thinking: *I always live I always live!* puffing, fleeing for the gate, the wild battle all around, men colliding, rebounding in the night, the nimble, deadly attackers cutting through and around like a diabolic wolf pack, striking, yelping incomprehensibly, someone tittering, penetratingly . . .

He was going full tilt by the time he reached the torchlit gateway and burst into the jammed men there like (Skalwere thought, watching from the wall, perched with a fistful of spears) a stone through a straw roof, and rolled into the yard, shrieking:

"Shut the gate! Shut! Shut! . . . Demons from hell! . . . Gate!

Gate! You pissbuckets!... Shut! Shut!..."

Skalwere searched for a target (not forgetting to consider Howtlande himself for a moment), then fired a spear and thought he scored...saw another climbing the wall like, he thought, a spider, shockingly long, swamp-pale limbs creeping rapidly up: threw and watched the climber writhe and twist down into the earth's darkness...

I have to live, Howtlande told himself, racing for the castle, massive belly heaving, *I have to live...*

As he reached the steps a spear spat sparks and clattered loosely beside him.

No, his mind said, *Not yet...not yet, you filth!*

Plunged against the massive portal, yanked and strained at the handle expecting the bite and shock in his back every sweating instant...

And Skalwere, wild with outrage, fired another in a high arc, hissing:

"Coward! Fat coward!"

Knew he'd missed again and raced along the wall and down the stairs as the fighting spilled into the yard. He was holding two spears now. Nothing would stop him. He'd slay the fat sack. He'd slain far better among the Vikings and nearly got to Prince Tungrim himself...bad luck had ended that and he'd fled...a swordstroke away from being a great lord himself... that was fate...But this fat coward would not escape...

Parsival hesitated. Didn't know and never knew why. He held the long mace part lifted. Saw the faintly glowing armor three feet before him. Didn't strike. Shrugged. He'd let him go past, followed and then hesitated...then they had their strange conversation.

All throughout he thought about Unlea. Kept watching an image of her that hung in his inner sight, a shape that delicately hinted at subtle things, hopes, touches, washes of sweet light opening into soft landscapes that took his longings deeper, deeper into partial forms and exquisite colors, and he wanted to talk or sing or do something about it, some gesture or shape to hold the ecstatic delicacy...felt the blow coming and instantly realized this knight had succeeded where unnumbered

others had failed and he was actually going to die here and now
with that flowing magical vision drawing his attention...

Lohengrin, his son, saw brilliance that was blinding white
pain as though his skull had burst and the light streamed not
in but out through the fragments and he felt the something, the
burning cold and bright and agonizing something there, feeling
even the shape of it like a steel splinter under the skin or a
sliver in the eye, and he knew something was in there, in the
wound: all this virtually timeless in perception as arms and
back cracked with the supple strain, slamming the cut home
as everything went fluid and slow and flimsy in the terrific
bursting light and himself and the other seemed shadows, part
of the dark that was part of them both, his own movement
mechanical, meaningless (he somehow saw) momentum...
pointless...pointless...disconnected from life...who was
this fellow shadow?...What was himself?...Too late to
check the absurd blow, except he didn't realize until a shock
of time later that his hands had already (as if briefly separate
from his will) released the hilt...

He'd partly doubled up before he felt the narrow shock of
pressure along his side, felt the steel links shear, and the pain,
and was still trying hopelessly to wrench away as the ground
slammed into his face and knees. Felt the slosh of blood as the
blade (he didn't know) spun, bounced and skidded away in
rebound and the man (he'd just realized was impossibly, in-
sanely, but probably his son!) was already fleeing as if in horror
and ultimate repudiation of what he couldn't have known was
attempted parricide, fleeing blindly (he heard him past the pain
and desperate breathless sucking of his lungs), crashing and
clinking across the field through brush and saplings and moon-
less obscurity, and he tried to call after him but his lungs felt
flattened and his mouth gaped like a beached fish's, only his
thoughts racing on:
*My son...Was that my son?...Sweet Mary, was that my
son?...*

Parsival sat on the hard ground for a while, listening to the
night. The distant sounds of fighting had faded. His son, he
thought, if it really had been he, lost himself in the dark woods.
His fingers discovered the wound in his side was superficial.

That surprised him. He'd been winded by the blow but there wasn't much blood. The fellow must have misjudged, he decided...

He stood up after a time and went on in the general direction taken by Gawain and the others. After dawnlight he'd be able to pick up their trail.

Those ribs will be sore as the devil's whang tomorrow, he realized. *That bastard was sly enough to be Lohengrin...Taking me like that...I'm getting to be quite the ordinary great man,* he thought, sarcastically. *If this keeps on I'll begin to believe I'm mortal after all...whoever he was if fate keeps up this game we'll meet again...*

He moved carefully through the trees, somehow (he never questioned it anymore) feeling where they stood and avoiding collision.

The next problem would be Unlea. What to do about that? Well, another bridge to wait to cross...

"Anyway," he muttered, "if that was my boy I hope he gives me time, when next we meet, to say I'm sorry." Smiled, wry.

Parsival, he told himself, *you collect problems like dogdung breeds flies. And even if you don't think them up they leap out of the dark at you...*

XXV

At a certain point Broaditch realized they were trapped. He let himself and the others be led without resistance towards the great fire. The madman they now knew was Clinschor had stopped speaking and the other man (John, the leader) came forward again on the ledge. Pleeka was just ahead of Broaditch.

Close to the fire the blank rockface was impressive, the two figures on top commanding. At first Broaditch didn't realize they were being discussed.

"Brother Pleeka brought these creatures here," John declared, reedy, annoyingly insistent.

Broaditch was sure who he was now and yelled up at him: "Are you not John of Bligh?"

"By Christ, you're right, I think," murmured Alienor. She held both her children before her, surrounded by the dark masses.

"I brought them as converts," Pleeka was answering. No one paid attention to the interruption. Pleeka's remarks seemed to amuse some of the crowd whose breath and stink swelled around them. The flames popped and hissed. The smoke seemed to hint at strange shapes as it sluggishly rolled overhead, great creeping things with many heads and twisted limbs . . .

"Ha!" somebody called.

"Hoo!" another.

"The brother has been away," John said, with easy humor. "He knows not the new ways of the holy people."

"What new ways?" Pleeka demanded. "Our ways were founded in truth and God's light! What new ways need we? And who is this—"

John cut him off.

"God's will changes at His pleasure," he announced. "There can be no converts because the brothers and sisters are a whole folk. The lost race of Trueman from the days of the prophets!" A sighing; a breathstink went up from the massed holy ones, still a little numbed from Clinschor's insane but matchless rhetoric. "We are the inheritors of the earth in these final days! The final days of the old world!" Sighing. "This is the day of Armageddon! The twilight of time . . ." The crowd was swaying and humming a strange dirge or universal keening of infinite and primal pain. "This is a time and a half time!" John suddenly screamed and Broaditch squinted hard past the flames at the shaggy-looking, dark-eaten figure. "A time, time and a half time!" Sighing, sighing . . . "We are the people of the judgment! We are the mouth with teeth to chew the sinners!!" Sighs and outcries and moaning and the dirge . . . "To chew and swallow the sinners and the accursed of God!"

The mass went into a frenzy, blotting away Pleeka's shouts, his sweaty, fire-shaken face tilted up, mouth struggling soundlessly.

Things rarely flow easy and smooth, Broaditch thought, *but here's all rapids and falls . . .* Leena stood, eyes shut, holding the boy.

Finally Pleeka's hysterical voice broke through and Broaditch heard:

"You've profaned everything!" he was yelling. "Everything!"

"Seize them all!" John ordered. "For their tongues are as the tongues of serpents!"

Broaditch dimly saw Clinschor's long head bobbing, nodding madly as if in agreement as the other spread out his hands in nervous benediction, pacing slightly, erratically from side to side through the entangled shadows and flameflashes.

God, Broaditch thought, *what a crew! Every madman's found a home at last . . . even the plague seems to shun these creatures . . .*

His spear had already been snatched away and he decided not to struggle hopelessly to save it. Watched flailing, vociferous Pleeka overcome by a swirl of them, broken pieces of his shouts audible:

"... betrayed ... promise ... promise ..."

As Broaditch and the others were lifted, yanked and bound with wirelike cords, carried into the darkness, the organlike tones of Clinschor swelled over all in immense disproportion to the stick figure form:

"I will create the new kingdom and overcome the evil forces of weakness and sickness and confusion! This triumph shall outlive the ages! We shall raise in stone the final monuments of blood and time!!"

And the rest was lost in cheering howls, clashing of metal and the curses and gratuitous buffeting as several blows rocked his solid head and the sounds became the music of some lost and maddened world of plague, seas of blood, drying, dying earth ... how could any bear it, he wondered abstractly, how could hopeless and fragile flesh bear this crucifixion of all nature? ...

Then a dark, closed wagon, the door slammed shut behind them.

"Are you intact, Alienor?" he asked.

"Torky," she was saying, soothing. "Torky." As he wept.

"Mama ... mama," Tikla clung close in the black, musty place.

They must keep pigs in here, Broaditch thought.

"Where are you, papa?" Torky scrambled around, tensed. "Papa ..."

Pleeka was still raging:

"Betrayers of God! ... Betrayers of God! ... Children of Gog and Magog!"

"Torky," Broaditch said, "we are all here and still live. Come to my voice." Heard the boy moving then felt his hot, surprisingly hard touch. Thought how he was changing with the days and hoped these times would not wound his heart forever ... He held him silently now ...

"God will be revenged," said Pleeka to no one present. "The beast will be cast down and broken! ..."

Leena was embracing the young boy. Only the full adults had been bound. She crooned to him, not thinking about the blood. The fire had showed it everywhere, splashed on all of them in running rose stains. The fire was bleeding ... She calmly didn't think about it.

All Broaditch believed he wanted, as he strained carefully against his bonds, was not to surrender to this. There had to be a sane moment in every madman, a clean spot in every leper. So, he concluded, somewhere in this wasteland, there had to be a garden, in all this broken, bleeding, burning life . . .

He sighed and sank back on the foul-smelling boards. Pleeka muttered inaudibly now. His head stung and was starting to ache . . .

"Never mind," his wife was saying, "You tried. You have always tried, Broaditch."

"Woman, I . . ."

"Never mind!" She was fierce, almost harsh in her tenderness. Her head touched his solid shoulder. "Say no word, husband. Say no word to me."

He nodded. Rested. Let his eyes gradually tune into the faint strands and blots of light that showed at cracks and around the door. Sighed and sat, not even thinking anymore. Just waiting, patient and still, terrifically intent, nothing in him even asking for sleep yet. Sitting solid as carven, indestructible granite. Felt his son's hand on his arm gradually soften as his tense breathing steadied . . . waiting . . . not thinking . . .

Leena was praying, fingers twisting the rope belt of her garment as if it were beads. The dark made it hard to keep the shapes away, the faces in the gusting torchlight, harsh beards, unlooking eyes, the metal smell of the blood sticky on their clothes and faces as she pushed at the closing shadows, flopping, arching, kicking, raw sound bursting from her without words, begging her father and mother for relief from the hands that kept coming back, from stonehard bones, the sheer heaviness of men, pulling, pushing, grunting, blood and suffering, her own blood draining down there darkly beyond help or reach (masses of stony shadow crushing her flat as though not just the raping men but the whole world lay on her, the horse snuffs and smells nearby, laughter . . . a barking dog . . .), her painful blood draining down her wrenched thighs . . . draining into a void that sucked her down too past all struggle and outcry . . . the savage, rhythmic pain prying her from her body . . . And now she pushed the images away, forehead resting on the planks, eyes pressed to the thinnest crevice where almost light showed edgeless as water, praying, the boy across her lap, hands twisting the knotted rope as if to tell or untie it, soundless lips steady, praying the way another might strike blows . . .

XXVI

The sun was setting behind a wall of violet-dark clouds. The fields opened before them, silvery, water-vague. The mules, horses and marching men seemed to float along.

"We don't stop tonight," Tungrim had announced. She was riding next to him again.

"I don't care," Layla said.

"We eat on the march, as Norsefolk should."

She wasn't looking at him.

"And drink," she said. Waited. She knew he'd be frowning. He was, she'd previously reflected, a serious barbarian.

He said nothing.

"What can you still want of me?" she asked. "Think you have not had all?"

"Mock me not," he returned, gruff, uncomfortable. He shifted on the steady mule. Their shadows had melted away into the silvery wash. One of the marching Vikings called over to him:

"Tungrim, we're far from the sea!"

A few others guffawed.

"Aye, right so," one added.

"Peace, my brothers," Tungrim said. "I promise it will wait for us till we return."

Laughter and a fairhearted cheer. Someone began singing, lilting, high-pitched, haunting...another joined in...Long grasses rustled softly...fireflies scribbled obscure, hinting twists and streaks on the dimming air.

"Well?" she finally said, still not looking towards him.

"Here," he said, ripping the wineskin free from his mount's

withers and slamming it blindly at her hand, and then she, unhurried, uncorked it and held herself still, except (and she knew it) something inside was at the edge of frantic.

"You can say it," she informed him, tilting it up now, amazed at how she relished and sustained the moment, the first stinging, bitter wash over her tongue and burning warm in her throat... She shut and opened her eyes. Shuddered. "You can say what you like, my lord Tungrim." *Dunggrim*...

"I ought to have left you where I found you."

Held her in his thick arms in front on the unsaddled horse riding down to the beach where the longships were drawn up in line like, she'd imagined, mysterious giant fish in the bright moonlight. Barrel-bodied horse hissing through the sand, the burning stronghold far above and behind them now, the sea air helping, clearing her lungs and mind...

"I am called Tungrim," he'd told her. "Prince in the north-lands." Reined up by the dragon-prowed ships. "I am come to this land to find a damned kinsman." They'd dismounted and she'd fallen on the cold, damp sand and he'd helped her up and held her. His head came a little above hers. He was very wide and thick.

"You're a fine-looking wench under it all." He'd given her a swallow of rich sweetness (it didn't burn until far down within her) that was mooncolored and she later learned was called honeywine. She'd coughed and looked into his face, eyes deep, dark and lost...

That was... and now she took another swallow. The impact was less this time. She felt very comfortable and even a little amused. Men were silly beings. All of them. This bear wasn't so bad... Fuzzy-backed... but what did he expect from her? That was a question... No, not what, but rather when would he say it out because all he had was her body and time and few of them would ever be so satisfied even when it was all they actually wanted after all.

"Am I still a fine-looking lady?" she wanted to know. "Have I not stolen your heart, sir?"

He didn't respond. She wondered if he was going to rage again. She felt almost giggly. The peaceful night drifted past marked by the silent yellow streaks and spots... as if in echo the stars were showing. She smiled.

"Tungrim?"

"Hmm?"

"I never told you my name."

"Did I ask?"

"Ah."

"What is it, woman?"

"What seek you here, in this country . . . besides loot? You once said . . ."

"Loot? There's precious little loot. This land is cursed unto death."

"Then?"

She drank again knowing he was watching, though his face was set straight ahead. She smiled within herself because these were her best moments, when first it took hold, before the memories spilled into it too and then she had to drink to hold them away and mute . . . but now it was still fine, light and easy as being young and courting in the castle garden to music and tender candlelight, except . . . except there was always a small stone under her back, she thought . . . always a stone . . .

"It were once a single thing," he replied.

She thought he meant well. Felt warm from the drink. Meant the best he could. He might have chained her to his bed if he'd liked. What a shock she'd suffered, torn away from everything. She'd never really understood how unyielding and chill the outside was, until she was dragged from her home. The world finally closed down around her to a few blank feet of dimness, filth and misery . . . *No, no,* she thought, *not yet . . . I care not to remember yet . . . leave it smooth and blank, for Jesus' sake!*

"And what is now, Tungrim?"

"I seek Skalwere, the traitor. This be a blood matter. And Viking men turn not aside from such!"

"And what is not a blood matter?" she murmured.

"Do you mock me? You said I were . . . pompous."

"Did I? I remember not . . ." She felt his hurt with strange surprise. Reached and touched him gently. "I mock you not, sir."

He turned to her, features an edgeless gleaming. The soft light brought back one of the memories: a phantom face on a twilit lawn, kneeling beside him on the silky, warm summer grass, tentatively touching his bared chest . . . the phantom, beautiful face, long hair a watery sheen gathering the blurry light and she said, both to the ghost and to Tungrim, tenderness, lostness in her tone:

"My name, though you haven't asked, is Layla."

XXVII

Howtlande ran through the dark passageways and unnumbered chambers of the castle, feeling his pursuer like a tangible pressure at his back. He choked a scream as something caught his legs, violently tipped him up and over and he rolled across cold, battering stone.

A chair, he realized, *a chair!*

Got up and plunged on, sweating, panting...up stairs...around bends...on...

Skalwere crossed the yard at the cost of one thrown spear that clattered harmlessly past a bowed, shadowy attacker who went after someone else anyway...through the door that Howtlande hadn't dared pause to bar, and slammed the giant bolt home before moving into the dark interior.

Outside, the silent, cynical Sir Galahad was slashing, banging, looking for breathing room, armor dented, head ringing from a dozen blows, only his bent shield keeping death at bay as the deadly men leaped in like wolves at the sluggish, frightened mass of victims.

He knew he had to get inside. Backed, turned, made short fierce charges, chopping his way again and again and he vaguely wondered why he kept trying to live, since he had no particular aims left. He let it be his body, purposeless, instinctive . . . clawed past the last men in his way, knocking one flat in the dark with swordhilt and pushing another into the obscure fray where he seemed simply sucked into the frantic fury. Then he fled, backed under the main stairs through an arched portico, panting, leaning on the wall, letting his lungs pull deeply at life.

"All right," he whispered. "I live for the moment again . . ."

Aye . . . since before Arthur died . . . oh, my king . . . my king that was . . . You taught me emptiness as love taught me hopelessness . . .

What point, since death had to close in a few heartbeats one way or another . . .

Brute that I am yet I wrote verse for my love . . . yet everything must always come to be lost, that's beyond prevention . . .

Time took all, as from the merchant who clutched his gold and coppers in a fantasy of permanence and then but passed it to the next hoarder of scraps . . . like keeping life's breath in a sack . . .

Under the arch he found a grillwork and was slightly surprised when it skreaked inwards. He went through into total blackness.

And I slew for Arthur. I loved him. I slew in such momentous and pithy causes that are now all long lost . . . It was no better than fighting for this fat man . . . Why must I still think? The curse of Eden was the rambling brain that left animals in peace and man in pain . . .

The dark was so total that each step he expected to crack his face. Each unblocked stride into the cool, mudsmelling depths was a minor surprise . . . His mind freed by the blackness, leafed through the past uncontrollably.

His life began to fail with that boy, he suddenly decided. The half-naked, blond, beautiful boy who'd knelt before him praying to him as if he were a God . . . The boy Parsival, so long ago . . . He'd said knights hope to have shining glory and the words were stone that hurt his mouth to speak. He'd spoken of glory to that blue-eyed innocent, kneeling there ready to believe as a sponge to drink . . . It began to fail there, with having to say *glory* . . .

Remembered Parsival at court, years and years later. Adult at last. Coming to a feast with two deep scratches beside one eye and the story was his wife had literally chased him down the corridor with the teenage boy (Lohengrin) waving a dirk, his younger sister clinging to his legs and weeping, the mother raging too, and the famous knight holding his hand to his bloody face, fleeing down the stairs to where only her tongue could still rip...so he'd been told...

He groped ahead down a slippery slope into utter lightlessness.

The wife, Layla, had shouted, they said: "You're not even a man anymore now, you son-of-a-bitch!" And the great hero had supposedly wept into his streaming blood. Saying nothing. Standing in front of everyone, servants, men-at-arms, knights and ladies. Cried out: "Forgive me...I tried...I tried!" And his son trying to crawl down the steps with the sister still clinging, bushy black hair shaking as he yelled: "I hate you! I hate you! I hate you!" And then (they said) the father ran out into the castle garden where he just leaned his face against the far wall in cold autumnal drizzle that gradually soaked into his silken robes, pounding his fist over and over into the cold, wet gray bricks. His wife at the door now, frozen as if an invisible barrier blocked her in, shouting across the fallen, colorless flowers: "You failed at everything! Face it! Be a man for your own sake, Parsival! You failed and all I asked was some little sweetness...Face it now!" And (they said) he stood like a penitent lad who'd blundered lessons, face to the wall until she silently went inside...stood there as the rain went on...

Had that been my wife...But I never had nor ever will have...no matter...well, mayhap he were praying at that wall, for short after he fled to join, they say, the monks at their untiring nonsense...

He realized he was in a large space. Clinked his sword on the scabbard and heard the hollow, rattling echoes. There was still mud underfoot.

I went on crusade with Gawain instead...Oh, that was lovely, that had rare meaning...Groped on. Great Christ, is there no end to this darkness?...

Skalwere believed he would actually smell the fear of his fat quarry. He was asking himself why he ever listened to any promises of obscure triumphs or heeded his flabby orders. He snarled thinking about it. Howtlande, the fat, pompous toad! They would soon meet and that idea soothed his mind...

He had to get a ship again and escape this miserable, wasted land. The sea was the only way... He remembered, with a kind of longing, night raids on the coast, the excitement of moving in with careful oars, aiming through the faintly luminescent surf, the longships leaping, cracking, holding steady all the way into the grinding sand... splashing over the side, up the beach, each sense ready, into the sleepy village... a pair of quiet voices, a drowsy watchman with his pale torch, then the surprise, sudden flames, blundering men trying to fight, women... panic... fleeing... out to sea again, counting over the loot on calm, slow swells, the gathering of dawnlight on rimless water, feeling sweetly spent, a little drunk... at peace with life... the smooth roll and lifting on...

He froze, listening. Was sure of a slight sound ahead, squinted, his night eyes probing down the long corridor, saw the thin outline of a chamber door.

You'll greet the heatless sun of hell this morrow, he said to himself.

Padded on, delicate and terrible, over cool, stepworn stones, last spear ready. He never questioned this. It was man's life, ritual, a kind of formal dance where now his thrust was necessary. He was actually without deep malice, even cursing the enemy was a formality, proper manners for the kill. Fate played and a misstep was formally fatal...

Howtlande found a slit tower window overlooking the dark courtyard. The rich, dry summery air puffed over him as he leaned out. They were milling indecipherably in the castle yard, the cries and banging muted by the height.

The thing, he was still thinking, *is always to live. No dead man ever raised a kingdom... I live for more than my mere self, that's the point even if few believe in me yet...* The idea was somehow a comfort. *They won't stay here, whoever they are... there's no food... I'll wait and when they move on I'll begin again... find stouter fighters... that's the advantage of being alive...*

XXVIII

The unseen planks banged, crackled, hissed with strain as the dark seemed a solid thing jolting, battering at them.

Broaditch never ceased to struggle as the wagon rolled on. Until morning light drew a blurry rectangle around the door and traced a few cracks across walls and ceiling.

Torky moaned in his fitful sleep. Tikla snored softly. Alienor rested against him, napping a little.

He twisted his numbed wrist and thought he finally felt a strand give slightly...a fraction...a fraction...He grunted and winced with fresh pain.

"Peasant man," Pleeka suddenly said.

Broaditch regathered his breath and responded:

"What wise words have you now?"

"All has been betrayed," the man said from the far end of the rocking, battering vehicle. Outside the hoofbeats were steady and not so rapid as their exaggerated inner movements suggested. Broaditch assumed the road was especially rough (this was true) and the rig badly constructed (also a fact).

"Are you working on your ropes?" he asked Pleeka.

"I cannot see how all this happened. Here I lie in disgrace . . . betrayed by good John . . . I cannot see . . ."

"While you ponder these things," Broaditch suggested, "why not struggle for freedom?"

"Freedom? Only through God can freedom come, peasant man."

"Getting loose here will be a start and give Him less to do."

"I will tell you these things."

"Don't feel . . ." Broaditch twisted and tugged his numb, aching forearms violently. " . . . don't feel you have to . . ." His muscles cracked and he arched his brawny back. The rope gave again. His hands felt about to burst, swollen with blood.

"This is the hour of the beast," Pleeka confided. Broaditch went on with his strainings. Fraction by fraction through the searing constrictions the bonds were yielding . . .

"Unn," muttered Broaditch.

"The hour of the beast and his dreadful reign, I say . . . Aiiii!" he suddenly cried and Broaditch heard him hit flat on the boards. Alienor fully wakened and Torky groaned in his dreams. " . . . I have seen it and have been the right hand of the beast . . . aiiii . . ."

"I think," Broaditch told his wife, "he has lost his fondness for John the Silver Duck or Farting Eagle or what you will."

"Methinks he's taking a fit," she said.

There were rhythmic thumpings and bangings and gasps against the slow careening of the wagon. Leena and the boy crouched near the door. They were gray, ghostlit by the fuzzing of dawnlight.

"Aiiii! . . . and the beast hath seven heads . . . aiiiii . . . and ten horns and crowns . . . and all the nations followed the beast . . . for who is like unto the beast and who can make war against him? . . . aiiiiiii . . . aiiii! . . ." Crash, thump, thud, gasp, gasp . . .

"Can I help?" Alienor asked.

Torky was sobbing a little and she comforted him in the lurching dark.

"I'm nearly free . . ." he panted. "but . . . nearly . . . is . . . not home . . ."

"Aii . . . I have his mark upon me . . . upon me . . ." Thump, bang . . .

"He's off and bent," she commented.

An inch more, he thought. *An inch ...*

Leena began to pray, fierce, steady, not quite loud or hysterical, as Pleeka raved on:

"The beast was my brother and behold I knew him not and saw not ... aiiii ... saw not the word *blasphemy* writ on the crowns ..."

"That John," Alienor said. "That bastard John."

Broaditch paused for breath and to ease the burning, cutting. "What?" he wondered.

". . . the word and the blood of many ..."

"John the priest," he said. "I knew him on first foul sight. Him who raised the peasants and let them perish. Him."

". . . brother ... brother ..." Growling now and Broaditch imagined him chewing the floor and foaming. ". . . the beast were my brother whose number be six hundred threescore and six! ... Aiiiii!! ..."

"I knew him too." Two decades ago. He'd followed John to betrayal and outrage of what had been a promise, a shining hope for freedom after all the horror of those days ... *Of all days,* he thought. *Of all days ... How could nature suffer such a thing to live on?*

With an intense explosion of air and a shriek Pleeka (Broaditch knew instantly) burst his bonds and began caroming around the confined and pitching space.

"*Ave Maria,*" Leena was saying, chanting, "*gratiae plena ...*"

And then he was free himself, a rush of tingling agony pouring into his hands, which he held as if in disbelieving prayer before his face. Locked his teeth tight together.

Pleeka was flopping weakly now, like a fish, Broaditch thought, on the dock. The girl's litany went ceaselessly on, almost uninflected ...

"They are lower than the lowest low," Pleeka was whispering. "Lower than the slime worms and offal of the deepest dark ... they have shat in the clear well of the heart ... aiii ..." His screeches now were bizarrely conversational. ". . . all foul practice is their delight and their abominations have fouled the waters ... all the nations follow blasphemies and the beast ..."

Broaditch sat up, realizing the lurching motions had ceased.

He barely noticed the girl's voice or Pleeka's raving.

Well, he thought, *here we are somewhere but where and for what? By Mary, I may regret the answer more than the question . . .*

"Give me your hands, Ali," he told her, painfully moving his fingers. "I'll free you now."

Clinschor had insisted on riding inside the only other closed wagon. He'd had them lay bedding on the floor and drape the inside walls with hangings, tattered garments, rags, anything they had (to him they seemed the rare and perfumed silks of his past) until a soft, smoothly hushed interior was created. He further commanded a single chair (though it had but three gnarled legs) to be nailed to the floor facing the single slit window in the rear door he'd had them make by removing a single board and now he sat there in the muffled obscurity peering out at the grayish-pale morning, watching the narrow strip of already passed field and hillock and forest flow away . . .

He felt suffused by peacefulness. Rocked slightly with the long swaying tilts of the quite stable wagon—unlike the one where the captives rolled and tossed. His big, soft hands gripped his knees and his stomach griped with pain, ground and squeezed his first substantial meal in weeks. Burped. The gas pocket remained. Grew with slow probings. Pushed deeper. He drew unsteady breath and sweated from the pain. Understood he was being attacked magically again . . . Burped . . . Which one of them, his mind wanted to know. Then he knew this was the work of Morgana the witch! Snarled as he bent forward in agony. Clenched and unclenched his long, wide fingers on his knees . . . strained . . . cursed when he couldn't move the wind. Pictured her pale redheaded face and began muttering a spell which he periodically broke off in fresh attempts to fart as lines of marching, dark-robed Truemen passed across the slice of vision before him. Groaned, strained and muttered . . .

Once I reach the fortress, he kept reminding himself, *my power will know no limit! Then Morgana, you'll see what you'll see!* Gritted his teeth and pressed his bony knees tight together. Still no relief . . . Stepped up the spell's intensity. Thought of others who would suffer beyond imagination when his time came: that blond fiend who'd cast him from the shining heights into that freezing, deadly, stinking muck! That one, that wizard's form who'd defiled him and drowned him into unconsciousness so he'd forget who he was because he could not be slain by them. Vast, immortal beings had charge over him and he felt their unseen presence always. Shut his eyes and called them, sensed them reaching to him from far, far below the earth's surface in their great halls . . . Parsival had thrown him down and he sent them his image and asked for his destruction . . . Parsival and Morgana, he sent, concentrating, swaying.

"Destroy them, O mighty ones!" he whispered. "Destroy them!"

Tightened his hands, pale, bony, wide forehead clenched, not even feeling a long, hot push of gas bubble and fizz slowly from his narrow, bony hams . . .

Outside, John, tall, erratic-moving, brushed his wild, stiff hair back with a nervous hand. He was walking, keeping pace with the captives' wagon. His captains in their shagginess and robes were close around him.

They were just crossing a thin drool of river where the waterflow barely topped the wash of smooth, pale stones.

"A month behind," a short, red-haired, bulge-eyed man commented as the two wagons banged and scraped over the crumbling banks, "this ford were knee deep."

"There's been no rain since," another put in, a stout longbeard. "And Lord God has sent us great heat."

"To fulfill what was written," John broke in. "The world shall perish in great heat."

"Praise His name," the first asserted, crossing himself and rolling his eyes with a strange seeming of joy.

"We are the reapers, brothers," John went on, jerking along, elbows tipping out after each step, splashing through the spatters of water that felt sweet on his feet, "of all the burning earth." He headed for Clinschor's wagon on the other side. In the first touch of sun he felt like iron on an anvil.

"And," said a quick-faced redhead, "He has sent His oracle of flame to guide us! Praise Him!"

"Amen," added the second, blotchy-cheeked, blinking, moundishly formed.

"What do we do next, Father John?" red hair called over as they topped the far bank and headed into the pale, sparse trees.

"He goes," another said from under his beard, "to consult with the angel."

John glanced back. His eyes were like polished pebbles. But not bright. The light seemed unimpacted in them.

"Each sign," he told them, "will be greater than the last."

His expression showed nothing but determination, abstract, unswerving. He turned to the slit in the wood. He looked neither reverent nor afraid, just intent, expectant under his bushy white-stained hair. "God," he told the slit in the wagon, "hath given us meat and drink in the parched desert."

"What is it?" the muffled voice rumbled within.

And John quoted:

"'Come and gather yourselves together unto the supper of the great God: That ye may eat the flesh of kings, and the flesh of captains, and the flesh of mighty men, and the flesh of horses and they that sit upon them, and the flesh of all men both free and bound, both small and great!'"

Broaditch had freed Alienor and was crouched over Pleeka, who was kneeling now, facing a crack in the wall.

"Will you stir yourself to save yourself?" Broaditch demanded. Nothing, no response.

"What ails him now?" asked Alienor, holding the children as they tilted and slid towards the back. Though they couldn't know it they were mounting the embankment of the drying stream. The sun was a hammer on the exterior and the stale air thickened. They were all soaked in sweat. Leena was silent as the young boy, now. The creases of sunlight lit them dimly. "How fare you, child?" she asked Leena. No reply. "And you, boy?" she went on.

"I want to go home," he said.

"Ah."

"Yet," said the girl, suddenly, "he has none. There's naught there save blood and ashes."

And then she was silently praying again. Pushing the red away from her eyes, looking away from the sunbrightness at the crevices that held tints of that terrible color of flame and bleeding. Shut her eyes tight and rapidly, hoarsely prayed...

"What are these *Truemen*," Broaditch hissed, "that they follow a crackbrain killer half-dead of plague and hunger? Tell me that, by Christ!" He was angry with disgust.

"They'll give him food and drink," Pleeka said into the lurching wood. "Never fear."

"Truemen, shit!" said Broaditch. "We have to escape." He pressed his eye to the plankspace and winced at the sun's impact. Finally made out, in the blinding day, lines of them marching across parched, nearly treeless fields, the wagon rolling almost evenly now in the baking heat. He wiped his eyes and stared again. Couldn't see more than a narrow strip.

"Where did they come from?" Alienor asked Pleeka. He twisted around. His face flickered with tics.

"Ah," he said.

She touched his forehead, his wiry hair.

"Poor soul," she said, "you trusted them."

"Ah," he agreed. "Him."

"Him?"

"John . . . For God was with him. He gave blessing to many . . . many . . ."

Broaditch half-turned to take this in.

"Blessing," she murmured. She thought what a blessing it would be to sit under the trees at twilight after supper. Have long Bym come visit with his pipes and all sing and nibble sweetcakes while the children ran and played in the mysterious dimness feeling the amazing promise of time.

"He laid his hand upon me," Pleeka said, "and I felt the grace of Lord Jesus pass into me . . ."

She kept her hand resting high on his skull. He was more or less kneeling before her.

"You can open your heart," she told him, "if you choose."

"Ah . . . gracious woman," he sighed, very sane for the moment.

She felt tears and pity. No one could ever become accustomed to real suffering, she believed. Any lost soul, like a starving child, touched what was lost in your own person and would bring any but a stone to hot tears.

"Poor, broken man," she murmured.

"He had the power and the word."

"John?" *Why must there be such men that all believe them and they prove ever false? John . . . Men ought not to believe other men but seek good only in their private hearts and if they find it keep silent . . .*

"Where are they taking us?" Broaditch demanded. "What will they do?"

Pleeka said no more. Rested his face in his hands as the stifling wagon sagged and swayed on and Broaditch sat down in furious frustration.

"Well then?" Alienor put to him.

"Let it come dark," he said, at length, "and we'll see what may be done."

If, he reasoned, *they don't kill us by daylight first . . .*

XXIX

Skalwere wouldn't admit he was beaten and frustrated. He padded on through the twists, dips and knotting of corridors until he found himself by an outside wall where a long sunbeam tilted across the straight dusty hallway that ran into empty obscurity. He peered through a windowslit and saw deserted fields with the sun well above the bluish shimmer of horizon hills. No sound floated up to him. Here, in the upper levels, he felt safe from those dark devils of the night. This place was barren, he realized, long unused . . .

And Howtlande would feel safe too. Somewhere up here. He padded on. Up a circular stair now, in a wide tower . . . came out in a bright room, crouched forward, noting tracks in the floordust, moving with a slight smile and gritted teeth towards a closed, canopied bed that sat between two sunbright windows. He squinted, held his hand up to the shining as he teased back the faded silk hangings with his spearpoint, saw the glare blurred figure lying there.

"Bastard coward!" he hissed.

Thrust in a violent spasm of contempt and fury, shouting:

"Sleep on then!"

Then knowing it was wrong even before he felt the weapon

pierce the too-thin body and no blood gushed to the pale covers on the pale lord, because the bearded face had fallen in on itself and was past pale to waxy bluish, and the whole frame shook stiffly under the blow and flopped stiffly when he yanked the spearhead free and now the corpse lay starfished on the elegant bed. He saw that one hand was missing and that the flesh was desiccated without real rot (except the eyes were not good to study) and he thought:

Why didn't they bury him? What Briton strangeness. Because he couldn't know that this was Unlea's husband, left unburied when the plague decimated the castle folk . . .

Snarling he turned because he'd felt it and knew he should have felt it sooner and was raging at himself, thinking:

He let you believe he's altogether a fool!

The massive figure in the doorway was already taking dead aim with a bow virtually pointblank, weary, determined, spiteful, flabby.

But he'll have to talk, the fat hog, trust him not to just dispatch a man . . .

"So, Skalwere," Howtlande said, aiming steady, "you traitor. The quarry takes the hunter, it seems." Waited, aiming. "What say you to that? Hm, treacherous one?" The Viking crouched and watched. When the finger let go the string he would twist. There was always a chance he might not be mortally struck. "Silent, are you? I followed *you.*" Nodded. The voice was just under hysteria, the other noted, waiting. His mouth tasted like metal. Dry. "All is not lost, Skalwere, that's the point. Which is why I'm loath to slay you. What think you of that?"

He wants companionship, Skalwere thought. *Fire damn you and let's have done!* He was concentrating too hard to speak.

"I say all is not lost," Howtlande insisted. "We bide our time. Find a new company of stout lads, you see? The point is to live! What do you say to that? You're too good a fellow to waste."

He's all cunning and no heart at all, Skalwere thought. *Why wants he life, what savor can it have for such a one? No sense in waiting . . .*

His chances seemed better than he'd imagined.

"And betray the next crew too?" he wondered, playing now. "What use to merely add our deaths to the rest?"

"We all die anyway. It's all in how you do it, Briton."

Dipped his knees fraction by fraction.

"Then why did you flee the north, Skalwere? For honor's sake?" He grinned.

"Never mind that. Shoot and be damned." The spear shook in his hand but by the time he raised it he'd be hit.

"Why make pretense?" Howtlande asked, feeling on surer ground now. This was something well within his province. "We're fine fellows to prate of honor and death."

Skalwere ground his teeth and clenched his fists white with hate.

"Coward," he managed to say.

"Yes, yes, and you were brave to flee your homeland."

There was foam at the Viking's lip corners.

"I flee no more," he mouthed. *It will be seen . . . it will be seen . . .* "We'll be alive," Howtlande was saying, quite unheard now, "and the living have all the advantages . . ." and broke off because the little, stooped man was coming straight on, spear leveled, not even charging, not even trying, coming step by step, eyes popped, and Howtlande realized this vicious barbarian was walled off from any touch save death's, knew his arrow couldn't miss at this range and suddenly feared the demon within the other might not die, thinking this wasn't just a man stalking out of the dusty sunbeams, but his own ruined fate, and he could have wept thinking how nothing ever really worked for him, not at home or with that wipeass Clinschor . . . and now this . . . this . . . always thwarted . . .

"Damn you!" he screamed at the stupid madness of his sullen fate as this final, senseless-as-stone representative of unreason lurched towards him.

Skalwere, not hearing, mind going on and on:

No more . . . no more . . . here's an end . . . let this be the final holmgang, myself with myself in the deadly circle . . . Bared his teeth and howled like a wolf and charged . . .

While far below, the knight in the cellar was leaning on a pillar in fetid, total darkness. He had no idea how many hours he'd been wandering. It had been faintly amusing at first as each attempt at a straight course failed and left him groping from pillar to pillar unable to reach a wall without circling, so that this chamber seemed boundless . . . His thoughts bothered him. They were too vivid in the silent blankness, memories flashed unbidden . . . far away ringings and whistling . . .

random images as if he were about to fall asleep...

He decided to try again. Why not? He let go of the stone support and tried one step at a time. The blackness was an actual pressure. He went on, counting his steps this time, trying that, and had reached ninety, groping, heart racing when he struggled not to run because he knew he'd hit a pillar (they weren't actually round and had sharp edges) and then lost count and heard himself shouting like a frightened child, the cries sucked to nothingness as though the dark were a sponge of all sound and movement and he felt the panic growing...

No echo... no echo...

How far could the walls be? His body had just started to run while his reason hammered at it repeating he'd seen the building by day and it wasn't *that* big except the panic replied: *You're far under the earth by now there's magic here you're on the road to hell... there's no bottom...* He was running now, staggered as his shoulder glanced, ringing, off stone with a sparking scrape and still he ran... then stopped, seeing light... panting, seeing light up ahead... warm, reddish-yellow gleaming.

Torchlight... even if it's killers I'd rather die in a fight...

Closer, the light was diffused. Blinked, strained his vision. No torches... the illumination was stronger at the edges of sight and it revealed no forms, neither roof nor earth nor support, nor his hand held up to his eyes either.

Witchlight, his mind decided.

And then they were there, emerging without perceptible edges from the darkness, faintly reddish, squat, massive, hinted. He drew his sword.

"In Christ's name," he said, "keep your distance, I adjure thee!"

We know thee, Galahad, something somehow said without a voice.

"What? I have lost that name forever."

Now it hath found thee.

"Who are you?" He strained but made out only rounded, almost limbs and perhaps skulls with possible eyes.

What you see, came the reply.

"I see almost naught."

This is the bottom of the world, Galahad.

"No. This is a cellar." He was afraid but fighting back. That gave him security. "A cellar."

Flee as thou willest, all the world will hold thee here. All the weight of it above. We will deliver unto thee all its measures and secrets, Galahad, and make thee great among men.

"I want none of it."

At thy feet are rare and precious gems. But stoop and load thy hands, knight. Stoop! Stoop!

He found himself bending and gathering his hands full. Stood up and filled his pouch until it hung heavy at his armored side.

Believe in us!

He trembled, losing the fight . . . losing . . . He found himself nodding. Others had spoken of the Holy Grail . . . might such things be real and close at hand? Was that why he was led here, was there truth and purpose in the world still? Could men be led in fact by beings from beyond the veil and childhood tales tell soundly and reason fail? Was his life to be born new henceforth? . . . Trembled. Was it possible?

But stoop now and take up the food of eternal life!

He did, gathered handfuls soft and warm, a caressing, rich and soothing to his hot hands.

"Yes," he murmured, "yes . . . yes . . ."

Pass on and behold the glories of our kingdom!

And he realized he'd been still walking. How long he couldn't tell. He was weary . . .

Now there was faint grayish light filtering in from somewhere above. Blinked, focused and found himself in a wide, brick hall. High up there were streaks of light, and he thought:

God, I praise Thee for Thy mercy!

Looked around. Saw a litter of iron and steel, rusted helmets, bent blades . . . suits of armor . . . broken wheels, shattered pottery . . .

A junkheap.

. . . rotting mattresses, broken beds and chairs enmeshed by delicate massings of spiderweb that wisped at his face and further grayed the air . . . all these disparate items were joined and blended by this immense network . . . faded tapestries . . . even a smashed wagon and stacks of mildewed clothes . . . a shattered sundial . . .

He went on.

. . . rusted chains, broken scythes . . . a bent saw . . . a peeling portrait on wood of a roundfaced, jowly man wearing a crown with a seeming scepter in his hand, standing while others knelt, a sleek dog with lolling tongue looking up with adulation . . . Then a wooden door, ajar, brighter light behind it, and it wasn't until he reached for the handle that he recalled the holy food in his hands, held them up and then flung away the muck that coated his fingers and palms, pushed through the door and emptied his beltpouch on the dusty earth in the yard where sun glared as though the ground were melting into flame. Watched the dull little rocks clatter, bounce and scatter . . .

He smiled. Shook his head.

I've been a fool . . . wasted so many years . . .

Headed outside, squinting. Stood in the courtyard staring at a few pale, dried weeds that pushed up through the cracked and dusty earth. Their shadows flicked lightly as the breeze shook them. Those near the failing well under the outer wall where they'd found more precious wetness, he thought with strange wonder, had more gracefully arched forms and were greener. He stared as if the dark he'd just passed through had blotted and soaked up troubles, memories, years, and now, pondering these delicate spears of attempted life, he realized he wanted to make things grow, suddenly, to take land, dig and plant, reap from the miraculous earth! And he knew he wasn't mad. Possibly, he mused, for the first time in his life he wasn't mad . . . Remembered now:

All the fleeing and blood and dead faces and suffering, lost faces of kings, lords, knights, serfs, women, children, all the ugliness he'd gathered since manhood, kneeling finally, not even weeping, by Arthur's body wrapped in furs on the stones near the broken Roman wall where the black and white horse (that stood nearby, restless in the falling snow, tail jerking) had started at a snake and tossed the already wounded lord high (himself and the rest of the party watching in helpless shock) and he seemed to float down, his mind saying *nonono,* as his king rebounded once and then again.

And with the tip of his sword (he could see them now up on the walls and behind him in the yard but he didn't even glance back) he cut a furrow in the hard, harsh, pebbly soil, leaning into it as if this were the real beginning of a new life and hope, thinking how at last he'd found his fit work because he'd left the deaths and bitterness behind in the dark that had changed him and there was only the baking hot sun . . . he stuck the blade upright, tossed his helm aside, removed his mail shirt, then took up the sword again in his light undergarment ... the sun and earth ... all the battles had become one slaughter and all the lives one single outcry and outrage that he didn't even need to weep for ... just the terrific sun on his neck and the now dusty blade cutting, turning the ground, and him digging it along, straining, because he wanted to have done this once, as if he really meant to cut to the world's heart or leave a mark in the marklessness of it ...

Felt the sweat, heat and sweet strain, and knew he wasn't mad, thinking how this was his final work, that he'd been lucky to find it, that few men ever found it even for a moment and he wished, if he wished anything, he'd married and had a family ... but ... and he actually said (they were close around him now, silent, dark), as the first slash bit into him and the shallow line in the dirt wavered, zigged and stopped and blood like rain beaded suddenly in the dust and pebbles, said:

"Thank you for all of it ... for all of it ..."

Thinking as the next and next hit and the sun staggered with the sky: *Even for what was not, thank you for that too ...*

Howtlande's head was already turning with his massively fleeing body, so the arrow hitting home was the last image, hitting dead center in the vagueness under the savagely clenched face that froze his eyes until he broke himself free with the bowtwang and rocked and skidded crazily down the stairs, around and around, the windows and door arches flashing past as finally the great mass of stone itself seemed to immensely spin around him ... down ... down ... fleeing not just death but the absurdity and curse of his life, begging Devil or God or any between for succor because he didn't dare look back in case he'd missed that contorted, mad face. Imagined Skalwere (even dying) on his heels until, at bottom, in the huge main hall, he careened wildly from the stairs and looped and revolved across the room trying to check himself on the slick tile without having to fall, watching the tilting windows and walls speed sickeningly around, feeling the spasms in his vast gut ... brightening windows ... gray walls ... dark figures ... windows ... walls ...

No! he cried out silently. *No!*

Figures, beards, weapons ... windows ... walls ...

Reeled to his knees, already heaving burning bile and foulness into his throat and mouth, crying out through it in a liquid,

explosive howl that spewed out as if the cry itself were a
stinking splash, because fate had him again, on hands and
knees, rage in the spilling too, the vaulted space still rotating,
then pitching over and rolling as the wildly black-bearded face
and wiry, bent, pit-eyed little man with missing toes (the same
who'd attacked Parsival by the stream) came closer and leaned
a shaggy hook of a face inches away (spinning...spinning...),
dark caked short sword touching the floor cane-fashion.

Uarrrrgggghh!" Howtlande heaved out of himself in a final
spasm.

Lohengrin had come out of the trees into grayish dawn-
glimmer and wandered across the fields away from the castle.
He wasn't thinking about anything, just moving on, suspending
all decisions and letting weariness gradually tug and grip at
him and blur and press at his eyes...

By midafternoon, helmet off, sun beating at his black, curly
hair, too thirsty to be hungry, he kept shutting his lids for a
few steps at a time as the fine dust gradually coated his black
and red armor and filled in the gaps and rips where loose links
swayed and flickered.

Dusty fields unrolled, on and on, with spare, browned,
failing trees. He kept hoping for even a trickle of stream or
something that would afford real shade.

A mile or so ahead, low black clouds were packed above
what seemed a dark forest. A long, low wall crossed the stony,
dried field just ahead and he thought, vaguely, he might rest
there...

He blinked and swayed slightly at what he first took for heat
shapes as little dark-cowled men rose behind the wall, dozens
of them, armorless but all armed. He looked around and saw
others at a distance, moving, enclosing him in a kind of bag.

More troubles? he thought. *What a world this is that I've
forgotten...*

Waited, motionless, broiling hot. Winced his painful eyes.
He had no urge to fight. It had all been a miserable dream,
one senseless scene after another rising around him over and
over and himself with only a name attached to nothing, no real
history or purpose to place him in the reeling nightmare and
he knew it was, somehow, deeply unreal, and that he had to
wake from it to...to...to what?...The splinter of pain still
creased the side of his head throbbing in the violent sunbeats.

The bearded men were closing in, some creeping, some walking, some careful, others vacant, starey. He didn't want to fight and he saw no point in dying. His hand suddenly drew his dagger and plunged it into the hard, harsh soil. He stood there, waiting.

Even if I tried to battle, that pain would probably block my strokes again.

He was strangely uneasy as they led him toward the gray, paintless wagon that seemed equally made of dust and wood. The cloaked folk kept close and pressed him on when he hesitated. These bore no weapons and were equally mixed men and women, even a pair of long-limbed adolescent boys in the cluster. There were thousands in sight, moving on steadily. They seemed fairly well fed for these times. Raised an immense cloud of dust that shimmered in the fiercely cloudless sky where the sun beat like hot bronze. The vast migration of them was now approaching the dark hills and forest he'd seen from the wall where he'd surrendered.

Coming closer to the closed vehicle he noticed a narrow plank was missing from the rear door. A pair of dusty yellow mares tugged it along at a moderate walking pace. He'd just stepped over a fresh nest of droppings that appeared from under the wheels. Suddenly he knew this had happened before in the other lifetime, the lost days before the constant pain at his temple. His nerves tensed, heart ticked harder. This seemed important and he was afraid . . . why? . . . tried to remember as the soft pack of people pressed close around him, murmuring indistinguishably among themselves.

Stared at the dark slit, felt watched, wanted to struggle away . . . felt a chill and memory of sickness and shame. Tried to push through the massed, robed people, remembered something: a flash, light . . . lightning . . . fire, a solid blackness opening, a terrible voice commanding or raving . . . wincing internally now away from the hollow, muffled words already sounding inside the slit, rattling the planks as if the laboriously creaking and jouncing wagon itself animistically voiced the inner pain and fury of tortured wood:

"Come closer!" demanded the slit.

It's him, his mind knew, *it's him.*

"Closer," it said. "Closer."

XXX

"Come then," he said, reddish mane swaying around his face above her. She reopened her eyes, not really looking at him, blurry, warm, far away. Oh, it wasn't his fault, she told herself again. Outside the tent she could hear the night sounds, wind flapping the loosely tied opening... voices singing soft chants with a strong beat... They were always singing, she'd noted.

Dour, dour, dour, this one is always dour... always watching me and every least nothing stirs him into deeper glooms... You'd think I'd captured him or whatever was done...

"Layla," he asked, "you do not want to?"

She tried to focus his face. The reddish-dark twilight shook steadily at the opening and shone on Tungrim's pale, stocky, nude torso.

"Oh, Christ," she breathed. "Why don't you just do whatever pleases you?"

Instead of chilling her, the easy, warm wine-sea she floated in softened her bed of stinking, lumpy hides into one of silks.

She felt sly—knowing there was a stone jug of mead under the edge of the straw.

"You're laughing," he said.

She pulled the top covering away from herself and showed him her lean, graceful body.

"Here," she told him.

"I cannot take you thus, Layla."

"My lord, I know no other way."

What does he want? Except she knew. Love. As if she were still a girl at castle Tratinee and this were the naked young fool Parsival kissing her, fumbling, baffled, while she thought: he's a dream stepped from the world of sleep that clothed itself in strong, smooth limbs and sweetness . . . She reached now and stroked, far away, over twenty years away . . . kneaded between his legs, surprised to find softness, began to rhythmically work at it, feeling him stir and gradually fill . . .

"Ah," he said, positioning himself. "My dear, fair one . . . my sleek fish . . ." His beard brushed her face. "Ah . . ."

"Am I?" she asked, opening her legs around him, directing the now straining hard, burning hot curve, letting it work around a little as he gasped and began to thrust. "Easy," she told him. "Not yet. I'm not wet yet." Feeling a brief pain as it caught in a folding of flesh and then (floating into the images so that she opened in a sudden flooding) letting him spear into her with a breathless shock. "Oh." She held him and watched the images: she was in a warm soapy bath among rose petals, the water soothing, sweetly draining, and a beautiful woman with long blond tresses wearing a pale shift soaped and oiled her body and there was daylight at the large, sunny windows where roses moved slightly in the syrupy air and she watched the lady's seacolored eyes reflecting her own nakedness in the perfumy suds, gave herself (as even in this fantasy) with a small thrill of something sweetened with sin and fear . . . let the image fingers slip smoothly down across her body to where she ached and sighed, softened . . . burned . . . desperate . . .

"Oh," she said, as he rocked on her, into her in the now blind dark. "Oh, Lord Christ! . . . Lord Christ! . . ."

The fingers flicked, stroked, circled . . . then probed . . . paused . . . pinched . . . vibrated faster . . . faster . . . clawed . . .

I need this, her mind insisted, *I need . . .*

"I love thee!" he cried out. "Layla! . . ."

And now the mouth, hot and sweet and sucking into hers, the honey taste triggered by her loins (beyond the beard and harsh, rhythmic bones, knotted elastic strength and fierce mass of him), the sea eyes absorbed her as the slick tongues probed in echo of the long, easy, slick sliding down below, between . . .

"Ahhhhh . . ."

Beard, pounding, arched gripping maleness, plunging maleness melting into the edgeless resistless taking in and in . . . always in . . . deep . . . deeper . . . deepest . . .

Later the air was dark and cool. He was sitting up, squatting on the covers beside her. She wasn't even trying to see where he was. His voice floated out in the tide of dream and recollection surrounding her, sleep overlapping, lapping at her mind, body feeling boneless, saturated . . .

"I want you for wife," he said.

She moved only her toes, very interested in the process. He almost had to say it twice before she responded.

"Everyone in this bed is married already," she said, murmured.

"I have considered these things."

She was trying to wiggle just the big one without moving the others.

"How something or other," she said.

What a dour prince he is . . . in truth . . . Prince Dour of the North . . . They make love well and except . . . I don't know what? . . . Men have strange minds . . .

"I say I've pondered this," he insisted.

"It's impossible," she murmured, trying to move the toe, tensing her calf too now.

"Nay," he said, gravely. "There's a way."

"The others move no matter what."

Try as she might the little ones winked with each attempt.

"What, woman?" he asked. "Hear me. This is a hard thing. But I will put aside Jana according to just Norse custom."

She gave up on the toes.

"Why?" she wondered vaguely, drifting again . . .

"Because I want you."

"I have a husband," she murmured, closing her eyes, thinking she also said: *The son-of-a-bitch . . .* "But it's the bleak country you come from," she said into the draining seapull, thinking: *Makes you so dour . . .*

"What? You speak oddly, woman. Are these not important sayings we say? Not many Vikings would make such an offer to an outlander. If he lives I'll find and slay him."

Wonderful, she thought. *There's a ready answer . . .* She felt pressed flat, numb and more numb . . . She couldn't even move her foot now. *Slay him that's a fine dowry . . . dour-ry . . . what does this man want? . . .*

"Christ," she said, as the numbing dark washed over her, sinking her at last. "What do they ever want?"

"Who?" he asked, somewhere far above the surface. She felt her lips move and that was all. Sank into silence. "I freely do you this honor."

Then just sat there staring at the invisible tent wall before his face. He held her firmly with both hands but felt he gripped at running water or a wave and would be left with a few mere drops of moisture on his fingers in the end . . . Brooded over this in silence now. She resisted nothing and that may have been the worst of it. He wanted to leave a mark in her. He realized that. She never struggled and he wanted . . .

He sighed. Baffled. Shook his head at himself. This was just a woman, why did it matter so? . . . What did he imagine lay in her flesh or mind to so draw him on?

"Do you sleep?" he wondered, huskily. Listened to her breathing. Wondered how it would be there with her under cold skies beside ice-green water . . . timbered huts, long snug nights . . . dancing, singing, drinking, fighting . . . snug by the coals while the snows sank the world in ghostly silence . . . How warm life was there . . . how clean and bright fire was there . . . sighed . . . yawned . . . lay down as if to sleep and stayed furious, tensed while she snored . . . murmured sweet formless phrases . . . shifted slightly, eternity away from him . . . waited as sleep fleetingly batted at him from time to time . . .

Waiting hot and bleary for the agonizing dawn and knowing he couldn't talk himself out of it, that he'd want her again tomorrow because he didn't know and couldn't face what he really needed, what lust was merely a mask over.

Love is such comfort, he thought, savagely twisting to the other side, away from her. Lay on his belly. Felt himself hard again. Rocked his hips a little, part consciously. Felt painsweet pressure . . . pictured her body and wanted to do things he'd never imagined with Jana: press with his face and reach with his tongue . . . rocked his hips . . .

Next morning he stood with his captains, eyes swollen, haggard. She was still in the tent. They had camped in the dark last night at the border of what they now saw was a strange country that rolled away into the horizon's sunglare. A land, he was thinking through his headache, of ashes, of charred, limbless trees like poles row on row, crumbling, blackened blightscape.

"I say we turn aside from here," one of the stocky men was saying.

"See how sudden was the ending of the fire," a bald man put in, "as if it struck a wall . . . see . . ." Pointed. ". . . there are other trees untouched a few steps from that rim of blackness." Shook his head. "I like it not."

"Mayhap," Tungrim added, "all the rain was used up at once and now there's none left to ease this country's parch."

"Give me the sea," the bald redbeard said. "Leave this for the Britons."

"We go on," announced Tungrim without even emphasis. Shielded his eyes.

It's the right direction, he thought, *to come to the water again.* Because the rest hadn't realized they were in serious trouble yet. No flowing streams for days. No rainfall since they'd left the coast. He'd given up on finding the traitor, and the booty he'd insisted they were after was chimerical because this land would yield nothing.

"We go on," he repeated.

"I think you err, Tungrim," redbeard said, scratching his shiny pate.

"You trust me no more?"

"We love you," said the first man, the roundest.

"One may love deeply," Tungrim said, "and trust little."

"I think you err," the older man said and shrugged this time.

"Well, let time teach us that too," Tungrim concluded. *Who never taught me wisdom either . . . what can a woman be to so draw and intoxicate my thoughts? . . .* "Strike the tents," he commanded, "and yield but a cup of water a day to any but the sick."

As he reentered the tent they watched him, the morning sunbeams hot in his red-blond hair and beard.

"Back to the woman," the round one said. "She looks not so lusty."

"Ah," said a third, dark-haired, slimmer with a lipless mouth, "his eyes tell the tale. He's like a guttering torch."

"The sea," baldhead stated, "the sea will clear him."

"Not of that," said the third, shaking his longish head. "Or hills or snow or sleep." Kept staring at the tent as if to read some further truth there in the bound and tethered hide walls. "Nothing."

XXXI

The sun was beating noon into the hardening earth under the scorched weeds and bleached, spindly underbrush.

They stopped to rest by a long, thin curve of what was recently a stream that fed the river, now mud and scattered pockets of watery silt. The peasants, men-at-arms and others were arranging themselves in spidery scraps of shade.

Gawain had removed his helmet and had wrapped his bandagelike, vaguely oriental headdress over his mutilated skull. He sat near Parsival and Unlea, who were standing side by side not directly looking at one another.

"I always have news for you, Parse," Gawain said from the shadow of his strange turban.

"Which this time?"

"You know I spy things out."

Parsival nodded. He was thinking about being alone with Unlea. Noted a broken wall running along the opposite rise parallel with the vanished brook.

"Yes." He waited.

"I think your family . . ."

"Family?" Thought of the knight in the dark who said he was Lohengrin. But that seemed absurd . . .

"Wife and daughter."

"Yes?"

"One, I think, is living."

Parsival remembered the chopped bodies, chopped faces, his wife's necklace as he tossed the grave dirt over them . . .

Unlea was staring at him. The sun beat like a hammer on an anvil.

"Which one?" he finally asked. Gawain's good eye was bright under the hood shadow.

"I know not. I met a raider, a Norseman. Lost from his fellows, he were." He shrugged. "It came to blows . . . a matter of a horse."

"Where's the steed?" Parsival smiled.

Gawain shrugged again.

"Fate is uneven," he said. "But we drank together at first and said a few things, tightlipped though these barbarians be."

"He spoke of *my* family?"

"Not in so many words . . ." Gawain raised an expressive hand. "But you know my ways." Shrugged.

"You ever tell me things to change my life."

"Why believe this?" Unlea put in.

Gawain leaned back, the shreds of shade flicking over him.

"It may be true," he answered her. "He were drunk at the time he spoke. The facts were blurry. He said the *woman* was with his chief. But mother or daughter, I know not."

"Or much else for certain, sir," she said.

"Like many things," he said, "it may be true or false."

"I think it false," she said.

"Which may be true," Gawain was amused to respond.

They went up to the wall together and sat on the shade side. Parsival was quiet for a time, reflecting on Gawain's information. He'd looked for his son, found a murderous shadow in the night who called himself Lohengrin. Now his wife or daughter might still live.

They reclined in silence, hands almost touching on the hot, brittle ground. The twisted, burned trees squeaked slightly as they creaked in the light winds.

"So," she said, at length, nothing showing in her voice, "you'll have to look for them, too."

He stared and she watched him stare.

"Too?" he answered, abstracted.

"What about your son?"

He shrugged with his mouth.

"Hm," he responded.

"That's passing fine. I can go home."

He touched her hand, which she neither gave nor withheld. It felt cool and smooth.

"What?" he wondered.

"I've a fine future before me."

He touched her cheek next. She looked weary. There was discoloration under her eyes. He remembered how she hated to travel . . . Her nose was sunchapped.

"Unlea," he began.

"Did you come back for me?" She didn't look at him now.

He hesitated and knew she knew it. It was so hot. Heat waves shook along the stones just above his head. His whole body was sweating.

"I came back," he said. "But I need your help now . . . in this business . . . I can't turn my back and forget . . ."

Her hands rested at her sides. Kept her profile to him. Her hands were soft, pale, not even tense . . .

Later, the sun slanting down the far side of afternoon, in roughly single file, they were crossing into what already was being called the "ashlands." Miles on unending miles of forest country destroyed during Clinschor's war for the Grail. An immense chunk of the country had been charred to dust, even their unhurried footsteps raising a fine, black, choking dust. Some, like Unlea, had tied light scarves across their faces.

Parsival and Gawain were at the rear.

"The problem," Gawain was telling his friend, "is coming clear."

"How much water is left then?"

"A half-cask and some skins."

The ashes whispered underfoot and billowed a little whenever a hot breeze stirred.

These are the worst, thought Parsival, looking at the almost limbless trees that stood oddly stripped into isolation where there had been a dense mass of forest. *They poke up like poles in hell . . .*

"You're sure," Parsival asked, "this is the best way?"

"The shortest track to the coast, which is our best hope."

As Gawain walked, the charpowder gradually dulled his armor. "There'll be food and water there if anywhere. The ocean trade . . . and, mayhap, word of your son or whoever."

Parsival grunted. After a few more steps:

"I don't know what to do," he confided.

"About what? In the main, we have few choices. When in the sea, sink or swim."

The sun was at their backs now, pushing shadows gradually out before them. Parsival's reached nearly to Unlea. He thought the sunheat was like bearing a weight.

"No," he said.

"The woman," Gawain didn't actually ask.

They moved uphill and deeper into the black desolation. Following what might have been a riverbed or a wide road, fairly straight, ankle deep in ash. There was a structure ahead, dark, massive stones, a broken turret and high wall. Gutted.

Nothing but rock, Parsival reflected, *not even steel could have kept shape in those fires* . . . He remembered the unbelievable wall of heat and fury, howling, hissing, booming, melting armor like wax, bursting flesh . . .

"Smoke?" Gawain was surprised. "Here? What's left to burn?"

A crease of faint vapor rose behind the soot-stained walls into the fiercely blue sky.

"Hm," muttered Parsival.

"Where there's smoke there's folk, the peasants say."

"Where there's folk," Parsival amended, "there's murder and misery, more times than not."

There was no gate, just the open archway into the castle yard. Unlea and the surviving peasants waited outside as Parsival and Gawain went in.

Nothing stirred. The castle was squarish, not large. The terrific heat had cracked the foundations. Several sections had crumbled, opening into vacant dimness. Here and there were shapeless spatters of metal. Gawain suddenly stopped.

"A well," he said.

They peered into blackness driven straight down into the earth. Water smell, no doubt about it.

"Here's fortune," Parsival remarked, looking around for the fire now. Studied what he must have been a formal garden beside the inner wall. What looked like statuary, standing or fallen, grouped where the walks and prospects must have been. The smoke rose from there.

Except what he'd taken for statues were young men and women, lying, sitting and standing so perfectly still it seemed a spell must have held them. Gawain, who was not in the least traditionally religious, crossed himself as they came closer.

Stopped by a young girl, slender, hair long, stringy, oil-twisted, quite naked and covered with soot except for startling clean streaks around her mouth and hands. Her eyes were shut, hands held over her head, long fingers hooked as if to grip the hot, substanceless air.

"Well," Gawain wondered, "does she breathe?"

She was pretty, Parsival noted, under it all, but hollow-cheeked as if she ate shadows. The lids suddenly snapped open and large, blue eyes glowed at them without seeming to focus.

"Girl," Gawain asked, "how long have you stood thus? What ails you?" When she didn't respond he poked her side with a blunt forefinger.

Parsival was looking the rest over: a nude boy with clean flesh showing too, where he'd obviously cupped the water to drink, was sitting on a stone staring at the blackened wall, head nodding continually as if in perpetual agreement with something unheard. Another male lay on his stomach, undulating slowly as if (the gray-blond knight thought) miming a failing snake, grinding himself into the black dust. A girl lay on her back, just her hands moving, clenching and unclenching in the ashes that had practically covered her so that she seemed to be growing or slowly dragging herself out of the lightless ground.

"Can none of you weird creatures speak?" Gawain demanded. Then drew his sword and aimed the point at the buttocks of the undulant boy. "We'll probe for truth," he announced.

"Nay," said the other knight, "they're all mad. Leave them."

And then, without looking at them, the first, standing, blue-eyed girl was speaking, staring over the stony wasteland before her.

"Ah," she said, without a peasant's accent, they noted, "men of shadow."

"What?" asked Gawain. Sheathed his blade with almost regret. "Say on, girl."

"Girl?" she wondered.

"What else?" Gawain cocked his incomplete head, artificial hand resting on mailed hip. "She's bent for sure." Turned to go. "Let's take some water and proceed apace. This country is a nightmare." He headed for the well whose blackened stones poked out of the ashy swells of ground.

"Where are your people?" Parsival was searching for a point of contact. Her strange madness kept pricking his fear. Gawain had lifted a bucket on the end of the pole.

"Shadows," she intoned, rocking slightly back and forth. Then she screamed with sudden violence, blackened hands over her face. She screamed into them. Gawain glanced up, pouring water into a leather bag. "Thirst!" she screamed. "Thirst!"

And Parsival turned thinking a demon from hell's heart had risen before him: a round face, all massed black beard and a preposterous beak of a nose that looked as if the whole head had run into it. Short, covered with soot, genitals a black obscurity. Unlike the others, he moved with purpose. He was chewing something (clearly he'd made the fire, Parsival concluded) and holding a gourd in his hand. Gawain was just taking a long pull of water and then strapping the waterbag across his shoulders.

"Let's be off," he called over. "Leave them to their writhings."

"Horror of shadows," she was moaning, fingers over her face.

The gnomelike man (the only adult Parsival had seen) gave her a long swig from the gourd, which she lapped down, greedy, trembling. Sighed and shut her eyes, weaving as if to music.

"What does this mean?" the tall knight asked the beard and nose. The fellow silently held out the gourd. "Can you speak?"

"Do you not thirst?" he wondered.

"I'm content for now. Who are you people?"

"Parse, come on," called Gawain from under his load.

The nose-faced gnome kept the drink up to Parsival's lips.

"This is the water of life," he said. He seemed a man made of charcoal.

"Parse!"

The girl rocked and rocked, hands on knees, clean mouth smiling now.

"I came for the children," the burnt-looking man explained,

offering the water still. "This is haven for the lost folk. Freedom for those in chains."

"What? To grovel in filth and burned dust, raving?"

Gawain shouted this time:

"Cannot you part yourself from these delightful companions?" he wanted to know.

"A moment," Parsival called back.

"The world is burned away," the nose and beard informed him, sloshing the liquid slightly. "Here it is ever springtime and all wounds are healed." The undulating boy had reached the base of the blackened tower and was wriggling his head into it again and again like some blind worm . . . the girl on her back had reached behind her head and was gripping a massive chunk of wallbrick, caressing it with long, bizarrely tender strokes . . . "Drink, shadow-knight. Join the peace of the children."

"I fear I'm tasked with the strife of the adults," he told the strange being.

"Mmmmmm," sighed the girl, rocking in rapture. "Mmmmm . . ."

The gnome aimed his face of bristly darkness at him, letting the drink drop back to his side.

Parsival licked dry lips. His saliva felt gluey. The sunheat was sucked into the dark earth. The air pulsed as at an open furnace. He wanted to drink but something said: *wait*.

"Come to my sweetness, shadowman," the swaying girl said. "Come to me . . ." her hollowed face flickered with tension.

"She invites," the nosebeard said. "Taste the sweetness, the honeywater of life." His voice was whispery. The boy still writhed his head into the wall . . . the girl twisted and embraced the stone . . . and there were others stirring here and there around the yard . . .

Parsival turned and strode away after Gawain, who was heading for the road. Something in him was still drawn to them and feared . . . feared . . .

Went out the gate through the ovenlike afternoon. He thought he understood and was saying to himself:

It doesn't help. None of it helps . . . they try but it doesn't . . .

The stars were bright over the dim wasteland. Unlea had just gone into the silken tent. Parsival stood, uncertain, just without. The peasants were sitting quietly, depressed by the unrelieved desolation beyond anyone's imagination. Heat, thirst, weariness was wearing and wearing... He was surprised to hear someone singing and realized it was Gawain.

And not a dirge either, he thought, smiling a little.

He rasped, but not unpleasantly, a lilting ballad. You might have danced to it... Then Parsival's mind refocused on his own situation. Stared at the closed tent, while Gawain's incongruously merry voice shaped itself in the hot, close evening...

After a few more restless moments Parsival pushed the flap back and went inside. Sensed her sitting in the empty dark where his straining sight touched nothing.

"You honor me," she murmured.

He knew from her voice it was all right. He let out a long breath.

"Unlea," he said. "Do you want me to leave?"

"Make not a farce of it."

"I'm sorry. Forgive me." He sat down near her voice. Felt the wisps of her breathing, a faint, sweet scent. She managed to keep surprisingly clean, he realized. Knew he must be getting fairly rank, himself...

"Never mind sorry," she said. It was still in her voice. Obviously.

"Unlea, I—"

"Nay," she cut in, touching his lips unerringly in the dark. "Pray, say so little as you might."

"I..." his lips tried under her fingers.

"Nay. Naught, I say."

He stopped and then felt bare flesh, soft and shockingly limitless.

Ah, he thought, *yes...*

Things were suddenly running too swiftly... too much was unexplained... what did he really feel? Her hands were plucking at his linen shirt, touching soft, sleekhanded.

He kissed her, held himself into it, shifting his nose to better breathe. She pressed herself up into him. Even in the dark he seemed to see her there, apart from himself, somehow surprised by the idea that she was so intensely, desperately groping, drinking at him as if sweetness would flow from his flesh, and he couldn't release himself into it, thinking she was somehow dreaming him, that her end was a dreaming and he wanted it too, the comfort of losing himself in it... thinking too how many tears he'd kept for this moment (he still heard Gawain's roughly lilting song over the ashy stillness of the night), missing her, missing the dream of her...and now, locked invisibly out, he knew it was going to be hopeless even as she helped him with his shirt and tight-fitting pants...

He shifted around beside her, naked, and her hands kept gripping and pressing his smooth, muscle-thick chest and wide back, thrashing her loins over his leg, startled (because he was cool) by the wet, burning contact, and he kissed her breasts and belly, arms, hands, shoulders, neck and felt hopeless as she struggled herself tighter and he tasted sweat too and inhaled her musky sweet and sour and his own harsh smell...thoughts were too rapid because he was trying to convince himself:

This is good and sweet look how beautiful she is and all yours to use as pleases you...

Ran his fingers between her legs, probed rhythmically into the hot wound, felt her open to him and gasp into that frenzy and still he floated far, hopelessly, above it...

This is good this is lewd and sweet...

Touching himself (turned so she couldn't tell what he did), hand racing, trying to hold the lewd images of whores in stews and fucking...tense, sweating...aware he'd created this problem because he believed it was too late to relax and start again...And then there it was at last in spite of his mind floating far from the locked coolness of his body (his sweat lay on him like ice), there it was, growing, filling, slow and sluggish but definitely improving...he concentrated on it, half oblivious of her except to keep free of her limbs and hands so she wouldn't know. There was moist heat and perfume on her breath as she licked his neck and face with intense abandon that seemed to push his mind even further away so that he could, nervous and desperate, only long for relief, wish it could be as in the past...remember from far away what it had been like to be fused in the forever of loosened moments...straining, pulling, testing and turning his indecisive and treacherous organ with her breath at his ear:

"...my love...take me...my love...I give myself...take me..."

Strumming himself now with almost fury against dull and spiteful flesh he levered himself over and between the thighs that she reflexed wide and he, afraid to wait, chanced everything on a semi-flaccid thrust and was amazed to find himself sealed safely within and next began to violently, tensely jerk his lips into her fluid outlines (as if all the love-skills of twenty-odd years had never been), gradually lengthening his strokes as he rode more securely and finally, confident again, holding himself back from the edge, feeling strong, smooth and easy and then, remembering her at last with a start of guilt:

"I love you," he told her quickly, "ah, sweet, dearest Unlea..."

Except he somehow missed himself in the middle and knew it and the fear multiplied suddenly... Unlea rolling her head back and sobbing and squeezing her legs together, asking in sighs:

"Where are you?... Have you spent? Love?... I cannot feel you..."

Stopping now, cold and furious. Silent and hopeless above her, all muscles tensed and rigid but for one, not even able to be amused yet when she said:

"It's all right, Parse... peace... just a moment more..." Rolling her futile hips against his futility. "A moment, pray, dearest love..."

"I'm out of moments."

"Oh... very well... it's all right..."

"It's not all right."

"Your hand, my love," she softly pleaded. "Please... your hand then..."

As he was moving aside he heard it and went to his knees, frowning, and silenced her:

"Be still, woman. Wait..."

Listening and then the strange cry repeated. Something between a wail of torment and awful joy. He went to the flap and leaned out into the warm, burnt-smelling air, blinking at the failing moon just over the eastern hills... voices... then the cry again, closer, falling into a strange, infinitely prolonged sighing.

He clutched his tunic and went out, scanning the lessened darkness, now silvery, cold-lit. His shadow showed and a blot: a figure stood on a rock outcropping against the wall of dark beyond that was impervious to moonlight.

"Gawain?" he called, watching the figure. A woman's voice, a commoner by accent, spoke nearby:

"He's lost his wits with the moonrise, me lord."

The figure on the rock (that he now realized was his friend) howled again and began to emit long drawn-out hums:

"Hummmmmm...Hummmmmmm..."

The woman's voice floating, directionless in the pale night:

"It were the moonrise done him. He come loose in the brain when the light touched him." Voice smoothed by time and use, hard like a polished stone.

"Gawain," said Parsival.

"Ahhh," was the apparent answer, "my mother comes."

"Gawain?"

"So fair to see sailing above the treetops in sweet white-silver..."

"Gawain." He could see he was watching the moonrise, arms upraised, pale linen head covering phantasmal in the gleaming air.

"Away! Away, you shadow!" Gawain cried.

"What's wrong?" Unlea was calling from the tent. The peasant voice answered:

"He come mad by means of the moon, my lady, as I have seen before. Meg Tweensel went to all fours like a dog... Have I not seen the like? Oh no, not I, not I."

Parsival gripped the entranced knight by the arms, shaking him where he perched on the ledge.

"Shadow of nothingness," he was informed for his trouble. Then a howl—terrible, feral: "Awwwowwwwwwwwwwwwwiii! O lovely mother I sing to thee! O mother of the night I thirst...I thirst!"

"What dread is this?" said Unlea, close behind him now.

Another peasant, older voice, male.

"He be drunken, then, the lord knight?"

"Nay, nay," said the female, "he fell to the moonbeams. In my village..." She went on and the man cut over:

"Mad then, is he?"

She was grave:

"In sooth. Mad."

"Ah."

Gawain leaped down from the rock and embraced his friend.

"Such beauty and wonder!" he cried from under his pale hood. "I am all wonders of light and time." He danced in an ecstatic half-circle. "The dark is all brightness..." And, uncanny, howled again.

"The Devil hath him," the male voice explained to the increasing, semivisible audience.

"Aye," another agreed. "And why linger we here in this place of hell? Eh?"

"It's the moon," the woman insisted, "not no devils."

"Drink the water with me, Shadowparse," Gawain insisted. *The water,* Parsival understood, *there's something in it*...

"Gawain," he said, "hear me..." Broke off as the older warrior was trying to stand on his head in the absorbent blackness of ashdust where the moongleam was swallowed totally. Then, falling, laughing, coughing as the fine powdery stuff caught in his throat. "Bring a light!" Parsival yelled. "Find that damned skin of water!"

Rushed past Unlea (a pale robeshimmer—feet vanished into the pitch, lightless earth) who asked: "What?" and stormed towards the steady charcoal fireglow, almost snarling: "Get that damned skin!" Because he was afraid and didn't dare even think that maybe Gawain had mixed it in with the main drinking supply because then he'd have to deal with finding fresh water here... "Find it, in the name of Jesus!"

XXXII

When the door opened and the hot, dusty light blasted into the closed wagon Broaditch crouched with his family, holding his arms (with the loosened bonds) as if helpless. Two men stood in the golden glare, armed. Studied their blinking captives for a few moments.

Pleeka worked his way towards them on his knees. A third man crouched between the other two, tall, angular, hair wild and uneven and without the beard nearly all the rest wore.

"So," Pleeka said, calm but tense, "you come at last. Brave enough to look at me now?"

"Ah, Pleeka, my brother," the tall man, John, said.

"Spare me *brother*," snarled the other.

"Peace. Our ways are God's ways."

"Mama," Tikla suddenly cried, "I'm afraid, mama."

"Hush, sweet thing," her mother crooned.

"Cease blaspheming, dog," said the man with an ax.

"Stay thy righteous fury, Garp," John commanded.

"Cracked John himself," muttered Broaditch under his breath.

"We were to save all we could and who we could," Pleeka accused.

"That's done with now," came the smooth, certain answer.

"Planting is done and now comes reaping." Broaditch saw his eyes, how they rested nowhere, like Pleeka's.

"Reaping what?" the ex-lieutenant demanded.

"Life," insisted John, in his best reediness. "Life!"

Leena and the boy were crouched by the door. She kept her eyes closed because the brightness pouring in had become the soft, water-rich fields surrounding her grandmother's castle (where her father had been raised, and it was a legend to her, a dreaming), where the flowers in the grass were jewelstain and the sun sparkled on old stone that seemed soft and she felt long sweet easy days under an almost moveless sun and quiet voices in cool shadows, as if all summers were distilled and suspended in yielding, goldenwarm crystal . . . there were no marks or rents and she could watch this landscape without darkness and the other terrible stains that she refused to name or color . . .

We'll get there, she was thinking, *soon . . . soon . . . God will light our steps and hold back the darkness . . .*

"Take these," John said and the axman reached in and dragged Leena and the boy out into the violent, streaming daylight. "I give you your chance, brother. Rejoin the Truemen or perish."

"It's always perish," Broaditch muttered. Felt a rising heat and hate. "With these mad bastards." Snarled. *Again and again and again,* he thought, hating.

"God will deliver me," Pleeka said with scorn (Broaditch rolled his eyes), "and cast you and the beast to destruction." He laughed, not pleasantly.

"What will happen to those children?" Alienor called out, cold, furious.

The axman, short, bushy-headed, leaned in, closing the door, the halo of sun left his face a hollow blackness. His voice was fanatical, stony.

"The brothers and sisters will take them to themselves," he informed her.

And then the door slammed the darkness into them, blank and palpable.

"Well, husband," she said, "what do we do?"

She felt him stonestill and concentrated.

"Wait for nightfall," he muttered. "Wait for nightfall."

Pleeka began to sing quietly, madly to himself, mumbling . . .

"Just wait . . ." Broaditch said again.

"We cannot help them . . . not a grain's worth," she said to no one. She didn't weep. "Not a grain's worth . . ."

Walking behind Clinschor's closed wagon, surrounded by Truemen, Lohengrin was leaning close to the slit in the paintless door and made out the figure within, sketched in the dimness by vague and dusty fingers of light: the bony man rocking on an uneven stool, long face and madly twisted moustaches plastered to the sweaty, grimy, greasy face, pale, washed-out, bluish-gray eyes peering from under the terrifically knotted brow, graying hair stringy across the forehead.

"I know you," Lohengrin said, with wonder, bushy brows raised, setting off the beaked nose.

"I called you to me," Clinschor asserted. "You have returned to me." He saw his magical fire reaching out and touching the young knight.

Lohengrin thought the unwavering eye had a spectral glow, as though its light was not all reflection of the day. Lohengrin vaguely recalled a deep dark place and this voice commanding him and strange terrors whirling all around.

"I know you," he murmured again.

"I need my loyal ones." The eye was close and he moved it as if screwing into the other's, inches away on the other side of the crack.

And as Leena and the boy were being hustled past they saw the knight following the dilapidated wagon, as if his nose had been tacked to it, and she opened her mouth already crying out before even shock or tears (because she knew that hooked profile from the cradle), struggling for the first time since capture, tugging towards him as they pressed her away into the black, choked, advancing horde of beards and hooded women, shouting:

"Brother! It's Leena! . . . Brother . . . Lohengrin! . . . Lohengrin! . . ."

He pulled his face from the eye in the slit for a moment, looking for the voice he thought he'd heard. Clinschor's bass rumble had muffled all other sound . . . saw nothing but the somber marchers wading through the clinging dust in long, uneven masses like, he thought, insects over the parched fields at the border now of the skeletal, black forest.

"Look at me!" Clinschor demanded. His forehead was flat against the inner boards so an eye seemed sole and suspended in the dark strip. Lohengrin blinked at it.

"We near the end," the rumble intoned from around the eye. "I have been resurrected," it confided. "My forces are gathering about me. My day is come. A few have been chosen to survive these days whence I may bring the golden kingdom to pass! I have been resurrected to this end."

Lohengrin blinked.

"Tell me, if you know," he said. "Who am I?"

He saw the flames again, everywhere . . . billowing, massed smoke . . . crashing like hell's surf, armies sinking under and bursting into flame . . . heard this voice raging, ringing hollow like steel and stone above the bursting fury . . .

"You are my right hand," came through the slit. "My angel of power. My loved one."

This seemed colorful but unenlightening.

"Is my name Lohengrin?"

The eye grew sly. Squeezed its lid.

"Son of him," the voice rumbled, "who kept it from me. Son of the Grail-thief."

"Whose son?"

Things were coming back, pushing to come back through the again mounting pain in his head that was a white-hot wire drawn through the left temple, searing, beating through the skull, blanking, damming back floods of remembering. He sighed with pain. The sun beat and beat and beat at the back of his head and he staggered suddenly, leaning both hands on the splintery wood that rocked and tipped and fell on and on away from his twisting, intercaught steps as he reeled and weaved and tried to grip the flat wall . . . falling away . . . away . . . caught somewhere, falling, saw the light-haired man (he knew now was his father) riding in rain and mud out of the castle gate, his mother, Layla, following and himself, shouting something, in fury and misery, then words too:

"You don't love us! You never loved us!"

And then that fell away and his mind was all alone in darkness crying out:

Father . . . father . . . father . . .

And then it was night; the march had paused. Broaditch crouched by the space in the wood he'd managed to enlarge by fingerchapping scraping and prying for hours with his belt buckle. He could see the campfires, the glow sucked up by the charred earth and trees.

Unsteady silhouettes moved past the flames like beings of shadow. There were fragments of what seemed garbled singing. He tried to see how many stood near the wagon. Didn't have enough angle. In any event, there was no choice but the risk or stay here. Spoke over his shoulder:

"You," he hissed, "Pleeka. Your hands are free. Will you join with me?"

As he spoke he set his powerful grip around the edges and braced his torso into it.

"Aye," Pleeka said, flat, inflectionless.

"You wait," Broaditch told his wife. "If I come not back by moonset, find your way north by east and trust to God. If I live I'll follow after. I always do."

He pulled, slow, steady, hands swelling with blood, until his sight was rent by white flashes and then...then the old boards gave, twisted...snapped dully. Cool air washed over him. He stepped, panting, carefully out into the firegleaming darkness.

"I am your father," the lanky, beardless man was telling Leena, sitting stiffly upright on the burlap tent floor, dark robe, pale face and hands lit by smoky lantern light that redly gleamed on the expressionless faces of two girls in their midteens, lips set, big eyes darkly watching, robes tight to the necks.

Leena just watched him, on her knees close to the hide wall.

"Where did you take him?" she wanted to know.

"I am your father," he repeated, touching the girls.

"My father is Parsival," she said. He paid no attention.

"All things are holy. We celebrate life in all things." She saw his meat-red tongue slip out and along his underlip. "I wish you to join the sisters." One of the girls reverently kissed his hand, eyes dark, showing nothing. The other smiled faintly at Leena or perhaps at some secret...

Leena shut her eyes to see what would be there: the bright vision of the castle or the stained, bleeding landscapes... nothing...just the purplish dark of her flesh. Reopened them.

"Come here, child," John told her. His pale hand made a softly jerking motion.

She stared. Didn't move. The girl who'd smiled crossed over to her.

"He's the father," she said, quiet, confident.

"The world is over," the other one said.

"He leads us out of the darkness," said the first. "I knew this when first I heard his voice."

"I knew too," said the other. "I knew."

"I was alone on the road fleeing with the others from the fire and the sickness . . . My parents had traded me for grain . . ."

"Ah," murmured Leena, sympathetically.

"I passed through many hands," she continued. Her dark hair hung very straight behind her. Leena impulsively touched her arm: cool, dry. The girl went on in her strange, hushed fervency: "Father freed me from the dark life. Father freed me. I have found peace. We all were hungry and now there is food."

"Yes," John said, smiling and opening one long hand to her. "We are Truemen. Keepers of holiness and the scourge of the unrighteous. I shall be the father of many nations. I am that am, the father and the blood of Christ and His flesh also." His hands shaped at the air and his lean head tilted from side to side as he spoke. "I give my children holiness and life. The life from within me. The father shall give you sweet delights to heal your pains." He shut his rapt eyes. "Child, come to the father, bring your torn heart to be healed."

And the dark girl held her hand, swaying her across the red-lit space, feet bare and quiet. Leena stared, doubting, for a moment, hoping:

Heal . . . can he heal?

Everything was blurry from strain, sleeplessness, hunger and fear . . . blurry . . . She staggered and the slim girl held her . . .

Broaditch moved carefully across the charred, whispery earth, staying behind the bare, depthless treeshapes as much as possible.

They were moaning or singing again. Chunks of burnt wood and branches crunched softly underfoot as he worked around closer to the banked fires that were mostly charcoal glow and little flame.

He hadn't had to debate it with Alienor because you didn't start deserting children. Not in a dying world where all you had to keep was how you felt about what you'd done with life.

They seemed gathered in a compact mass around the long pits of hot coals. It looked like a pig roast and then he smelled it broiling, sweetish, fat rich and he realized how hungry he was.

Fresh food, no wonder they moan like that...Speculated about carrying some away with him except there never was a safe way to do anything.

Found a stone after poking around in the sooty ground: the size of his hand...Moved closer to the crowd. Heard a terrible, muffled scream, tearing, frantic, drowning itself in a sloshing gurgle. His neck hairs prickled. The droning chant went on...

He moved around a dim treehole and was almost among them, holding the stone inside his loose shirt. The wavering coal-light melded everything into general shadow.

Stepped, jerked his foot back from sudden softness and squatted over what he instantly knew was a body. One of them. Dead? Asleep? Poised the rock to strike. The limbs were quivering and Broaditch stemmed a cry of pain when his thick finger poked into its chomping mouth and (because Broaditch hadn't identified it yet) was shocked by the snapping gnash, and then the man went on quietly thrashing through his fit and Broaditch stripped off the garments (sweating, straining as one suddenly stuck), then tossed the cloak over himself and tramped on into the crowd, thinking:

Fate or chance?...Fate or chance?...

The wind veered and the heavy, sweetish smell from the pits broke over him. The strange moaning song was all around.

Someone (not John) was calling out a blessing and the crowd stirred as steaming, dripping hot hunks of meat were passed from hand to hand:

"Here is the gift of life from the father. Let the father hear our gratitude that we perished not but were fed by his word and wisdom! Amen!"

"Aaaaaameeeeennnnn," swept through the crowd. Broaditch winced at the heat billowing up from the pit. Shadowy figures with poles were laying what his mind was still trying to see as hogshape, the outspread, cloven trotters, the tapered snout, except his eyes were insisting against his brain on the long legs and arms and the face, illumined by the puff of burning hair as the already swelling, charring features writhed in hideous parody and madness and he knew he wasn't going to escape because he wasn't going to be able to stop himself (thinking of the girl, too, afraid to look or not look), turning, unaware of the stone in his hand, not hearing the half scream

of disgust, fear and fury so intense as to blast his movement
into a white, silent, obliteration, two of them already down,
not even feeling the impact on their skulls, kicking, smashing
into the shadowy crowd, roaring as if to hold off weeping and
pain, flailing on, converting even shock into a mad charge,
doomed, the rock already lost somewhere in the shouting,
screaming, only stone fists and feet now (too late to stop or
flee, thinking of Alienor moments too late to matter), fighting
suddenly for life and whatever slim chances were left to break
out of the crowd into the open night . . . too late, hearing finally
his own bellowing voice; sucking breath and screaming; snarling:

"Slime! . . . Slime! . . . Slime! . . ."

Striking, veering as blows jarred him, lanced light into his
head . . . endless hands caught at him, bodies jamming closer . . .
closer . . . biting, foaming, clawing now . . . and then he was
face down in the choking ash still fuming and heaving in un-
quenchable anger, the voices a meaningless rushing all
around . . . spitting the bitter dust from his bleeding mouth, still
trying to curse them . . .

XXXIII

"We were set upon," the long-haired Viking said, breathing hard but evenly, the soot coating him in patches, running with sweat and blood. "They slew Rufflo and Walgrim. There were too many so we fell back." Three others stood with him facing Tungrim, bloody and blackened as well. The sun was coming up towards high, white, violent noon over the desolate black landscape.

"You slew in turn?" the bald, red-bearded captain asked.

The soldier nodded once. Pointed.

"A great many. In dark robes. Half a day's march ahead."

Layla and the mule were stained, as was everyone, by the dark strokes of this terrible place. She watched Tungrim covertly. She had a headache and no appetite today. Felt drained and remote. She looked at him and thought, without phrasing it, he'd won . . . she wasn't going to struggle about it . . . no struggle and strain . . . there was no better way to go, and since she wasn't dead yet what difference did it make?

At least he's a man, she told herself. *At least he's that . . .*

Watched him push his hair from his eyes as he spoke and gestured, one fist tilted into his hip. The men, at his commands, moved into compact packs, spreading out among the black, ruined trees, raising the fine black dust like smoke, round shields cocked, horned helmets flashing the relentless light. Hundreds of unflinching, untiring fighters moving with grim accord; here and there were shieldless berserkers with axes only, moving apart from the others: mad shock troops ready to race at death, to welcome blows and destruction as others might sink into a lover's kiss and groping soft sweetness of arms...

She watched him mount his bare-back pony and turn to her. She wanted to say something but couldn't yet. Was still accepting everything with a kind of numbed hope because all her dreams had bled and burned away to this char and there was nothing better or worse so she'd live... and wanted a drink of wine. Licked her dry, chapped lips as he pointed to the circle of carts.

"Follow behind with these," he told her.

A few camp followers, wounded and one or two older warriors were occupied there.

"Yes," she said.

Two of his chiefs waited as he shook his head, baffled, annoyed.

"You think me so dull," he said, "after your Lord Fops."

"No," she said.

"You anger me, woman."

"There's a hole in me nothing can fill."

He squinted through a frown, then smiled. Guffawed.

"You still think this," he said, relaxed for a moment. "I must mistake my size like a fisherman the catch he lost."

"Not that," she replied, not even amused outwardly. "This hole I pour wine into without end." Then she smiled too.

"Come, lord," redbeard said.

He snapped the reins and started off, the dust smoking around him.

"Well," he called back to her, "like a stripling, with each fresh hope my spirits rise. Let me go then, with hope, my strange, fay Briton lady."

"I cannot prevent hope," she said, still smiling. And as he rode on ahead there were words in her mind:

You may hope indeed, rough sir, but you'll need to hold up my end of the pole ... She looked towards the carts. *One drink is all, to soothe me* ... *I'll have but one...it'll quicken my appetite...one only*...

Howtlande was all sweat and soot, tottering, corky arms lashed to his sides, prodded by the spearbutts of the epically unkempt Truemen. His captors drove him and several other survivors of the fight across the sea of ashes, wading and tripping, the sun on his head like, he thought, a metal hammer.

He walked behind the single bowlegged and filthy horse they'd loaded with half-a-dozen corpses. The limbs and heads jounced and rocked stiffly where they poked through the ropes. They'd buried all their own dead, left the rest to rot, so why bear these along? It was baffling but that was the least of what troubled him.

Even with a swollen tongue, blurred eyes, mouth half choked with soot, he kept trying. That was his nature. Kept cocking his head and squinting significantly, raising his eyebrows, running through his various routines like a spring mechanism, desperate and widely ignored, still at it even as they reached the loosely bounded, inching mass march:

"... you see, my friends," he was saying, "you see, I could have great value, a man of my years and knowing..." panting as the mallet sun beat without cease and his head floated a little and eyes blinked futilely at the bright shimmering blackness everywhere. "... you see, never to waste a man like myself... for I've plans... great plans... for great deeds!..."

One of the bleak fellows, eyes like glass chips sunk in wild beard matting, tall, stooped, spoke sidewise at the bent, steel-sprung older one who'd attacked Parsival by the foul stream in the swamp that now seemed a precious camp to have given up, for they'd seen no thread of water since.

"Rozar," he was saying to the other, "here's rare feeding for the brothers and sisters."

Rozar ground his gapped teeth together, reflectively, bouncing along, steel and fluid quick, shin-deep in the oddly slippery, grinding stuff. One arm swung low, anthropoidic.

"Why bring'm back?" he wondered. "Why not stay as was? That's what I ask."

"Because it's for the folk, Rozar. For father."

"Arrr," was the reply as he jammed the long, warped spearshaft into Howtlande's sweating fatrolls. "I ain't so certain."

"You don't believe in father and all? Him what brought us to succor and safety?"

"Arrr," semi-shrugged the older man. "What was we before? We do the best we can, mate. And what we must to live. This John be not the first wight to promise all and more to come, and yet see the world's to all a cinder still... arr..." Prodded Howtlande again. "What care I about *believe*, lad? I cross the bridge seems soundest and go on."

"Well," remarked the more theoretically-minded youth, scratching his frizzy beardling, "we serve father in diverse fashions."

"Right now," Rozar allowed, "he's got the mill a-turning so I'll grind me bread at it. The rest of you be free to mumble prayer as you best please."

"Well," said the youth, blowing his nose into his hand and flicking the results into the black dust that seethed like smoke under their feet, "I believe God blessed us and what we do. That's what I believe."

"I ain't putting my hand in your mouth, lad. Say what please you."

"Else we'd be the worst than beasts," said the frizzybeard. His glasschip eyes flashed fanatic, nervous. "God blessed us, as father says."

Howtlande glanced behind as they neared what he didn't know was Clinschor's wagon.

"You seem a fellow of sense," he directed at the older man, whose eyes were like black pits. "A fellow of my own innards, I think." Caught his breath. The day danced and swayed. "You'll find . . . good use for me."

Rozar tittered.

"We will, we will!" he practically shouted and in an excess of glee struck him a terrific blow across the back that puffed the coalblack dust as if he'd exploded and Howtlande fell on his face, weeping with agony. "We'll find a fine use for this partridge." Tittered. The other helped Howtlande rise.

"When father leads us to the land of plenty," he said, flatly, blankly, "we'll eat fit things again." His eyes were widened, pale through his scraggles of beard. "We do what God wills!"

"Reap the crop that grew," said Rozar, grinning. "Dream not by the empty furrow."

The chip eyes stared. Howtlande tried not to really understand what lay behind their words. He felt sick, chill panic deep within . . .

"I believe these ills will pass away," the young one said. Others were now cutting loose the corpses up ahead and tossing them into a flatbed cart as the march crawled on.

"Meanwhile you feed like a churchyard worm, lad," Rozar suddenly snarled. "Don't dream of dainties! You're a worm and that's that! Look what we are . . . your fancy God smiles on us?" Rozar tittered. "Look what we are, you simple ass.

Think you Christ guides mad John? Aaarrr! Know you not your
true master, worm? Eh?" He gripped the other by the greasy,
sooty folds of cloak and pulled him off balance. "Your griping
belly, is what! This be all there is! No more . . . We're all
graveworms. You silly shitstick!" He flung him away and
strode on, one arm swinging low, hooked below his knee as
he stooped along, furious, kicking Howtlande and the other
pale prisoners on. "The world's a grave and we're the worms
in it." Face locked with concentrated rage as the victims cow-
ered away from the blows. "Some eat and some are et!" Howtlande had lost his speech at last. "You kept enough fat to be
sweet," Rozar let him know. Grinned. "I know not how you
kept it. The stars bring fortune, it would seem, even to mag-
gots." Tittered suddenly in fine (if mad) humor again. Howtlande said no more, struggling to keep, he hoped, ahead of
more kicks and blows . . .

John was riding one of the bony horses. There were a few
left here and there. They'd been saved when God revealed the
new diet.

The widespread horde was funneling into compactness as
they moved into a gradually narrowing valley, following the
ashchoked bed of a lost river.

Howtlande was roped like a strung fish with a line of others
behind one of the two closed wagons. He kept squinting at
John, who wasn't far away. They were all near the head of
what was becoming a lumpy column. At least, he realized, the
terrible sun was now cut off by the steepening walls.

About a dozen Truemen came limping and straggling towards them. Most were wounded. Howtlande watched them
reporting (just out of easy earshot) to their leaders.

"How far was this?" John demanded. He glanced up at the
darkening blue sky.

"Few miles, father."

"And?"

"We left the fresh meat ahead."

John still was looking up.

"Good," he said.

"Savage men," put in another. "Norse bastards such as I've
seen on the coast."

Howtlande looked away, restless, agonized, exhausted.

He was first in line and stared randomly (through blurring
skullpain) at the black-stained boards bobbing along a few feet

in front, and then started, stung with fear, because the eye was watching him out of a strip of blackness and his mind said: *It's an animal!* And then he remembered exactly what it was (just as Lohengrin had) and was just trying to shake off the notion when the muffled, unforgettable voice vibrated the wood, earth and his insides too and he thought:

No . . . Good Mary . . . How? . . .

"The unseen hand reaches out," the voice was saying, "and brings all things before me that were far off."

And then, after panic, he understood it wasn't addressing him at all.

It's he . . . it's he . . . I should have known the Devil wasn't finished with him yet you don't throw away a sword with a chip or two in it . . .

Lohengrin braced against the rocking, crouched near Clinschor, who was still staring back at the narrow slice of dark ground and toiling prisoners.

"I have a circle of magic surrounding us," the bony man confided in a confident rumble. "Nothing may penetrate it."

Lohengrin could see Howtlande when he shifted his head, arms stretched out by the cord as if in prayer or supplication.

"Tell me about myself," Lohengrin demanded again. Memories shifted and pressed around him. He reached for one; saw the blond knight he now believed was his father holding the slender dark woman (had to be his mother), only this time both of them were crying as the image eluded him, blurring where he most sought to focus . . . like rain on reflecting glass . . . they were speaking and he strained for the words that blurred away . . . "Tell me," he insisted and felt the large, soft hand touch his shoulder, flutterlight.

"You are my chosen son and heir," the big voice suddenly decided.

"Your son? But—" Winced as the wagon banged and a lance of pain sawstroked his skull.

"I make you heir to all my fortune and power . . . I name you Bungamarl! That's a magical name and will set your enemies in terror . . . Understand me, boy . . . understand me . . ."

"But I want to know about my past, I—"

"At the end of this road lies my hidden power and wealth untellable!" He nodded. Outside Howtlande was cocking an ear through his misery, catching a certain amount of this conversation. Enough to stir deep-revolving thoughts. Clinschor's eyes rolled without particular focus in the thin strip of paling light. His hands fluttered and shut in midair as if he meant to grasp the sunbeam. "Yes, yes, yes, all my enemies will perish soon . . . Men have all turned to beasts but I'll learn the spells to restore the golden world . . ." Sat there and rocked and now stared out at the bloated, filthy, bloody face of Howtlande.

"What road?" asked Lohengrin.

Clinschor saw it again, with an obliterating vividness: there were no walls, no outside or inside, just the sweet tropical trees bending over a motionless blue sheen of water in a city of white tile and graceful bridges where golden bells and jewels sparkled in the boughs and graceful, tall, fair men and women strolled and sang and ate sweet dates and admired the massive statuary and all the white roads led and climbed the central hill where the soaring temple sat on intricate columns and the Grail pulsed in there like a great dark heartbeat filling the air and earth with power, saw his body upright on a magnificent throne above the Grail itself, smiling, unchanged with centuries and the people of his empire never ceased to come and marvel and weep with love as each generation told and retold his story: the maker, the founder, the father of the great, golden race . . .

Yes, mother, if you'd lived you see it too, he thought, suddenly cranky.

Remembered her round, indrawn face . . . remembering was suddenly unchecked and he saw her clearly, saw past days in the south of Italy where he'd become a knight . . . not recalling what had been sealed over, the hurt he never touched or looked at, not seeing again how he'd waked, blinking in the torchlight, the flames thrust in his face as he struggled to sit up in the tangled bed, the woman just covering her face, shadows leaping along the yieldless wall where he now stood, pressed back from the bearded faces, the glitter of eyes that were cold and amused too at his naked flesh as he panted with terror, distantly imagining that the wall would open and he'd be free, racing away through the dark, safe corridors that were so close, just a foot of stone away . . . safe and dark . . . trying to talk, say something, not really registering the voices, his uncle there just a harshness, a hopeless wall of chill words and then he was fighting because he couldn't flee, flames jarring, no blade touching him, just gripping, hard, terrible hands and garlic-creaking, sweaty brutes bearing him down, spreading him out on the bed, screaming like a child as he absurdly swung the pillow at them, trying

to kick away the hands, just hissing breath now and the grunting
voices, on his back on the silken sheets. His uncle had just tossed
her out. And she vanished into the darkness beyond the torches.
He kept imagining he would suddenly escape, they'd forget and
he'd get out too or she'd bring someone to help him except there
was no one . . . felt the cold armor close all around as they pinned
him motionless and his uncle's voice suddenly, sinkingly, hopelessly clear: "Your father's sister. My wife. Make no plea to me.
If you would live, hold your peace. Say nothing about love, you
unnatural monster." And then (he'd sealed it all over) the knife
blade glittered like ice in the wild, smoky light and at first it felt
cool, slicing quick and sure and then the terrible pain and his
wordless throat bellowing, bursting as the edge sheared between
frenzied, locked legs and the blood drained into the sheet and
from far away (because he couldn't even lose consciousness yet)
he heard her voice too, high, shrill, quite mad . . . He stood in the
hall, pacing in his robes with the lucid sunlight soaking into the
dark rugs and Italian tapestries while his mother watched him,
stolid, unmoving.

"You may go without me," she'd told him.

"Mother," he'd said, sawing the air with his arm, "you don't
understand."

"I understand. You and your great plans for everybody else."

"Come with me. See for yourself how I deal with the world."

She shook her head.

"I care not," she responded, eyes tracking his pacing, lean
body as he passed back and forth before a blue shimmer of window.

"I shall triumph," he insisted. "Nothing will stop me. I am
called to this."

She shut her eyes. Now there was sadness.

"Oh, Clinschor," she murmured, "Clinschor . . ."

He stopped and stood there, blocking the daylight.

"Mother," he said, "there's no reason to . . ."

"Pity you?"

"Nonsense!" His big, thickfingered hands began plucking at
his robe. "I won't fail. I have renounced ordinary life. Men like
me—"

"I've heard all this, son. Next you'll tell me about the secret
power. Sooner or later you tell everyone *that*. I wonder they believe you in anything."

"Mother, you have no imagination. There's the Grail. I . . ."

She was within herself and the weeping was invisible from where he stood, and not quite in her voice either as she overrode him.

"You were always a lonely child."

"Mother!" He was furious, hands leaping into fists. "Stop it!"

"And then that terrible thing was done to you." Her tears were steady. He rolled his eyes and turned his back.

"None of it matters," he said. "None of it matters . . . None of it matters . . ."

"You never listen . . . I've borne it . . . everything . . . Christ knows! You . . . your father . . ."

"Leave him out of it!" he yelled into the painted, red tile wall between the windows. "He cared nothing . . ."

"That's not true. You were hurt and lonely and—"

"It doesn't matter! It doesn't matter! It doesn't matter!" Suddenly he was hitting the bricks, fists slamming. "Leave me in peace!" Winced slightly as he cracked his wristbone and the pain drove through his arm and then he was standing there, leaning on the wall. "Just leave me alone," he sighed. "I beg you. Please . . ."

She blinked away the last tears.

"You're my only son. My only . . . So I'll bear this too . . ."

"What did I do for you?" Lohengrin was asking, repeating. "In the past."

Suddenly Clinschor was holding the young knight's beak-nosed, dark face with both hands, pale gray, strangely luminous stare pouring cold, almost frenzied intensity into the other, who blinked as if suffering a palpable shock.

"Ah," the aging man said, "good Bungamarl, I feel it . . . I feel it close at hand . . . the Grail is close at hand! . . ."

As the soft, large fingers squeezed over the scar Lohengrin winced and this time the pain was a clear memory and he tore himself free as if to reject the image with the moist touching, fumbling fingers, seeing the troops he knew had been his own, chopping down women and shrieking children by a burning hut and felt himself gone cold thinking: *They die sooner or later what matter when?* Saw himself leap out of a glitter and tangle of berry bushes crashing his mace into a mounted man in a group of others and knew it was done for pay, without even hate . . . all the hunting and hurting flowed over him, burning his mind . . . saw a young girl looking up into his face with eyes refusing to weep as he thought: *Hurry, little slutling, I long to spend . . . spend into your fair face* . . . and then, wordless, she took the hard, curved length of him and let it slide, hot and salt-tanged, between her bruised lips and he heard himself saying: "That's good, you whore." And saw the tears now and rocked in and out thrusting himself deep into her flushed face . . . "Work your slut's tongue!" he commanded . . . and now, still flinging the puffy hands away from his face and saying:

"No . . . no more . . . I want no past!" Scrambling, scrabbling at the door, pushing so it banged and flipped open and he was already leaping (Howtlande actually calling his name and starting to talk) and running in one motion, tearing through the dusk-mist that was gathering in the blackened valley, thinking rapidly as his body acted of itself:

No past . . . no past . . . I don't want it . . .

Not hearing Clinschor's cry behind him:

"Bungamarl! Bungamarl has been caught by the enemy!"

The head pain was maddening and he saw more flashes, memories, earth and air twisting, bouncing as lightning hit and ripped everywhere on the high place, figures all shiny black with fiend faces, all silver snapping teeth, steel men, all battling on a narrow strip of ledgelike trail, a batlike shape, great wings billowing and flapping around it . . . no . . . a robed man flourishing a thin spear . . . coming closer . . . a big man, peasant, bearded . . . and he knew (as the tilted landscape leaped in shocked light and wind and rain exploded) the man was fighting him, slipping, dodging backwards on the slippery trail. He rebounded off the cliffside, as he closed, slashing through the blunt wall of storm, blade sparking on the stones, flinging open his vizor to better see (suddenly realizing the robed figure was Clinschor) the massive peasant (shown frozen and freed with each strobe of light) whirling something around his head (a sling?), and then it leaped through the violent air (*a stone*, his mind said), caught by a flash, flash, flash, and twisting his head too late, white violence tearing into his mind, blanking it utterly in a soundless blazing stun . . . his whole life lay still and open before him, as if he watched from a vast mountain height, and saw himself within himself saying wordless and absolute: *No more, I won't feel that anymore no more* . . . And there was nothing but the feelings now, as if a cloud gathered edgeless, weightless, shaped by itself, shadowed and lit . . .

He paused, running, and shook his head, blinked at his memories . . . then there were little horned devils taking form out of the twilight and he blinked at them, suddenly hearing the shout-

ing all around, and screams too, and clash of arms; whirling he
drew his sword in pure reflex as the savage little men (not *that*
small, however, he realized) drove him back and he hacked and
ducked for life and backed into something, a wall behind him he
didn't realize was the second wagon: stroked, kicked, stabbed
at the round shields . . . blocked ax strokes . . . spear jabs . . . cuts . . .

John was just remembering the new sister. Remembering
the scene in the tent last night. He was still hoping to master
the need, in time. It was the devil's tempting . . . a terrible
struggle . . . It would ever build gradually so he'd keep his mind
lifted over it, refusing even the memory for a while, as if it
had sunk forever out of knowing . . . kept his mind on their
goals . . . everyday planning . . . just as now he'd been concentrating on the best way to use that madman he let them believe
was a spirit. It was in God's interest to do so. What a piece
of luck it had been. For a moment he'd almost believed it
himself . . . almost . . . well, after all, God had spoken through
him, in a sense . . . well, they'd follow the poor wight's path,
for now, since one direction would serve as well as another
until they swept up whatever sinners were left living in the
name of the avenging God. He wasn't thinking about the girl
now . . . in the name of avenging God of this Armageddon . . .
eating the flesh, consuming the ungodly . . .

He half-consciously rummaged through his pack and drew
out a strip of salted meat. Began chewing, idly, thoughtful.

Shifted in the saddle, squinted into the gathering evening,
the too warm breeze steady in his face. Purpose, he reflected
(keeping the girl far away now) never let the brothers and sisters
degenerate into purposeless brutes as had the peasants he'd led
in abortive and bloody revolt so many years before. They would
fulfill the avenger's wishes and remain pure. Pure and clean
with minds on clean God!

Chewed, swallowed. Reached up his waterflask from the
mount's withers. Shook it, frowned as he sipped. They were
thirsty. It would get worse. God was drying up the earth. The
chosen would be known by survival alone. Looked up again
at the darkening blue between the valley sides where a few
traces of cloud drew a subtle red glowing like droplets of fire
or blood. He smiled and one of his captains nearby nudged
another and said:

"See, he is pleased."

He had a new sign and felt the thrill of it. He felt an almost rapture. All thoughts of the girl and that business were remote now. His hands came together of themselves.

"He prays," the second man, stumpy built, observed.

A sign... how sweet to feel this intimacy with the vast, mysterious form of nature... how far he'd come from youth when he'd raged in frustration at his father who sat smug in his castle life... then as a priest to a silent God... later stirring up the dull serfs, stuck in hopeless mud and failure after failure... hopeless pursuits... and as the fangs of invasion, plague and social breakdown closed around the land he'd followed that crazed knight, Gawain, and sundry cutthroats on the trail of what they'd sworn was the Holy Grail that would change the world . . . nothing changed . . . years, black, empty, silent years... and the new war that at first he hadn't understood was the judgment come at last and an end to bleak time, cold stars and unconcerned suns marking his vacant life off... an end to stupid, meaningless eating, sleeping, boring knights, dry scholars, blunted monks... he might have died a miserable little priest working a vegetable garden and losing his sight over stale books while great lords went hunting and got drunk and plotted petty overthrows of equally uninteresting neighbors or to set a silly king on a tottering throne, while peasants hoarded grain as best they could and merchants haggled for gold to line their coffins. And now the world and time lay all around him like potter's clay to shape and finish, and the heart of it whispered inmost secrets in his mind's ear with voiceless certainty... Now!... At last!...

The blood, he was about to say, *we will drain off all the blood and seal it...* He stared at the droplike clouds high up. *Oil to keep it from thickening... in clay jars!*

"God has shown me," he began, "that our people may not thirst and perish in the wilderness and dark places of the earth! Until our wanderings are done we..." Broke off because no one heeded and at first he saw only his own people running back and striking blows in a senseless frenzy until the horn-helmed men (he instantly knew were Norse warriors) charged out of the gathering shadows, yelling, and clashing their weapons...

Broaditch sat up in the dark, rocking wagon, his body merely successive knots of pain that no posture could ease. They hadn't even bothered to tie him this time. Alienor leaned close.

"Alive yet again," she murmured. It was hard to believe.

He made a sound, then spoke:

"Spare me words . . ." The interior tilted one way, his brain another.

"Poor man."

"Need I say," he groaned, "all went not to perfection?"

"What of the girl and boy?" she asked, holding tightly as they banged over series of deep bumps and wood creaked terrifically.

He saw the image and refused to hold it, replaced it almost desperately.

"I didn't find her . . . I suppose I was an ass again . . . You ought to have fled while you could."

"Aye," she said. "And what of the lad?"

He shut his eyes.

"Let it pass, wife. Ask me no more."

Tried to get his feet under him and the pain came in series like (he fancied) pinching stone hands. Blinking hard he realized one eye was closed and one tooth at least was wobbly. His tongue found yet another broken. Her hands were gentle on his head and still he winced and heard her gasp touching the lumps there . . .

"Sweet saints," she whispered.

"Peace," he whispered, faint and sick to his stomach. "My top is better . . . better than many a knight's helm . . ." And then he felt soft as water, slid, somehow, out from under himself and only dimly felt the hard boards bang into his wide back . . . then he was awake yet again.

Just let me take a moment, he thought he was actually saying.

"I'm up," he finally articulated. ". . . a moment . . . don't drag back the covers like that . . . I'm up . . ."

XXXIV

Gawain was quiet now. Parsival hoped he was sleeping it away. The madness. The peasants had settled back down near the last, purplish coals. Someone was snoring, steadily, rattlingly.

"He drank bad water, you say?" Unlea wanted confirmation. She was stretched out on the rumpled sleeping silks in the dark tent. He sat by the open flap, staring out towards where he knew his friend was lying, not really visible, a yard or so away: just now and then a hinted metal gleaming seemed to surface when he may have stirred slightly.

"Parsival?" she added, querulously.

"So I think," he told her.

"Will he recover?"

"Am I a leech to know this?"

"No. You're the great Parsival."

He folded his arms, eyes tracking in the hollow darkness.

"Need I be mocked?" he wondered.

"Do I mock?"

"I know not if you do not," he sighed.

"Mayhap you pained me."

"Forgive me then."

A pause. The snores went on. There were no insects, no normal night sounds in that wasteland.

"Will you not," she said, slightly hesitant, "come over here?"

"Hm?" He was preoccupied. "In a moment..."

Now what? he was asking himself, staring at shapes so vague that the night seemed to press flat and close against his face. *Now they say my family lives...I used to dream of this woman and now she's here...my life is an endless wandering...now what?...Content lies not before or behind for if it be not with you where you are you'll never come to it...*

After a while he moved within and touched her. Though it might never be recovered, he would try because she was alone and needed...him?...Something, needed and that was reason enough.

And then he heard the first scream out in the darkness and thought:

Gawain!... Then: *No, that's a woman...*

And then he was charging outside into tumult, panic, another scream, raw and shrill and terribly long...

He drew the dagger (he kept for woodcraft) and raced past where Gawain had lain (not registering that he'd moved—only later realizing he would have tripped otherwise), plunging down towards the sounds into and among dim forms, demanding:

"What is amiss, curse it?"

"My lord?" A man.

"Yes. Who cried out."

"My lord." A woman. "My sister. Here all cut and horrible!" She was hysterical but quiet. "All wetness and terribly opened...oh...oh...oh..."

"What? What?" he snapped. "A light here!"

Gawain? Gawain?

And the greasy, sudden torchlight (lit on fanned coals) showing the woman, belly ripped from chest to groin by half a dozen ragged strokes.

He grabbed the torch and raced through the night, blindly angry at everything and for the first time in months (perhaps years) ready and ripe to kill, sick of madness, horror, frustration...

And then saw the steel gleam ahead through the wildly shifting tree shadows his light flung everywhere and charged on up the crumbling, charred slope, the fire ash in his nose and mouth, yelling now:

"Gawain! Gawain!"

And the big knight turned, helmetless, head uncovered, single eye bright; the dark a deep pool in the missing side of his face where the bared teeth were terrible . . . and then he realized Gawain wasn't even looking at him.

"What have you done?" he said, raged. "What have you done?!"

Panting, holding the dagger up like a pointing finger. The staring eye didn't see him. "Gawain!" He stepped closer, not looking at the horrible side of his friend. "Gawain . . ."

"There's no such name," the other said, bending the half of his mouth that could into a smile. "He's gone at last. WE drove him off."

"Why did you slay that poor woman?" The light boiled through the smoke, the flesh seeming to melt and reform in the flameflow.

"Woman? I need no woman." The terribly bared teeth glinted dead white. "I am both and whole now . . . whole . . ."

"Whole?"

"Behold!" he suddenly yelled, pointing the handless arm at the virtually halved face. "Whole! Whole again!" The eye was streaming tears, over the creased, handsome cheek and jaw. "At last . . ."

"Show me your sword, then," Parsival insisted. "Show me!" He didn't know why it mattered so tremendously but it did and he wasn't really focusing on the rest yet.

Gawain seemed in ecstasy, looking far beyond the shadowy figure before him whose part-naked form shook like a mirage in the flame.

"Gawain is gone," he was saying. "Gone . . . and we're healed . . . Task not us with what Gawain did . . ."

Parsival jerked the other's sword free and saw it unstained, a clean glitter

Who ripped her then? he asked himself.

"Gawain," he said, "come back and rest for a time. This spell will pass. It was but the strange, tainted water you drank."

"He's gone and we're free, being of no substance." His voice was exalted, serene. He seemed, Parsival finally realized, deeply sober. "We're going away. What matter the means so long as there is healing? This is all poor Gawain ever sought . . . This is all . . . and now it's found. His body and soul restored again. This has now been done." The single eye shut and reopened. Next he began walking into the night, leaving the other knight standing there holding the superfluous broadsword, watching the other melt beyond the ring of flame into the leafless, limbless trees...

On the way back to the fire Parsival felt eyes in the darkness: swung the torch a few times and stepped aside. A hint...a dim gleam that might have been eyes, possibly an animal, he reasoned. But who ripped the woman? Why?

There were other torches now and the little group huddled near his tent. Unlea was wrapped in light robes, streaked with the inescapable soot. They'd covered the slaughtered woman with a pale fabric.

"Is that his weapon?" Unlea asked.

"Yes."

"Did...where..."

"Gone," he told her, still taking it in, understanding it, thinking: *It may be better who am I to say nay? Of all poor, hopeless, sad men, who, by Satan's piss, am I to say any other nay? Let him be whole and so please him*..."Gone," he repeated. "Gawain is gone..."

"This place is damned," somebody was saying.

"I say we fly now," another male added.

"At first light," Parsival said, "we go on. Build up the fire. I'll stand watch." Lifted the sword and bent and flicked the torchlight. "None will come too near." He tried to spit the black dust out but it sucked the moisture from his tongue. "Bring me water," he said, seating himself on a round stone, his back to the tent. "Try to rest, Unlea," he told her.

He was suddenly thinking about Layla, his lost wife, remembering the first time they'd drunk too much together, so many lost years past...rolling in the grass together under a sweet, clear autumn sun...in bed winter nights, discussing the trivialities of the day, the absurd pomp and silliness of court...analyzing the infighting and lecheries of the castle... and her revealed hopes told in trust, dreamings, remote to his knowing, yet fascinating childhood wherein she'd once walked and it gone past anything but a reflection of a reflection, something he could never know, roads he would never walk...and he knew she was still there, had always been there all along and it had been all right until he found Unlea again and she was really free this time and now he had to face that as well...that she was really free...and Layla was still there too...

He half-consciously took the flask someone handed him, tilted it up and drank, barely noticing the water was slightly bitter, almost fizzy...drank deep and set it by the rocks.

"Might I stay by you, my love?" Unlea asked.

He didn't look up.

"Better to rest, I think. You'll need all your energy come the morrow."

Sat with the sword resting across his knees until he knew she was gone. Set the flickering torch in the earth before him, watching the flames shifting on the absorbent blackness...the others settled down again away from the dead woman. Sat waiting for the dawn.

Took another drink. Blinked at the slow, starless night ...Blinked again sometime later...the heat was steady and thick and he felt wilted, a film of sweat soaking into his shirtlike garment...drifted into sexual thoughts...wondered if he'd always have trouble. Blinked, then kept them shut and then was struggling to reopen them as if they were somehow sealed skin to skin...he felt deadly watchers close around, keen steel looks cutting from the darkness...couldn't feel the stone under him now or the hot night air...couldn't feel himself, as if (part of general numbness) he'd melted into the surroundings without being able to feel them. He struggled to wake up from what he believed was sleep and then he knew, saying or thinking:

The water...the water...they gave me the water...

Sat there locked in night, afraid, shadow-watched, losing all sense and shape of himself, not even feeling the heart he knew would be racing on, only the words in what had to be his mind giving any proof that anyone existed there:

The water...the water...

XXXV

Sounds of battle, clash, screams, raging curses, indescribable tenseness everywhere, unmistakable, and this time he got his haunches under him and brushed Alienor aside. The wagon was stopped now. Moved to the door through the stiff bursts of pain and heaved against it, then stood up, giddy but intent, and kicked once...again...on the third it gave and the twilight (bright to him for an instant) showed the swirling fighting and then a bareheaded, link-armored knight appeared, panting, several horn-helmed Vikings leaping and cutting in at him like a wolf pack, and then the knight rolled up into the doorway as a wave of robed, shrieking fanatics broke between them, and the fighting swept away for the moment...

Broaditch looked at Lohengrin's aquiline, brooding face, bush of black, curly hair, eyes like onyx stone, and knew him instantly. For some reason he wasn't surprised: remembered that face leaning out from the canopy in the whore's bed long ago...the old nobleman lying there, blood bubbling from his stabbed chest, the woman trying to slide away, Lohengrin's cold black eyes holding Broaditch as the steel-wrapped arm almost absently flicked the dagger into her and the cold voice hissed at him where he stood between the rows of tentlike beds, saying he'd die if he spoke...and then the next memory, the battle on the narrow ledge above the Grail Castle in the in-

credible storm that seemed to tear the earth apart, dissolving
it into wild clouds that broke in lightning-rent surf over the
peak, rain a near-solid mass, the beak-nosed face glaring in icy
fury out of the opened helmet as Broaditch spun the improvised
sling, flinging the dull, heavy ball (he'd found in the Grail
Castle) in a last, desperate try, the hurricane wind veering it
as the knight twisted away. It seemed to follow him and then
(because the lightning was suddenly intolerable) explode in
brilliance as the wind took Broaditch over the cliffside and
hung him on the air in impossible suspension...

All this in one recall and he was already saying:

"In a stew how can you tell fat from lean?"

And Lohengrin crouched and watched outside and inside
at the same time, sword half raised.

"What?" he asked, stared hard. "Know you me?"

"More to the point, sir, is the reverse the case?"

"They say I'm Lohengrin."

"What say you?" put in Alienor.

He watched the blurry, continuing fight.

"My memory is torn," he said, "and I'm no longer sorry
of it."

"Do you serve these...foul..." Broaditch had trouble
getting it out. "...*things?*"

"No," said the young man. "I serve no one. I want to lose
myself."

Broaditch nodded, painfully shifting his thick legs out the
door.

"There's an ambition to commend, sir," he remarked. Studied the dark gleaming eyes that seemed less cold than he'd
remembered. Clapped his steel shoulder with a big hand. "Let
me get a spear and we'll lose ourselves together." In the last
wash of day the battlers raised a terrific cloud of black dust.

Some cover, Broaditch noted, as he helped his family down.
They all moved around past the halted mules: ears and tails
jerking, eyes white, the driver hanging upside down from the
traces.

"You knew me too?" Lohengrin asked.

"Lightly, Sir Knight."

Tikla was whimpering. Rubbing her face.

"Stuff in my eye," she said.

"Well," Lohengrin insisted, "tell me nothing. Do you hear?
Nothing!"

"So please you."

And then the knight rushed past, as Broaditch was picking up an abandoned spear, and met two charging robes, zipping their daggerlike blades, springing from a long roll of ashcloud.

"You are not brothers," snarled one.

As Lohengrin raised his blade and Broaditch came charging up, a flurry of Norsemen turned the confrontation into chaos. The little group moved on, Lohengrin and Broaditch covering the family. To Torky it was forever a dark memory of choking ash, rock-edges against his ankles, the big bulks of his father and the warrior, cries and clashings in the dark, strange voices, strange warcries . . . huddling in closer to his mother and sister, struggling on into seeming nothingness . . . invisible action and then brightness just ahead, flames suddenly high and fierce, and for a moment he thought of sunrise, and the big fires at home when the farmers burned autumn leaves, the smell in the cool air that always excited him, sent him running to the blazes . . . walking home at dusk on the suddenly mysterious, rutted road, moving with prickles of fear as he passed shadowy bushclumps . . . then smelling the cooking food and hearing his mother's voice across the cool, violet fields . . .

The Vikings had closed in all around. John, his best men, plus a mass of hundreds of sparsely armed women, boys and girls were bunched together in the steep-walled defile around Clinschor's wagon. A wedge of horn-helmed figures were hacking their way through the packed defense when John stood up in the stirrups and yelled:

"Save the father! Save the father!"

And the cry spread rapidly over the din of battle. The brothers and sisters stirred out of a kind of lethargic panic and began moving, chanting it now, louder and louder, led by the younger, the weaponless, chanting it with swelling purpose as if it were a tangible mace to smite with:

"Save father . . . Save father . . . Save father . . ."

Pushing, packed, into the terrible blades, axes, spears, clubs, the front rows screaming, falling, flopping in pieces, vomiting blood, tangling in their entrails, brains spattering sticky and strange, the dead unable to fall so that all the bodies advanced in a rolling, horrid, groping wave pressing the horned warriors back as by a lavalike, inching, irresistible wall of bloody meat and bone as the twilight was sucked away to utter night and only the screams and curses and butcher shop sounds rose over the weakening, now shrill cry:

"...Save...father...Save father...Save..."

The sounds revealed where the believers were still being ground and minced...and then several open supply carts puffed into flame as fabric, wood, tallow, oils went up under Truemen torches, the blazes holding the flank as John and his inner guard fled into the twisting valley while the almost motionless pile of chopped dead secured the rear, the gushing blood turning the ash to sticky muck...

Leena had been marching among the younger sisters and brothers. They'd tied a black robe around her shoulders. Her pale blond hair was gritty with soot and lay flat along her forehead. She kept looking upwards where the day glimmered and died.

She was enduring all this now because the luminous sky was a sign to her, a hint of what waited at the end, when she would finally sight the little castle across the golden wheat fields where the pure air was rich, beating energy. So the other pictures were blinked away and she concentrated on the light that the very fading made more intense and precious. Blinked away even last night because it hadn't really touched her, just another strangeness that didn't matter: all of them nude, praying, and John stroking his bent, hard member with both hands and gasping out fragments about Jesus and whores and shame...

And when the horned heads appeared (she knew they were devils and this hell's gateway) she was unsurprised and kept her sight on the thinning light as the dark and choking hellsmoke rose among the expected screams; raised her eyes because she knew there was nothing else, nothing more she needed to take in ever again, just the light she knew she'd still see after the choking, dry, hot dark closed altogether everywhere. Barely felt it when the cry went up and the mass of them packed together and began heaving into the demon's weapons, the bodies slamming together, bones cracking and popping around her, the vast weight and pressure closing, small children shrieking and vanishing underneath the mass, some carried along, feet not actually touching the ground, barely feeling the crunch of her own body because she was now able to shut her eyes and still see it, the brightness of it, actually stepping now, walking on the yielding greenness beyond the rippled fields among blazing flowers where trees soothed in the liquidity of breeze and light; actually there in that luminous land where nothing had edges, where each moment enfolded you with a tender, endless kindness and you yourself melted and flowed into the kindness, closeness, and she and the day were one thing and the kindness bore her up as she lightly ran forward like waterflow, destinationless, floating within and without straight into an unbounded softness where she had no thoughts, memories, just followed one pattern of color and music after another, each new, totally absorbing, color, music, scent, softness . . . each step an infinity of wonder while somewhere forever away swords and axes ripped and there was screaming lost under the least whisper of tune and breath and chaotic blood and blackness lost under the least flickering of ecstatic light . . . and her racked bone and flesh finally fell away from her, freed her at last from all it could not escape . . .

Clinschor kept his eye pressed to the opening and watched the battle in the dusk and soot, recognized the creatures of weak softness, strange butterfly-like, bright and flimsy, begging for gentleness, creatures who'd been conjured by the enemy wizards. *Cowards all*, he reflected with livid hate. Safe in their remote mountain lairs they sent forth their foul minions . . .

He sneered a smile and decided he'd soon put a stop to this: felt his power stir as he leaned back on the uneven stool (the wagon had just halted) and locked his hands in mystical position and began his first invocation . . .

Outside, strung on the rope with the others like fish suspended from a skiff, former lord general, Baron Howtlande, of Clinschor's disintegrated forces, rolled his eyes, sick with fear and fury.

Sleep, he thought, *has more reason than waking* . . .

Because by some inconceivable thrust of incomprehensibility there he was roped to that lunatic's cart about to be slain as part of some profitless horror where there was nothing to gain save more dead—nothing rare, not even food, nothing but blood and buckets of ash and he didn't know he was moaning under his breath . . . for nothing . . . and it struck him like (he didn't think) St. Paul on the road only this was a dark, not bright, flash when he understood there was nothing to win or preserve but breath and the few days you lived, tasted, touched, nothing to dream about or perish for, nothing to keep but choking ashes as death rose slowly over everything like a tide of mud . . . so he raged and wept now, heaving against the rope, shaking the others, sawing them back and forth, straining as the fanatics flung themselves on the Norsemen as onto a steel and bitter wall and then some slash or parry had cut the cord and he tumbled with the flopping rest into a gully, onto brittle, crackling branches of char as the fighting lost itself in lightless clouds and he was actually praying because there was nothing else now, nothing but breath, coughing and prayer . . .

John was shouting in the thickness and confusion:

"Drive the mares along!"

The wagon driver, over the muffled din of slaughter, now heard what John was aware of: a booming thunder (that no one believed yet was human), rhythmic, a bellowing blowing, shaking the wooden sides of the vehicle as though, John felt, some leviathanic creature were trapped inside, and suddenly he was afraid he'd made a terrible error about that madman and flipped his finger across his chest in a cross-sketch. The booming pounded at the sides like vast, soft fists and the driver stared back once, twice, then leaped over and fled into the thickened darkness as John waited in puzzled shock. The mule team strained on undriven as if to flee the sound they bore behind like a tinpot on a hound's tail, delicate hooves flicking knee-deep, slipping and tugging, the noise pounding harder and harder, faster and faster.

"The fire lord speaks," someone called out.

"Father," another shouted, "release him against our enemies!"

For a moment John almost believed it as the terrific chant-booms seemed to strike inside his belly and chest, somehow match and supersede the heartbeat as if, he sensed, the sound alone could take him over, rule and disport his limbs, drive on his thoughts . . . He shook his head in sudden fear, then he and the others fled, riding and running ahead on the twisting, narrowing way, seeming chased by the muffled, tremendous echoing that had no more words in it (save what imagination might impose) than breaking thunder or knotted wind . . . fleeing on, drowning out the horror and tumult of slaughter at their backs . . .

XXXVI

Perhaps an hour later, Broaditch wasn't even furious anymore. It went past that. He felt tight clenched around himself like a fist over a stone. They weren't going to break him because it had gone too far, too many escapes and recaptures and miseries...no more...too many years of wandering and wars...deaths, lost homes, friends, hopes...it was absurd, they were absurd, futile, simplebrained and even roped in a row (to the second cart), in senseless thrall again, cut away from wife and family again, he felt safe because he'd become stone. There were men strung in front and back of him as they stumbled and waded into the twisting, descending ravine.

John, riding, held a torch. The shadows ate at his long head. Other flames showed here and there. They seemed to be looking for something besides escape and Broaditch didn't care a fractional damn what it might be.

At some point they stopped and all three flopped down. The man behind kept panting and coughing. Black-robed Truemen flitted here and there in the flamelight. Broaditch's wounds were stiffening but the bleeding had stopped. He gritted his teeth and looked at nothing. He sensed that all his troubles and absurdities would simply fall away from him like water spilling around a boulder. He'd outlast them. Suddenly he murmured as if alone:

"We were away. Safe," he said, straight into the night. Reset his jaw. It was a curse or inscrutable purpose again because he'd had to talk at a perfect time for silence. "I said to him, I know not why, even as we moved low and crouched among the trees..."

The man still panted on one side, the other, equally invisible, rested motionless.

"Said what, brother?" the silent one suddenly said.

"Am I your relation and know it not?" wondered Broaditch.

"We're the family of doomed bastards," was the reply which the other found excellent.

"Aye," he said back. "How came you here?"

"I used to..." He suddenly tensed. "I...I...lived ...I..." Paused. Then: "But what said you, brother? Nay, a tale may take my mind from its pains."

"But make mine fresh," Broaditch replied. "It's not even a tale. Just madness." His voice was hard. "Or a poor joke of fate, which may be one thing, in the end."

"You remind me of him I knew."

"Who?"

"What died this recent . . . died..." Voice trembled. "All died...all...all...He were called Flatface for his face were like unto a Lenten cake ... we used to farm the land together... but the land died too and so we planted dead and grew hell's crop...poor Flatface, he dove deep for his meanings, now he's deep..."

"He dove deep, did he? Well, I sink for mine...Hear how the fire flared up and showed us, Alienor...my babies... ah...ah...but if we'd moved on apace..." His tone was flat, hard.

"Up," someone said out of the night as the rope suddenly heaved at them, yawing their wrists around. "Up and on."

The other wagon banged and strained a bend or two back. The booming thunder voice had stopped by the time it (driverless) caught up with them. Above the ravine walls a few hazy, swollen-looking stars showed. .

"Go on," Broaditch was continuing, talking at the invisible shape of the man roped ahead of him. The other still panted behind and said nothing. "I said: 'Go on,' to Lohengrin but he wouldn't move. The fire showed us..."

"Why not move?"

"He had to ask questions."

They lurched and swayed around a bend. The ash was shallower here. The fire had not come that far.

Because Broaditch didn't know why he'd had to say it after so long a silence. Yet, he mused, over and over, that was his special flaw, the error he had to commit in the wild red flaring light of the blazing carts and goods, Lohengrin dark against it, his family crouching behind him, saying an hour ago:

"I struck you. On the mountaintop. In the storm." Wishing he'd chewed his tongue raw instead except, perhaps, he'd sensed the young man had needed to know this and that it was the beginning of a kindness...

"I remember," he'd said, excited. "You were the peasant... you threw the stone. I was trying to slay you."

The ash and smoke boiled around them, the red flaring on the dead-black earth. Alienor was dragging at his arm, children muffled close to her. She said nothing, just pulled. Lohengrin was blocking the way forward but this time he went at him, actually pushing the armed knight on, saying:

"We cannot speak here, for Christ's sweet sake, lad!"

But it was too late and robe flapping, lithe figures seemed to spring up from the lifeless ground everywhere at once and the last thing he saw, in the tortured glare, was Lohengrin hit in the head by a red-spinning flash that merely (falling himself a moment later he understood) was a tossed ax this time and then he was on his face, choking again, darkness lapping over his consciousness...

The rope whipsawed his bound wrists as they rocked around another turn. His feet kept slipping.

"Fly," he'd screamed into the ashes. "Alienor, fly! Fly!" Screamed until his choked throat failed him and the darkness all ran together...

Alienor stood still, a hand on each child's shoulder, the black trees around her, the flamelight, a wisp of color on their faces, was swallowed to nothing everywhere else. She'd hesitated as the shadowy men pounced into her shouting husband (she saw the others, the horned ones, battling through the fires and heard the agony behind them) and she was just whirling when someone gripped her by a wad of clothing and yanked all three of them (because her grip on the children was locked) as the little girl cried out in pure and terrible hurt:

"Father! Father! Father!"

Torky struggled to free himself as she writhed in the violent grip and her mind flashed that this was death, the dance of death, *he* had them as the night closed in and a voice whispered, repeated at her ear with breathless pain:

"I'll get you away . . . I'll do this..." She recognized Pleeka's strained tones. "The times have done it...the times have made them mad...I won't let them feed..."

And now they were running into the blind night because of the children...the children...feeling the staggers in his gait even as he fiercely yanked and balanced, hurled her along past the limbless, lifeless dim trees, her mouth raw with thirst and dust and each breath and foot impact shocking, flashing pain...

They were climbing the steep side of the valley that had become a ravine, blundering, snapping through small trees and fallen branches, charred brittle; scraping their hands on edges of rock, moving part up and part parallel.

She was half-carrying Tikla again. Pleeka stayed in front. She heard him scrambling on, almost continually muttering. She caught few of the words...*just live*, she told herself when she told herself anything...*just live*...

They passed through my body into all this so I'll keep them as long as I may...I did it before...I did it before...

Because she was dreaming now (though she hadn't realized it) of the water...

We've used up the gift, she thought in fear, *she'll not save us again...She* of water, *she* of all benediction, because to Alienor it had a face and form, an almost face of wet light all clothed somehow like summer and spring, and clutching her frail daughter, the male at her other side, uncomplaining (as if she willed it so because she was half-helpless, beyond her limit, driving herself up into darkness) behind the mechanically muttering ex-believer. Alienor could almost see the image almost above her, neither beckoning nor rejecting, almost luminous, almost palpable...

"Onward," she told her children.

"Thirsty, mama," said Tikla.

"Soon," she answered, firming her voice for their sakes. "Just onward now. Soon..."

Not far behind in the same darkness the Vikings descended into the stony, burnt-out cut. Few of them had been killed or wounded. Tungrim was on foot now.

"It's serious," he told Layla as they went side by side near the head of the column. He'd ordered all the animals slaughtered for food except for her mount.

Several men with torches were out in front, casting strange, horn-headed shadows among the dark stones and pole-like trees.

"Hmn," she replied.

"We're lost," he told her.

She rested her long hands on the mule's ridged back and didn't think about there being no wine left. The animal was gaunt and chewed its lips together with thirst.

The mountainsides had become actual cliffs here. Their feet ground over smooth pebbles. There was little soot suddenly. Obviously this had been a riverbed.

Layla looked dully at the fat man who called himself baron. He'd clearly been grosser but hard living had loosened his flesh into great pouches. She didn't like his stony little eyes. He was smiling, of course, holding a torch and gesturing intensely.

"Gentlemen," he was saying, waving something in the torchlight, holding it up to Tungrim's face. "Here's solid proof enough."

"Keep still your hand then, slayer of Skalwere," the Prince said. Plucked it from the other: a bone, freshly chewed with scraps of gristle. It had obviously been cooked. "This but proves some go before us." Squinted at the fragment in the shaky glow.

"At least they have meat, my lord," Howtlande pointed out as the captains silently watched him, expressionless. "That's worth following after these days."

"The seas, fat one," redbeard baldhead put in, "are full of fish and not such land-garbage."

"We'll come back to the sea in time," Tungrim told them, flicking the bit of flesh and bone away as they went on, crunching over the streambed, the sound almost as though water flowed there . . .

"Do you believe this fat cheese and his tales?" the lanky captain added. He walked ahead with his torch flashing over the pale wash of pebbles and ever-narrowing walls.

"Which tales?"

"About treasures of the great wizard."

"They're sooth," Howtlande insisted, "sooth."

"We should have slain you," redbeard added to the discussion. The flames gleamed on his smooth skull.

"Peace, Thorere," Tungrim quietly commanded. "This fellow smote our enemy."

"This load of gull droppings?" the lanky captain snorted.

"I never lie," Howtlande lied, with firm dignity. Prince Tungrim raised his eyebrows. "I knew the wizard. I heard him telling countless times about this place, this hidden fortress he'd made in the earth. This be where all his treasures are kept secure." He was trying to distinguish their expressions in the fugitive orange glow. "I heard him say the secret of his magic is there."

"What might that be?" Tungrim responded laconically.

Layla felt chilly though the night was warm. Crossed her arms over her chest. Each sway of the mule irritated her.

At least let's camp and sleep, she thought. *Thank God for sleep. There's little to say for waking . . .*

"The Grail," Howtlande was saying, "The Holy Grail of power itself."

"Eh?" Tungrim was baffled and faintly disgusted with the conversation. "The what?"

She was already twisting around in the saddle, almost shouting:

"Grail? Grail?" she said. "Kill him! You hear me, Tungrim? Slay this gross fool!"

Their faces were shadowhollowed as the torches rocked and the flames bent and puffed. The four stared at her with eyes blotted out, gleamless.

"I'm a Norseman," Tungrim began, tediously, "and Norsemen are bound by their honor to—"

"It's a curse!" she raged, arms refolding over her slightly shivering body. "A fucked curse!"

"Lady, I—" Howtlande began but was cut short by the Prince.

"I want no accursed magic," he bellowed. "I'll have no such—"

"Fool!" she said, shivering so that her voice shook. "I had my life spoiled by that nonsense . . . that Grail . . ." She spat out the word. "Slay the fat fool for his own sake . . . It's a disease that eats your husband's mind and leaves you loveless with tormented children and—"

"Woman!" he said. "Woman!"

"Clinschor," Howtlande insisted, "swears it's real."

"Oh, yes," she went on, cold with fury too. "No doubt. They all believe it . . . all of them . . . Slay them all, I say!" She twisted around to stare into the blankness before her. Saw him, Parsival, the long, bright hair flamed with rose-red from the sunrise, mounted on a blur of horse, red armor (helmet in his lap) like quickening coals . . . remembered only her feelings, wordless . . . remembered begging him to stay and he said something and something . . . the red fire in his hair, the clear, blue remoteness in his eyes, and she'd felt death was like that: seed . . . growing . . . filling out . . . drifting into goneness . . . gone . . . she'd shouted something about how they'd lied to him to get him lost following the Grail . . . and he went and the old, old tears of that long, lost morning had really been wept because she'd been walled off from her love dreaming . . . the wall never came down again . . .

"Grail," she whispered, refusing to look over at them again, clinging to the bony back of the staggering, mincing mule. Shivered and felt no appetite.

I cannot ask him either . . . Wondered if some warrior in the column might have a skin of wine put away in his pack. *The son-of-a-bitch* . . . The hooves lightly and unevenly clicking on the bed of stones . . . *Now they've got me too . . . even me . . . they've finally got me following it . . .*

"Grail," she almost spat in to the blankness beyond the wavering torch glimmer . . .

XXXVII

Now they had no water. Gawain had poured part of a flask into one of the two kegs the men bore by turns on their backs. Parsival had shattered it with his sword. The other was finished. He held it up. Shook it, smelled the sweet, damp wood. Flicked loose a few drops that vanished into the black, burned soil. The sun was high and fierce in the stifling haze.

They were alone now. The peasants had fled on before dawn when a second woman and a man were killed despite the fires and watchers because Parsival had been struck down by the poison water: he'd paced and stared, the blade across his shoulder, peering into the darkness beyond the charcoal glow . . . and then his sight blurred, ears roared, teeth rattling together madly for a moment and then a silence as if sound, sight and all senses had been sucked away into a vast blot of nothingness: he heard screams, terrible screams of panic and pain. He'd run at the sounds, seeing . . . not seeing . . . seeing again . . . the terrors echoing strangely around him as if he were closed in a walled chamber.

"Unlea," he'd shouted. "Unlea!"

Suddenly the woods were daybright and he had an impression that he'd slept and dreamt everything except it was wrong:

211

the trees were in full bloom, lush with heavy, midsummer greens, earth a softness of deep grasses . . . deserted . . . silent except for the pleasant winds wooshing across the fields . . . he knew that he knew the place and tried to recall it: a thin stream, banks in an aura of sunlight, a long, smooth crease and then he saw the mounted knight coming down, the giant horse rocking through the grasses as if breasting seawaves, faceplate shut, armor a blood-red glint on man and mount and he believed it was someone dressed to look like Sir Roht the Red (remembered slaying him so long ago with a thrust javelin in the throat, blood misting and leaking down the shaft over his own pale hand as he braced against the shocking weight of the toppling man, his hot rage already run out, and he was bewildered, curious, hoping he was doing what was expected of a knight, the hot blood drops on his face and fool's garments . . .) or a dream yes, that was it, he was still asleep . . . no . . . the water, the poison water . . . the knight lowered a red lance and began a slow, flowing charge straight at him and he felt cold draining fear, trying to raise his blade and finding it tremendously heavy as if he now moved underwater . . . the red warrior came on, massive, silent, three-edged lancetip dead on his chest . . . closer . . . closer . . . trying to move, fight or run . . . frozen to the spot he finally watched the spear come ripping in, piercing his heart and his heart burst and flooded him with warm, golden, soothing light . . . then blackness . . . then the dark fires again and Unlea, one leg up as if suspended in midflight, even her garments fixed, silks billowed out and still in the night air, and beyond her, in the orange-red glowing, moved vague, dark, threatening shapes . . . then all gone and he was kneeling over the fallen knight, the helmet freed, javelin pulled out from the round hole where the blood gurgled in a dying trickle, the redhead's blue eyes looking at him, suddenly free of their deathglaze, blood clotted, mouth moving, speaking:

You've done me, boy.
I had to become a man, like you, sir.
Now you have to bear it.
What, sir?
This suit of steel. It's heavy, boy. I can no longer rise
in it.
I have to be a knight and know the brightness . . .

Forgive me, boy, for I brought you to this.
Forgive you? But I slew you...
I wasted all my moments until this one and this one is my best.

"But you died," Parsival was yelling into the darkness. "You never spoke a word!" Saw Unlea running, then motionless again, as if (he thought) in a childhood game of "Trollstill and Scamper." "Never a word."

And the night was gone again and he faced a stone wall laced with ivy where the sunlight tangled the shadows and flashed hot and bright and he recognized the priest just coming through a low, barred door which he shut and locked behind himself. Straightened and watched him.

I told you, he seemed to say, nervous hands adjusting his robe and patting at his tonsured hair, *you truly have no choosing. Now you're locked in here.*

"No!" he yelled, or thought he yelled.

You're getting more chances than ever a mortal was given before. How many can you waste?

And Parsival rushed past him at the door, through which he saw a long shimmer of water. Stooped down, face near the close-set, thick bars, staring at the scene: long hills where flowers were golden flame and clouds unwound in slow, mellow light that seemed a condensation of all childhood summers; a single sailboat out in the blue stillness winked smoothly away into the haze where a castle stood on an island, delicate spires mounting high and clear white with golden trim like sun flashing... and he began to weep, face on the cold iron...

The night slammed back and screams were still ringing, Unlea fleeing past and he followed, shouting:

"Unlea! What?! What?!"

And she spun into his arms, panting, shaking:

"They were in the tent!... The tent!..."

And he suddenly was seeing two worlds at once (or was mad), where dark, stunted creatures stalked among the blasted woods, things like fish with clawed, reptile feet dragged themselves through the ashes, pop eyes gleaming in the coal light; where birds with human heads hopped on long legs and grimaced... howled... where things like giant bees hovered beside winged lizards... where vast greenish fires raged in the distance in what seemed burning cities. He knew they could

see him too. He blinked and shook his head as she trembled
against his cold metal side. The visions remained. He was
trapped again, the other world leaking through everywhere.
That deadly water, he believed, had washed away his defenses...his fortress walls were crumbling...

"The tent...Oh, Parsival...Parsival...save me, my dear
one...Please save me..."

"You?" he wondered. "Save *you?*"

The screaming had stopped. The peasants were gone. In the
other world, terrible distorted creatures were following them.
A monkeylike thing with a sharkface seemed to caper around
the glade, banked rows of terrible teeth bared.

"Stay here," he commanded, plunging off to where he
glimpsed a humanish form bending over what appeared to be
a flopped sack. A girl spun to face him with drawn dagger,
eyes wide, bright, and the monkeylike shape leaped between
them and Parsival struck, missed or cut through a shadow,
twisted back, and the girl was gone into the confusion of darkness and overlapping worlds. Now Unlea was backing away
from another girl with the horrid fish behind her. A pushing
stream of liquid fire flowed across the rocky ground. Parsival
charged back and the girl ducked aside and then still another
leaped in, cloak outstretched except they were batlike wings
and he slashed and shouted, hit nothing, and then Unlea was
clinging to his legs, howling sobs.

The poisoned earth let them in, his mind somehow knew.
We all did it...we poisoned everything...He held her, shut
his eyes. Bent and kissed her uncombed, slightly sourish hair.
Held her with Gawain's drawn sword as nervous as a youth,
feeling awkward and slightly incapable. He kept his sight lowered, denying all terror and vision, gathered his will and waited
for dawn to gradually fill the woods and wash all the blackness
away. Watched the two new corpses gradually emerge from
the background, sprawled in the ashy earth: a woman and man.
He didn't look closely. The effect of the water seemed to have
faded. He sardonically wondered why Gawain seemed so
pleased with it...well, he'd had more than a mouthful and no
doubt was mad in proportion. He sighed...Unlea stirred and
he soothed her with a touch.

All his life, it came to him, he'd lived as if his steps could
always be retraced. He'd clung to that. Expected the second

chance, a place to return to . . . except there wasn't, time ran one way only . . .

Now it was hazy noon. He shielded his eyes and scanned the desolate hills for movement or a change somewhere to green . . . nothing. He worked his dry tongue and sucked it for moisture. It was sticky. He was glad he'd spilled the bad water because the temptation would have been immense.

He held her arm as they trudged on through the shadeless forest. Followed a dry streambed leveled with the omnipresent soot. Hoped vaguely that the far end might still be wet. Glanced at her: the gown was rent and blackened, her hair in knots. Sweat had streaked the ashstains on her face. She was footsore, limping.

"Is there hope?" she asked.

He wondered how he looked himself. Each step jarred his head.

"Hope," he repeated, looking ahead at where the banks wound on, sinking slightly, steadily. "For what? There's ample room for hoping."

"To live," she said, licking her cracked lips.

"Unlea . . ." Squeezed her hand.

"I thirst so."

"Yes." Felt responsible and wondered if that was what love always became, because what had been love before was gone: he could look at her and see a fragile, often silly, fear-ridden person; see the sweet good and tart ill mixed all at once without the tender elation and melancholy of the past, without jealous need to possess all her moments . . . it wasn't just the miseries of their situation either. He was used to loving, he thought, amused, under the worst possible conditions. His loves had survived everything but marriage.

"If there's water," he told her, "we'll come upon it."

"If there's none?"

"Need I answer?"

He noticed something moving, squinted: it seemed a brightness, a shimmer like sun on ripples. Blinked . . . it was gone. Decided it had to have been a heat mirage. As he looked away it came back and he studied it indirectly, still walking, and then realized what he'd drunk last night was still active. He watched it take form and something like music sounded from within a space resembling an open door where a womanshape floated as if glowing colors had taken flesh, cool greens, rare blues, flowing golds spilling and sparkling...

No, he thought. *Sorry...but I say you nay. Haunt me as you please I care not.*

"Who slew those poor folk then?" Unlea was asking.

"I know not," he replied, slowing, spotting what he hoped were the banks of the main river crossing into them a few dozen steps ahead.

"There was a young girl in the tent," she said, "with a knife...She was so young." She shuddered, slightly. "There was blood on her face. The candlelight showed it plain. Oh dear God, what days are these? What days?" Shook her head. "Children do murder...the earth is seared to dust. Will we find any towns or castles left?"

He shrugged.

"I know not." Stopped now at the edge, looking down into a deep ravine. He heard no water sounds in the bottom shadows.

"Sweet lady Mary," she murmured, "now what do we do?"

He was irritated, hot, headachey, thirsty.

"I recommend we leap," he snapped.

"Parse," she said, hurt.

"Oh, Christ, don't weep, I beg you."

She looked at him. Opened her mouth but held her words. The tears gleamed, unfallen.

"So this is it then," she said. "Your heart is plainly read."

"What?" He took her hand to lead her on so they could walk on the rocky rim of the cut except she jerked away and stood with fingers pressed to her mouth. He knew she was chewing the knuckle. She always did when upset.

"Very well, then," she announced, voice unsteady, nodding. "Very well."

"Very well what?"

"Go on," she said. Nodded. "Go."

"Unlea," he pleaded, "seems this a fit time for—"

"You never cared, that's plain to see. I'm ashamed... ashamed...You're helping me from pity only...pity!"

"What dung and nonsense, Unlea."

"Ahaha," she cried, "yet I see it plain enough!"

He saw her teeth nervously working on the finger. She wasn't looking at him.

"This is absurdity!" he suddenly yelled, hoping for effect and frustrated too. "I love you!"

"Ahaha."

"Oh, God in heaven!" He grabbed her wrist and she was struggling, wild, awkward, frantic out of all proportion, yelling:

"Free me! Free me, you bastard knight! Free me! You smug bastard! You faker! You sod of shit! Used me like a whore and murdered my husband..."

"No! Be still!"

"Used me used me used me! Faker! Smug bastard...Oh, God I'm alone with him...with him...I have nothing... nothing. Oh, God!"

He shook her violently, screaming now into her contorted, weeping, wild face:

"Be still! Damn you, be still! Unlea! I love you! I love you! I love you!"

And then they were both on their knees, her wrist in his hand, both sobbing, her greasy hair flopped across her face, reddened eyes running tears. He was gasping hoarsely for breath and remembering his life with Layla. He felt stupid, guilty, helpless...

"There's nothing," she kept saying, "nothing...nothing... nothing...I want to die please let me die...please..."

Though he believed he loved her he'd felt no truth in saying it. Looking at her he felt a sad, deep shock, thinking:

Oh, all the pain...the pain...so needless all this pain ...here we are at the end of the world and there's still this pain...

He knelt and gathered her into his arms, pressed her hot face close, the wetness and unhappiness and pungent breath...holding her in the dried-up stream under the unrelenting sun, sobbing and kissing one another...then pulled and twisted and tore their garments free, stretching themselves out, gasping on hot, baked, sooty mud, ears roaring, blood beating, feeling himself arced hard, spearlike.

"Oh, darling Unlea," he moaned, "Oh...Unlea... Unlea..."

Help us...we take what we can...help us...help...

XXXVIII

"See here, see...see for yourself!" Clinschor was exulting, squatting at the fallen knight's head. The brief flash of day was over, though it was barely past noon, because the canyon here was so high and narrow and twisted that the sun only showed when pouring straight down for a piece of an hour and then dusk rushed into dark down at the barren bottom. So he held the sputtering torch over Lohengrin's gashed head, one long, thick finger aimed down, washed-out eyes reflecting the shaky light, hollowly, catlike, while his flesh seemed eaten to bone by the rocking shadows. John leaned in the wagon door to look on. Outside the remnants were squatting and sitting, chewing food and sipping from flasks. Broaditch and the other prisoners were close under the rock wall. One of the Truemen was handing out strips of dried meat. Broaditch dropped his piece without comment, staring with steady fury at the bent, bearded man who was grinning, mouth-breaking. *His nose seems so lost in hair no air can reach it*, Broaditch commented to himself. *My own beard at least grows in a general direction and not looking like it be attacking my face*...and then the man handed him a drink and this time, gripping it between his bound hands, he grunted thanks.

Took a slug and it wasn't just warm and clotted but metallic too (*As though I cut my gums!*) and he was spitting and gagging and snarling a curse. There was enough light left floating in the dusk to show the thick black-red on the pale pebbles and spattered over his hands and lips.

Just as, within, Clinschor turned Lohengrin's head on the dim planks and placed his pale finger in the glancing slice of a wound. His pale eyes rolled up and he shuddered and for a moment there was an image, a feeling, his mother's round face across the table, his burly father working a beef bone into his beard and mouth, small very white teeth grinding and ripping into the flesh, and her voice too:

"Nay, my lord, that's too hard a thing."

"Be it?" the dark man replied. "What say you, boy?" Speaking now to Clinschor who was looking up at the big face and small, hard eyes. "He's free with brag and boast most days."

"Let him remain at home," she insisted.

"But he claims to be a man already. And quite a one, eh, boy? Are you a great one, boy?"

He thought: *even then the dark magicians worked their spells against me* . . .

"But no more," he muttered . . . the feeling, the feeling standing there at the massive table, arms folded across his thin chest, nervous hands drumming and twisting, candlelight touching their faces with quivering fingers as if the flesh itself were loose, uncertain . . .

"What's wrong with him, eh? He spoke large enough ere this!"

"Let him be, why can't you?" she said.

But he refused to answer and felt his power gathering within, knew he was growing taller now and more massive moment by moment, concentrating on it, and knew his father would soon see his error and would feel the terrible strength of his son . . . felt himself towering, filling the hall with the massive force of himself.

"Clinschor," she was saying, "are you ill, son? Son? . . ."

"I said no word," he informed John, "and soon I smote the Devil with my magic!" The torchfire hollowed his sockets. "First there was only myself and then a time came of hundreds of thousands, yea, and more! A time came!" One large, pale hand flicked through a complex gesture expressing all these things. "And then, again, I was alone and betrayed by weakness, cowardice, stupidity!" Took breath.

John smiled a secret smile because he suddenly saw this being's true form and this amused him and touched him with awe as well. It had instantly come clear to him. All the blood and pressure of the night had led him to this: here was no wandering madman, this was God's own instrument. He saw splendid limbs and flaming eyes under the twisted, skinny, filthy, blasted guise and knew the pig face that spoke to him in secret, the pig that stood upright as a man in the shadows of his tent or on the lonely mountain trails, the red eyes fierce, commanding, the divine pig who'd found him in his wandering misery long ago and with stern compassion taught him God's true and deepest will had now possessed this broken creature with his infinite spirit, force and wisdom.

"I lived in darkness," he confided in Clinschor, who cocked his head to the side to listen, long finger still poked into the knight's wound. "Aye, master." Gazed with deep pleasure into the red pig eyes behind Clinschor's sockets. "I was a priest, praying and blessing, hoping to heal the world's pain... but I was young, master, and saw well the folly and wickedness of things, so I gathered the serfs and smashed at the foulness..."

The other blinked rapidly. This was a good servant, whatever he was saying he said "master."

"Now it's in my hands at last," he said, "this scrap here—" Wiggled his fingertip in the shallow slash in the knight's head that exposed a bright strip of metal, wedged into the temple bone, neither quite cool silver nor warm gold, in the changing light. "I bent close and lo! I read the writing in this hurt... Lo!" Moved his face near and peered into the split flesh edged with bared skull as if gazing into the head itself, it seemed to those men behind John who perched birdlike in the doorway.

John frowned, hearing these holy words from He whose name was known to him. He knew these were parables.

"Lord Sixsixis," he said, leaning close to the upturned snout, that poked from behind the human bone, "divine one, I know it is written in the blood and flesh that we are to feed and drink from the substance of the unworthy. I have led my people to this. When all failed, when I were left helpless, searching in vain... in vain..." He was weeping. "... for truth and power... even then, lord, you showed me and lit my path... even before I knew Thee in Thy form, dread lord, Thou came when all my reasonings had failed, my plans confounded, and with a blade put to my throat by my selfsame hand to end this sorry life, Thy voice spoke unto me and shattered the false world and all appearances into shivers!" No numbers added, nothing grew straight, stars wheeled planless, men whirled among themselves like dustmotes in a turn of wind, babbling nonsense, dying for insubstantial dream after dream and he knew the madness was health because there was no sense save in nonsense. He found the end of all science and philosophy. And only nonsense freed him at last because there was no pity in anything but only the great grindstone of death smashing all things to meaningless dust and this pitilessness freed him from all inner conflicts. He saw the truth was pitiless and so became the truth and the pig whispered to him: *Feed and live! Feed and die! Feed and live! Feed and die!*

Clinschor squinted one reddened eye at him, face still close to the wound as if listening to it now. He clearly was listening to nothing else.

"I read the words and lo my strength multiplied," he said. Reached his arms wide as if everything could be embraced. The thundering voice suddenly rose to full force and shook and snapped in the confined space.

Broaditch, at the end of the rope, had moved close enough to the wagon to hear and see and then smell: a reeking of excrement poured from the doorway and he realized Clinschor must have been relieving himself without ever stepping outside.

"All things are my things!" the voice exploded.

As Broaditch edged closer one of the black-robes gripped him by the hair, yanked at his head until tears welled up.

"Back, sinner," he snarled.

But the sinner stepped into the terrific pain so he could watch and saw Clinschor hook his fingers and rip the bright metallic shimmer out of the skull as the knight screamed and flopped wildly, horribly (Broaditch felt a shiver through his own blinding pain, hardly noticing the kicks raining on his dense body), thrashing in the torchlight like a man with falling sickness as Clinschor held high the sliver, yelling:

"The Grail! I have the Grail!" Seeing the host surrounding him, the calm, bearded giants and pale magicians weeping despair; female fiends with terrible, tender faces stretching out soft hands (he knew) to weaken him, tempting him to softness... he felt coming history shift towards strength and away from pale quoters of poems, singers of sweetness... prayers... held history in his clenched hand... away from soft arms and lying peace and empty embraces... away... Clutching the bloodwet fragment, he danced.

Lohengrin still howled and flopped around his feet. John crouched, transfixed, beholding the pig rise, expand trunk and trotters until it stooped, immensely filling the wagon, red eyes fist-sized, dimming the torches with their glare as the voice, beyond, he believed, anything human, cried:

"Hail victory! Hail victory!"

And Broaditch, stubborn and amazed, watched (head still sawed back and forth by the hair as the blows hit) John caper on the steps and gleefully raise his fist in wild salute, crying out between Clinschor's boomings:

"Praise... all... the glory... all praise... highest pig... the pig!... Thine eyes surpassing... bless... bless... wonder... Thy form..."

As Lohengrin spasmed into Clinschor's legs and sent him reeling forward into John, who beheld the holy one reaching to embrace him and held him on the wagon step like a lover.

Broaditch finally gave ground and stumbled back with the others on the rope. Lohengrin suddenly sat up, blood streaking his face as Clinschor squealed, gibbered and frothed, snapping his teeth, clutching the metal, clawing free of his worshipper with the other hand, screaming and raging:

"It's mine alone! Mine! None else may touch it!" Rolling and scuttling back into the recesses of the vehicle, squatting, gesturing with his free hand in intricate passes, massive voice intoning now, harsh, abracadabric...

As John stood still, nodding rapidly, blinking, understanding the meaning, parabolic hints, saying:

"Yes... Yes... I see... I see..."

Here was the mystery he was not perfected to grasp yet: "None else may touch it." That question needed pondering... was there truly an "it" that could be grasped? He smiled as he reasoned. There were many subtle points to be considered... the divine one was taking him yet another step on the path to wisdom and perfection... He nodded as Clinschor frothed and spasmodically scribbled on the flame-shaken air, voice muttering like stormwind in a chimney.

John turned to the remainder of his followers, raising his

arms, benedictory (as Lohengrin was still trying to rise) and victorious.

"Brothers and children, the spirit has made it plain. Nothing can be possessed for death flows among us like water among weeds and the strong wind leaves only the best trees so those who've perished have left us stronger than before! And we go forth again to devour the sinners!"

The men cheered. Broaditch found energy to dryly spit, which brought back the blood taste. His companion on the line, the gatherer of the dead, Vordit, touched him with bound hands.

"Why did you bear those blows?" he asked.

Broaditch shrugged. They were moving again.

"They're going to slaughter us like sheep," he said.

"They're all dead mad."

"They eat human meat. I saw it. And swill blood." Spat again.

They followed the tremendously creaking wagon, crunching over the dry pebbles. John still stood on the steps, arms gripping the doorframe. Inside it was dark again.

"They'll find little enough on me," Vordit said, "as things stand . . . anyway, I'm dead . . . what matter?"

"There's no humor in such horrors."

"Hah. You say so. There's nothing horrible no more. It's all one thing . . . all one thing . . ."

"No."

"They can roast gooseshit. What care I if they bury us dead in ground or in themselves? We all come to be death's dung in the end . . . So there's nothing neither way . . ."

"No," his massive companion repeated, gritting his teeth, thinking about the walled arbor he'd built at home, the clustered grapes in mellow sunlight . . . quick birds gusting and rattling the leaves . . .

Never, he thought, *all one thing . . .*

The rope bit his raw wrists, his new bruises starting to ache.

"Never," he muttered.

Father, Lohengrin was saying, the tall blond man with blue eyes like dew on crystal leaned above him, and he felt himself reaching up slowly as if the air were liquid, arms too short . . . *Father* . . . helpless under a great, soft weight, reaching for the remote face framed by the shoulder-length shimmer of fine hair and then the warm, firm hands gripping him . . . *Father* . . . tipping, lifting up into magic terror and exhilaration, thrilled in fear and joy and surprise as the view unfolded, the rich brightnesses (he knew to call candles), the vast blank and shadowed rushing into mysteries and strange perspectives . . . an open space, white hard white light points quivered around a perfect glow, . . . *moon*, he thought, *moon* . . . and then he felt himself scream as he spun and floated in gripless nothing and then the safe hands closed, soft, irresistible and then tossed him again and caught him and he screamed with the fearjoy this time and wonder: *Father! Father! Father!*

And then the tilting sway banged his head again . . . the hands were gone and he sat up, shuddering in the blackness, in the terrific, slow creaking and sequence of blowing, bubbling snores that he first took for suffering.

All Lohengrin's memories were back. He just sat there with his past slammed into him as if, he thought, it had been rammed through the hole in his head, because he remembered that too, the agonizing fingers clawing into his naked skull, incredible fire and rasping.

So he snores now, he thought, *like any other*. Stared with contempt into the unrelieved darkness and now he suddenly became aware of the stink. Clapped his hand to his nose as if that would help. He believed he must be sitting in it and scrambled his feet under him. Or had he soiled himself? He touched and saw he hadn't.

This saves your life, he thought, *you swine!* Because he couldn't endure this reek (gagging now, tasting bile) long enough to act. It felt semi-solid, flowing, filling his nose, throat, chest, insides . . . he scrambled for the door, half-doubled over. *The bastard sleeps in his latrine!*

The pain was dull and fading in his head. A healing pain, which the other never was. He rarely sickened from wounds, in any case, even without treatment. God knew he'd felt enough of them.

Outside he crouched on the double step as the wagon labored on in the darkness. In dim torchlight he made out flickers of dark shapes.

The Truemen, he thought, *must be very afraid to push on by night*. He grinned. *Well, I'm myself again* . . . Frowned. *Or am I? . . .* Paused. *Do I stick here or wait for those coming?* He coolly contemplated the situation. *That dream troubles me . . .* Gingerly touched his wound. *Everything after that blow seems a dreaming now . . .*

Make up for lost time, that was essential. He'd . . . what? . . . where to start? It hardly mattered. Licked his lips. Was very thirsty. One place was as good as another given the world's present circumstances.

There was a third alternative: beat these bastards to wherever they were rushing. Get whatever it was first, whether food, water or Devil wonders.

He dropped lightly down and ran into the rope and then into Vordit and flashed his dagger to the man's throat.

"Not a word," Lohengrin hissed, then felt the bound hands and understood. *Sow confusion*, he decided, *and reap chaos* . . .

And cut him free and moved to the next and next after, warning them all to silence. Then the guard came up in dimly fluttering flamelight which just showed Lohengrin's beaked, harsh-boned, curly head and the silver flicker as the short blade ripped an arc through the fellow's neck, dropping him soundless in bloodspray and a quiet gurgle that accompanied his flapping, meaningless gestures.

As the torch rolled and went out, Broaditch stepped near him.

"You're free," the knight said. "The rest is your business."

And moved off into the darkness, hugging the near wall in order to bypass the dim, bobbing lights . . .

XXXIX

He'd shifted her on top so the stones and dried mud dug into his back and buttocks and he angled his heels and rocked her as she lifted long and slow, firm around him each ecstatic fraction, each stroke concentrating the thick sweetness, the pressure building...building...burning...she swayed above him, terrific sun brilliant...everything went away, the hard, cutting earth painless now, relentless brightness mere background color...near his face a few spears of quivering green were poked through the blasted soil. Past and future hung there, the only time measured by the beating of blood, bone and flesh, and he shut his eyes and watched the images flash and let thoughts wander...

All the time...we'll just do this all the time... AH...all...

Then he could hold no longer, lifted her on his vibrating, arced body as she twisted and throbbed, sloshing her loins, and he felt it rush, pump, burst as inarticulate words spilled through brain and mouth, pulses, blazes exploding, and then instantly in imploding silence she was gone and earth too, sky...everything gone into silence...and he stood in a soundless place where clouds rushed up to immense pastel heights. The effect was of an open hall, horizon wide, that lost itself in shifting banks of gentle luminescence. Trees with jeweled leaves shimmered musically . . . far away the vague, almost outline of himself and Unlea entwined and struggling together almost showed . . . A young girl flowed from the cloudy gleamings among the strange boughs, behind her scenes forming and unforming, lacy mountains rising, gleaming rivers of rose-pale melting . . . naked children supple in violet air, playing as if childhood summer twilight were forever sustained, forever dying . . . flowers sucking slow life from the teeming earth as golden butterflies filled the electric blue air with a sweet chaos of color . . . and then darkening, ripping, rending . . . and his eyes were pain in the hot, savage blades of sunlight that razored at his brain and he thought it was his own voice screaming until he saw Unlea over him, crying out and shaking in what he still believed was passion as she twisted his head to the side on the baked, sooty, stony streambed.

"Stop it," she cried, "you'll be blinded!"

And he realized (in the wildly batting, flitting globes of fierce afterglow) he'd been staring straight into the sun and he wondered for how long . . . He could barely see what was around him, a blotting, blurring dimness . . . blinked and blinked . . .

"It's that water again," he told her and himself, sitting up on his heaped clothes. "The poison still works in me."

"You fell over in a faint." She was pulling her clothes back around herself. "Fie," she said, touching between her legs, then wadding the hem of her tattered gown and dabbing there.

"Did I give you pleasure?" he wondered, holding his hands up and squinting through his fingers.

"What?" she murmured distractedly.

He heard the tittering before he saw the young girl's face peering over the embankment a few feet away. Strands of her stringy blond hair caught in the burned bushes that walled along the top. Her eyes were blue and strangely blank. He recognized her from the burnt-out castle miles behind: one of the mad children posing in the ashes. He somehow was certain there were others, knelt his legs under him and reached for his clothes (not out of shame) squinting and blinking as Unlea just stared.

The girl tittered again. The soot streaked her dead-white skin as if it had been painted.

"You belong to the beast and the bad," she said. "The seals are all open now." Tittered.

He didn't bother to answer, jerking his tights and leg mail up, cursing his sight because he couldn't tell how many more there were as the violent suntorn brightness danced and bounced, veered and popped . . . and then the other strangeness was superimposed over the swarming inner lights: shapes in the dried, burnt brush and close-set blasted trees beyond: the craning, crawling fish, the red-eyed monkeyform with shark-mouth working . . . insectile creepings, a pig crouched in the crotch of a tree . . . things with human faces . . . the porcine fore-limbs swayed slowly . . .

He pulled Unlea up beside him. Back slowly off, holding his sheathed sword over his shoulder. Watching everything at once as best he could through his uncertain sight.

"You belong to the beast," she called after them, just her head still poked out of the dark, shiny, crumbly bushmass. The fish had crawled beside her, pop eyes goggling at them in a welter of dancing, orbiting specks.

Still looking back, Parsival and Unlea moved across the far bank into the bare, black trees on the rim of the deep ravine whose bottom was blanked in shadow.

When the girl's face was just a pale spot, featureless, he paused and called back:

"Why did you slay them?"

And the immediate response from off to their left, came in a deep male voice that Parsival remembered from the well — the stunted-looking leader, or elder anyway, with the thick beard:

"They belonged to the foul beast as do you. You spoiled all the green and made nastiness. Hurt the children . . . Your world is all gone now. Now the children hurt you!"

"Come," Parsival said to Unlea.

"Who are these?" she wondered, adjusting her garments again.

"Throat slashers."

"Unless," the male voice said, invisible in the charred trees, "you drink the water of cleansing and holiness."

"Send me only atheists!" he snarled. "From this day on."

"They refuse to be clean," the voice announced, unsur-prised.

At the rim of Parsival's sight where the fading sunbursts still danced and spun he saw the fierce fish creeping where the voice was sounding. He yelled over:

"If any come near let him make ready to greet hell, you poison children!" He saluted the black wall of ruined forest with his drawn blade. "I am Parsival, son of Gahmuret." He half-smiled at his boast. It was unlike him. But his distorted consciousness was taking its toll. How long would it last? All the realities and imaginations were mixing and pressing in. "Stay near me," he told her. "Bear with me if I am strange and wake me if I sleep out of season." She nodded. "Poison children," he muttered. Gripped her firm hand. "But did I?"

"What?"

"Pleasure you."

She looked around.

"You always do," she said, "more ways than you know." She kissed his sooty hand. Rolled her eyes and sighed. "I drip again," she realized. "Well, no time for that . . . I think I grow tougher than when last we wandered in the forests together . . . Heaven, but things repeat themselves."

"I think it's until we learn from them."

She seemed calmer.

"Can we escape?" she wondered.

He shrugged.

"Go far enough and there's always an end."

No, he thought, *you never escape . . .*

XL

"The point is this, my lord," Howtlande was saying as the Vikings marched down the ever deepening crack in the earth by fitful torchlight. "The point is, training, organization ... I learned a great deal from that madman. For all his errors he was a remarkable bastard. I was not lightly won to his cause, at first. There was a promise then, a call to greatness that seems, in these times—"

"You must have slain Skalwere with your weight of words," Tungrim cut him off. "Make your point. You'll need breath for better things than breaking wind from the wrong hole."

"My point, Lord Tungrim, is simple."

"Make it then and have done, by Thor's frozen balls," the redbeard captain interjected.

"My point is this," Howtlande went on, studying their expressions in the wavering reddish flickerstrokes. "Organization. Training. Men become what they're taught to be. We take hold of the remaining youth of this land and raise them away from everything and teach them only what *we* want. Give them a new faith, a new outlook." He was quite excited now. These ideas had been perking in him for some time. Clinschor had shown him the way. "The lord master—" Caught himself.

"—the clever bastard wanted the whole world destroyed so he might rebuild it, you see? Eh? He was right. And now it's been destroyed and we—"

"What better training can there be than being born and raised a Norseman?" redbeard cut in. "Eh? You fat sack of contending winds."

"Well, well," put in Tungrim, "a man ought not to be afraid to learn a new thing from time to time. Even a Viking." He glanced over at the pale, mincing, wobbling mule that bore Layla, her face still in fixed profile to him. "Anything ahead?" he called to the lead torchbearer.

"Nothing yet, Lord Tungrim," was called back.

"If they'll move day and night," Tungrim stated, "then so will we."

"With your support, my lord," Howtlande continued, "we could begin such a project. Eventually we'd have people with total faith and no weaknesses. Totally loyal. Dedicated to you like monks to God!" He knotted one big fist. He saw Tungrim was musing, turning these ideas over within himself . . .

"It may prove a greater feat, fat talker," redbeard pointed out, "just to find food and drink." He leaned into the torch aura shifting around Tungrim. "Unless you mean to chew stones." He laughed without mirth. "There's a diet to support your fat."

Layla was sweating chill drops. She kept rubbing her tapered hands up and down her forearms. Licked her lips.

Now what? she asked herself. *I feel ill . . . what do I do? Bear him children? Hah . . . more of that . . . do I dream he's a fine prince and lives not at a court of mangy dogs in crumbling huts where I may spend long evenings chatting with his people about salting fish? Oh, Christ Jesus, be this where I end? . . . or just follow while they chase grails? . . . not without wine . . . I'll perform nothing sober . . . sober raise little beast brats if ever we reach his chill homeland? . . . among amazing bores . . . nothing without wine . . . who sees clearly cannot endure life . . . Parsival seems not so bad to me now . . . those days seem sweetened . . . bless the wise fellow, though mayhap it were a wife, who first thought to trample the grape which brings sleep's ease to those who must be waking . . . I'm so cold . . . and ill . . .*

She shivered in a shudder. Almost called out because something had moved against the high rim of the canyon where the bright, twisting strip of stars showed. Something huge moved with spiderlike springing, clawing. She kept staring.

"What do you see?" Tungrim asked, moving nearer.

"It moved," she told him.

"What?"

"Something. Up there."

"Um?"

"Something terrible..."

"Terrible?"

She shuddered. Nodded. Didn't look at him. In the wavers of illumination he saw her hands wringing her arms.

"What troubles you?" he gruffly asked.

"Ah," she replied, "what indeed."

"Is something there now?"

"I won't miss it," she said, voice too high and light, he thought. "Terrible things are coming...terrible things..." Kept her stare fixed at the crease of stars.

"You need rest," he said. In the background Howtlande was talking to someone else now. "We'll halt before long, Layla," Tungrim soothed. "We'll catch these silly fish and see what we see."

"No," she said, "it will catch us first."

"What will?"

She laughed, too high and light.

"Oh, it will, it will," she told him, staring. "It will."

"What's that, mama?" Torky asked.

They were nearly to the rim of the ravine now. She could see Pleeka ahead against the stars. She heard it too: a deep roaring above them, stormsound.

"Wind, it would seem," she told him. She could hear Pleeka still raging flatly, independent of listeners, as he clambered on.

"...so...so...so," he was saying, "all was betrayed and stained and let the great mouth swallow all except these I've pulled from the jaws...the jaws....I save food from the jaws...all will be eaten save these and let them be stones against the teeth!...so...so...so..."

She was easing Tikla higher on the fairly easy incline they'd reached. Pleeka was just mounting over the top and the wind struck at the same moment, like a black wall blotting out the stars, and he seemed to hang, float free and dissolve as driven ashdust blotted him away and he passed over them, his sounds swallowed by the terrific, pounding howl that shook the cliff stones, and then soot was pouring down and she was desperately sliding and scraping with the children towards the far bottom, the dry choking stuff, that seemed the dryness of the dark precipitate, spilling down like rain in hell . . .

Lohengrin realized one of them had kept pace with him as he ran ahead down the twisting channel that was now about an armspan wide. He had a fleeting fantasy it would end in a blank wall.

He heard the other coming closer. Suddenly stopped and turned, skidding a little on the smooth pebbles, silently drawing and holding the blade straight out before him.

The following foot impacts stopped.

"Who are you, sirrah?" the knight demanded, then realized: "Ah. The big fellow." Smiled invisibly. "You helped me. My memory's back now."

"Does that content you, sir?" Broaditch wondered.

"You're a shrewd Jack," Lohengrin decided. "How are you called?"

"Broaditch of Nigh."

"You were nigh onto my back . . . Well, walk on with me. I mean you no hurt. All that's run water . . ." They headed on, fast, though the big freeman kept a few cautious steps back. "Anyway, I think you did me a great service."

"Did I?"

"You snapped the halter fate had round my neck. You broke my memory, I mean, fellow." Sheathed his blade and kept one hand stretched out before him now. "Where there's a top there's a bottom," he commented. "Beginning has an end."

"Must it, Lord Lohengrin?"

"What did you throw at me?"

"On the hilltop?"

"Where else? I told you, my past is back with me. But what was it, nay, come out straight, I say."

"I cannot tell for certain."

"What?" Their pace had slowed as the walls closed in. They kept bumping and scraping around zigzag turns. "You hurled that mystery well enough to break my head. I love you not for that part."

"Your sword was not idle, sir."

Well behind there was a sudden silence: the wagon obviously could go no further. The outhouse on wheels, was the gist of Broaditch's thought. There were faint shouts.

"They're all mad to the pate," Lohengrin declared.

"I knew your father as a boy," Broaditch told him.

"Ah. Him..."

"And his mother too, for all of that."

"If this narrows more..." They went sidewise now. "It's good we've eaten little lately... You knew grandmother, did you? They claim she was queer of brain too. It follows the family. I don't follow the family." Glanced up and saw no stars at all now, a void... "I was the bad one. Blasphemous and so on. Well..."

"You were none to meet in a lonely place, I think."

"What? Oh, I remember. I sought your life for a time."

"I pray it's a habit you broke."

"Strangely enough, it ceased to matter after I became duke of now nonexistent lands." Chuckled dryly. "Or lord general of an annihilated host." Shrugged. "The past turned to ashes. What matter you saw me slay some long lost phantom?"

"Unless it trouble your conscience."

"I dare not feed one at this late date. The bill would break me." He groped along. "But why did you follow me?"

"I didn't." Which was true, because he assumed Alienor and the family had enough start to be well ahead.

And it's not likely a dead end else I'd of met them coming back...

"Hark," commanded Lohengrin. There was a steady roaring.

"If that be water," Broaditch muttered as they worked their way, bumping and scraping, through the jagged zigzags, "we'll shortly have more than we can drink."

"I think it be wind, Jack."

The sound was building, coming on as if flowing down the ravine behind, embellished now by screeching gusts.

"Right enough," Broaditch agreed, clawing around a bend. "What next?"

"Trust the Devil," said the panting knight, "he'll provide."

Vordit was alone near the deserted wagon, sitting in the dark. The Truemen were gone and now he heard the Vikings coming behind but didn't look up. "You're free," the big peasant had told him after the knight had cut them loose.

"Free," he now muttered. Listened to the storm building up behind the oncoming shouts of conversation. He rested his back on the rough wall and waited. "Free..." His mouth was too dry to spit or he would have. "I'll just step home now and plant me crop...Freedom's sweet..." Would have spat. Didn't look up from his sullen contempt when the horned warriors charged past, torches whipping out in the sudden, black, strangling gusts of ashdust. Didn't move as it flooded over him...

Cursing, Clinschor popped out the door in a rush of fecal stench and was jumping up and down in the twisting torchlight, left hand clenched tightly around the metal fragment of what he was certain was the Holy Grail. He felt its force pulsing up his arm into his bony frame.

The wagon was jammed tight between the walls. Hopelessly. As the thundering voice raged at the beasts and driver and finally at nature herself, John watched, in awe, the terrible, flashing, glow-eyed fury of the holy being that possessed him.

"Use your powers," he cried out in sudden ecstasy, "mighty one!"

The mighty one paused in his raging and lifted one contorted hand as if to reach and rip the dark walls apart, then closed his fist.

"Not yet," he said. The torch flames phut-phutted in the first fingers of wind. "We are close...close..." And with surprising, spidery agility he clambered over the vehicle and down the far side. As the others followed, he raced and vanished into the lightlessness beyond. "Soon we are home...soon..." He saw the hall of the earthgods where power rose from the deepest foundations of the world, a vital darkness like flame that needed but the touch of the Grail...the touch...the wordless voice was explaining, showing him without images, teaching without precept, the voice within the bones of his head, intimate, infinite, hollow with chill force, made clear that he and the power would be one at last, the earth itself would be his body, subterranean fire his blood and stone his bones...

Aiiii, he thought in trembling delight, *yesyesyes*...actually running now as the voice urged him on and he tripped and bounded off the narrowing sides, spinning and half-spinning, laughing...just one touch of the Grail and the hollow force...just one touch...

And then the storm hit, blasting and sucking air, washing floods of ash (because there was no rain) down the streambed, the first invisible puff already among the rearmost, choking, eye-stinging...

Alienor and the children, who were well behind even the Vikings, had crawled halfway down the slope and found a deep crevice in the rockface. They'd crept within, safe, as terrific gales puffed, billowed and snapped.

They held one another in silence. She didn't even pray. And the children didn't cry. Just held each other...

XLI

Parsival and Unlea were right on the rim when the first blasts came ripping and crashing through the powdery forest. They could hear the brittle trees snapping. The first spray of dawnlight was in their faces as they fled along, panting, not speaking, as if they ran to greet the sun.

He sensed the fierce children still behind and parallel to them but the windstorm was already muffling any lesser sound from that direction and an instant later had blotted out sight as well in swirling, tortured clouds. Dead black tendrils coiled and uncoiled reaching ahead of them. He thought of a vast spidery thing clutching at the world. The air stung and puffed around them.

The outline of a fortress jutted against the molten horizon at the edge of the ravine. He'd spotted it in the first light and planned to make a stand there one way or another.

Half-supporting her he fled on hoping the poison in the water would wear off because he could still feel it, lambent, within him, his perceptions a shadowfall away from the other worlds ... visions ... whatever they were ...

"We're nearly there," he reassured her, panting. "Hold the pace."

The black swirls hooked and clashed closer.

"O Mary . . ." Cough. "O . . . Mary . . ." Cough.

She stumbled to her knees on the broken bricks where the first wall lay shattered. As he lifted her he saw them taking shape out of the coil of jet dust, totally blackened figures, young people mixed with nightmarish shapes: a thing like an egg with a face racing upside down and backwards on stump legs beside the fearful monkeylike thing; birds with lush breasts above the walking fish with eyes like pits to utter, unreflecting nothingness . . . and now in the roaring masses of cyclonic soot he saw deeply into their world, a strange greenly glimmering landscape . . . and he saw, as he reached the outskirts of the castle grounds, lungs fire, limbs dead, a skeletal army of them massing and pouring forward towards where the glowing border seemed to shimmer within the stormdark, and he had a vague idea that the wind might drive them all through into this world.

Illusion, he thought. But what did that mean? A feeble shield, for at these outskirts of reality visions had the weight of stone. And the storm seemed to be gathering and literally blowing from that green-dark world where strange fires flashed like lightning flares (he and Unlea reached the fallen inner wall and were scrambling up the loose blocks and firecrumbled rubble), revealing tall shapes, shadowy outlines that seemed to preside over those mounting forces.

He set her down and turned on top of the pile. The brightening sun showed three of them charging up the loose slope, long knives drawn, long hair flying, eyes and teeth alone white as they rose from the bottom of the gusting blackness that was mounting, twisting, opening the other world everywhere now, the livid masses of horrors swelling forward as if borne by the contorted gale . . .

Three teenagers came on, skidding, falling, clawing upward. Others appeared, staggering through the stifling gusts, and the empty-eyed fish and prancing monkeything were at their heels and seemed rock solid.

"Unlea!" he shouted, "make for the castle! I'll follow! Go! Go!" And saw her stagger down the far side of the shattered wall, and then the great, stinging cloud heaved vastly and blotted out the sun and they all reached Parsival at once and he drew his blade and something seemed to say in his thoughts:

Hold back the darkness, Sir Parsival of the Grail.

And the whole, incredible, mysterious landscape fell over

him and he stood among the greenish glinting rocks and spectral hordes in raging stormfury, knives flashing and zipping at him from blurry shapes. He strained, blinded by the driving dust, swayed, ducked and twisted, reflexed as if the sword itself could see...struck...struck...felt a slash across his back mail...struck saw the fish raise it's foreclaws, the monkey snatch at his face, terrible steel birds rip through the blasted air...

"You're all real!" he howled at them as the wind lifted (or was it the creatures?) and drove him backwards. "Yet false!" as though it were a war cry or deadly incantation...

Broaditch and Lohengrin were just ahead of the storm when the knight, as he'd feared and expected, crashed and rebounded with a muted groan from the inevitable dead end.

"Christ!" muttered Lohengrin. "If your head hurts, why that's the very part you hit."

Broaditch was already groping over the rocks, thinking:
The water got through when there was water...

"Always," Lohengrin was sighing.

"Here," Broaditch said, on his knees. The soot was spilling over the high, narrow sides in semi-solid gouts, hissing around them. He'd found a low opening that seemed to dive into the belly of the earth.

"A rat's hole," the knight said over the mounting wind-sound.

Broaditch was already squeezing in because, he reasoned, if he hadn't passed them yet why then they were ahead. These sides couldn't be scaled so his logic was seamless and, as is often the case, safely enclosed no truth whatsoever.

"Better to live a rat," he called back, struggling in on elbows and knees.

"Than die as anything better," Lohengrin completed, creeping in behind. They could hear the dust piling up behind, filling the cleft like a snow of blackness.

Clinschor was a few yards behind, prancing, following the contorted way as if it were bright-lit, long bare feet and bony shins swishing through the already calf-deep sootfall. He was tittering and chatting and coughing as the fine powder caught in his throat. The last time he'd entered his stronghold this way he'd had to wade through the water, but his memory on such points had become increasingly sketchy . . . normally you came in through the fortress above where Parsival and Unlea were struggling.

Concentrating on what he was going to do with the power of the Grail, he'd totally forgotten the blind wall until he hit it, cracking his nose, and burst into a frenzy of curses: the wizards were blocking him out again; well, they'd soon see!

"Still trying, you bastards!" he shouted into the drifting soot, swallowing the noseblood and coughing. Shook the Grail fist at the wall, prepared a spell to burst the rock asunder . . . then remembered, stooped and skittered under the overhang in a gush of ashes. Heading forward into the total blackness he resumed planning the great games he would institute where all in the empire would have to fight and prove their worthiness to exist . . . except, naturally, the slaves who would tend the gardens. The gardens were a major project, would cover countless acres with flowers of beaten gold as tall as men, trees of pure silver, hung with little bells shaking in the breezes . . . no night! He would banish night with a million candles lit from dusk till dawn. Nodded his head fiercely. Always music and light and the most beautiful people. He was walking upright in a space where Broaditch and Lohengrin were still creeping along on their knees, and they heard him going past, talking steadily.

"We stay behind him," whispered Lohengrin. Clinschor's voice was booming in the obviously large space. "Of all men on earth he's the easiest to follow."

"And gives the worst results, eh?"

"More than true, but now is there choice?"

". . . the breeding will take place out of doors in the heavenly gardens," the voice was elaborating. "Each male and female I select will bear a brand on the left arse cheek . . . an excellent idea, and those with corresponding marks will be allowed to mate! Excellent. Offspring will be examined and the fit will live and be sent to battle at the earliest possible age. Excellent. What warriors I'll produce. Who will stand against the survivors of such training? The breeding will take place in certain beds and I will control the weather with my invocation . . ." And on and on . . .

Broaditch knew that Alienor would keep silent and hoped that she'd hear and follow that voice too. There wasn't much choice. The dark was solid enough to make the eyes flash as if trying to create their own light in compensation.

"Do you hear all that?" Lohengrin wondered quietly as they tried to stay directly behind. "That's the kind of thing I used to have to listen to. Till your blow freed me, Jack."

The mule needed no urging. It jerked and plunged along. The ash was sucked into whirlwinds and torrents, dimly visible in the feeble dawnlight high above the ragged cliffs.

Layla had pulled her scarf over her nose and mouth and was hacking and choking less than the Vikings behind her. She heard Tungrim shouting something, and then it was lost as the dying animal careened around the twisting way, all sound sucked away by the muffling sootfall and raw mutter of the wind...

Howtlande heaved along in a massive panic, pushing ahead of Tungrim and the others, thinking:

No...no...not like this...

Rebounding off the rough walls, falling in the powder, lurching on, hands pressed across his mouth, sucking air that caught in his throat, eyes mad with fear of suffocation.

No...

Tungrim cupped his hands under his ample nose and went on steady and stocky, shouting for Layla as the black dust rose knee high and more...

So by the time he reached the gully cave it was almost chest high and he believed he was doomed. The downpour showed in slight touches of glow that seeped through the great black gusts.

He was startled when a great blackened head lifted from the drifts and turned a glazed and hopeless eye on him, and then he knew it was Layla's mule. It was kneeling, up to its chin in the stuff.

He kicked around to satisfy himself she was not actually under the surface.

In something closer to panic than he'd ever experienced he sucked in a last dusty breath and ducked under because he knew she hadn't climbed out. No one could have. And he half swam, half dug to the base of the cliff...

When you cannot retrace, why you go on, he said to himself. Down into the indescribable black, as if the core of all darkness had precipitated into dry substance...

He dug, clawed, scraped along the rockedge, felt nails rip and peel away, head butt-butting. His brain flashed and flickered like a stifled torch, and he saw a bronze shape that his mind named Odin swinging wide a massive iron gate set in a towering wall in a cloudy violence of sky among wailing, melting voices and the voice like bronze:

"Strip off thy flesh-armor. Put aside all goods. Remove thy remembering and enter here cleansed of every yesterday."

No, he thought, *not now, not yet, hold off I pray! Hold off!*

His limbs scraped and groped far, far away from his seeing mind and sensed the two about to snap apart forever...and then he was somehow through the gate into an unending softness grayly soothing and draining him away into soft darkness, draining the last scenes: flashes of sea, rocky hills, women and playing children and shocks of season among huts in thin sunlight...his life drained, whirled out into the bottomless sidelessness...

He didn't know he'd broken through and was rolling inside the cliff, lungs flattened, body thrashing volitionless.

Parsival got up, leaning against the wrenching gales that tore at him, fluttered his light mail shirt, staggered him in the last livid streaks of lost sun, the air screaming as the flapping children and fiends reeled as if dancing the maypole (he glimpsed Unlea crawling up the steps to the fortress gate), the quick, bearded male leader shouting in glee words that were sucked away at his lips, falling, rolling as the knight braced and cut at them with furious disgust; the other, livid green glowing landscape fading in and out around him, the hideous army pouring through flanked by many-headed flying things that seemed all jaws and ruby claws and leathery, crashing wingbeats...

A naked girl danced, shrieking at him, dagger whizzing, and the wind veered her beyond his sword's point, her own slash a mere symbol...Two others crept towards him as if imagining they were invisible. They wriggled up the stones, knives in their teeth. Their actions, he strangely perceived, were like words, a scatter of messages...

And the leader shrieked, choking and hoarse:

"...seal...seal...opened!..."

The great fish leered and tilted; the monkeyform capered

on the crumbling walls as the other things flapped and crept and hopped...

The leader tried to handstand and was blown over. Parsival turned, ghostly troops, blurred, glow-eyed, gathered between him and where he could dimly see Unlea pushing inside, the door suddenly flinging inward in the terrific draught. She was gone as the killer children wriggled and plunged hopelessly at him and he just ran now through the fiend army, the shimmer and whirlwind of biting, blinding ashes. For a heartgripping fraction he was totally there in the harsh chill green world and felt terrible hands and claws pluck at his body and fall away like charred twigs... and he charged into the welcome stillness and lightlessness of the castle, yelling:

"Unlea! Unlea!"

Slamming the huge portal against the gale as though it were a bedchamber door, then the slam echoing in a time-frozen stillness as otherness surrounded him again: the sweet shifting pastels, the cloudy scenes, the watersmooth women taking his hands, stroking his knotted, aching body; silver music sounding; kissing with lips that melted from his tongue like honeyed mist, featherlight fingers where everything soothed soft and invited him to linger, drift in unending, changing cloudiness that could take any form he imagined, where all dreams took instant substance...

The interior was not quite black, so she could see him vaguely where he stood, still in the center of the floor, swordpoint dropped. Outside the storm thumped and heaved and light powder drifted in the thin, high embrasure.

She heard them scraping and rapping at the door.

"Parse!" she cried. "Parse!"

She flew in a frenzy to the door and slammed the great bolt home. Their voices seemed part of the mad blowing that rattled the wood.

"What do we do, Parsival?"

Fled back to him, pushed, pulled, shook him, beat her small fists into his lean hardness, hair loosely glinting.

"What? What? What?"

And he came back, the women melting into a general misty dusk that was the room too, walls and arches... studied her pale streaked face, sorrow of bone and desperation. Caressed her gritty flesh.

"That water still has me," he told her. *It may be*

forever . . . "But I won't betray you, Unlea." Sheathed his blade
and led her across the chamber through the widest archway.
O lord, draw me on, he thought, *for all my own ways have
failed . . . my skill foundered against children and empty wind . . .*

Went down the wide stairs, ignoring shattered skeletons that
tangled as if fallen while descending—weapons tilted and broken. Stepping over shields and armor fragments, kicking aside
a skull (as she shuddered) that clattered down a long way before
them . . .

"I'm thirsty, Parse."

The stairs wound in wide turns, like a corkscrew driven into
the earth. The light from above the shaft was wisping to nothing.

"There's always water in cellars," he suggested.

"Will they follow us?"

"No doubt."

"They were but young people."

"Yes."

"Yet so terrible."

"Yes."

He paused to take a torch from a wall holder and strike flint
and steel to it several times until finally it flared into flame.
He heard her gasp, clearly seeing the broken bones, but he
didn't react because the light had soundlessly burst inside his
head and the afterglow seemed to shine through the dark stones,
and while he could still see her his sight went deep beyond into
scenes that slowly rose, formed, absorbed his attention . . . he
gripped her hand tight . . . he understood these were more than
memories as he rushed down the well-like stairs with her. Felt
them drawing at him, rich, layered color collecting into movement: antler prongs glinting, a brownish-roan form balanced
on delicate legs, floatleaping, gusting from green-blue brush
where sunlight lay broken and coinbright in the vivid density
of shadows, the angled spear clattering, blood jetting into mist,
eyes like dark jewels, profoundly calm . . . The steps flew underfoot and Unlea swayed into him . . . Blood mist was only
color: the spear had slain nothing, simply changed life and
substance to new forms and splendor as the deershape collapsed
into the rich wonder of brightness where death was a melting
from shimmer to shimmer . . . Saw the Red Knight again rising
above him as the big horse reared and the blood jetted down
the spearshaft over his own hot face and he felt himself melting

into the death, into the bright blood, the other forever a part of him...

Suddenly he knew the children were on the stairs. He didn't have to hear them. He wanted no more violence. The steps spun by. Unlea gasped and clung.

"I can't..." she was crying out. "Help...I'm falling..."

The torch fluttered as they whirled and it seemed that the stairs and walls moved and they were suspended motionless in the vortex center...

"No stopping," he called into the rushing spin, watching the next images gleam and shape themselves...

And then the stairs were over and they kept whirling out across a tiled floor, the wisp of light lost in a great hall. She fell and he went to his knees beside her looking (through his cloudy skull itself) at a dense pine forest and other trees tossing flames that were autumn red-golds under ice-blue air by a castle wall...

So we're back to this, he thought, recognizing the Grail fortress the way it had been when as a teenage knight he'd first found and lost it. Sick and weeping, Unlea clung to him as everything rotated. Then he helped her up, holding her hand and the torch, and they walked and wobbled a little.

"Come," he said, leading her through the woods towards the yawning gate in the warm little center of their flame, empty darkness all around.

Heard their voices coming down the stairs and was surprised by their speed. Why were they so persistent? What was the point? Madness fed on madness, he supposed...

"Hurry," he urged, as they crossed the deserted castle yard, though her eyesight showed only a narrow passageway lit by a fluttering torch. They were descending again on a long, smooth slope.

"God," she said, "but I cannot...I'm weak as a child..."

But we must, he thought, *or we'll start to really feel our hunger and thirst and once stopped too long she'll never rise again...*

"Never mind that," he insisted, but compassionately.

"Why? To perish in pits and tunnels?"

"Lean on me at need," he said. "There's a bottom to all pits."

No plan, he insisted, *no thinking...no trying...*

Because they were inside now and he saw the vaulted chamber lit by thousands of candles, warm, bright, rich, and saw his young self in blue and white silks drinking with the keepers of the Grail and falling asleep, his face so smooth . . . so fair it startled him . . .

Lost shades, he told himself, except he was there again in the stifling room, staring at the bearded, pale king propped on cushions, pages kneeling around him, one holding up the bloody spear. *King Anfortas*, he remembered, *poor man* . . .

And some blurry one uncovered some blurry thing on the table in the center—something round like a metal ball. Someone seemed to open it and all form dissolved and it was a hole in air, in walls, light, mind, sight itself, something the eyes couldn't fasten and focus on . . .

Is this it at last?

Paused and felt her slump against his legs, gasping, spent.

He stared; avid, tense, because he believed he was going to see what he'd missed that night long ago, discover what revelation he'd forever regretted. Tried to look at the strange, spheric absence and then he knew they all were watching him, the king looking painfully up. (Had this actually happened in the past? Was time a sleeper's dreaming of movement and scenes while he stirred not an inch from his bed?)

"Well," he cried to them in the soft brilliance of candles and white-blue silks, "let me see it! Show me. Here I stand waiting!"

And a long, slender woman rose in a fluffing of shimmer-gauze and pointed to the blankess that swallowed sight, saying:

Look.

"See . . . see," Unlea half sobbed. "What do you mean?" She climbed his legs and torso until she stood there weaving. "I hear them coming . . . what are you looking at?"

"There it is but . . . show me . . . show me the Grail, damn you!"

She was trying to pull him away from where he stared at the blank passage wall that dimly glinted in the steadily failing torchlight.

"Come," she said. "Oh, I thirst, Parse . . . come . . . I hear them . . ."

A steady padding coming fast like cat feet.

"Show me!" he shouted. "Curse you!" Raging at the markless stones.

XLII

Lohengrin and Broaditch headed for the warm spot of light. Entered a tunnel into a foul-smelling draught. They could see the bounce-walking skeletal figure of Clinschor ahead against the rosy fireglow. Could hear the echoing mutters.

"Ugh," Lohengrin said.

"At least there's light," Broaditch put in.

"To see what stinks by . . . that maniac has friends or family here."

They stayed in close to the dampish walls. Clinschor was just visible where the corridor turned. His bony, flame-wavered outline seemed to be towering over a pair of dwarves. His voice rumbled and rattled, the words jumbled and lost.

Broaditch's thirst kept distracting him as they worked their way closer. He idly wondered if there were enough moisture on the stones to soak off on a bit of damp cloth and suck.

Lohengrin made out some of what was being said up ahead:

". . . at last. So, where are the rest of my people?" Clinschor seemed expansive.

"What's that?" a squeaky reply.

"I've serious business here."

"Ah," said one of them. Lohengrin could see he was poking

his finger into the mucky floor, squatting. The other he could have sworn was urinating against the wall under the smoky torch set there.

"Attend me," Clinschor commanded, and strode on without looking back at the two, who just watched him for a moment, the squatting dwarf seeming to lick his fingers. The dwarves stooped along after the great conqueror, more, it seemed to the knight, out of curiosity than anything else...

If they came this far, Broaditch was thinking about his family, *they're likely captured*...

"I see no better road than the one ahead," Lohengrin said.

He decided his memories meant very little. Even reviewing the murders he'd done, battles fought, plans planned, even then it stayed dreamlike and, as amnesia taught him, might as well have happened to another. Memory was not such a great gift. A man called himself his memories and they were largely a trick of the mind. No wonder a condemned man felt innocent at the scaffold: the crimes were only memories and if all men would forget, then nothing would have happened...

Clinschor watched the short, jerky, limping figure labor towards him through the torchshadows. His robes were rent, patched, filthy. The almost lipless mouth parted in shock and went slack. Little hands fumbled nervous with ragged tunic.

"Lord master," he said, mouthbreathing. Blinked his restlessly rolling eyes.

More of the male and female dwarflike people had dully gathered from farther ahead. They were largely naked in the humid air. Some carried clubs or warp-shafted spears.

The cripple, Lord Gobble, formerly of the great, world-shaking armies, looked apologetically around.

"Most of the others," he murmured, "fled... Cowards and deserters. I..." He gestured emptily. "I've organized this cave folk as best I could... I did the best I could but..." He gestured around expressively at the dull-eyed, grubby, wormpale faces of the little people. Some were picking lice and staring blankly, a few carrying on murmured guttural conversations which were totally obscure to Gobble. "... you see what I'm up against. Nevertheless I remained loyal to you, lord master..."

Clinschor kept his left fist tight shut over the blood-crusted fragment he'd ripped from Lohengrin's head. He more or less recognized the drawn, wolfish, avid features twisted up to look at him. He partly smiled. Was thinking of the tunnels twisting down and down the labyrinthine ways to the common center, where the well was sunk to the center of the world where the vast, implacable, magnificent lords of time and power waited frozen in the dark...he felt the Great Lord calling him, aware of the Grail fragment, that could melt the ice and pry back the stone and free them to rise through the shaft to the surface...

Clinschor's grayish-blue eyes showed troubled fires that the twisted Lord Gobble drank in with delight. He was recovering from his surprise and general depression.

"Lord master," he breathed, "you have passed through much. Mayhap you have returned greater than before."

Clinschor went past him, rapt, absorbed by distant things. The toadlike people looked incuriously at him as he passed. He was vaguely aware of them and made a note to chide Gobble (whose name he kept forgetting) for not keeping their gleaming black and silver armor spotless. He was sure he noticed specks of stain and rust here and there. He didn't glance back and assumed the tall and terrible elite warriors with their fierce face masks had fallen in behind. He pictured thousands of them filling the chambers and galleries of this stony warren.

"I know you've done your best, Gob..." he said, forgetting the whole name this time.

"I've done all I could, lord master," he replied, twisting his frail body to hurry after his lord, the bent, lumpy foot crashing down on the loose planking that partly covered the mucky floor. "Let us wash some of the soot from you. I think I recognized you only by your eyes, lord."

As from far away (because he was striding through great jewel-dazzling halls beamed with silver and gold over deep, rich fur rugs) he heard him.

"The great days are come again, Gobble," he thundered suddenly and the little man, as if injected with fire and fury, jerked up his bulge-eyed head and nodded once, instantly excited, pressing close to the spindly, blackened, twitch-stepping conqueror.

"Yes," he said, "yes! Thank God you lived! Thank God you're back! I crouched here helpless and alone with these...these lumps...betrayed, deserted, eating filth to live..."

"The great days have come forever." Bounced along with Gobble struggling to keep pace, a few of the half-naked dwarves ambling, semi-interested, in their wake through the foul halls, past feeble, scattered torches. One of the dwarves stooped, bent over what seemed scraps of food lying in a mass of rotted straw.

"Arrr," one grunted, poking at it. "Very like... very like..."

"This here's where the kitchen tunnel cuts over," another mumbled. "Them dogs feast an' we sweats and starves..."

The first sucked his finger, tasting.

"It's good flesh," he said, judiciously. "Not above a day old."

A third crowded close, amazed and delighted with the find. The first held up a pointy head with part of the neck still holding on. With many looks ahead and behind the lucky three gathered up the bony fragments and wrapped them in the hides they wore.

Up ahead Clinschor and Gobble were just passing a group of bowlegged women and sickly pale children sleeping, nursing, creeping on heaps of uncovered straw.

A few steps beyond all the wall torches were burned out in their sconces and Clinschor strode on in the shifting oblong of Gobble's flamelight, bouncing his shadow across the rock floor and walls. His left fist stayed locked closed around the scrap.

"My armies stand ready," Clinschor declared in stern thunder. "I've been too merciful in the past but that's all over. They all mistook my compassion for weakness... no more..."

The darkness before was luminous with his vision of all the defiant nations, all the thick-brained defiers of truth laid waste by the searing fires of his magic. His powers would find out every traitor in his very thinking and smite him. He tossed his arms well back and virtually hopped at the end of each stride.

"Where are you going, my lord?" Gobble called ahead.

He was nervous about going too far into the unmarked and untraveled maze of carved passageways that no man knew the end of, or when they'd been constructed. Did Clinschor know, he wondered? He went on without hesitation. Anything was better than rotting back there with those filthy degenerates, he decided... he had wanted to die for months here, and now... it had to be a miracle.

Clinschor went straight down a long, straight slope ahead of the flickering light, the immense voice muttering on like wind in a drain.

All the old force is still in his eye, Gobble assured himself.

He remembered the irresistible flow of their armies sweeping over the green earth, the wild excitement and sweetness of it; a new age about to be shaped from the sullen lead and dough of the old . . . and then the flaming accident that destroyed them, caught in their own fires. Crawling here to hide in the earth without hope . . . and then, thinned to bone, blackened, the master had reappeared from the cindered world, coming out of the darkness while Gobble was dragging himself on his hopeless, meaningless rounds in a parody of his old activity. And then, as if taking form in the reddish light, solidifying into tight, ironhard substance with all the force of an omen or a dream. *I will follow and forget . . . Follow and forget . . .*

"Parsival," cried Unlea, bracing herself, yanking at him, dragging him out of the glowing Grail Hall—she didn't see—towards the nearest archway. "For mercy, come! Come!" Because she heard the footsteps rushing faster . . .

Except he was in a dim, mistladen forest of towering, dark-wet trees. Moved in a kind of twilight silence. He felt her hand and had a dim sense of the actual darkness they hurried into. He felt the deadly children following behind among the trees that were chilly corridors and empty stone . . . a mounted knight floated out of the mist, greenish armor wetly glinting . . . familiar . . . calling something . . . his name: *Parsival Goddamnit!* . . . cantering past . . . *Parse! . . . Parse!* . . . and as he vanished into the shifting fogs he recognized Gawain . . . features whole as they were twenty-odd years ago, and next there was himself (he half-expected it) helmetless in the red armor, riding the thickformed charger he'd won from Sir Roht the Red. *So young,* his mind noted, *and so fair, by Christ, I seemed a woman.* And he remembered what was coming next. From far, far away something (he didn't realize was Unlea) was trying to pull him out of this scene. He remembered what was coming next as the young Parsival, golden locks flowing, rode through a wall of mist and reined up as the old man stepped into his path, dark, big, bald and heavy-bearded.

Merlinus, he thought, and, arm stretched out, pulled unseen Unlea along in the other world that was less than shadows to him. *Merlinus . . .*

Spoke over his young voice (saying something about gray-beards interfering . . .) and saw the wizard's deep-set eyes flash to him, looking past the youth.

"Merlinus," he called through the fog, "I need your help again!"

From a ghost? the eyes somehow said.

"Yes. Am I not a ghost as well?"

Do you trust me at last?

"I need help. I'm lost."

Then let yourself be led.

"Where? Where?"

He was still moving into the swelling grayish veils, drifting away from the scene, though he still struggled to get nearer against the invisible grip he couldn't understand, because his own body seemed but a thickening of vapor...

The last door is at the bottom.

"Bottom? Bottom of what?"

And then he veered, tried to duck away from the fanged and taloned monkeyshape that suddenly sprang out of the dark trees, struck and bounced him reeling, and something screamed in a wailing voice: the dark world came solid again, flashed painfire, and he saw the stone pillar he'd crashed into and heard Unlea's desperate cry clearly now:

"Parse! Great Jesus . . . are you struck blind? They'll be upon us!"

She held the torch now as he groped for his bearings.

"All right," he told her without conviction.

"Are you come mad to hold fierce converse with nothingness? My God, lost in this terrible place with—"

"All is well. It's the poison water!"

He headed across the long hall, set with hundreds of pillars in echo of the dark forest from the past.

All is well except it will come back...

"You stumbled like a blinded man," she was saying, "straight into that pole though I pulled at you."

"Yes. All is well now. Come on . . . come . . ."

They entered another sinking, twisting corridor. He gripped her arm. Heard her laboring breath.

"O God . . . Parse . . . Parse . . ."

"If the poison grips my brain again just guide me as best you can. Do you hear, Unlea?"

"O God . . ."

"Do you!?"

"Yes . . . O God . . ."

"I love you. I love you, Unlea," he said. "I'll do what I may..."

"O God..."

He could hear the slapslapping of the following feet, and voices too now.

Why must they follow? Let them but come close when my brain is all mine and I'll instruct them in regret...

"Fear not," he said, but perhaps to himself mainly, because he felt the other world coming the way a dreaming is already on you by the time consciousness grasps the change. Heard the voices and the padding bare feet...

Layla felt it was a comedy. She only wished she were drunk enough to laugh. She realized she needed water but her mind was on wine, even here in this black cavern under the mountain. She kept recalling the last few swallows she'd managed after discovering the gourd in a discarded pack as the ash storm broke over them in black whirlwinds. There'd been just enough to flush her with delicious numbness and she knew she could deal with all other problems, even here buried alive. It was a comedy running and hiding and chasing through the desolate, pitiful world...

Tungrim...had he survived? She decided he wouldn't be easy to kill. He was a man, that one, no mistake...pity he was so crude and that they'd not met in early years.

Except all years have been dismal in their fashion, she reminded herself. The winesoft blurring lay around her like a soothing touch. She wobbled slightly and wasn't particularly concerned at seeing nothing in all directions and having no formed notions of what was to come...*A man as others weren't if it comes to that. But do I go to his frozen lands with him and become the lady of his longhouse? Imagine what his mother must be like...At least Parsival's was dead...She* frowned now that she was thinking about him. *The bastard...did he ever trouble to stir to my side of the bed?*

"No more," she muttered, "no more..."

Hugged herself suddenly, feeling the dank draughts that sucked foul stinks along with them. She believed, without having to phrase it internally, Tungrim would find her one way or another, simply because that was another unsatisfying alternative to nothing better. She believed the calamities would somehow run their course (they always had) and strand her again in the wrong place in the wrong life with the man who wasn't quite right enough... not quite, though good...

She wasn't really aware of the sickly torchlight until she was already sloshing and stumbling over the half-submerged planks that served for flooring in the inhabited sections of the tunnel system. Blinked at the flames... went on... blinked at the runty folk who suddenly emerged from a cross-corridor. The shortest and widest of the crew had a beard that coiled in patches along his jawline like coppery wires, face fishbelly pale. He gawked at her with washed-out eyes widened in something between awe and outrage.

What repellent little things, she thought. *Do they grow them in the slime here?* She giggled. There were even females, she noted. No shorter, the near one was, but laced with fat and sags like, she quipped inwardly, a bound roasting beef, half-naked as the rest.

What charms...

"Have you tongues?" she asked. It turned out not all did because the wide one yawned his mouth and pointed at the stump.

"Blaaaaerr," he said. Then smiled. Gawked. Moved closer, still smiling. Touched her stained leathers with stubby fingers as if wonderingly.

How well spoken, she thought, *and what fine teeth...*

"You live here?" she asked, raising her voice pointlessly.

Scatterbeard nodded with vigor and tugged at the fabric.

"Blaaahhher," he explained, gesturing, smiling.

"This is no doubt your court," she said. "Is there feasting and dancing this morrow?"

She walked past the group and wasn't really aware that they were all closing in around her until she caught her foot between two boards and reeled forward, half-running, and several sets of hands clutched her and she was down, kneeling, staring into the flabby woman's faces, shadows setting off the bulges and sinking the tiny eyes out of sight.

Layla didn't struggle. Wondered why they didn't help her up or release her.

"I have a thirst," she told them. "Have you any wine?" She shrugged in the softly firm gripping hands. "Or ale, for all of that? But wine's a noble's drink... still..."

The woman, almost face to face with Layla on her knees, stood there, expressionless, nothing moving but the flame-

wavers. The hands kept firm. She was only just beginning to
be afraid.

"Alllbhhhhooo," the voice said in her ear now and some
one of them laughed. The breath in her face was like soured
flesh. "Blaaatoooo!" Violent, spittle spraying.

She somehow knew he'd still be smiling. Reality was penetrating as no one moved.

Oh, she thought. *Oh ... oh ...*

The pig stood there, upright, scarlet gaze glaring, spacious
head near the roof of the passageway, great body gleaming,
a pale reflection of the baleful eyes, and John trembled with
awe and fell to his knees, hands gripped, interlocked against
his lean chest.

"Thou hast preserved me in the midst of Thy wrath, Lord!"
He felt the terrible look penetrating him, burning his soul naked.
He felt exalted. Felt an inner trembling surrender. "Thou hast
brought me whole through the storm of Thy darkness. I serve
Thee only, Lord!"

The vast shape remained fixed. Eyes glared, blank fire. John
waited for its voice to sound ... waited for a sign ... Felt no
hunger or thirst. Watched the sleek, luminous, towering porcine
form as if all nourishment flowed from the raised front trotters,
the thick snout itself: the mystery of its substance ...

Clinschor and Gobble and several ragtag dwarves came out
of a cross-corridor. The pig whispered and John called out:

"Wait!"

And Clinschor turned, eyes tracking, vaguely.

"Who's this?" Gobble asked.

"We must bring the Holy Grail—"

"What?" Clinschor focused, frowned. "What?"

"I have been told. By our Beloved."

"What?"

"Where did you come from?" Gobble wanted to know. He
was wondering whether these two might not be brothers, both
emaciated, filthy and wild-eyed. While he believed in lord
master's greatness, he remained concerned by his condition.

"We must take the Grail with us and raise statues of the
Mighty Beloved in every church in every land."

Gobble watched Clinschor ponder this idea with deepening
frowns.

"Who's this mad creature?" Gobble wondered.

Clinschor was now making intricate passes with his free hand.

"Back, devil!" he commanded. "Grababebble Grabab Grabab!" He incanted. "You cannot steal my power. Begone, devil, begone! I adjure thee!" Leaped up and down and flailed his bony arm in the other's face. John stood, swaying. Clinschor spat next, frothing with fury. "I've been too soft and tender," he said, nodding. "No more of that . . . no more . . ." Whirled and walked away. Gobble followed and then John staggered after, skinny fists clenched.

"Betrayer!" John cried, frantic. "We must save the churches! It's His command! Men's souls must be cleansed! This is our work!" He clutched at Clinschor, who swung the Grail hand just as Gobble whacked the fanatical priest with the flat of his blade. John fell flat, raging, agonized, clawing at the mud, blood in his eyes, cried after them:

"Betrayer! . . . Betrayer! . . ." The pig voice whispering instructions.

Clinschor was smiling, holding up the fist that prisoned the sacred splinter.

"No magic can stand against me," he explained. "You saw with your own eyes."

Gobble's own eyes were watching his master sidelong as he sheathed his sword. Blinked. Frowned faintly . . .

"I think we should rest and eat something, lord master," he suggested.

"Nonsense. I need no mortal sustenance anymore." Smiled. "I have returned from the land of the dead. I cannot die again."

"Ah," breathed Gobble. Frowned and watched as they labored deeper into the tunnel. Then his eyes went back to their customary restless rolling, as if ever searching for an exit or watching for a foe.

"I belong, as soon as you will, Gobba, to the powers." Smiled and stuck out his chest with simple pleasure. "Soon all will belong to them," he added, chipper, refreshed . . .

Broaditch actually heard the scream. He was holding a long, thin-stemmed mace. He'd just found it leaning against a damp wall as they carefully moved from torch to spread-out torch.

"A woman," he told his companion.

"What?" Lohengrin, who was nearly past the entrance,

wondered. He peered ahead hoping to sight Clinschor. He assumed he'd find the nearest way out.

Broaditch, thinking of Alienor, was instantly heading down the darker passage even as the knight hesitated a step.

"It makes little sense to go this way," he called after him.

"At this point," the other responded over his bulky shoulder, "it makes little sense to put one foot before the other."

Around a bend . . . another, no torchlight here. Broaditch banged and scraped along, ripping his hands on the gritty stones . . . heard another female cry, much closer. Lohengrin, losing ground, cursed and rasped his chain mail until sparks flew . . .

Broaditch was suddenly standing, panting, in a low, squarish chamber lit by a central fire that smoked back into the place as the flue sucked the flames into the rockroof. He thought:

The picture's come to life!

Remembering instantly (what he hadn't been likely to forget anyway) the bizarre paintings on the walls and ceiling of the wagon full of whores he'd traveled in before reaching the country where he'd found the famous Grail castle. The paintings had amazed him and now he froze, seeing the slender, long-haired nude woman shockingly outspread in the smoky light, limbs stretched in four directions (he couldn't see the ropes on wrists and ankles yet), a small, flaccid-bodied female bent forward between her legs as if drinking from her groin while several (*children*, he first thought) pale little naked males writhed around and over her, small hands plucking at her flesh and one another's, joining together like acrobats, grunting and gurgling, the bound woman yelling as Broaditch broke his brief trance and moved forward as Lohengrin crashed through the last twists of the passage.

". . . you fucked, foul, diseased mute filth!" she was yelling. "Oh, Christ!! Remove that fat asshole of a face from my private garden else I'll piss in your scummy mouth! You pig bitch! Fat, fat dwarf filth! Untie me, I say . . . you pack of dwarfed degenerates! Free me, I say!"

And Broaditch was even laughing a little as he raced past the flames and heard Lohengrin's stunned expletive behind him as he stopped and uncertainly shifted his mace in his grip. He felt vaguely like a parent finding children in the hayloft while he resembled, in the flameflaring, a demonic judge of hell's remoter pits.

Some of them looked up, pale, interlocked with organs of
action that large men might have envied, and beckoned him
into the heap with grunts and choice, proffered flashes of anat-
omy, while the fat little female licked and slobbered in the
bottom of the lady's belly . . . they tugged and sucked at her,
reminding him of kittens round a dam.

"Great God," Broaditch said.

". . . disgusting, loathsome," Layla was going on, then,
seeing him: "Are you another of these *things?*"

"Free her," he told them. It had little impact.

Lohengrin had arrived. Broaditch heard his breathing.

"Well," he said, "this once would have been to my taste,
before I was hit by the Grail or whatever . . . but I like not all
the fellows to the feast here so well—" and broke off as he
and Layla stared at one another. Broaditch was now scraping
and kicking the others away, though they simply continued
their sport wherever they fell in the heaps of hay and sacking
spread everywhere.

"Lohengrin!" she cried. "Lohengrin!"

Broaditch paused, dagger poised to cut her cords, and stared
at both.

"I . . ." the beak-faced knight began.

"Great God," she said.

"Mother," he said, "I . . ."

Broaditch just stared in the jerky reddish-dark waverings,
the pale heap of entangled dwarves on one side (he'd tossed
the fat shimmer of pendulosity into the center of it all), mother
and son, incredibly reunited, on the other . . .

He found nothing (as he later put it) in his mouth but a
stunned tongue and so, wisely, kept it shut . . .

The torch was sputtering to death. Parsival hadn't actually
registered anything as he skidded to a halt on the clay semi-
mud, locking her close to his side with his free arm. The pit
at their feet filled the tunnel from wall to wall. Here the bricks
were loose and slimy muck pushed out between them under
the sagging roof.

He held the flame down and stared into the soundless gape
of darkness.

"Mayhap," he murmured, "the bottom is in Satan's bedchamber."

"What can we do? What—"

"It's not too far to overleap." About seven feet, he guessed. What had that vision of Merlin told him?... *The bottom door ... or something ...*

"Oh ... But ..."

"Peace, woman. What may we hope to go back to?"

I'll take a good start ... with armor and a woman ... Christ lend me succor ...

"My God," she said. Repeated.

He heard the relentless feet splashing behind. He didn't dare face them, not if the other world flipped back and blinded him again.

"I won't have all my roads end here," he told her. "Not in this sewer."

She gripped him then, looking into his face, desperate, intense, eyes showing the guttering flame in a face of shadows and black filth, a last, lost tremble of brightness squeezed by the absolute dark.

"Hold around my shoulders," he commanded.

Persistent, disgusting maniac children! he thought.

She kissed him first and took it in to herself with closed eyes as if for eternity.

And then he drew back with her and charged for the rim, trying to gain traction, pointed footgear slipping, and he knew halfway it was no good and dug in his heels, hoping to stop without going over, and at the last moment, shrugging, flinging her off, gasping:

"Let go! Let go!"

Even as his legs went in he tried to twist around and push her to safety except she clung with such fierce strength (that would have amazed her had there been time), and so he hung half in, half out as the mad children, in a flashing and flutter of torches, arrived screaming and howling as if they'd just won some game ...

He clung to the slippery lip, Unlea holding one arm, his tense, weary, furious face contorted, glaring at them with terrible bitterness. There were no fiendish shapes this time, just naked boys and girls, dancing and cheering with glee, flashing daggers.

"Why?" he cried at them and the walls and the dark too. "Why do this?!"

She didn't look, kept her eyes on his face.

He saw the leader, the stoneblank expression, the bunched

beard. He was panting. The rest watched him for a sign.

"Death in life," he pronounced. The group sighed. "Life in death."

The sighs suggested ecstasy.

"What mindless wretched nonsense!" he snarled. He struggled to claw himself up and draw his blade, his legs swaying over emptiness, fingers scrabbling, slipping.

The naked mud-and-soot-stained crew capered closer, smoky light leaping around them, at least a dozen blades snick-snicking, and then Parsival saw the dark shapes around them, growing out of the smoke and fitful fire, hovering, possessing...

"Bathe," the leader cried, kicking his heels together in the air, "in the blood of love!" Sighs and gasps. *Lustful*, thought Unlea with shock, not looking, not taking her eyes from her lover.

The fish, the monkeylike thing, others, others, bodies of greenish smoke, clawfaces, clawing-eyed... The world dimmed again and with a kind of sobbing he let go and gripped her, pulled her over, clutched her to him, as the blades that were teeth too arced and ripped in vain, and they fell in silence, locked together, plunging down... down...

"I was here once," Howtlande was telling Tungrim. They shared a torch tugged from the tunnel wall. They'd met on one of the bowel-like turns of the inner warren.

Now they were working (to the best of Howtlande's recollection) their way around the main subchambers, although what lay farther and deeper than these was a complete mystery to him. "I spent the best part of a week in this miserable hole two years ago. This place was bustling then, let me tell you, fighters everywhere... part of my command, the best lads ever to march... that bentbrain led us all to hell... bad strategy, you see, Lord Tungrim, threw away the—"

"If he's such a fool," the other demanded, "why do you drag us behind him like this?" He was thinking about Layla. She was down here somewhere. That was the point. Go on with this fat flapmouth who knew something of the territory, until he found her.

"Here," Flapmouth said, stooping by the wall, holding the torch high. There was a steady rill of water tracing down the mossy stones. He leaned in and pressed his surprisingly thin lips there as if sucking at a shadowcrease.

Tungrim's body pressed close almost without his will, about to yank the bulky man away before he caught himself into his prince's dignity. Waited, feeling his tongue fat in his ash-dry mouth as the other man sucked and coughed and lapped at the stones. Finally he pulled back and the Viking drank deep, the icy trickle splashing over his face and neck.

"So," Howtlande went on, "mad as he be yet he's *cunning*. When you think of the loot he took!" Nodded. "And it's down here, by Freya. We all knew that. Why has he come here save to gather his wealth to raise a new army? Eh?"

Tungrim straightened up, panting a little, leather and steel tunic now soaked and chill. The fat ex-baron was vaguely less respectful, he noted. He watched the flabby, beak-nosed, desperately earnest face. He was still talking, he suddenly realized, amazed . . .

". . . and make ourselves masters of—"

"Masters?"

"Yes! What can stop us? We take the booty. This island is a field left fallow, you see? All we need do is march—"

"This island is a clot of shit, mad talker."

"But—"

"Be still, walrus. Keep the door shut and your fancies within."

"But—"

"Peace, I say!" Tungrim laid a hand on his sword hilt and they went on in the shifting, dulled torch aura. "Masters," he muttered. "By Odin's bleak stars . . . masters . . ."

Gobble was panting hard, struggling to keep pace as Clinschor bounced along the brickless tunnel. His deformed leg hurt with each splayed impact on the ringing, hard floor.

"I want the army shining with readiness," lord master was rumbling cheerfully. His recent triumphs left him expansive and warmly serene. "You will bear witness to great acts, Gobbo." His big, soft palm stayed closed over the sharp, blood-stained fragment. "Great acts . . ."

And then the passage ended under stalactites at a blank wall. They stood together, the flame shifting their shadows back and forth as if they rocked in bizarre unison: a skeleton beside a bent toad.

"So still you would thwart me!" Clinschor suddenly

screamed, so wildly Gobble nearly dropped the torch.

"Know you not where we are, master?" he wondered, uneasy.

"The wizards, who soon will suffer greatly, have shifted the turning to confuse me." He laughed. "No matter. I cannot lose my way, for all ways are mine, Golba..." Smiled and raised the Grail hand again. "I might open this wall with a single stroke, if need be..."

"Need it be?" Gobble was wary. Mad or not, this was Clinschor the Great. Who knew what he might do?

Howtlande saw the light whisk past down the cross-corridor and heard the unmistakable voice, thundering.

"... you see, I've found a new way to the lowest level and foiled my enemies once more..."

And the rest muffled away as Howtlande said:

"That's him! We've stumbled onto him. What a fair fate I now follow!"

Tungrim raised both eyebrows and deemed this as good a direction as any in these ropy coils of confusion.

"Why," he sullenly mocked, "we'll be masters in the space of a seagull's fart."

Get the woman, he thought. *Go home. Find the rest of Skalwere's kin before we find the longhouses burned...*

Broaditch had found Layla's robes and helped her into them. The three of them stood there, Lohengrin, as the shock wore away, smiling and shaking his head. The swarming dwarves rolled and spread and regathered in their heap like a single creature many limbed and headed, struggling in the quavering light...

"Well," said Layla, shaking out her matted hair, "there's so much to say I'll close my mouth over it."

"What a delightful place to find you, mother," her son commented. "I'm pleased you've kept from idleness."

"I'm glad you kept from death, my boy. I've heard much of you."

"Not much, I think, as was pleasant, mother."

She shrugged.

"Either of you have a good direction in mind?" she wanted to know.

"No, mother," he said, "we thought it best to stay here with your rutsy friends."

"How like yourself you always are."

Broaditch tapped his foot and cleared his throat and wobbled the mace, trying not to look at the constantly shifting, reforming mound of sex.

"I like a family reunion as much as any," he put in. "But I think, lord and lady, there be other holes down here just as foul as this and not so filled up, so please you."

Layla approved his irony and pondered him.

"Like your father too," she said to Lohengrin, "you're thick with the clods." To Broaditch. "But you're a rough old rogue, uncle, to have witnessed my shame."

"Say, rather," he suggested, "inconvenience, my lady."

Holy mother, he thought, with a sigh, *I tracked through all the earth to find trace of any of these and here at last in this snake's palace and mole's delight* . . .

"How well he speaks," she said, with surprised condescension.

"Is your husband here?" he asked.

"What?" put in Lohengrin. "Him too? Is all Britain in this sewer drain?"

"Your father?" she was humorous and scornful.

"I know not. I asked you, mother."

"So did this great chunk of peasant." Leaned close to Broaditch. "But say, fellow, have you such a thing as wine or ale about you?"

"Ha," added Lohengrin, "father's spirit is certainly present."

He lit a torch at the big fire and then pulled several burning sticks from the coals and straightened up.

"Have you?" she persisted.

"Eh?" Broaditch was watching her son.

"A drink, clod Jack?"

He gestured at the orgy lump.

"Try them," he suggested, "my lady."

She took his advice so far as to stoop and peer around their garments, as suddenly dozens more of the pallid, voiceless folk emerged from the shadows (*one must have gone for others*, Broaditch reasoned) and advanced, surrounding them, gesturing towards the unceasing action. Several males and females exposed their genitals, fingering themselves and dancing, swinging their hips to unheard music.

"Right enough," said Broaditch, pulling Layla towards the fire where her son had started hurling burning sticks into the obscene mob. "Christ on high!" he cried.

"Mother," Lohengrin yelled, laughing, "they mean to have the lot of us!"

They were burbling wordlessly, ducking the missiles that fell in fluttering, rushing arcs around the chamber.

"Christ," was all Broaditch could say, lifting his mace and leading them towards the archway.

"Had they fairer forms," Lohengrin declared, "I might be tempted."

Suddenly falling was suspended, the darkness gone, and Parsival was sure he floated on a soft cushion or was supported by gentle, unseen hands. Unlea was gone again... he felt himself rising as a feather on a draught... and then he was in a place he knew, a hall with thin, slanted lines of light fanning in from high up, past dim pennants unstirring in the still, cool air. He moved up the hall and saw, with a tremor, the woman on the highbacked wooden throne, pale light washing her form into the stone dimness. Her head suddenly tilted back and he heard her say something he thought had his name in it, but he couldn't quite make it out and heard his own voice:

"Mother... Mother... What did you say, mother?... Can you see me?"

Her extended hand went stiff into a violent clench and he knew she'd just died.

"Help me, mother... tell me... tell me..."

And then mud and water rained down as his lungs sucked for air, and he heard Unlea's outcries in the total blackness clamping in around them as they clutched and scrambled into the muddy edge of an invisible pond or sluggish stream...

"Stop!" Clinschor shouted, holding up his arm. They'd just entered a chamber where shriveled carcasses of what might have been goats or sheep hung swaying in chains over low fires. They were obviously being smoked. At the far end of the room was a low wooden door. "What wizard's work be this?"

Gobble shrugged and took a deep breath, grateful for the rest. His leg was almost numbed.

"We must have circled back," he offered. "I know this place."

"Thus you've been the more deceived!" his leader thundered. "This chamber is enchanted. These are the bodies of the heroes before me who tried to do away with the lies and stupidities and corruptions of men! This was their fate. Endless torment!"

Gobble rolled his restless gaze around, unsatisfied.

"But—"

"Silence, Goppa," insisted Clinschor, watching the colorforms that menaced him, wizard things to seize his soul, forms of soft butterfly confusion, cloudy purpose... shifting shapes hinted wonders of light and peace... He forced his eyes to the pure dark shadows. "They tempt me still," he muttered to Gobble, who was just watching now and massaging his cramped, crippled leg. Clinschor stared at the swaying meat and began a muttering drumroll of incantation.

"I will burst the spell that seals the door," he said.

"Master," Gobble put in, "I can open it, I..."

"Make ready, men," Clinschor said. Gobble wondered which men he meant. Looked around at the smoky, dim chamber and saw none.

"But..." Gobble began and then was checked by the smouldering, pale, hypnotic eyes.

"There are powers here, Globa, you cannot imagine, whose lightest touch would shrivel your bones to dust." Gobble nodded, locked to the strangely vacant stare. Felt the threats around them now, the nameless shapelessness of unfocused terror. Clinschor could see them pressing against the door, fluttering, soft, stupid touchings, like women's hands ready to stroke, sap, lull him to weakness... "Once we pass this barrier nothing will stop me!" He flung this challenge at all of them and advanced on the exit, incanting under his breath, his vassal tilting along uncertainly in his wake. "The corruptions gather against me. The cowards who fear the prisoned king chained below. I'll free him and woe to you all! You weaklings who cannot bear greatness will pass away forever!" The soft, tender cloudiness rose up before him like a cloying perfume... he thought of his mother for some reason... "Behold, I smite!" He roared and lunged at the door, struck it with the Grail fist and it sagged and wobbled open effortlessly outward and he stood facing the terrific, chaotic frenzy. "Behold them put to rout!" Where his dark lightnings flayed the rose-soft, cloying sweetnesses and amorous, dying tones to whimpering shreds...

Gobble stared, tried to see something in the musty dimness beyond the doorframe. Saw musty dimness.

"Follow me, men!" his leader cried. "To final victory!"
What men? he still wondered, following . . .

Now they were sloshing on, clinging together, groping calf
deep in the slimy spill that Parsival realized must be draining
somewhere ahead as it flowed steadily over their feet.

She seemed strangely calm now, he noticed. She'd passed
hysteria. Realized she'd given up and so would be all right for
a time . . . until her hopes returned . . .

The visions seemed to have ended again. His eyes beat
hopelessly into the blank wall of absolute lightlessness and
wondered where this would ultimately empty . . . in any case,
as ever, there wasn't any choice.

Tungrim batted his eyes.

"What's this?" he muttered.

They'd come out in a high-roofed, cathedral-like hall lit by
hundreds of candles.

"I know not," Howtlande said. He was depressed. They'd
lost Clinschor's trail a few corridors back and had circled use-
lessly since.

There was something like an altar in the center of the floor,
where more of the stunted people were gathered in seeming
worship. A massive, unshaped chunk of rock lay tilted on the
pedestal. Several of what looked like priests (in robes that
dragged behind the diminutive forms) stooped, knelt and appeared to place small objects around the stone. He squinted as
they went past. Some of the congregation wore fragments of
black armor with tarnished silver trim; some wore what he took
for masks until he realized he was looking at helmets with
hideous silver faces. The little priests (if that was what they
were) chanted out of phase.

Howtlande was tugging at him.

"Here's a way," he said.

And they hurried away into this new descent.

"What a place," Tungrim muttered.

"Determination is everything," the huge man meditated
aloud. "All things fall to the determined man. He never sur-
renders to adversity. That's the key to greatness. Not being so
smart and great of wit, who cares? Eh? Who cares for genius?
Eh? Better to sink in your teeth and hold on to the end
. . . determination . . ."

Determination, the Viking thought, *yes, by Thor's eyes. I'll crawl through all this stinking pit until I find her . . .*

The sex-maddened little people were following at a distance as Broaditch, Lohengrin and Layla went on quickly through the fetid passages, each with a weak torch. The knight would suddenly turn and catch flashes of their eyes as they fell back and waited for him to go on.

"They just creep and crawl and cling at you," he muttered at his mother's slender back. "How can you even kill them? They don't really fight."

"Being both men," she suddenly said, "you no doubt need no counsel from a woman."

"Much less a lady and mother," said Broaditch from the lead, thinking:

I began in this family's service and mayhap I'll end at the start . . . I feel it . . . I'm not free yet . . . I'm being forced into something again . . . the tide and waves still bear me on . . . (remembering how the sea had once gently borne him through a tremendous storm, past fanged, dripping reef-rocks, restored his life as a gift and a debt to the invisible, less than a year ago . . . and from that moment he'd known no one is ever free) *but on to what? I would ask were I still babe enough for asking . . .*

So he accepted he wouldn't find his family again (they— or it, or he—always withheld them like stakes in a gamble) until he'd done whatever it was the invisible demanded . . .

"Mother," the knight was saying, "I, for myself, am eager for any help I can get." He glanced back, hearing a shuffling scrape. "Keep from my reach, you shrunken sodomites," he called into the ambiguous blackness. "I've been changed, mother. I had no choice in the matter."

"Have you, Lohen?" she said, not untenderly.

"Something caught in my brain," he ironically explained, "and let the old things run out and much new come in. Him, that burly, aging rogue who pants before us, he'll testify a piece of something holy laid me low."

"With what holy, pray?" she asked.

She was vaguely worried, reminded of his father. Was he going to flip full over and cross-kiss like the rest of that uneasy line? Better if one of them could find some solid footing in the middle . . .

"A piece of the Grail, mayhap," Broaditch said, and she couldn't tell how seriously.

"O great God of spiders and windmills," she cried, one hand reaching inside her soiled robes and touching the flask that jogged and sloshed there. Because even as Broaditch was jerking her free from the pale, stunted seducers, she'd been able to snatch it from a heap of their things. Touching it took the tremble out of her sudden fears. "Not that," she said.

"We know not what for certain," Lohengrin said.

"Just like your father and mad grandam," she said.

"Mother, please. Spare—"

"What advice?" Broaditch put in as they moved across a deserted chamber, unlit, where the torchflickers showed a giant erection scratched into the wall and decorated with smoke-stains.

"A question," she said, "merely: what gain is there ingoing ever deeper into this maze?"

"Or," put in Lohengrin, "what happens when these sketchy flames go out?"

"We walk in the dark," said Broaditch, "noble folk." Smiled. "Or light these others I've thrust under my beltcord."

We all saved something, she thought.

Lohengrin made a slight, sudden rush backwards and was rewarded by seeing a few of the leaders scurrying away.

"Still hopeful, eh, rats?" Laughed. "If we die of weariness at least they won't devour us. Guard your nether eye, big ruffian, if you fall."

"Wherein have you changed?" his mother wanted to know. "You still laugh at things unfunny."

Her hand closed around the firm neck of the leathern flask that rocked against her thighs.

"That's a private matter, my lady," said Broaditch, "as to what's funny."

"Never say 'Grail' to me, by Christ. The Grail swallowed my marriage without chewing! Gulped your mad father down."

They were following down a tight spiral now, unmarked, monotonous walls passing, a dank smell rising.

"Hm," grunted her son.

"He, whose mother was daft, and Christ knows how far back ran the taint."

How like my Alienor, Broaditch thought. *Noble or plain, a wife is the same . . .*

"Everything has a bottom, my lady," he called back up half

a turn. "Babies, holes, even griefs . . ."

"Did God swear it was so?" Lohengrin added, a full twist above. None of them was in sight of the other as they descended.

"If not we'll soon prove it," Broaditch answered.

He couldn't stop in time, because the turning was too steep and tight, so he flung wide both arms, dimming the torch, just as his legs and belly hit the stooped, strangely bent, hollow-faced creature (so it seemed in a winkflash) and he knew he was going over and down, crying out in shock, anticipating claws at the very least, the flame going out entirely as he sailed into the blackness and tumbled around the following bend, trying to kick himself clear of the thing behind him (seeing burning light as his skull cracked into rock), hearing, as from far off, a screeching that at first he took for the woman, then the creature except it was saying (Lohengrin coming, metal jingling, passing his mother), raving:

"Aiii! Aiii! Slay me not! Pity! Pity!"

And then he righted himself as Lohengrin's torchlight flashed on his drawn sword and outlined the grotesquely twisted figure Broaditch had fallen over . . .

John's head still hurt from Gobble's blow. He followed the glow of the pig through a dim and dark complex of chambers and ways. The giant form moved before him smooth as floating. The reddish eye-glare was like a torch to John, who was filled with calm. His soul was washed clean and polished smooth and there was no need to think, fret, plan, hope or fear: the Master would make it plain . . . the other one was false, and had sinned in the sight of the pig and sought even now to take the pig's holy power for himself in his foul blasphemy. The voiceless voice explained it in deep, rushing clarities within his brain. He laughed out loud, though by the end it had become a kind of moaning, and then he spoke, shrill, harsh:

"O blasphemer, thou shalt be set at naught!"

He barely noticed he was crossing a firelit hall where numbers of the runtish folk and a few normal-sized (though no less filthy, pallid and torpid) men and women gathered around steaming kettles, plucking out boiling things, scalding and sucking their hands, hardly looking up as the gesticulating, mumbling man, sootblack, jerky, went out the opposite archway.

"All thy work," he was saying, relishing, "shall lie dust and thy get and generation shall be as ashes and naught shall remain standing one stone upon the other in the sight of the Master!"

Went on, as if booted forward, head and neck wobbling, following the reddish phosphorescence of the tall, bulging shape ahead, not really feeling or noticing each time he blundered into a pillar or wall, smiling, confident, intent on the voiceless voice...

Parsival heard the sloshing roar ahead and felt the quickening flow of the thick, stinking water around their legs. Unlea simply clung to him. She'd vomited several times and now her legs just hung unflexing as he dragged her through the thick blackness.

And then he knew it was coming again, felt the first strangeness, faint flickers of light that brightened nothing.

Oh, God, he thought, *what do you want of me?*

Then he could see the walls of this foul tunnel, solid and dripping, dark water gurgling past, oily-looking, streaked as with dribbling spittle... then the rock faded...

There was a speck of brightness ahead like a droplet of sun burning deep in the heart of the world. It dimly echoed the fire within himself and he found he could look at nothing else now. It was like the door of a dungeon open a crack... He felt himself moving loosely, floaty as a butterfly, a blueness of sky exploding above vast, swaying golden-white flowers that condensed and shimmered the air that was thick and soft as honeyed water, curling, caressing under his wide, bright, sail-like wings. His eyes saw everything at once in crystalsharp shimmers... he was floating, swept into the melting golden softnesses and whispering flower touches, the tender shock of tasting the taste of himself too as he buried his face in the blossom, drinking deep, wings shuddering in ecstasy...

He turned, forced his perception away; strained, and the dark rushed back and slammed into him as though the walls had crashed closed; then, in fear, he begged the vision back, gave himself to the everchanging, speaking, touching brightness, the only opening in the unending mass of night's crushing stone...

It was so sweet, he half-saw a great winglike flash around himself, catching the streaming rays, and he was almost weightless, barely conscious of carrying her, almost sprinting through the stinking spill that here and there woke golden facets where a stray beam caught it... he fled... fled... locked to the distant shining. He rushed as the stream gathered speed and saw the waterfall he'd expected, glimpsed the sheer, terrific plunge of it, felt Unlea (all sound lost in the roaring) struggle in his arms, knew with tenderness that the foolish child was screaming as, without hesitation, he opened his silksmooth arch of wings and leaped out into the crashing abyss, feeling everything, world and water, stop so that while he saw it moving it hung within a stillness that suspended everything beyond comprehension . . . movement and time went on but went nowhere, progressed nowhere . . . meant nothing, touched nothing essential beyond the flimsy shadowflicker of the world as those delicate wings filled with prismatic flame, color and beat firm, lifted.

"Hark!" Tungrim said, gripping Howtlande's thick, softish arm where the short mail shirt ended, stopping a lengthy talk on the value of building from small beginning to enormous enterprises.

"Eh?" the ex-baron general grunted.

Tungrim had cocked his head to listen down the passageway ahead.

"A cry," he murmured.

"Ah," breathed the other as they moved cautiously on. He drew his broadbladed sword.

The darkness opened to the left: a crossway, flare of firelight, shadows and struggling forms . . . shrieks of pain, one light gone and then the other bobbed away as some fled and some followed . . . darkness . . . a diminishing rattle and chinking of steel . . .

"Things are stirring in here," Howtlande decided.

"Who are . . ." Lohengrin began and then, peering closer, recognized the twisted man on his knees. Pushed the flame closer to the wolfish face with the ever-shifting gaze.

"Lord Lohengrin," said the almost lipless mouth. "Hear my words."

"I'd sooner hear your screams," was the retort. But the young knight waited as Broaditch righted himself in the narrow turning.

"The master's mad," Gobble insisted, rising partway.

"Christ," mocked the young man, "here's news indeed."

"Who is this creature?" his mother wanted to know. In his

shadow she had just taken a pull on the wineflask, felt the hot, sourish trickle and soft impact within her, as if it instantly reached a soothing touch to each part of her body.

"Hear me, he's mad, I tell you!" His eyes bugged and wandered. "He will destroy everything."

"Is there aught left?" Broaditch considered, looking with faint disgust at the furtive little man, "he overlooked, perchance?" Because they all knew who the *Master* was.

Gobble's eyes flipped back and forth in the smoky, shifting flames. The slashmouth never entirely closed.

"There are terrors below," he said, his hysteria evident. "Terrors beyond terror."

"Below," commented Broaditch, setting his teeth. "You think what's above us here's a Sunday feast? Choose your own doom, fellow, I cannot decide. The menu's too rich for me."

But most of what he said was covered by Gobble screeching:

"He means to release the terrors, I tell you! He makes for the hole that reaches down to the demons in the earth! The well!"

"He goes to dip out friends," Broaditch said, "instead of water?"

"Well or ill," Lohengrin sneered, "I never cared for you, and I weary of your cracked master. Clearly your own brain's been bounced sidewise." Except he remembered first meeting Clinschor in the pits beneath the castle he'd won for himself by slaying the duke; remembered strange and fearsome visions . . . but nothing, he assured himself, substantial . . .

Gobble fastened on him, tugging, spittle flying, desperate, Broaditch trying to pry him loose, the crippled little man raging, pleading:

"Listen! Listen! Heed me! He has a charm to free them . . ." They had him all but loose, one bony hand still clinging as Broaditch shook him free. "A . . . charm . . . in his fist . . . fools!"

Behind them Layla took another long, slow pull on the wine. Blinked down at the absurd tableau.

"He must be stopped," Gobble screeched, "or they'll come. Cannot you grasp this? They'll come up the well! Up the well!"

The unerring pig shape in its smoky glow led John into a section where the way tangled and twisted into a hundred corridors like a knot of intestines.

The screams and outcries echoing around bends meant no more to him than water dripping or the flashes of torchlight as

he crossed passages, sight fixed on the floating, massive orac-
ular form that moved its slow limbs, wading through dim air.

He didn't take note as he stepped over and around a sprawl
of bodies, the blood splashing his filthy bare feet. A black-
robed man, dagger in one hand, torch in the other, stood
widelegged, little stonedark eyes squinting through his madly
flared beard. Stared as John went past without a pause.

"Father," he said. There were others behind him among the
little dead people. His scattered teeth winked in the dimness.
"Father, we are here." Stared as he passed, hands clasped
across his body like a meditating monk. "We devour the ungodly," he called after John, hopefully, as if to draw him back
as that lank, erratic prophet veered off into a side passage. One
of the others was bent over a woman, sawing and hacking
chunks of meat from her runtish limbs.

"This looks a tender bit," he remarked, brightly.

He was kicked for his pains by the small, rockhard, gap-
toed foot of the leader (the man who'd first chased Parsival),
who then pointed his bloody knife into the shifting shadows.

"We follow the father!" he told the dozen or so of them.
"We're serving him and not ourselves!" And went, loping on
legs like springy steel, and the rest, not quite howling, followed...

Lohengrin went up a few turns of the spiral, listening, intent.
They were gone. Down below, Gobble raved on as Broaditch
and Layla (whom he noticed seemed strangely content to lean
on the wall and watch proceedings with a faint smile) waited
developments.

Where did our perverse little friends get to? Lohengrin
wondered. Shrugged, ready to start back. Heard muffled
shrieks and clashing higher up... went a few turns more
...yes...no question...and something that sounded like
barking...he crouched as a little naked man came spinning
around out of the blackness, then stood, leaned a moment,
seeming to speak in gouts of blood that spilled over him as his
mouth formed shapes, and then he dropped flat and dead on
his face.

The sounds were coming: yapping, raging, howling, rattling, banging...

He went down, catching his mother by the elbow (she nearly
fell) saying:

"Let Lord Stagger lead us," he ordered. "Death comes behind." He kicked at Gobble, who huddled back along the curve of wall. "Take us to Clinschor," he snarled, "where he goes there's always a way out. Thus have I seen." Gobble was still stark pale and trembling.

"I tell you again," he said, more calmly, "what he'll unplug down there will eat the world."

"And this troubles you, Gobble?"

If I'm led by heaven and truth, Broaditch was thinking, *why then I'll have a miracle in time . . . if not . . .* His mind shrugged as he followed the others, last in line now.

"You don't understand me," Gobble was protesting around the bend, "I believed in a great dream, never in this . . . never this . . ."

Howtlande and Tungrim, swords in their fists, backed through an open chamber, stinking greasy smoke eddying from somewhere. All around echoes and outcries, blows, racing feet: dozens of tunnels fed into this space and the sound shifted, leaped . . . it seemed they were surrounded, about to be attacked . . . a swarm of semi-armored men of mixed sizes flooded into the chamber.

Too many, Tungrim thought.

"Fly," he said unnecessarily to his companion, who was already well under way and surprisingly fast, sparks trailing from his thin torch. Tungrim had hesitated because fighting would be a relief.

As he followed the fat man he glanced into the echoing openings that flashed by, fragments visible: little people in fire, smoke and shadow, glints of whirring steel, screaming . . . fragment: indistinguishable mix of tall, short, naked, armored, fleeing from one passageway to another, back and forth . . . suddenly half-a-dozen of what he took for adolescent girls and boys charged from somewhere holding daggers and short swords, laughing and whirling in dancing glee, holding (the last thing he registered as he ducked into a tunnel mouth and realized without concern that he'd lost his companion) what seemed human heads in their upraised hands . . . each way crossed a dozen others in an insane maze . . . smoke and terrific heat blasted into him . . . *Not that way . . .* tried another full of screams . . . *No . . .* pulled back . . . another . . . ducking through the mounting, incredible chaos . . . another: saw what he took for the black hounds of hell slashing and barking, fangs bright... leaped over charred and bloody tangles; raced through a long room of dead women and children sprawled over a pit of hot coals, the blood still hissing and bubbling... another opening, a blade zipped at his face as he spun back and a blur followed, panting, screaming. He cut and ducked into a shoulderwide creviceway, in the flame shudders glimpsing robes, wild beards, metal flash, blood spray... ran... ran... and then the teenagers, hair flying, yelling, waving weapons, chasing down the squealing, terrified, slashed runts just as a tall, jerky-stepping man lurched (Tungrim had an impression he was blind) right across the thick of it, oblivious, seeming pushed forward into a cross-corridor by an invisible hand as Tungrim charged into another lightless opening, ran sweating, panting, groping, away.

"Layla," he called because that was at least something to grip at in this whirling, stinking, bottomless nightmare. "Layla!"

Past an opening: flame, shadowy struggles... fleeing ... boiling, biting smoke... another opening: blank... he plunged in...

"Are you there, Layla?" He faintly knew that if he saw daylight he would run out and probably not stop until he reached the ocean.

Another opening: the teenagers squatting, kneeling, dancing and clapping their hands around a heap of fallen, flinging blood and chunks of flesh overhead, spattering the dark walls. Some were rolling over their victims, bathing in the hot blood. He knew now he was circling, caught in this knotted labyrinth... raced up a short flight of steps, heard shouts to his left down a short, straight stretch as shadows flew towards him out of reeling torchflame, shouting:

"Father! Father! Wait! Wait for thy children!"

And his powerful, stocky body, racked with cramps and raw lungs, carried him on, pounding away, skidding on blood and water, tripping over the dead, weeping now in blocked rage.

Get me out of here... out...

Around a bend and everything in flames and he thought this must be the dark burning rock here that took fire like charcoal: thick black smoke billowed and the air lost its virtue in his lungs.

Burning stone...

Dull, creeping flame-fingers that groped and grew . . . Flew into another hole, the madness singing shrill in his ears and he tried to distance it through all the sudden jolts, flashes, howls, warring, death and darkly flaming rock . . .

Clinschor felt light and free, bounding down the slope where (though he didn't know it) Gobble had deserted him. He was sure this was the way to the bottom. He perceived his enemies in a vast ring surrounding this place; saw their pitiful pastel, fluttering demonstrations at the rim of his swelling power, and he bubbled and mouthed his exultation because in a few mere steps he would unleash the full force of earth, spit long light-nings, rain fire and vomit irresistible armies . . .

"Gobble, Gobble," he told the twisted lord he clearly imag-ined hobbling along behind him, "what joy is mine!"

Coming out in a huge cavern between two gigantic statues, his wink of torchlight hinted only at the feet, great, deep clawed toes of brassy green stuff. He hurried along a processional aisle of these figures, whose bent shoulders supported the roof that seemed the mass of all the world. He clearly saw the long limbs, titanic shoulders, long, cold faces . . . his armies behind him, steel glinting in the sourceless light of darkness concen-trated. He gave his voice full force now, letting it burst into these muffling spaces that soaked up its thunder:

"All you who have followed me with faith and strength are near your reward!"

He watched them far, far below. Saw them begin to stir their immense, recumbent limbs among spell-dark stones at the bottom of earth and time. Eyes like dark jewels shifted. He kept his fist sealed close around the metallic splinter, believing it would vanish if it broke contact with living flesh. Had it not remained embedded in Lohengrin's skull, he believed, it would have been lost forever. But his destiny had never given him up and never would . . .

"All of you!" he cried.

"This way!" shrieked Gobble, veering suddenly into a side passage, body seeming (to Broaditch) to head two ways at once.

"To where?" he called after.

"Matters it?" Lohengrin asked over his shoulder, leading his mother.

Broaditch shrugged and followed. At the outskirts of the

ruby-orange illumination, Gobble seemed to be dissolving into mist as he walked, and then the filmy strands were flashing back from the flames and coiling in the air around them. Layla exclaimed with disgust. Broaditch waved his hand and caught up hundreds of fine threads: *spiderwebs*, he realized. A few more steps and they were covered with the sticky stuff. For some reason Layla suddenly found all this very amusing.

"On through the webs," she said, "to save the world..." Giggled and wobbled.

If she be not drunk, Broaditch reflected, *I'm a sow's get...*

She giggled and spun like a child, waving her slender arms to catch the glinting gossamer. The stuff trailed behind them all now, wrapping and flowing like robes.

"I'm pleased you knew this way," Lohengrin told Gobble who beat on ahead.

"We've all become ghosts," Layla observed, brightly, spinning, "so we must be dead." She glancingly reeled into the wall. She looked like she was spinning a cocoon, Broaditch thought. Lohengrin had closed his helmet. He kept picking to clear the eyeslits.

"This is a light weave, indeed," his mother announced, holding up a shimmering arm. "Well, fellow ghosts, whom do we first haunt?" Skipped a little down the steepening slope. "I'll choose your father...the bastard...I'll haunt him..."

"If still he lives," said her son in his muffling helmet.

"Never fear, boy," she assured him, "he always turns up. You think he's gone and there he is scratching at the gate again...all innocence, the bastard..." She wasn't amused now. Brushed violently at the endless, filming webs. Wobbled. "I'm not going this way...This is the way to the dead lands..."

Gobble cried out, stopped, a short bent shape (reminding Broaditch of a melted-down candle end) in the palely gleaming spidermist, feeble torch held high.

Something was standing in the deeper web fog beyond, massive, menacing, long arms reaching down as if to seize the shrunken cripple.

Lohengrin drew and stepped closer, slicing through the dense stuff, opening his helmet. Behind him Layla giggled again, irrelevantly. Broaditch saw her tug free the flask this time as her son, in the strange, cloudy pall, poked at the tall figure with his swordtip and heard it ring and scrape.

"Stone," he said. "Come on."

A carven man whose arms seemed to hopelessly clutch at the myriad strands that enveloped him. And Broaditch thought that could have been any of them turned to stone . . . any of them . . .

"Where?" wondered Broaditch.

Layla giggled. Gobble lurched on into the misty wall that endlessly tore and clung and dissolved in the torchfire. Lohengrin paused, thoughtful.

"Haste," said Gobble, "haste." He spun around in his strange, gleaming shroud.

"What tells you this way leads anywhere?" Lohengrin demanded.

"This is the spiderway," he screeched. "The spiderway . . . they all speak of it . . . it leads to the bottom . . ."

"To find what?" Lohengrin pressed him. "No one has passed through here in years."

"To find lord master," Gobble said. "I told you that. His sickness changed him! . . . made him mad . . ." Turned and went on.

"I trust not your sneaky mind, runt," Lohengrin said. Watched him lean on ahead, torchflames spurting the gossamer. His mother took another semi-furtive nip. Broaditch shook his head.

"Does he believe what he says?" he wondered.

Up ahead, Gobble shrieked again.

"Now what?" asked Lohengrin. "A statue of a dog's ass? A heap of batshit?"

Howtlande suddenly was in a wide corridor, steeply tilted, and as he stared into the blank openings filled with shouts and cries and smoke, the main din and maddened horror came around the near turn like a flood. He realized that the passages on this level had funneled them all here. The stinging smoke packed them together. He backed against a wall as several lithe black-robes came bounding out of a sideway and stood baffled and panting, bloody, blackened, some snarling, some afraid; coughing, choking as the smoke boiled out behind them from every hole now.

"Every way leads nowhere," one said, chest heaving, waving a bloody knife, facing the approaching mass of runts and normals, a few racing desperately ahead of the pack as others began spilling from the side corridors and colliding, falling, rolling, screaming and cursing: the naked teenagers were caught with the rest, ripping their blades around frantically now, trying just to clear room to run. Howtlande was backing away, half-running, as the space filled with death and pain and rage and fear. The panic became a force, a thing of torn and broken flesh that now drove down a single, smooth tunnel with no more openings lining the sides, a tilt that had half of them rolling like a snowball coming down a winter hillside. And he didn't hear his own voice saying, shouting:

"Wait! Wait! This is senseless! We can all join forces! Listen to me! Fools! We can all join forces! We..."

He didn't see the opening behind him...the sudden staircase...

The pig was descending the sheer, immense set of steps, with torches set every few yards, only a few lit, and then total blackness after that. John was pleased, gazing down into the chasm, because the betrayer would soon be delivered up to inexorable vengeance...

He barely glanced up as a big, blurred form (everything was misty save for the awesome being guiding him) went spinning past, shouting a blur of words too, rolling and flopping down the ten-yard-wide staircase as up behind an incredible din exploded. The smoke and insane battling had driven hundreds more into struggling clumps that jammed the halls and all were caught in the savage panic...

John paid no mind. Spoke and listened only to the vast intelligence before him. Heard nothing but mumble when Howtlande crashed past him, bloody, blackened, rolling helplessly down with crunching spattings, shouting:

"...I...aaaa!...help me!...aaaaa!...it hurts...it hurts meee!..."

His loose clothes and fatroll shook as he bumped and bounced out of sight, faster...faster...

The wordless din mounted at John's back but he didn't turn or care.

Howtlande was on his belly now, starfishing like a boy on an icy hill, spinning, screaming, futilely clutching the racing stair edges, fingers snapping...down...down...body vibrating, rattling his bones, friction searing now, clothes starting to smoke as he sped at incredible speed (stomach keeping his head safely high) past the last torch, his screaming a hopeless bleat against the final dark...

*　　　*　　　*

Fountaining light poured down in gold-tinted vibrancy, poured over and into him. The liquid colors bubbled and pulsed into his blood, filled his throbbing heart, burst into his head, washed away every shadow, every stray thought and now streamed, he felt, from his eyes as all things floated in radiance and ringing music. He held his wings still now, letting the light rush lift him as he turned, soared...saw Unlea adrift beside him in this shoreless, unending exquisiteness, saw her glowing limbs and streaming hair of fire and gold...time without time moved without passing. He kicked himself gently forward through the lucent billows, tenderly taking her hand (that felt like cool flame), rushing towards the mysterious land where deeper, darker brightness lay, where mountains and valleys were fractured bloodruby jewels...the golden-tinted overlight spilled down and then he saw the fortress. The source of the light was within it, streamers of unbearable brilliance spewing from behind black walls, and he caught a glimpse of the shape that stirred there for a moment, and then something within the sweet glowing, shifting rays that were his mind too, said:

The beast waits.

Because something was rising there against the darkly burning sky. He sensed it crouching over the pulsing, singing light source and he followed, floating her along, riding the golden rays, letting the reflected light within draw him to its source and bear him (because his body was but swirling colors) like a feather on a breeze...

Unlea screamed all the way down through black vacancy where the invisible waterfall crashed. Clung to Parsival...and then the impact stunned and blanked her...then the pounding, deafening foaming booming...choking now...Parsival, she didn't realize, towed her by one hand to the jagged rocks they'd missed by fractions—where he saw the rugged, dark lands filled with blood-colored fire and the ineffable light that was being blocked and dimmed...

"...help," she babbled. "...help...oh...oh...oh..."

It was dawn outside. Alienor had just started to dig at the packed ash sealing them in utter blackness. Tikla was sobbing; Torky was beside her, scraping his fingers into the dense, gritty stuff.

"Mama," he asked, "will we die in here?"

"No," she said, grim, digging her hands in as if the stuff were solid rock and her fingers chiseled steel. "No."

Her husband, meanwhile, and his companions were all staring through the misty webbing (he kept wondering where the flies could have come from to have justified so many spiders) at where Gobble was limping backward, pointing.

Layla was amused again.

"We all look like cocoons," she announced.

Broaditch studied the shape there, a massive shadow like something seen through a fog. The dense strands glinted in the fireshine.

"Another statue," Lohengrin said, passing Gobble, who'd stopped screaming. "Looks to be a knight . . . a good ten feet tall . . . if carvings scare you, what happens when they're real?"

Before Gobble could respond, Lohengrin was already ducking back, sword drawn, as the dim figure struck at him, and Broaditch, shocked, was just registering the sound: a scraping bray of creaking stone and metal as the six-foot blade lashed around and rent the cobwebs with awkward speed.

"It comes to life!" wailed Gobble. "We're doomed . . ." Limping behind Layla. "It's *his* spells, he's bringing the very rocks to life! He has the power now . . ." Gobble was imagining mountains moving and smiting cities, the earth suddenly sentient as the forces of the deepest world rose to the surface . . .

Broaditch and Lohengrin were side by side, the big peasant crouched behind his spear. After the stiff, shrieking movement the thing was motionless. Broaditch noted the feet hadn't moved.

They both went forward, carefully, holding the torches high, eating away the webs . . . suddenly the giant blade snapped back the other way. They ducked. Broaditch held his ground as the next chop came overhand, squeaking, grinding, and Lohengrin threw his torch at it and in the brief flash they saw the jointed, naked figure that barred the passage and glimpsed the exit gaping behind it.

It was still again: a naked male carving holding that outrageous sword.

"There's no room to pass it here," Lohengrin noted. "Clumsy as it be, it's quick enough." Was amused. "Only the arm seems to move."

"Aye," agreed the other. "And only when we come in range."

"We'll have to go back," Gobble said. "But then the first we passed will be living now as master's spells spread . . ." He squatted down, panting, eyes wobbling restlessly.

Layla took another drink. She felt more than justified. What next? she wondered . . . She blurrily watched Broaditch and her son draped in phantom, fluttering robes.

"It's a machine of some kind," Broaditch asserted. "Like the toy knights at fairs."

"We'll have to charge it, I suppose," Lohengrin said, grimly.

"Solid stone and steel? And then what?"

"One of us might pass the sword."

"Unless the other arm decides to move as well."

"Mnn," Lohengrin grunted.

Layla had wobbled closer. With most of the webs cut, her torch clearly lit the deadly machine.

"Quite a fellow," she remarked. "Look at that prong they gave him."

"Stay a distance, mother."

"Never fear," she answered, "I have known enough like him, who might as well be stone, to keep away . . ." Giggled. "A pity that one part were not carved and unbending on a man and the rest . . ." She shrugged. "More soft . . ."

Broaditch had been studying the thing carefully.

I should be used to this sort of business, he told himself. Because he saw it was another riddle. They had probably trained their warriors here, whoever *they* had been . . . *It sees nothing yet it strikes . . . how like a great political lord. . . .* He was sure he had the answer. Measured the distance with his eye. *God knows, if I'm right, our retreat was cut off by some worse mechanism . . .*

"Hold this, my lady," he said, handing her his torch and setting down his spear. Then he took Gobble's sword and scabbard, his expression brooking no argument. "As you don't use them," he said.

"What are you about?" Lohengrin asked.

"You'll learn, if I live, my lord." He took a good start and, holding the sheathed blade, charged past Lohengrin, and about ten feet from the statue he leaped, hung in the air, waiting for the grinding cut to take him, and then his heels hit and he careened into the thing's smooth, hard body, banging his shoulder, panting. Layla thought the webs trailing from him had looked like wings as he jumped. She tentatively flapped her own arms, shaking the torchlight.

"Well done!" yelled Lohengrin. The statue hadn't budged.

"Like a great moth, he flew," she murmured.

Broaditch reached up, both hands gripping the sword and scabbard.

"It's the floor there," he called over, "sets it going. Take a step to make it move and then fall back." Which done, Broaditch was almost stunned by the explosive rasping grind as the arm flailed stiff and terrific at the young knight, whose mother, he noted from the corner of his eye, seemed to be weaving forward into range. He leaned into it (feeling what must have been vast weights shifting and turning in the floor) and jammed the sword into the shoulder joint so that as the stone arm crunched back the steel was twisted. Before Lohengrin could grip her, his mother had taken an extra step and the blade chopped back and forth, back and forth, the arc restricted now so that she simply swayed past it, each backswing missing her waist by inches. She reached Broaditch, who still clung to the grinding, squeaking, naked, blank-eyed carving, and said:

"Just look at that outrage . . ." Gestured between the stone legs. "Do you think there's a gear to make it move?"

The thick, oily smoke from whatever was burning had choked off every corridor, forcing Tungrim down from entrance to entrance, trying to break out of the twisting, sickening maze of insane fighting, naked children, black-robed killers, crazed dogs, thrashing, screaming runts . . .

Finally he was forced into the main passage. Torches guttered on the muddy floor among mangled bodies . . . and then, choking and battling, they all came flooding in, and he instantly was waist-deep in dwarves (who stank of fear, blood and bathlessness) as the smoke and fighting packed everyone together, bigger ones climbing, running a few steps over the others before being dragged down into the swarm that filled the hallway, tearing, frantic. He fought to keep upright because to fall was death. Then, as the mass spun him, he glimpsed Howtlande up ahead, mouth wide, as the flood of flesh poured around the next bend . . . on the following spin he saw the fat man gesticulating wildly, backing away, seeming to harangue the bearded, blackened and bloody crew retreating with him . . . and then the mass careened in a flopping, howling wall of madness.

Tungrim was striking at everything, blood and flesh splashing from his short sword, his mind falling...falling far far away...from this...himself too, and he didn't hear Howtlande's arguments blotted over by the howling of this feral horror that his own wordless, flat, ferocious cries melted into as clubs, hands, teeth, swords were shocked into one ravening heap that spewed like a burst bungplug, vomiting onto the steps, popping Howtlande first to roll and stagger and finally slide and sail past John (and his guiding shape), then the rest bursting down the sheer staircase to the depths. Tungrim, as he failed desperately, saw his home, the hills...bright water...and Layla there, as in a dream...very clear and impossible...

Clinschor could see the dark geysering into the tremendous chamber as if this were the source of all blackness shot from the stomach of universal night, and he could see, somehow, the giant figures supporting the arched and jagged roof, saw the wondrously delicate but powerful stonework.

He moved straight towards the streaming, palpable beams of blackness, clenching his fist in spontaneous salute as he drew near the gigantic lip of the well.

He felt them gazing up at him, stirring in the lucent dark, eyes like the last red stain in a dying coal, aware, quickening...He knew they felt the beating light prisoned in his cramped left hand, which had been locked closed since yesterday. The speck that would free them as it fell, like the one touch of white artists drop into black, to make it the more rich...

Now he had even forgotten the massed army he imagined at his back, and he spoke only to those at the bottom of the frozen gulfs.

"I am come," he announced, prancing forward to the raised well-like rim, and suddenly weariness dabbed at him like a dark sponge, and a rush of feverheat...he wobbled...felt himself dissolving, name, memories floating into cloudiness... floated over the chill gulfs, his body far, far away..: he felt them, felt their dark, intimate words, and he understood his own meaning, understood that Clinschor had been one provisional word, for what was never twice the same...when did the raw, shapeless metal become "sword"?...in the partly beaten block, or in any rough shape along the way? or when an edge was first honed or polished...buffed...or when it was ultimately drawn and swung? Which was the sword? Which name meant it all? When it broke and lay rusting in ages to come or remelted to another and greater? Which was "Clinschor"?

Far from his ravaged, swaying body their souls reached to him, flowing on the dark beams...

"We are come," he thought or said, feeling excitement and power lash the dimming clouds of himself. "We are come!" like thunder, as if the black air pumped through his thick throat without his will and formed the speaking itself...

Past the now crippled mechanical statue was an open space where darkness massed beyond the feeble spill of their torchfire. They all stood there, dabbed over by the misty, clinging webbing. Layla kept blinking, trying to focus.

"Now where, you stinking shitball?" Lohengrin asked Gobble, who rolled his restless gaze around.

"Shit," muttered Layla. "Shit he surely was..."

"What, mother?"

"He was...Your father...Sir Part-of-Shit..." She giggled.

"Peace, mother. Peace."

Gobble was moving into the open darkness, not too fast now.

"This way," he said, hopefully, uncertain. "This way..."

Broaditch supported her arm as they followed. He assumed they were wandering in a curve but there was no way to tell yet. Thought he looked a strange, limping goblin, the pale shimmer floating around him.

"What do *you* think?" Layla was asking him.

"Eh?"

"Of my son here? He's not like his father, is he? Hm?...I raised him to be nothing like...nothing..."

"Mayhap you did too well at that, madam," her son responded.

"Do you care for him, sir?" she went on, plucking at Broaditch. The wine was strong on her breath.

"I am no 'sir,' my lady," he replied.

"Do you care?" She leaned her head against his shoulder. "Not many did...Life among the great is a cold business..."

"Gobble," raged the knight in question, "you rat fecality,

your steps wander! Where in the Devil's hind are we?"

"This is the great hall at the end of the spiderway," was the reedy reply.

"That much I knew already. Have you ever seen this place?"

"No."

"I knew that too."

"We're a sad and broken family," she was saying, lilting. "I took lovers . . . but that's a great smoke and little fire . . ."

"Mother! Why not have a scribe write it all down as well?"

"Wait," commanded Broaditch. "Hear that?"

Layla suddenly tugged free and staggered a few steps on her own, admiring how the gossamer flowed. The stuff clung stubbornly to everyone.

They listened to a booming, muffled pounding roar that seemed to be high above them and moving down . . .

"Christ, what now?" Lohengrin asked no one, rubbing his beaked nose through the faceplate.

"What then?" his mother commented, reaching over and patting Broaditch's cheek above his grayed beard. Looked, serious and sad, into his clear eyes. "You're a good fellow . . . you cannot fool me . . . none of them ever could . . ." Shook her head with sleepy violence. "Not a damned one, I tell you . . ."

XLIII

The awesome shining shape moved closer and enfolded John in its own ineffable vitality, as he went down the sheer stairs that angled straight into the darkness. The rich piglight now pulsed around him as the packed, knotted, struggling spill of slashed, crushed, unspeakably mutilated, rending, snapping beings came tumbling in a nearly solid plug down behind (Howtlande had just vanished far below, still accelerating), limbs and heads twisted and tangled together, blood dribbling, teeth gnashing, mouths gaping in indescribable suffering.

But John barely noticed. As the balled mass slammed and snapped him into itself he felt the warmth and porcine power embrace and protect him, murmuring maternal, tender promises. The torches and stairway spun as hands clutched and teeth bit. A bearded Trueman face, eyes running blood, rose and sank again into the churning. Mouths raved blood and foam, knives and swords glittered, as though the careening lump, gathering crushing speed, sprouted steel fangs to chew all before it, flowing down on the shattered bones and slick blood of itself. In the madness and reek where Tungrim still howled, clawed and tumbled with the rest, it caught and wadded, leaving a solid stain of blood and meat as shapeless pieces, once human,

were torn away by mounting momentum—the bloody children
and dwarfed, lost followers of Clinschor all squashed into a
single bleeding. Truemen...Viking...indistinguishable, all
one at last...John rested serene as volitionless hands clutched
and tore, embraced in chaos and ultimate spasm; rested in the
calm glory of his protector, the thrilling touch of the trotters
around his tumbling body, the supernatural glare of the burning,
ruby eyes...

The hard, darkly shining landscape passed smoothly as Parsival and Unlea floated towards the tremendous fortress. He
sensed the thing behind the walls was trying to grind out the
streaming glory that was singing and caressing him home...
Walls and towers suddenly loomed, filling the vast, opaque
luster of ground and air, miles on miles high. Then the first
spawn of the beast sped forward to meet them as he worked
his gleaming wings, gathering the musical light as a butterfly
would gather air. The prismatic rays poured through chinks in
the stones and above the jagged walls, outlining the vast thing
as it moved. Suddenly the part-blocked radiance dimmed and
he sagged; the insectile forms swooped closer on waves of dim
and dark, darting to avoid the golden-tinted beams. As the light
faded he felt a shock as when a lover is found untrue, a sinking
dread...then the flame was free again, the shadow drew back
slightly as the first spike-winged creature (all smoothness, claw
and whipping stingers) closed, cut at them...

Unlea staggered, bare feet torn by the rocky flooring, clutching him as he dragged her along through the total blackness
of the cave.
"Please," she kept protesting. "Please..."
He was half-running, crying out unshaped sounds, bounding
and rebounding from unseen walls, rocks, stalagmites, tripping
and dragging her down and up. When a rock edge caught her
knee she screamed and he dragged her along a rough wall for
a few steps and she screamed again.
"O God! He's mad! He's mad!"
And then they staggered in an open, echoing space, and
when next she fell he stooped and lifted her and she pleaded
as his voice now went on breathless and smooth too:
"Ah, what glory! What glory! Ah! Try this then, you crud-
wet fiend!" Struggling, whipping at the air and she sailed free,

fell and heard him struggling on, shouting, grunting as if he
fought palpable foes. In panic (because being lost alone here
counted worse than being with Parsival mad) she crawled and
groped after him, except his footsteps arced in wide circles as
he yelled:

"Fiends! Foul fiends! Away! Away!" And then his trium-
phant laughter as she ran now, groping, desperate in the hollow
space that seemed boundless to her, crying out:

"Parsival! Parsival . . . come back! O God! Help! Help me!"

He discovered how to bank his wings into the light as the
hissing, rasping, dark-gleaming insects slashed at him with
razor claws and stingers like jousting spears, blank, burning
eyes more baleful than malice in their stony indifference. He
soared, doubled and circled, wings breaking golden air into
blaze—saw her on foot, far below on the cold, jagged plains.

Zooming near where a dark ray crossed close, the creature
rasped like scraped iron and snapped the curved stinger into
the light at him. This time Parsival caught it in his hand and
wrenched and tore as if snapping a green stick. The thing
shivered, and in desperation clawed into the bright beam where
it found no support. He smashed his free fist into one opaque
eye and watched the creature spin and drop, spraying smoking
poison blood; then knew he'd hung still too long as others came
straight down with terrific speed, tearing through the shifting
light-rays, and even as he banked desperately one hooked into
the translucent shine of his wing and he fell, spinning, from
the sustaining gold above the gigantic, pitblack towers and
outworks where obscure wheels and holes spun and sparked
fire; where countless coal-gleaming wingless things toiled and
great, spiked beams tilted on massive iron structures; where
axblades revolved like windmills . . . spinning down flatly he
glimpsed miles of walls and squatness . . . sensed the crawling
fish down there somewhere, the monkeylike monster,
others . . . immense constructions chugged along like beetles on
hundreds of stubby, stiff metal legs. Gouts of flame burst from
within as if they were animated furnaces. The workers here
and there mounted into tremendous pyramidlike heaps. Vast
masses toiled to raise the dark walls higher and higher around
the central pit to close out the golden light that poured almost
straight up to flash among the roiling mountains of fumes. It
was poised on top, straddling the rising tower, iron feet gripping

the mile-wide sides, clouds swirling around immense black limbs.

The armored creatures ripped near him as he fell faster, the light dying like a sunset. He saw he'd hit within the wall among the fires and shadow-machines and he had to reach the light, nothing else mattered . . . he shook with chill now because the light was still himself and he was parted from it, and if it went out he'd be lost here with the rest, pinned heavy and cold in this unutterable bleakness . . .

The sound mounted, echoed, seemed almost directly above them: clatter, ringing, crunching, raving, screeching. Layla suddenly lurched free of Broaditch again and weaved rapidly into the dimness beyond the rim of their torchlight, falling forward, legs barely catching her each time, shouting this and that . . .

"Eeeeeee!" she cried as the dimness reeled and the din increased. She wanted to fly. She was clear on that point. She ran and dipped and spun sidewise, holding her arms out and flapping them, webs flowing, beating, feeling the warm soothingness that seemed without as well as within, as if the dark air were wine too, that was soft and gentle and cushioning. "Eeeeee . . ." Thrashing her arms as Broaditch and Lohengrin cut and dodged to follow her fluttery movements, the flame-tipped sticks whooshing, dwindling to near nothing from the draughts.

"Mother, damn you!" her son shouted over the mountain roar. "Piss and fire!"

She leaped into the air like a child (stung Broaditch with a sudden memory); again . . . again . . . fell and kicked her legs up, laughing . . .

"Eeeeeee . . ."

The world tipped and swung as Gobble came up to them. The torches lit the bottom of a straight, sheer stair carved out of the dark immensity of stone. Broaditch glanced at the small, web-shrouded, wrenched figure who was saying, shrill:

"Tarry not! It is nigh too late!"

"You're a vast help at need," commented the big peasant, puffing up one red-chapped cheek.

And then it was coming down the stairs: splishing, crunching, battering, ringing, howling . . .

"Ai," said Gobble. "The bottomless steps."

"An exaggeration," put in Lohengrin, "as life abounds with. Mother, I—" He had her half to her feet.

"Nay!" insisted the cripple, yelling above the mounting sound. "Leave her and haste! Or we be too late! The terror comes!"

His gesturing arm shook his ghostly covering. Broaditch peered up the steps, uneasy. Layla was singing.

"That's my mother, you son-of-a-bitch!" Lohengrin snarled and, snatching the gesturing hand, whipcracked him into the stairs about a dozen feet away just as something came spinning at blurred speed, zipping past sprawled Gobble and spattering down with a loose, hollow, sickening crunch at bottom. Blood flew, Broaditch thought, as though a wineskin had burst under a mace blow. The raw bonelessness that no one could ever know had been Baron Howtlande of Bavaria lay still in its fabric shreds.

Gobble shrieked and twisted to his feet, staring up as new horror came flopping, grinding, spilling into the dim glow.

A creature, Broaditch's mind said.

"Run," said his mouth, though Lohengrin needed no urging, and Layla's feet trailed behind as they dragged her away. Glancing back, Broaditch saw the carved sides of the staircase packed by a squishsquashing mass spewing gore where heads and limbs and shapelessness struggled and flopped and ground together, gnashing, clutching, and the last sight, as they drew the fireglow out of range, was the phantom shape of Gobble, dressed (he thought) for the part, lurch-limping, flailing and vanishing as the thing hit bottom with a *spatt!* that trembled the solid stone itself . . .

So Broaditch didn't see, if he could have lightly borne the sight, some of the incredibly still living figures, cushioned by the churning mush, gradually pull free and struggle, some still clutching weapons, trying feebly to slay . . . some babbling unceasingly like Tungrim who crawled, directionless, through the bone-ragged slush, dragging his crushed limbs, moving like a hurt swimmer, whimpering, vacant . . .

But none like John who simply stood obliviously upright, and waded through the gradually settling spatter, ribs painful, body gouged, hands locked in praying position, half-smiling in the darkness among the terrible screams, blowings, bubblings . . . past weakly clinging fingers; aimless slashes as the monster seemed to die in fitful parts...

But the pig-glow still summoned and exalted him, preserved for his task. The red, penetrating eyes seemed his own now, the red thoughts his thoughts, as if the death-impact of that ruin of violence had sealed them together and the supernatural senses fused with his own. He could feel the blasphemer in the blackness ahead, and he squealed within himself with blind, savage, sudden needs. Rushed faster, absorbed, making little snorts and grunts aloud, on the track of the betrayer, the denier, the enemy, the thief. Then the *thing* was suddenly in his sight and speaking with excitement he passed dim, red-lit figures, ghostly glows (that he didn't know were Lohengrin and the others), began to run, mouthing high-pitched rancor as fragments spun unrelated through his churned brain: images of himself as a young priest, praying alone, desperate for a movement, an echo in the cool, gray stone stillness where altar flames stood unwavering in banked rows, softly bathing the mansized crucifix whose Christ seemed always about to move, to speak to him... nights he'd prayed until blood ran from his fingernails... another time, listening, poised, his father in his highbacked lord's seat, fine white hair fluffy around his delicate wrinkles, sucking a ripe, red plum, lips dripping sweet juice and scorn... gritting his teeth, listening as if to the stone-gray sky above for God's voice to break and send his father cowering to his tailored knees... later standing over the massed serfs in the fields, listening to the still sky as his raging words went out and were lost... listening through all the bitter years of injustice and lost causes and wasted deaths, tensed, fierce, pleading... pleading with quenchless rage... listening...

... now running faster... faster through a pitchy night that opened all its opaque mysteries to him... squealing...

As another buzzing horror hurtled at Parsival, all slashing and stinging, he closed with it (above the jet fortress where the dark constructions crawled and creaked, tilted blades and beams and fire into the solid sky) thinking:

If you cannot ride a white horse try a dark...

Parsival gripped, smote in a furious whirlwind, the stinging spike lashing viciously, hard, sharp-edged torso knotting, taloned wings rending his back with searing stripes. Then he flung himself across the jewelsmooth back, clenching the thin, snaky neck that thrummed and whipped like springsteel, the chill beam of dark penetrating him as he locked his legs, fully committed to riding the killing thing before the others, banking all around, struck or his fading vital light was spent . . . spread his own wings to cover the others', his own head above the angled, terrible blank face and somehow matched his seeing and movements to the harsh coldness under him, superimposed his senses until there was a single fluidity and he saw darkness through dark sight, felt the power, the vast hollows of night, the safety of lightless holes, chilling magnificence of sawtoothed crags forlorn and lifeless; the excitement of sheer force pouring through whipsteel bodies clashing, soaring, tearing in stunning frays, ecstasy of wrenched forces; the vigorous beauty of hardness, sharpness forcing, ripping, shattering, leaving only stone. Felt himself sinking deeper into the edgeless simplicity and irresistible meshing of unyielding parts . . .

Wing on, he told it, which was part of him now, his golden shimmer gathered around the dark shell.

And it beat straight along the wide, black way, passing through fading wisps of gold, flashing at the gigantic squatting form on the towering lip of the pit where the light was slowly sinking . . .

Unlea followed the faint pittering of his feet. He was silent now. Her legs, breath, everything hurt. She wanted to lie down but wobbled on . . . and then went blindly to her knees as a terrific cry blasted the blackness and she couldn't tell if it were a roar or outcry of pain or exultant triumph, and she pressed her hands to her ears and screamed herself, in dubious echo . . .

Clinschor reeled on the circular wall and felt the rays of darkness streaming through him. Felt himself changing again, expanding his cloudiness until it encompassed all the massed stone of earth, all the grinding weight and pressure, slow shattering of faults and fissures, the incredible squeezing of blackness into diamond clarity; all this was suddenly *him* as limbs and torso became the dark icy waters underground, the hot bubbling too, the viscous darker fluids oozing like the ages.

Down below they clawed, scraped, fell back, climbing over one another. He held his clenched fist over the abyss and felt the fragment throb and sting as the infinite dark touched it even through his flesh. He knew they felt it down there with pain and hate, gnashing fangs in sharkish mouths as they swarmed around the Great One. He vibrated rapidly on the narrow rim, mouth wide, foam flying, waiting for the Great One to come to him, fuse together, waiting as the heat and pressure built in his fist, pain searing up his stringy forearm as if he held a drop of molten gold, burning its way through the flesh...yet he held...and held...Because he saw the Great One now, brushing aside the scuttling pack, struggling to clamber and flutter up the sheerness...saw how in Him darkness itself seemed to take ultimate substance, and unending emptiness found incomprehensible shape that even Clinschor (except Clinschor was now legion, ten thousand thousand names, faces, times come and coming) could only vaguely perceive, and endless yet totally compressed body that tossed like a hurricane, movements that flew and crawled, yet there were legs and arms too, heads and vast shapelessness, heads and flashing horns where night honed night to keenness...things that rose and fell and swarmed, flopped and changed...fire without light flamed and eyes glared that were holes in time and made black blacker...it lifted up in its chaotic might: spiked crowns adorned tossing heads, in solid emptiness and not flapping and not crawling, ascended, and he knew its vacant thoughts and chill cloud of heart...saw futures in amazing worlds where armies convulsed and skies broke open and the sun burst its heart and blood and fire rained everywhere...saw into future ages where foods would be made from filth and stones, and men drawn from iron with cold fire in their veins; where senseless steel tangles were worshipped and seemed to think...fruit eaten that never grew...creatures living that were never born...lumps of metal counseling the nations...the Great One ascended, not precisely like water filling a pipe or smoke a flue, and the churning thoughts of all the heads beat in his flayed mind: wines of poison distilled from springtime's sweetness...children hacking one another to shreds...cities crawling and rising and pressing back all fresh green until there was only squat stone, metal and stained, sour air...

The Great One ascended with lightnings in his grip; stinks and storms in his hearts. The first strands of darkness already coiled around Clinschor, gusting, as his hand exploded into golden flame and his body shrieked through clenched teeth, locked there, emptiness flooding his mind as the Beast began to eat the Grail speck and blackness squeezed him and pressed out all the myriad Clinschors into void so that void was now his own mind too, the shapelessness his.

As the first of many jaws gaped to grind off the burning fingers and wrist, his consciousness reached to touch with vacancy all living creatures, staining, seeping, filling, drowning them with palpable darkness. So his own pain (as he burned and was devoured) was his delight, because when the last agonizing shred of light was swallowed the world would be dark enough to receive and sustain the Great One.

He saw his people rising in joy at his coming: kings, generals and sheriffs, politicians, pontiffs, great merchants all dimming with delight... criminals, lawyers and judges dancing in ecstasy as the last illumination failed... physicians sagely prescribing nothing in the dark nothingness. Blackness sang hosanna as priests gazed down from blessing bloody swords... The black sun rose. He saw ten thousand poets, writers, artists of all kinds grip their tools, musicians tooting, as all shaped the spill of rich nonsense that poured from countless pens and lightless brains, sprouted from stages, colored, carved in stone and steel and spewed from the center of ascending blank while every drudge and scholar dryly rejoiced at last and opened the wan and narrowed eyes that light no longer could burn! The black sun rose as the bright heart sank...

The teeth snapped shut on his arm and the eyes that were holes in nothingness froze him... a gaze that emptied and emptied and yet was forever filled...

Parsival soared straight into the beast's squatting, grinding, flame-lit immensity, clinging to the hard, smooth beetleback. He willed the winged thing to arrow at where the strange heart ponderously crunched in the skeletal framework of what he now perceived was not an organism at all but flaming iron and stone grinding and creaking, rasping, all angles and fury; black lifeless bones stirring in frenzy, vast clockworks, gouts of fire and dripping sparks.

He flung himself free and arced on his own tattered wings past uncompleted black sheets of steel. It suggested a miles-high knight, the machine and flame within the hollow suit filled with greasy fumes. He flew past rattling and clashing groans... a clear space and there was the heart: a dark, uneven wheel that wobbled and dripped flame. He perceived it was the key point that locked the whole gigantic imbalance together, timed and checked the spidery, almost erratic tangle of dark bending angles that in turn shifted the vast, hollow outer limbs and the terrible head high above. Angles and beams slashed at him. The only illumination was fire. The deadly dark was sucking away the vague glow still throbbing in him. He was battered by the crashing metal, choked by the smoke, blasted by the raving gears . . . He tried to pick a way through the interior of the knightshape. Aimed at the faint golden pulsing beyond the wall: The titanic construction crushed massive stones down over it, heaping and grinding rubble with awkward, violent speed. Another swordlike mock arm sawed at him, he ducked aside, still sinking steadily in the almost total dark and cyclonic fuming . . . and then the thick air tore him in wild circles through the edged interior (like a leaf in a whirl of air), just missing razor ribs and frenzied gears and he knew if he perished here he perished everywhere and forever, just as a person who dies in his sleep, dreaming, dies in his waking too . . .

The ruby light from his eyes shone on the bony, tattered figure perched on the low, curved wall. John the Pig didn't realize the wall was the rim of what Clinschor saw as an immense well where the beast was emerging to claim his kingdom. The red glare of pigsight burned the blasphemous form into foul clarity and he leaped, squealing with triumph, hearing the scrape and clatter of his hard hooves on the slick stones, mouth chewing and foaming. The pig in his wrath ordained the punishment. As he leaped he dreamed of statues and massed worshippers packed and swaying shoulder to shoulder, copper, silver, brass gleaming, and the hot, raw, spewing blood as gongs raved and incense fumed and bodies, hundreds, thousands spurted, spilled, screamed and he drank deeply, grunting his prayers into the walls of silence:

Speak! Squee! Speak! Squee!

They were chasing Layla again. She'd suddenly sprung ahead, wildly animated, and raced beyond the faint torch circle on the heels of what they didn't know was John the Pig. A moment later, in the shadowy flickers (that seemed to partly suspend the flow of natural time), they saw bony, dark-hollowed Clinschor perched on the curved wall, head backtilted, arm outstretched as if saluting nothingness, vibrating and suddenly roaring great, tearing, wordless, irregular gasps of bellows breath as if monstrous and invisible hands squeezed his chest, bouncing there on his stiff legs.

Lohengrin hardly knew him: the uncut, flying hair, beard, fleshless stick of a body—but he recognized the long nose and the unforgettable voice.

"One of his fits," he muttered, and Broaditch said:

"They say the plague can do that."

. . . as the equally gangling shape of John jumped, piping an uninflected screech, arms wide . . .

But how did they find each other? Broaditch wondered. *By stench?*

. . . pouncing, fingers clawed, and then they were locked together, and as Clinschor's hand opened to clutch his attacker Broaditch saw a bright glitter that made him blink before it was lost down (he assumed) the shaft. He stood a moment watching the afterglow in his mind, dying colors that hinted images, memories . . . landscapes . . . distant figures . . . so it was Lohengrin who really was watching (even as he chased his mother right to the well's edge) the pale, skinny, obscenely mad pair battling on the arc of wall, spitting, clawing (*devour him!* the pig said, *devour him!*), and John chewing, tearing strips of flesh from the other's flabby, stringy arm. Lohengrin felt a rush of sickness. John was gulping, bolting the bloody meat, as Clinschor bawled scream after scream. Layla, falling forward, eyesight blurred, swaying straight at them, saw multiples; tripled, quadrupled hands and heads. She stopped and gaped at the struggling form, the crisscrossing violence of arms and gnashing toothed heads drooling blood (both were biting now, jaws locked in each other's chests), the fearful thing mounting, looming over her a mindless, mechanical rasping, squealing, screaming, blatting, foaming thing. Her own cries echoed as it twisted and multiplied and long arms lashed out and the thing senselessly plucked at her and she felt it was sucking her into its churning chaos and yelled:

"Save me! My God, save me!"

The boundless emptiness that had been Clinschor opened its burning hand as the great fangs tore the golden speck from him and the black throat gulped it down.

He made a sound as the last light winked out and the sleek, smooth, magnificent darkness swelled in a great wave lapping over the earth, and the wave was himself, and he was everywhere at once stirring life into vital action, drinking raw energy

and spilling it back again: the bird striking and spearing the
least worm, the jungle cat's joy as it sprang and became one
with its shuddering, crumpling prey...drinking the life that
drove the world on and on...the battling men, the thrill of
the victor, the mounting power and fear of success after success...Stormwinds shattering the rotten trees, the weak kitten
dying and the others feeding on the remains...more life...more
life...each weakness crushed and cast aside, the vital weeds
choking away the fragile blossoms...touching minds, whispering of stone, smooth, invulnerable, polished to dark
sheen...monuments rising, gleaming...whispering of steel,
of fire...whispering to all minds the grace of strength and
glory...how he would clean the waters of the nations and
smite the feeble and deformed and impure with granite fists,
all cowards, weaklings, crying out in a whisper: *Who can defeat
me? Who is like me?*

So Clinschor's body struggled on its own because it was but
a mote in the vast eye of his consciousness, which was spreading over the earth like ink in water. He was aware of a mere
vagueness, a shadowy movement as if he gazed down on scuttling ants at his feet, his body a discarded husk...expanded...
exhaled his immense message...dreams of striking sharks
shaking their victims to pieces, of a dark hawk pirouetting on
a cloud-edge then screaming straight down, talons aflame in
burnished air, slamming into the pale dove, blotting it out in
a bloodspatter and flutter of feathers...dreaming of crashing
bulls, crushing snakes...tigers...rising higher...higher...
dreamed a stone tower, the final monument, rising, compacted
of ground bones and cement, a tower rising through the clouds
into the void and blackness beyond, millions fed to its dark
blocks, generations slaving and breaking to lift it...
yes...the last dream as the body sagged in the other's arms
and the other rooted in his flooding throat now, chewed, drank
and swallowed, sucked as Lohengrin's blade hit them—zip
thwock! left and zip thwock! right—and they reeled and,
locked together, toppled in pieces into the seeming pit. Then
Lohengrin and Broaditch gaped in mutual terror (Layla had
fallen flat on her face) as a figure suddenly seemed to rise,
float up out of the abyss, arms outreaching...

Moments before, Lohengrin had watched (coming closer
behind his mother) the gorging mouth grinding into Clinschor's
strangely passive flesh as they tottered together on the rim, the

terrible gray-blue eyes glassy and remote with rapture as he was literally being eaten alive, and this was beyond even horror, and Lohengrin knew he had to stop the feasting. He had to end this thing, this sickening ugliness, the bloodflooded jaws, the eyes lost in their terrible joys. His mother was stopped and screaming. He dimly noted one of their tangled arms whipped free and clutched at her and his sword seemingly of itself chopped once, twice, again and again, and they were falling, erupting in blood and bone chips, a hand flopping up, a leg seeming to struggle a part-step by itself . . . in disgust, actually retching bile, he swung a last cut and the mess fell in sections into the gaped pit . . .

The steel angles crashed, whipped, snapped, sprung, cut through the cyclonic billowing of fumes and flames as the sentient black tower of metal groped and slammed to destroy Parsival. As he banked and dodged close to the ground, aiming for the last shreds of light poking like vague fingers from the rockrubble, the gigantic, twisted hands scraped for him, jagged stone shrieking and sparking. Then, flightless, he was running, ducking, climbing through the rubble, glimpsing the black mask face stooping miles above in the smoky, torn darkness, lit by the flames within its hollow blankness. He was heavy and cold and staggered now, feeling battered, bloody . . . half blacking out as he wedged himself between two rough blocks, gleaming steel spindle-fingers plucking around him; felt feverish, faint, stone dark everywhere . . . everywhere . . . The fanged fish modestly crawled from behind a shattered rock, pop eyes dull and round; the monkeyshape was squatting above him, clicking and clacking its claws together . . . kneeling in despair and weakness he saw a thin thread gleaming up from the loosely packed rubble, freed in the wake of one of the immense fingers that had just missed him in its frantic, mechanical frenzy . . . lifted, fell and crawled to the wan, golden trace, his mind saying: *If I dream on I die* . . . Heard the whirring scream of angles and gears crashing down to cover him and for a moment he gathered his will to fight, to smash back at the towering thing of dark and fire . . . *Stop dreaming!* . . . The rock ground together around him. Searing flame dripped on his back. The spider-steel hand closed over him and he understood and went calm and simply let it happen, and as the iron and stone crunched him to pulp he touched the wisp of gold at arm's reach before him and instantly melted, fingers, arms . . . all of him . . . closing his hand on the light, closing himself around it, his heart going up like a flame, like wax in fire, everything melting in golden spray. And all around he saw shimmers that were living beings faintly sketched (like mist near the rising sun) on the blinding truth, their light (like his own) reflecting everywhere. Now flooded by more and more brilliance that burst from heaven and earth, a blinding sea whose waves were music, currents joy, whose tides floated, lifted, moved and suspended everything, gave rhythm to each pulsing heart, filled each mother's breast with warmth and drink and kissed the flowers with color... all the vast darkness shrank to a speck... there was only light that dissolved and lit the thrill of each instant where time was a mist. Flesh and earth and all was song and had the same sweet light. He was absorbed now where the keenest orgasm of his sexual body would have seemed a dull deadness. He moved towards the misty shinings and saw one had a drawn sword and was holding up a guttering torch, staring into the shallow, walled ring where chopped and draining pieces of men lay at Parsival's feet. He looked around at the rest of them... Then he bent over the bodies mixed together there. The universal brilliance turned the massed mountain overhead into a shimmer of glass. He picked up a tiny speck of leaden metal that lay near someone's skinny, contorted arm. Then straightened up and flicked it away. Smiled. Understood.

"I finally found it," he told the living.

"My God," one said, "father!"

Layla went nearly sober with incredulous staring as her son brought his torch closer to the blond and silverhaired, blue-eyed face that looked peacefully at them. She managed to get to her knees by gripping the wall around what hadn't been a pit at all. She thought he barely seemed to be looking at them.

"Father," Lohengrin repeated.

He nodded. Through the shifting, streaming brilliance a cloudiness seemed familiar: Lohengrin. He smiled.

"Yes," he said. And was stunned out of thought and breath again by the glory that breathed everywhere...

Clawing, choking, Tikla weeping, Torky still struggling beside her, Alienor ground into the fine, gritty blackness, crawling forward, butting, thrashing kicks as if swimming, until one hand finally broke through and she lay still a long moment, just her fingers moving, groping into cool air...

Parsival still had trouble keeping focused on their expressions in the sparkle and shifts of radiance.

Lohengrin had stepped over the wall and was standing where he'd imagined only bottomlessness. He actually tapped the stone with his blade tip before he was satisfied. Glanced at the bleeding fragments on the floor, then his father. Recalled, for a moment, all his old resentment and it seemed so far away . . .

"Mother said you always turn up."

Parsival was watching the deaths as the last shimmers spilled slowly from the tattered flesh and floods of dark and light images fluttered away, and he knew those were the memories of these men draining back to the vast, roiling mind of existence. Watched their lives, blurring dreams, floating like windtaken leaves . . .

Even memories are dreams, he said to himself. *We're shells full of dreams* . . .

His wife was weaving her head and closing one eye to see him clearly.

"How," she asked, "did you come here?"

"Like every other fool," he answered her, seriously. "By dreaming." Looked at her now, and then at him. Noted Broaditch on the periphery. Tried to keep their outlines sharp. It was like looking through a rippling stream in sunlight. "My wife and son."

Creature locked to creature crawled and climbed over one another, swarming up from primal slime into an ever mounting, ever sagging tower, struggling into the best shapes for ripping and kicking free of the unforming mass . . . and what had been Clinschor felt all this within his outpuffed, cloudy reaches, the clustered frenzy his own body, and endless rage and roar his soul . . .

Suddenly his whole swarming self was falling to pieces, dropping, spilling as a razor brightness cut through everything . . . all his seething parts flopping, plopping down. He clutched and there was nothing to clutch . . . he scattered into ten thousand battling knots and there was no bottom, no sides . . . nothing above . . . all void and falling . . . falling . . . .and silence blew him away like a wind . . .

Lohengrin just stood there, sword in his limp grip. Flickering torch flipping its last wobbling glow around them. Broaditch was helping Layla keep her feet.

"It was me you didn't kill, son," Parsival said.

The young knight raised his eyebrows.

"In the woods?" he murmured.

His father nodded. His son rolled his eyes and nodded too. Of course. The final irony . . .

"Christ Jesus," breathed Layla. "Christ Jesus on high . . ." She clung to massive Broaditch as to a tree. "Jesus . . . Jesus . . . Jesus . . ."

Broaditch just looked at him in the weak and changing flameglow. He didn't want to laugh so he didn't. And he was thinking about his own family. He didn't want to laugh, but he'd set out to find this man when the man was still a boy . . . well, here he was. He didn't want to laugh. He stood there holding up his drunken wife.

When finally I am fed in a matter, he thought, *fate stuffs my maw to bursting . . .*

She's not dead, Parsival was thinking. *Then who was it I laid in the grave?*

He reached over and touched his son's head in a kind of wonder. Because of the streaming light the features kept changing. He was fascinated by the rich wonder of fired hair and eyes and the aquiline carving work of bone and flesh. He knew and didn't know this living being. Watched him, totally absorbed, as the past kept melting away and leaving him new again. He knew what to say and said it:

"Forgive me. For everything."

Lohengrin blinked at him. Silent, he nodded.

Layla pulled free of Broaditch and half fell, caught herself with both hands on the stone rim. Stared, kept her violet-dark eyes on her husband. He turned, watching the freshening light gather into her shape, her movements . . .

"Why?" she wanted to know, squinting. "Why did you have to turn up?" Waited.

"Layla," he said. Names were dreaming too, he noted. Flowered and passed . . . felt the brilliance shimmer in his heart and understood he existed only to know this, the way a flower existed only to be, unfold and fill and die, which was all a single shining . . .

"Nay," she virtually cried out at him, "don't say you're sorry or that you tried. Don't you dare . . ." She kept blinking to focus. "You haunt my life! Why must you do that?"

All he said was:

"Layla." Memory came back. It hadn't really mattered up to now. Gawain had believed one of them was living. "I thought you were murdered."

"Naturally."

"By *your* friends," he said to Lohengrin. Blinked. Expected the radiance to die at any moment, understanding it was tentative, and if his dreams returned darkness would pull the fused worlds apart again . . .

Gawain, he thought, remembering him, the bandage-like headdress covering the slashed, halved face, the single eye burning from the shadows, voice whispery and raw with pain:

"Parse, I had an hundred victories in my life."

"Yes," Parsival had responded.

"And women . . ."

"Yes."

"All I ever wanted . . ."

"Yes?"

The eye shut, winked away into the shadows of the head. ". . . was to love," he had whispered.

"Ah," Parsival had murmured.

"I never did," Gawain had said. "Never . . . yet I know what I missed . . . I know exactly what I missed . . ."

Ah, Gawain, Parsival now thought, remembering, feeling it . . . feeling . . .

"They slew Leena," his wife told him. Glanced at her pale son, who sheathed his blade.

"So I avenged her, I suppose," Lohengrin reflected, meaning that he'd slain Clinschor. *That's done her rare good*, he thought. Stared at his father, amazed, feeling nothing from the past. This was just a living man before him, trying . . . like himself . . . just a man . . . "father" just a word . . .

"I was rescued," she was telling Parsival, "by . . . by a decent fellow." She pictured him. Stared . . . sighed faintly, far away . . .

"Thank God," he answered her. "Where is he now?"

She shrugged.

"We were caught outside," she said, "in that stupid storm." Shrugged again. "I'm not so drunk," she added. "But I drink all the time . . . I'm not content in my heart, you see . . ."

Smiled. Batted her eyelids. The deep eyes were like mists glowing at twilight. "I like it well."

"Gentlefolk," put in Broaditch, "would we not do better to find our way from here?"

"Parse..." A woman's voice out of the dark. They all turned.

"Ah," said Layla. "Even down here?" she asked, seeming strangely pleased in a way that made Broaditch uneasy. "How little things change, eh?" She chuckled, humorlessly. "The great sage, he ever fell a-flop from wine when I knew him...which was but short time long ago...the son-of-a-rutting-bitch!"

Unlea came out of the shadows, limping on bloody feet, tattered, swaying, hair in a bundle that, Layla thought, needed only a stray rat for effect.

"A rare beauty," she declared, "this one."

Parsival was distantly amused. He wondered if his vision would survive these women.

"Parse," she said, "thank God I found you. I feared I were forever lost in these dark ways..."

"Well," Layla assured her, "you're found now, my dear..." Chuckled. "Are you the latest victim?"

"Unlea," Parsival said, watching the infinitely unfolding brightness turn all the massed earth to a thin mist of music and fire. "This is my family." Each overlapped the other in light, invisibly intimate.

She just looked at them, rapidly blinking.

"And an old retainer," put in Broaditch, almost smiling.

Alienor and the children were on top of the soot-choked ravine. The dawn sun was a hazy blur and a few sprinkles of rain spatted here and there from tin-gray, wind-tattered clouds.

If it meant to rain, she considered, then it was over. There was still healing in heaven. It was that simple, in the end. It was rain or nothing...

Parsival watched Layla's flame flicker and lose itself in Broaditch's fires, which were joined by Lohengrin's, Unlea's, his own. Like coals in a vast grate, he decided, each absorbed in all the rest...all beings burned in this cool sweetness and lit all creation...

They were going up a long, slow sloping corridor as the last sputters of torch wavered and choked out. Parsival found himself absorbed and fascinated by each moment: Movement, the sounds of steps and voices that echoed to endless depths of significance . . . the very sounds and not what they said stunned him.

"How can you be sure this way leads out of here?" Lohengrin asked his father, who could just follow the sense despite the overwhelming resonances.

"It's all simple," he replied, "if you don't trouble yourself."

"Like being born, you mean," his son returned, amused.

"That trouble comes later, my lord," Broaditch added from up ahead. "The first part is like resting in a haymow."

He was still supporting Layla's arm, though she was steadily sobering. Parsival brought up the rear with Unlea holding on, limping, in a daze.

"Do you want to look for him?" Parsival called ahead to his wife.

She half turned and watched him in the weak torchflutter. His eyes were bright, she noted.

"Look for a man?" She was amused. "Ha. They always find *me*, try what I might."

What must I do next? he asked into the brilliance that washed through the cloudy stones. *What?* Because he knew that simply to contemplate this unending glory wasn't yet possible. There was too much unresolved . . . there was Layla and Lohengrin and the past weight of all his days . . . *What?*

"Well," said his son, wryly, "is that what comes of not troubling?"

The passage ended. The last *fut . . . fut . . .* of the last torch showed a circular room like the inside of a well with no opening, not even a windowslit.

Broaditch tapped the blocks with the end of his short spear. Raised both eyebrows. Looked at Parsival, still bemused to be here. Remembered setting out to find him and ask about the Holy Grail.

Great God I was a silly man, I think . . .

"Well, my lord," he said, "last time I found myself in such a situation, I batted with the hardest thing I possessed and knocked a hole through." He shrugged. "I might have saved myself the trouble."

Lohengrin smiled, black eyes intense.

"The hardest thing you possessed," he repeated. "Well, how's your skull tonight?"

"How know you it's night, sir?" Broaditch wondered, innocently.

Parsival was rapt, losing touch with them again. The light was overwhelming, streaming, fanning, changing, singing, immersing their words and forms, thinning them, melting them . . . He watched. They were all shadowy, fragile husks that fell into death, dried, hollow . . . vanished in the restless cloudy substance until living light stirred the crumbled, time-chewed shells and filled, firmed and puffed them into shape again . . . He stood still, trying to hold this illimitable perception perfect, motionless, unruffled, hushed as a windless pond . . .

Unlea was shaking his arm.

"The torch is going out!" she said, and to the rest: "The water poisoned him . . ."

"Fear not," mocked Layla. "That's Parsival the hero. He'll save us."

"If we go back we'll walk in darkness and be lost forever," Unlea said.

"The hero," his wife repeated. "Darkness becomes you, lady," she added.

Parsival realized he really didn't want to get outside. He didn't want to move at all. Wanted to stay like a parched man at a fountain, nothing else real but drinking deep and deeper . . .

Lohengrin looked up from under his black hooked brows in the last shudders of flame.

"He wasn't there when Leena died," Layla said. "Neither of you were . . . you bastards . . ."

The light dimmed as if he'd blinked against sunlight and Parsival shook his head.

"I came later," he said. "I buried her . . ." He remembered the raw, chopped faces above the ripped and spattered gowns, colorless shadows in the chill moonlight. "In the yard . . ."

"My poor girl . . ." She gritted her teeth. "Did you know about his children?" she shot at Unlea who paid little attention.

"Well," said Broaditch, "this room will serve as a fine tomb for us."

Parsival watched their heartbeats, each sending a pulsing shimmer into the general glowing like water-ripples expanding, overlapping . . . each movement left a stain of light in light . . . each movement dying into the next... these wispy bodies would soon fail and fall but each life could no more cease than a fish could drown swimming. He would have just stayed there if he'd been alone. It was as good as anywhere else. But he felt their fear and a shimmer that was within and without and was and wasn't just his mind spoke:

Let it go this time knowing it. You cannot lose forever. You have passed through the door and now go back and do what is hardest, Grail Child.

And then the rapt touch died into a shock of total blackness and he was already walking (the torch was out) asking himself:

What do I do about the two women? Because he was back. *This is the most difficult of births, Lord, to enter the world knowing what awaits.* Crossed in the dark and reached the wall with his hands. *No more magic. No more dreaming...*

As if he'd always known this place his right hand found a handle. He tensed his massive back and pulled the arched door open. Stepped out into the fuzzy, blinding noon sunlight, his senses stunned into shatteringly vibrant life, hearing, seeing, smelling, tasting air, touching warmth, day, earth, sky... grass and blue sparkle. He took his first steps, as if entering a temple, into the hush and wonder of the day, drinking in his first breath there...

Alienor watched the storm front rolling, boiling on like dark surf, over the sunbright, green-blue skies. Lightnings flashed and flicked. The rain seemed to take breath, hold... then rush down. The children stood there with heads tilted back, the water spinging in, spatting on their sooty faces, the blackness starting to run off. Alienor opened her hood and spread it to catch the rainfall. It was cool and sweet. Bubbled in her knotted hair.

Gawain was on his knees, naked on the earth, crouched over the stippled water that had overflowed from the well. The lightning had passed over and the downpour was steady.

There was a pale, nude girl across the puddle from him, near the shattered castle wall. She stared into the water, smiling. Their reflections, alive with little impact-ripples, were pale, and both kept dipping up the coolness and drinking. Neither knew it as water, just sheen and glow, a flowing of soft, subtle tones, not reflection but a window, and the dipping

hands cupped light and form and they drank lush air washed
from lost springtimes where unweeping children played in unending mornings. His face floated near hers, each rainping a
perfect moment of color, their pale features watersmooth...

Gawain remembered Gawain like something lost in mist.
Drank again from his palm and felt the colors beat with his
heart and gush with his gleaming blood and waterflesh.

His face and body were finally unmarked by time or strife.
He dimly recalled another world of pain, confusion, darkness
and terrible sorrows back in the mists that were Gawain the
knight. Looked at his clean eyes, smooth cheeks, graceful arch
of neck... deep, deep, rich eyes where fields of newness swam
in flowering color.

And her face overlapping, her body overlapping him in the
rippling waterlight... everything going paler, silvering into
twilight... moon-color unfolding in her tresses as wavewinds
unstrung her hair where stars were caught... and he leaned
from the bank and let himself into the buoyant
reflections... falling into her and himself... drinking become
breathing... touching, feeling, thinking all drinking... he was
whole now drinking... whole... the incredible water filling
all of him and the her that was him too... drowning (though
he didn't know it) in her and in himself...

EPILOGUE

The rain was steady, washing the mucky soot into rivulets, creasing the blackened earth; running into gullies; gradually filling the streams as the world began to clean itself: puddles rising, cuts of waterflow foaming around rocks, some high ground already showing raw and clear, a rich muddy tang covering the bitter, ashy smell.

Parsival and Broaditch backtracked through the blasted woodlands. They were trudging up a moderate slope, water sloshing over their leatherbound feet. Their capes were tied closed and saturated. (Lohengrin had stayed with the women at the deserted fortress.) They planned to search for Alienor and the children, following the ravine at a distance and then circling back beside it. Broaditch felt it was as bad a plan as any other.

"Well," he said, conversational, "I hope you found the Holy Grail. You come in sore need of it, I think, sir."

Parsival was watching the softened rain tones blending in the mist. The rich, cool, wet air was a delight.

"Oh, so?" he responded.

"Aye. With two such ladies. How will you distract them?"

Parsival smiled.

"From what, Broaditch?"

"From yourself, sir. As wondered the chicken when the fox come up the yard."

"You don't fancy they'll rest content together?" He looked warmly at the big peasant. Thought him a fine fellow.

"I think nature's at war with it, Sir Parsival."

The tall knight rubbed the back of his neck, thoughtfully.

Glanced at Broaditch's ruddy features, grayed temples and beard.

"I remember you," he told him, "when you and that other...what was his name, the skinny one..."

"Waleis."

"Yes. When you gave me those fool's clothes. My mother thought they'd laugh me home again." A few more steps. The mist smoked around their feet. "I wish they had..." Sighed. "You've changed but little, I think, Broaditch."

"It's only fine helmets as show the banging," he suggested.

Parsival smiled with pleasure.

There's so many to learn from in this world, he thought. *Who needs magic? Each turn in the road, each new face is a wonder...There's your magic...* And it didn't matter whether it had been the water or not that had changed him this time. He didn't care at all. Layla and Unlea...Broaditch was right, except, he decided, it wasn't nature but brute custom made the troubles. They were really all so much the same that to fight was to fight with yourself, seek strangers as you will. All wars began in custom.

"Hold," he said at the top of the muddy crest. Stared through the thin, charred trees at shattered, blackened walls. Headed over, the big peasant a few strides behind.

He instantly understood, even before he totally registered the pale, naked body sprawled in the shallow pool around the well that stood there like a tower over a moat. The legs and arms were outspread as if trying to grip all the grayish-white and dark water where the wall and the sky showed...face down, the chopped short arm making a final, sardonic point, Parsival imagined, might have pleased the once tormented knight.

The long-haired, very thin girl had a hollow, haunted face. Her eyes were wild, wide, absorbed, tracking past them again and again as Broaditch came up on the soggy, flowing muck and stopped. Her eyes moved as if following invisible butter-flies...

"You won't believe it," he said to Parsival, "but I know this place. I passed it the first month I set out to follow you from home...long ago..."

"Ah," murmured the knight. He'd just realized he felt the light now without seeing it, without having to see it. It was there, a warmth within...all around, in mysterious flow squeezing each beat into his heart, each pull of rich breath...

"Aye," confirmed the powerful peasant, folding his solid arms across his thick chest, looking from the girl to the floating man. "I did. I keep passing over the same ground for all that I wander far." Reflected. Watched the pale body slowly turning in the greenish-gray water. "Do you know these?" The surface churned pale in the rain.

"One of them," Parsival said softly.

Ah Gawain, he thought. *Ah...*

The well continued to slowly flood. The downpour was muted and steady.

Broaditch remembered the place from that summer's day, misted (like the mist that ghosted here around the dark stones) through the twenty-odd years between, when the dead lay around the burned and shattered walls, dried, swollen in a field of goldenrod ashimmer with bees, the twisted forms awash in glowing lushness...

"I was looking for you," he repeated. "Your mother had just died."

The girl's gaze kept following nothing, over and over and back again...shifting...circling...

Broaditch kept following the lost image that seemed to drift over the wet, dark gray landscape. Recalled riding in from the road (that had been absorbed back into the markless earth), his mule's withers deep in the golden flood, the bees' drone a soothing murmur almost like riverflow...saw himself glancing back to where Alienor and Waleis (skinny, awkward, gripy, long dead, dreaming Waleis) waited on the now nonexistent road that led to vanished days and adventures...stood there, remembered, and hardly knew he wept or why...

The hollow-faced girl followed whatever it was across the tinflat sky, then down the arc and across the dark horizon. The rain pulsed steadily through her tangled hair.

"Well," said Parsival, "you found me."

"I no longer was looking, my lord."

Parsival waded knee-deep. His reflection was dim and cloudy. The water was warmish. He reached for Gawain . . . then checked himself. The rain whooshed quietly all around.

"No," he whispered, "you've drunk deep at last, old friend. I'll not trouble you now." Who did you visit in an empty house? "Farewell." There was nothing to it. He felt the spot of warmth in him that would never cool. You came and went and only fading, cloudy pictures stayed. "The tale is told at last," he said, motionless in the dim water as the day dimmed imperceptibly into mistgrays. "At last." As the girl furiously didn't watch him; and Broaditch wrapped himself in his own mantle of memory.